D1621795

"Liz Curtis Higgs's *Bookends* is witty, charming, delightful—this book will keep you up all night laughing."

"Delicious as Moravian Sugar Cake! *Bookends* has all of award-winning Higgs's warmth, wit, and charm. Brimming with fun and overflowing with Christian encouragement, *Bookends* has it all. Readers will love it."

"*Bookends* is proof that Liz Curtis Higgs's name will be indelibly written across the field of fiction. I am smitten with the way Liz dips her pen into the inkwell of her humor and her heart and spells out such captivating characters. *Bookends* is a delightful reason to declare a holiday and cozy up with this engaging novel."

"As a woman who fell in love with (and married!) a man who is nothing like me, *Bookends* hooked me from chapter one and continued to reel me in to the end. I want fiction filled with snappy, well-crafted dialogue, natural humor, and could-be-real characters. I want suspense, romance, and scenes that make me think deeply and spur me to grow in my faith. I want plausible struggles without easy, pat answers. I'll admit, I demand A LOT when it comes to fiction. The brilliant Miz Liz delivered it all, and more!"

"With a raw throat and an aching body, I crawled into my flannel jammies, took two aspirin, and curled up with Liz Curtis Higgs's newest novel, *Bookends*. Twenty minutes later, I was giggling, my aches and pains forgotten. And while this book may not replace antibiotics, it's a sure cure for sagging spirits and listless hearts. Liz has done it again: created real, likeable characters in a warm, cozy town, sprinkled the mix with romance and history and color, and topped it off with a recipe for fun and delicious sugar cake! You won't want to miss *Bookends*—it's a little bit of stardust and a whole lotta fun!"

"*Bookends* is such fun! It's a book rich in character, setting, and spiritual dimensions. Liz has given us a wonderful, thoughtful, yet humorous treat."

"This book sings! It's a flawless story filled with real emotion, conflict, and characters who live on in your heart long after the last page is tuned. The best fiction yet from this gifted storyteller!"

"Liz Curtis Higgs has done it again! Her new novel, *Bookends,* is a well-written, delightful concoction of romance, humor, tenderness, and fun. You'll want to savor it during your midday cup of tea, but may find yourself partaking of its delights whenever a spare moment arises. It's that good."

LISA SAMSON, AUTHOR

"From the first page Liz Curtis Higgs draws you in to a warm, wonderful world of small-town charm, Moravian culture, faith, and romance. She delivers the kind of characters you'd like to count as friends and creates the kind of setting you dream of visiting. This is a story you'll want to read again and again. Heartwarming and absolutely delightful!"

ANNIE JONES, AUTHOR OF *DEEP DIXIE* AND *PRAYER TREE*

"*Bookends* is a triumph! Laugh-out-loud humor coupled with moments that will turn your knuckles white as you grip the book. Liz has created characters so real, you'll swear you know them. Outstanding job by a novelist on her way."

SUZY PIZZUTI, AUTHOR OF *RAISING CAIN AND HIS SISTERS* AND *PORCH SWINGS AND PICKET FENCES*

PEOPLE LOVE MIXED SIGNALS!

"This is it! Liz's best work ever! A true home run…warm, cozy, truthful, compelling, and encouraging. Good messages about the God who rescued us, loved us without limit, and gave us a second and sometimes third chance."

VIRELLE KIDDER, AUTHOR OF *GETTING THE BEST OUT OF PUBLIC SCHOOLS*

"*Mixed Signals* is a real page-turner. I couldn't wait to get back to it. I loved Liz's characters. I've already recommended it to some fiction readers I know. She has a gift!"

CHERI FULLER, AUTHOR OF *WHEN MOTHERS PRAY*

"Christian fiction isn't known for humorous books, so this title is a special joy. This bouncy romantic tale of a devout Christian woman looking for love should please most readers searching for a fun read. Recommended."

LIBRARY JOURNAL

"LOVED *Mixed Signals*—I thought the characters were delightful and so very real! The storyline kept me up long after bedtime—couldn't wait to discover whose signals would get uncrossed!"

SHIRLEY GARRETT, AUTHOR OF *IT'S A FULL-TIME JOB JUST BEING ME…AND OTHER LESSONS LEARNED ALONG LIFE'S JOURNEY*

"What a heartwarming and soul-inspiring story you told! I laughed. I cried. I sighed. I'm having a hard time letting these compelling characters go. I'm ready for the next one."

MONA GANSBERG HODGSON, AUTHOR OF THE "I WONDER" SERIES

Bookends

Liz Curtis Higgs

ALABASTER
BOOKS

A division of Multnomah Publishers, Inc.
Sisters, Oregon

This is a work of fiction. The characters, incidents, and dialogues are products of the author's imagination and are not to be construed as real. Any resemblance to actual events or persons, living or dead, is entirely coincidental.

BOOKENDS
published by Alabaster Books
a division of Multnomah Publishers, Inc.
© 2000 by Liz Curtis Higgs

International Standard Book Number: 0-7394-0925-5

Cover illustration by Young Sook Cho/Scott Hull Associates, Inc.
Cover design by David Uttley Design

All Scripture quotations are taken from
The Holy Bible, New King James Version
© 1984 by Thomas Nelson, Inc.

For information:

Multnomah Publishers, Inc.•Post Office Box 1720•Sisters, Oregon 97759

In memory of my mother,
who made every living thing around her bloom,
including me.

ACKNOWLEDGMENTS

Hugs and kisses, blessings and thanks, to the following individuals whose hearts and lives have touched mine and enhanced the pages of this novel....

Peggy and David Jones, who kindly allowed Emilie to reside in their historic home on Main Street and prayed for this book from day one.

Jane and Don Rannels, friends and encouragers since my Girl Scout days, who welcomed Beth and company to live in their charming Spruce Street home and offered valuable information on Moravian matters.

Debbie Boehler of the Lititz Moravian Congregation, who compiled, faxed, and mailed more information about the church than one writer should require, and provided ongoing encouragement from the moment I walked through her office door one chilly December.

Dorothy Rutbell and Bruce Carl, birders both, who helped me keep our feathered friends straight.

Betty Siegrist, who truly *did* say she wouldn't mind having a golf course in her backyard.

Sharon Brown of the Moravian Book and Gift Shop in Winston-Salem for her guidance concerning Moravian music.

Margaret Bucher of Moravian Sugar Cake fame, for sharing her recipe with our Helen and her heart with so many for so long.

Bonnie Dills of Home Moravian Church, Winston-Salem, who walked me through a Moravian New Year's Eve Watchnight Service—the Home Church way.

Sharon Shaich and Tilly Shouten, for sharing their skills in the art of *Scherenschnitte*.

Richard Johe of Salem College, who kindly responded to a *most* unusual request from a stranger.

Donna Hammond of the Lititz Public Library who—bless her—keeps not only *my* books on her shelves, but lots of other authors' books, too.

Jim Hess of the Heritage Map Museum for kindly explaining survey maps and land draughts.

Nancy Sauder of the Moravian Mission Gift Shop in Lititz, whose enthusiasm for the Lord Jesus is positively contagious.

Stephanie Brubaker of the Humane League of Lancaster County for her cheerful answers to my many questions about animal adoption.

Jeanine Gehman, aesthetician, and Donna Stover, owner of Shear Sensations, who helped me experience a Grand Spa Escape over the telephone.

Glenn B. Knight, Web master of *www.LititzPA.com,* for knowing the answer to *everything* about Lititz and then some.

Courtney Yartz, for his expertise about irrigating golf courses and such.

Jane Clugston, book buyer for the Moravian Book Shop in Bethlehem, for helping me locate enough Moravian resource material for a dozen novels (and don't think I'm not tempted!).

Karen Ball, my dear editor, and Sara Fortenberry, my literary agent, two angelic creatures who made the whole process fun.

My hubby, Bill Higgs, for his own heroic efforts on behalf of our family, day in and day out.

Gloria Looney, office assistant, and Gayle Roper, novelist and wondrous writing teacher—two of the best "first readers" a writer could find.

And finally—always—to a precious sister in writing, Diane Noble, my best friend and encourager, who keeps my heart on my work and my eyes on the Lord.

Thank you, one and all!

You will show me the path of life;
In Your presence is fullness of joy;
At Your right hand are pleasures forevermore.

PSALM 16:11

One

◆

Success. Inform press. Home Christmas.
ORVILLE WRIGHT

It isn't possible!

Emilie Getz peered into the window of Benner's Pharmacy, amazed to find every detail exactly as she'd remembered. The soda counter where she'd sat as a child and ordered cherry colas, the stout glass jar stuffed with locally-baked pretzels, the racks of colorful greeting cards, the customers—regulars, no doubt—perched on vinyl-covered stools. Gazing out at her, gazing in.

She pushed open the door and found herself stepping into a time warp, like Alice falling through the rabbit hole into another world. Except Emilie knew this world—knew it inside and out, even after eighteen long years of self-imposed exile.

Home.

A tentative smile stretched across her features as she reached for the local paper, fresh off the press earlier that December day.

"Thirty cents," the clerk behind the counter said, then amended the price when Emilie added the latest issue of *Victoria*, one of her few monthly indulgences. On many a rainy Carolina evening Emilie basked in the magazine's artful depiction of life at its loveliest, then closed her eyes and thought of England and how splendid it would be to take a handful of her more mature history majors there.

Someday.

For the next six months, though, she was firmly planted in Pennsylvania soil, on a mission that could make a visit to merry old England—financially speaking—a distinct possibility. Who knew? The newspaper she'd just purchased might include an article about her arrival in town this very week.

"Merry Christmas," the clerk called out as Emilie gathered her reading materials and hurried down the steps. Slowing when she reached the icy sidewalk, she headed in the direction of her temporary lodging half a dozen doors east.

The cozy white cottage, built to last by John William Woerner in 1762, greeted her warmly. The town cooper, bleeder, and tooth drawer had left a solid legacy in the little house. Already it felt like home, even with stray boxes left to unpack and potted plants waiting for new landing spots. Emilie fixed herself a light supper of cheese and fruit, then unfolded the newspaper with guarded anticipation. Keeping one eye on the clock, she brushed stray wisps of hair out of her face as she scanned each page, hoping to discover a warm welcome there as well.

What she found was less than encouraging. Her momentous homecoming resulted in two short paragraphs, buried on page sixteen of the Lititz *Record Express.* The headline, set in modest type, simply announced: "Local Scholar Returns."

"Local scholar?" Nothing more? The story that followed offered little in the way of fireworks: "During her six-month sabbatical, Dr. Emilie Getz will write a commemorative book for the Moravian Congregation's historic 250th anniversary."

That was the whole of it.

Not a word about her being commissioned by the church or singled out from her peers for this honor.

No box around the story, either. No boldface type. No photo.

A tightening sensation crawled along her neck. *Oh, honestly, Em!* Swallowing with some difficulty, she snapped the newspaper shut as if to scold the editor for so easily dismissing seven years of doctoral work in eighteenth-century American history.

The weekly paper landed on a nearby drop-leaf table with a disappointing slap. "All things come round to him who will but wait," she reminded herself, her clear voice punctuating the evening stillness. As usual, Longfellow offered the perfect antidote to her blue mood. The Christmas Eve vigil, less than an hour away, would dispel any lingering melancholy.

Working her way through the house, snapping off lights and turning on small electric candles, Emilie reminded herself that there would be substantial headlines in much bigger newspapers soon enough if all went as planned. *And it will. It must.* She'd worked too hard, too long, to allow any other outcome.

The fact was, the *Record Express* didn't know the whole story. Couldn't know—not yet—or it would ruin everything. Her research on the original *Gemeinhaus*—"common house"—was strictly off the record until her suspicions about the location could be verified. It would take hard evidence—remnants of a foundation or identifiable artifacts—to ensure that her ideas were based on fact.

In 1746 when John George Klein donated part of his farm property for a building that would serve as school, meetinghouse, and parsonage, it was raised on a bluff on the south bank of a small stream.

A finished Gemeinhaus stood there by May 1748, no doubt.

But not the *first* one. If her painstaking research was correct, the first building—completed but never consecrated—was raised on a plot of land farther southeast than its later counterpart, and finished a full year earlier.

Now she had to find it. She had to *prove* it, if only to convince those confounded men in Salem College's history department that a woman—a *younger* woman at that—could play their game and win.

No mistakes this time. No hasty conclusions.

This would not, could not, be another incident like Bethabara, an academic disaster of epic proportions for her. She, who always triple-checked things, had missed a critical bit of information that sent an entire archaeological crew on a fruitless dig in the old Moravian village outside Salem, North Carolina.

The Bethabara dig had yielded nothing except sore backs and hot tempers. And a foundation stone that boldly proclaimed her mistake to the academic world: *1933*. Not a 1753 site, as she'd insisted it would be. "Getz's Blunder," they called it when they thought she wasn't listening.

It hadn't cost her tenure; it had cost her pride.

She would succeed this time, of that Emilie was confident. Not a single soul in her academic circle knew about her Lititz Gemeinhaus research. If she kept her nose to the grindstone, she might pull this one off without undue embarrassment. The endless hours she'd spent squinting at ink-spotted diaries and faded antiquarian maps were about to bring her the recognition that she'd waited far too many years to receive.

It was her turn. *Her turn,* mind you.

A glance at the hand-hewn clock mounted in the wall assured her that, if she left in the next minute, she would arrive at church at precisely seven o'clock, in plenty of time to choose a seat to her liking. Emilie stepped out the front door onto east Main Street and inhaled the frosty air, pulling her scarf more tightly against her neck. The temperature had already dropped a few more chilly degrees.

History swirled around her feet as surely as a hint of snow eddied about the tall lampposts standing guard over the busy intersection of Cedar and Main. Five-pointed Christmas stars framed the old glass globes with red and white bulbs, just as they had every December in memory. Across the street stood the Rauch house—its pretzel ovens still in the basement—and the corner house that once featured Lancaster County's first drugstore.

Home.

The slightest shiver of expectation ran down her neck.

Her parents were spending the evening delivering baskets for the needy in Lancaster, leaving her on her own until tomorrow. Solitude never bothered Emilie—in fact, the peaceful, orderly nature of living alone suited her perfectly.

Emilie locked the wooden door behind her, ventured down the steep brick steps, then turned right to pass the post office, keeping an eye out for icy spots. The evening was cold and starless, with a stout enough breeze to send her scarf waving like a flag on the Fourth as she hurried toward the church one block away. It would be good—wouldn't it?—to walk through those narrow wooden doors again. Long overdue, really, though she'd only been in Lititz for two days, all of which she'd spent unpacking enough resource materials to keep her busy through June.

Emilie noted with a smile of satisfaction that the old Moravian Congregational Store, circa 1762, hadn't been altered one iota except for the addition of dormers in the roof. There were laws about remodeling such buildings. "Remuddling is more like it," she murmured to no one in particular as she neared the corner and turned right on to Moravian Church Square.

In the chilly night, her heart skipped one beat, then two.

It was all there. The trombone choir, their elegant brass slides pointed toward the sanctuary doors, sounded a hymn as recognizable as her own name. The snow-dusted sidewalks guided visitors to the *Putz*—the church's annual diorama of Bethlehem of old. And hanging from every porch ceiling on the square were Moravian stars dancing in the wind, their ivory glow dispelling the darkness.

Nothing had changed. *Nothing.*

And that pleased Emilie immensely. From her wavy brown hair to her sensible leather boots, she was a woman who understood the importance of tradition. This was her hometown, after all. Her home congregation. Her people, as her Winston-Salem friends would say. The last thing she wanted was to find everything she valued—everything she loved—tossed aside in the name of progress.

Slipping through the door with a nod to the greeter, she made a beeline for her favorite seat near the front, blinking hard as her senses were overwhelmed with awakened memories. The lump in her throat felt like an orange stuffed in a Christmas stocking. She sank on to a much-worn padded pew and tucked her small purse beside her, careful not to disturb the couple to her left as she made a nest for herself with her cashmere dress coat.

It seemed that every minute of eighteen years had passed since she'd sat in that exact spot.

Not true. It seemed like yesterday.

Letting her eyelids drift shut, Emilie drew in a quiet breath, savoring the spirit of Christmas past that hovered around her. The lingering scent of beeswax candles—snuffed at the close of the earlier vigil service—still tinged the air. Behind the wide door to the old parsonage, aromatic coffee and sweet buns waited for the final love feast of the season, soon to be served to the chosen and the curious who filled the pews of the Lititz Moravian Church.

Home.

Eyes still at half-mast, her ears tuned to the faintest traces of Pennsylvania German in the voices murmuring around her, Emilie didn't see the man preparing to sit down next to her until he landed with a jarring thump, flattening one side of her cashmere nest.

Good heavens. Didn't he realize he was sitting entirely too close?

Not lifting her head to acknowledge him, she merely shifted to the left and whispered, "Pardon me," while she tugged at her coat sleeve. The black jeans plastered on top of it were the sorriest excuse for Christmas Eve attire she'd ever witnessed. *Obviously not a Lititz man.*

When his response wasn't immediate, she turned her whisper up two notches. "Sir, if you would, please. You're sitting on my—"

"Really? No kidding."

His full-volume growl sounded like a muffler headed for a repair shop. Young and old in a three-pew circumference turned to see who was disturbing the peace. When Emilie's gaze joined theirs, she found herself face-to-face with something even more disturbing.

The man—and he was definitely that—had impossibly short hair, enormous eyes with brows covering half his face, and a five o'clock shadow that darkened his chin line to a slovenly shade of black.

Before she could stop herself, Emilie grimaced.

Ick.

A lazy smile stretched across the field of dark stubble, at which point his narrow top lip disappeared completely. "Sorry, miss." He leaned slightly away from her, keeping his eyes trained on hers as he released her coat. "My mistake."

She snatched back her sleeve, chagrined to feel the crush marks in the fabric and the warmth of his body captured in the cloth. *Men!* Flustered, she fussed with her coat, trying to rearrange it just so without brushing against those tasteless black jeans of his, the ones that matched his black T-shirt and black sport coat, which, Emilie couldn't help noticing, displayed an unseemly number of blond hairs.

A masculine hand thrust into view and the muffler rumbled again. "So. I'm Jonas Fielding. And you are...?"

Blushing is what you are, Em!

She swallowed, hoping it might stop the heat from rising up her too-long neck, and offered her hand for the briefest shake. He was so...so *not* like her professorial peers at Salem College, buttoned up in their conservative shirts and ties. This man was—goodness, what was the word for it? Earthy.

Masculine. *Something.* Whatever it was, it unnerved her.

Still, she really ought to be polite. They *did* have an audience, and it *was* Christmas Eve.

Pale fingers outstretched, she nodded curtly. "Dr. Emilie Getz."

He didn't shake her hand—he captured it. "New in town, Dr. Getz?"

The oldest line in the book! And he couldn't have been more wrong. She jumped at the chance to tell him so as she slipped her fingers back through his grasp and stuffed them in her dress pocket.

"Not new at all. I was born and raised in Lititz. Graduated from Warwick High School, in fact." *Valedictorian, in fact.* She didn't mean to jerk her chin up, it merely went that way all by itself. "I've been…ah, gone for a few years."

His gaze traveled over her longer than necessary before his eyes returned to meet hers. "I'd say more than a few years, Emilie."

"Why…I…!" She was sputtering. *Sputtering!* The warmth in her neck shot north, filling her face with an unwelcome flush even as a sly grin filled his own devilish countenance.

An arpeggio from the pipe organ provided a blessed means of escape from his boyish wink and the chuckle that followed. *Heavens, what an ego he has!* With his dark features and all-male charm, he was undoubtedly the sort of fellow other women found drop-dead handsome. Emilie hoped he would simply drop dead. Or, at the very least, vanish at the end of the service, never to sit on her coat—or step on her toes—again.

"More than a few years"? Humph!

An out-of-towner, no doubt. The borough of Lititz, nestled as it was in the heart of Amish country, swelled with visitors over the holidays. Clearly Jonah—or whatever his name was—belonged among their number, which meant he'd be long gone before she turned the calendar page to January.

Calm down, Em. It's Christmas Eve.

An organ prelude by Pachelbel soon softened the corners of her mouth into a tenuous smile. The sanctuary dated back two centuries; the melody was older still. For historians, a Moravian vigil service approached heaven on earth.

Though at age thirty-six, Emilie herself was anything but historic. Wasn't that so?

"More than a few years…"

The echo of his words tightened her smile. *The nerve.* How old was *he*, then? Reaching for a hymnal, she stole a furtive glance at the stranger on her right. His dark eyes, she was relieved to discover, were focused on the printed sheet in his hands. His expression suggested bemused indifference. *The nerve!*

The man was easily her age. Older, judging by the hint of silver in his close-cropped hair. Granted, only two hairs were gray, but they *were* gray. Definitely.

His eyes shifted toward hers before she realized she'd lingered too long. "Counting my gray hairs, Emilie?" At least his voice was lower this time. Very low, actually. "I have two. Find 'em?"

"No! I mean, yes, but that's not what I was looking for." She sat up straight and pointed her chin toward the pulpit. "Never mind."

He leaned closer. "In case you're wondering—and you apparently are—I was born in the sixties. And another thing: You can skip the hymnal. All the words are in this program." He waved it under her nose, clearly enjoying himself. "Didn't you get one?"

"It's not a program, it's an ode. And I don't need one, thank you." She jutted her chin forward further still, refusing to look at him, and shoved the hymnal back in the pew rack. "I was born Moravian. I know all these hymns by heart, including the German ones."

Seconds later, when the lights in the sanctuary faded to black, *"Stille Nacht"*—"Silent Night"—floated down from the choir loft behind them. None too subtly, she mouthed the words *auf Deutsch* for all three verses, recalling her years in the soprano section.

"More than a few years, Emilie…"

That infernal man and his insinuations! He was at least as old as she was, she'd quickly calculated. Probably the very same age. It was quite obviously the *only* thing they had in common.

She'd seen his type all her life: athletic, popular, big man on campus, strutting around with a pretty airhead on each arm. The sort who wouldn't give a sober, studious girl such as she the time of day.

He was only talking to her now because he was stuck sitting next to her. Some things in life never changed.

When the congregation stood to sing "All Glory to Immanuel's Name," Emilie was amazed to hear a tolerably pleasant bass voice booming from the broad chest next to her. Not solo quality—not by any stretch—but fairly on pitch. Yes, she'd definitely heard worse. He also seemed to know the tune, even without printed music. Had he been here in years past?

Curiosity overruled her good sense. In the sparse moment of silence before the pastoral prayer, she whispered in his general direction, "Have you attended our Christmas vigil before?"

"Five years in a row. I'm Moravian too."

Her jaw dropped before she could catch it.

"Not *born* Moravian, like you," he chided softly, nodding his head toward the front to remind her the pastor's prayer was already in full swing. "You'll have to explain that one to me later."

Later? As in after the prayer? After the service? Later over tea in her cozy kitchen on Main Street? *Surely he isn't suggesting such a thing!* Surely not. She hadn't invited a man under her roof for tea—or any other reason—in a very long time.

Disgusted with the mere notion of brewing a pot of Darjeeling for a Neanderthal, she fixed her gaze on the enormous Moravian star hanging above the pulpit, spinning ever so slightly in the rising heat, and composed her features into an attitude of worship, even if her mind wasn't cooperating.

The man is not your type. At all. Another quick glance at the blond hairs on his jacket assured her of that. Still, his comment taunted her. Explain *what* to him later? Explain why she was back in Lititz after all these years? Explain why her whole academic career depended on what she might uncover less than a mile away?

Wrong. No explanations needed, not when there wouldn't be anything happening *later* with Jonah something-or-other.

When Pastor Yeager began reading the Christmas story from Luke, Emilie snapped to attention with a guilty start, determined to hear every word, to listen as if she might be tested on the material the next morning. Anytime a grade was involved, her concentration was legendary.

"And it came to pass…" the reverend read.

"Later," her rebel's heart translated.

Enough! She pressed her lips together in a firm line and busied her hands smoothing her straight wool dress, determined to cover every inch of her knobby knees. Not because of the man sitting entirely too close to her—certainly not! She was merely doing it for modesty's sake. And propriety. And simple good taste, considering her knees were beyond ugly.

Not that such a thing mattered.

What's the matter with her knees?

Jonas watched the woman next to him fretting over her skirt, tugging the fabric well past her calves as if the hem were in danger of crawling up a scandalous quarter of an inch. He rubbed his jaw to mask a broad smile and realized he hadn't shaved. This morning, yes. This afternoon, no.

Whatever.

She'd settled back against the pew and was still trying her best not to brush against his jacket. A nervous sort, this one. Prickly as a porcupine.

His eyes were drawn up front as the two dozen youngsters parked on small benches around the pulpit stood to sing the "Children's Te Deum." Their cherub faces—framed in short, white robes and big bow ties—jogged an unexpected memory of his three younger brothers, all in their early thirties now. They'd been about this age when the accident happened.

It seemed like eons ago.

Nah. It seemed like yesterday.

A ripple of anticipation moved through the congregation as proud parents craned their necks to watch the junior choir members in action. Emilie Getz, it appeared, hardly noticed the kids, so intently was she staring up at the Moravian star.

Counting the points, probably. Should he tell her there were exactly one hundred and ten? The woman was a serious piece of work. *Dr. Getz?* She looked more academic than medical. Conceited and prissy and arrogant as all get-out, which meant she was hiding something—and not just her knees. Women like her—uptight, no-nonsense, nose-in-the-air females—always had some dark secret they kept tucked away for a rainy day. He knew the type: "Look, but don't touch."

Then why don't you stick to that, Jonas?

Good plan.

Even if her pale, creamy skin did remind him of a porcelain angel he'd seen on top of a Christmas tree yesterday.

Jonas scanned the sanctuary looking for familiar faces, and found several.

Only one, though, snagged his gaze and hung on to it, whether he liked it or not. *Dee Dee Snyder.* The real estate agent who'd sold him his new house last year was perched on the end of a pew, her long legs crossed, her foot swinging provocatively, her short skirt hiked up too high for church or anywhere else.

Dee Dee Snyder didn't care who saw her knees.

She winked at him. *Winked!* What was this woman's problem? Did she think she could pick up men during a worship service?

He refused to acknowledge her except with a brief nod. Sure, the woman was a looker—short blond hair, bedroom eyes, and curves in all the right places. She was also dangerous with a great big D. As in Dee Dee.

No, thanks.

Besides, where was the challenge in dating the ubiquitous Miss Snyder? The woman had thrown herself at every single guy in Lancaster County before she'd decided to set her sights on him—again—this fall. He'd resisted being conquest #54, #97, and #122. He wasn't about to be #146.

It was more than that, though. He didn't have time for a woman who didn't have time for God. Dee Dee was only in church tonight because it was Christmas Eve. *And because she knew I'd be here.* He hoped that wasn't the case, but judging by the way she was dangling her red high-heeled shoe in his direction, it looked like the ugly truth of it.

Jonas made up his mind: The minute the organist hit the first note of the postlude, he was out the door. Santa wasn't gonna catch him kissing Dee Dee Snyder under the mistletoe. Not this year. Not any year.

His attention shifted back up front when the children's choir dropped onto its benches with obvious relief. The congregation around him settled in, prepared to sing half a dozen Moravian hymns while the traditional lovefeast was served. *Food in church. What a concept!* After five years and two dozen or more lovefeasts, he still looked forward to the simple meal and felt his stomach rumble as the kitchen doors swung open.

On cue, *dieners*—women of the church chosen for such service—arrived bearing baskets brimming with sweet buns. Taking their place at the end of the pews, the women quickly dispensed their fragrant wares. Passing the basket to Emilie, Jonas couldn't help noticing her hands, graceful as small white doves, and her concentrated effort to keep the powdery bun as far away from her dark dress as possible.

Which meant he was looking straight at her when she suddenly swung her head toward him and asked, "Jonah, is it?"

"Jonas." He bit his lip, fighting a chuckle. "Jonas. With an *s*." Few things entertained him more than an intelligent woman caught making a mistake. "Jonas Fielding."

"Ah...well, then. What...what exactly did you want me to explain to you...later?"

He took in a pair of light brown eyes, not quite focused on his, and rosebud lips, now pinched into a tight line. *She's already sorry she asked.* Her inquisitive, doctoral-degree mind had obviously taken over and insisted on fishing for an answer.

He grinned and swallowed the bait.

Two

Being an old maid is like death by drowning, a really delightful sensation
after you cease to struggle.
EDNA FERBER

"You said you were 'born Moravian,' right?"

You asked for this, Em. She dipped her head in concession, then forced herself to meet Jonas' gaze, furious that she hadn't kept her insipid question to herself. "And...?"

His dark eyes bore down on her. "When a woman tells me she was born in Lititz, that I understand. Were you?"

She nodded, keeping a steady grip on her lovefeast bun.

"Okay. And I know what born-again means."

She wrinkled her brow. *What kind of statement is that?*

He pressed on. "What I'm asking is, how can you be *born* Moravian?"

Is that all? "Easy. The Getzes have always been Moravians." Over the opening strains of a Herrnhut hymn from the eighteenth century, Emilie added softly, "I was sleeping in the nursery here before I was a month old." She inclined her head toward the front. "I sat in the third row of the children's choir for more Christmases than I can count. Attended vacation Bible school every summer in the Brothers' House. Studied for confirmation in the basement of the fellowship hall." Her gaze fell to the cranberry-colored carpet that circled the raised pulpit. "And that's where I took my first communion. Now do you see?"

Jonas nodded slowly in agreement, but his eyes told a different story.

What? Had she said something wrong? He'd only wanted to hear about her Moravian heritage, right? *Fine.*

Emilie leaned his direction a fraction of an inch to whisper, "The buns at Home Church in Winston-Salem are quite different." Surely a good Moravian would be interested in such things. "Their buns aren't sweet, like these. On the top, they have an *M* for Moravian—or a *W* for Winkler's Bakery. No one in Old Salem ever can agree on what the letter stands for."

His dark chin tipped down toward her, sending the oddest shiver through her system, while his low voice idled barely above a rumble. "Maybe it stands for *men* and *women*."

Oh my. The possibility had never crossed her mind. Vaguely unsettling, really. Historically, Moravians had always prided themselves on keeping the sexes apart. Their very buildings proved it.

The Single Sisters' House.

The Single Brothers' House.

One hardly thought in terms of men and women. *Oh my.*

She was grateful when a welcome distraction presented itself. A battalion of dark-suited servers—male dieners—marched in carrying heavy wooden trays laden with white ceramic mugs full of coffee with cream. Faces solemn, they waited at the end of each row while the worshipers passed the mugs down the pews.

After gingerly passing two steaming mugs to the couple next to her, Emilie reached for a third cup, barely meeting Jonas' gaze when his hands brushed hers. Why, oh why, had she ever started such a pointless conversation with an utter stranger?

Finally settled with her lovefeast in hand, she eyed the sugary bun and her navy dress, envisioning the worst. *Careful, Em.* Normally, she never touched sweet things, but this was different. She was in church, after all, and these buns were practically a religious experience. Balancing a white paper napkin under her chin, she cautiously nibbled at the edges of the flaky yeast bun made with potatoes, brown sugar, cinnamon—flavors that tasted like Christmas itself.

The tiniest moan of pleasure sneaked out before she could swallow it along with her dainty bite. How embarrassing! Surely this Jonas fellow hadn't heard her. Had he?

She waited, holding her breath, not eating and certainly not moaning.

Jonas didn't turn, didn't look, didn't move so much as an eyebrow, until he lifted his coffee mug to his lips. That narrow top lip of his—the one she'd vaguely noticed earlier—disappeared again in a grin so wide that when he tried to take a sip, he managed instead to pour scalding hot coffee down the front of his shirt.

"Blast!" Jonas winced, then stabbed at the spill with his napkin—a napkin covered with confectioners' sugar, which splattered numerous white blobs across the front of his black T-shirt. In seconds, the man resembled an oversized domino with teeth.

"Shhh!" Emilie offered him her pristine napkin and a stern expression. "If you'd worn proper clothing," she hissed, "you wouldn't be in this fix."

"No, I'd have ruined a sixty-dollar tie instead of a six-dollar T-shirt." He pointed at her lap. "Besides, look who's talking."

She glanced down and gasped. A virtual blizzard of white sugar blanketed her navy dress. This time, her moan wasn't the least bit tiny.

"Ohhh!" She patted, she fussed, she blotted, she brushed—all to no avail. Streaks of sugar mocked her every move. The harder she worked, the farther it spread.

From the corner of her eye, she caught a glimpse of the man in black snickering at her. Determined not to create any more of a scene, she peered at him through narrowed eyes and mouthed the words: "Your fault."

He mouthed back: "No way." His poor excuse for an upper lip was gone again, lost to a boorish grin. "*Your* fault."

Emilie yanked one coat sleeve over her powdered skirt with a muffled "Harrumph!" then sipped her coffee with as much dignity as possible under the circumstances. The man was ruining a perfectly wonderful service. She simply would not allow it. This was her town, her church, and her chance—finally—to earn the respect that was rightfully hers.

Nothing could stop her now, especially not a sugar-covered stranger who was clearly not her type. Nor she his. While the congregation sang, Emilie did her best to ignore the masculine notes resonating an octave below her own, and instead let her imagination spin a banner headline stretched across the front page of the *Record Express:* "Startling Revelation by Prominent Scholar Rewrites History."

Thirty minutes later, it was Jonas Fielding who was history.

Emilie didn't discover his hasty exit until she'd extinguished her beeswax candle and made a discreet canvass of the sanctuary, now brightly lit and filled with chatter....but not with Jonas.

Just as well, yes?

Most assuredly.

Hiding the last powdery remains on her skirt behind her purse, Emilie stepped into the aisle, her eyes scanning the departing worshipers for a friendly face. Good riddance to Mr. Fielding notwithstanding, the notion of spending the rest of Christmas Eve alone in an empty rental house left her feeling oddly out of sorts.

The vigil service had been everything she remembered and more, right down to the trumpets heralding the entrance of shimmering trays of candles while the choir shouted in harmony *"Mache dich auf, werde Licht!"* When the evening closed with the congregation delivering a fortissimo "Sing Hallelujah, Praise the Lord!" complete with a soprano descant that shook the hallowed rafters, Emilie's heart had been near to bursting.

Everything else that evening would be an anticlimax, she decided, aiming herself in the direction of the vestibule. Even if she did run into someone from her Warwick High days, visiting with an old acquaintance tonight would inevitably mean listening to countless stories of wedded bliss and cherubic children. Pictures would soon pour out of wallets, enhanced with witticisms allegedly spouted by the favored child and tales of perfect report cards presented at semester's end.

Wait.

Grade schoolers didn't call them semesters. *Terms, maybe? Grading periods?* She smiled to herself as she eased past the slow-moving crowd herding toward the door. How was she to know what children called things? An only child and a lifelong academic, she hadn't spent ten minutes around little tots. Didn't know the first thing about them. *Don't want to, either.* A shudder ran through her at the very concept of sticky hands pulling at her tailored clothes and crayon drawings cluttering up her spotless refrigerator door.

Ick.

From behind her, a decidedly adult voice caught her attention. "Emilie

Getz, don't you dare take another step!"

Pausing outside the front of the church, Emilie turned to find an old neighbor from Noble Street squeezing through the door—a page from her childhood, wrapped in a woolen coat.

"Mrs. B. How lovely to see you again."

Helen Bomberger was built like one of her apple dumplings: short and round. And sweet, as only four tablespoons of sugar could make a tart wine-sap sweet. Helen had lived two doors up from the Getz house all her married life, in a blue, two-story bungalow she no doubt still called home.

Loved by her neighbors and adored by their offspring, Helen had cooked and hugged and prayed her way into everyone's hearts over the last seven decades. Her porch light was on at all hours, her lap was always ready for one more teary toddler, and her chicken corn soup stretched for miles when company showed up without phoning ahead.

It was impossible not to like Helen, even if she did make Emilie feel six years old again. Preparing herself for a long winter's chat about God—Helen's favorite subject—Emilie concentrated on the cheerful countenance beaming up at her. "Mrs. Bomberger—"

"Helen," the woman corrected patting her gloved hand. "You're old enough to address me by my given name, don't you think?"

"More than a few years, Emilie…" Would the refrain haunt her all evening?

"Helen it is, then." Her gaze fell on the woman's too-snug plaid holiday dress and the wreath of wrinkles circling her sagging face. "Well, don't you look…the same as ever?" Emilie cleared her throat. "I mean… you haven't changed a bit!" She watched a crease of doubt crawl across the elderly woman's forehead and added quickly, "How…how are you?"

"Older." Helen smiled again and the crease disappeared. "As are you, dear. But the Lord has been kind enough to keep us breathing, hasn't he? What does your mother have to say about her only daughter nearing forty and not a grandchild in sight?"

"F-forty?" Emilie choked on the frozen night air. "I'm only—"

"Yes, I know. Thirty-six. Wasn't I there the day you were born?" Helen stepped aside as a gaggle of boisterous children hurried past. "Your father drove me to Lancaster General so I could see you in the nursery." She wrapped her hand around Emilie's elbow and steered her along the sidewalk toward the center of the square. "How proud he was of his baby girl!" she added with a twinkle in her eye, as the trombone choir reassembled for their last round of hymns before heading home to warm cider and warmer beds.

"So, dear." Helen's voice rose above the brass instruments. "How are you and the Lord getting along these days?"

"Uh…fine. We're…fine." Emilie had a sudden, uncontrollable urge to watch the French horn player, feigning interest in every note before her guilty conscience eased her attention back toward the woman by her side.

Helen's eyes shone in the lamplight. Not a hint of judgment was reflected there. "Stop by my place while you're in the neighborhood, will you, child?"

The sensation of being six years old returned with a hop, skip, and a jump. "Yes, ma'am. Any particular time?"

"My door's always open, Em. But then you know that." Helen patted her hand again, then turned toward the parking lot behind the church. Emilie watched the older woman shuffle away, tottering a bit, her round body swathed in a bright red wool coat that had seen too many Christmases, her curly gray hair exposed to the wind.

Without thinking, Emilie slipped her knit scarf from its cozy roost around her neck and hurried after her. "Mrs. B. That is, Helen…wait. Take this, please."

Helen had barely turned around before Emilie was tucking the still-warm scarf in place over the woman's hair, then knotting it neatly below her double chin. "It's too cold a night…" Emilie shrugged, suddenly self-conscious.

"How thoughtful, dear." Helen's wise old eyes blinked at her. "I'll be sure and return it when you stop by. Tomorrow, I hope." Her head tipped sideways, making her look more owlish still. "You're staying at the old Woerner place, aren't you? Run along now, or you'll be wishing you'd kept your nice scarf."

"See you tomorrow," Emilie called out, surprised to hear a small note of enthusiasm in her voice. *Must be Christmas. Good will to men and fa-la-la.* She shivered, aware all at once of the icy wind on her bare neck, and hurried down the sidewalk toward Main Street and home, certain she heard a hot cup of Darjeeling calling her name.

"Dr. Emilie Getz."

Jonas said it aloud, shaking his head as he watched her emerge through the church doorway. He squinted, trying to see through the darkly tinted glass of his Explorer, while his heater ran full blast and his bluegrass CD hummed at low volume for a change.

A walking, talking contradiction, that Getz woman. He wasn't spying on her on purpose. *No way.* After ducking out early to avoid a certain blond, he'd found his new vehicle blocked against the curb by another car—late-comers, probably—and had to wait for them to show up and move it.

At least here in the driver's seat, he was safely away from Dee Dee and her high heels on wheels. He'd spotted her as well, hurrying out the side door, obviously on a mission.

To find you, big guy.

It was not a comforting thought.

Emilie had ended up near the trombone choir. *Who's she talking to?* Unless his eyes deceived him, it was Helen Bomberger, the finest woman on God's green earth. When he'd moved to town five years ago, Helen had practically adopted him, stuffing him with pot pie and apple strudel until he begged for mercy.

She'd fed him spiritually, too. Prayed for him daily, she insisted. Nudged him onto the missions committee, then south of the border to build churches in Honduras the last two summers. Helen was the grandmother he'd never known, the mother he'd always remembered waiting for him when he got home from school.

That idyllic life had ended in his twelfth year, when out of sheer necessity his mother left their home ten hours a day to work.

Not Mom's fault, Jonas. Not yours, either.

Now his mother was gone, lost to breast cancer seven years ago. That made a woman like Helen Bomberger a gift from heaven. Even he realized a guy never got too old to be mothered on occasion.

He stared into the night, then nodded when he recognized the red coat. It was Helen, all right. Judging by Emilie's body language, the younger woman wasn't too pleased with whatever Helen was saying.

Better be nice to her, Dr. Getz.

Jonas tightened his grip on the steering wheel as the elderly woman turned on her heel and started off rather abruptly. If Miss Attitude Problem had said something unkind to a saint like Helen, she'd answer to him for it. His left hand dropped to the door handle, his right to pull the key from the ignition, as he prepared to step in and remedy the situation.

Wait.

Now what was Emilie doing? She'd slipped her scarf off and was wrapping it around Helen's head. *Well, I'll be.* Jonas sank back against the headrest, his hands relaxing again. *Never would've pegged her as the compassionate type.*

When the two separated, he noticed Emilie wasn't moving toward a car; she was heading full stride toward Main. On foot? Alone? At night? In the cold?

Not if he could help it.

He shifted the car into drive, then realized he was still blocked in. "Blast!"

At that instant, a laughing couple strolled up, keys dangling from the young woman's mittened thumb. She waved them in his direction, a look of freckled chagrin on her face. "Sorry, Jonas!"

Beth. One of the church secretaries. *So much for biting her head off.* They didn't come any nicer than Beth Landis. Jonas lowered his window and leaned out, striking a threatening pose. "Thought you could get away with this, didn't you?"

"Sure!" She wrinkled her nose like a playful pixie. "Drew and I knew it was your Explorer. We figured you'd be hanging around the vestibule fighting off female admirers for at least twenty minutes."

Her husband came up behind her, resting his hands on her shoulders. "Not tonight, Beth." Drew Landis, the tall, lanky type, towered over his wife. "He made tracks, or didn't you notice?"

"Nope. I was too busy helping with the children's choir." Her dark blue eyes glowed. "Weren't they wonderful?"

"Sure were." Jonas nodded, then looked behind them. "Where's Sara?"

"Home with a cold and a baby-sitter." Beth patted her bulging coat pocket. "I sneaked an extra bun for her, though."

The woman loved kids, no doubt of that. Probably anxious to get home. Flipping on his headlights, he waved at their Nissan and tried to sound gruff. "If you lovebirds don't mind, I have important business waiting for me."

"Really?" Beth rolled her eyes. "What's her name?"

"Bet I know." Drew's lazy smile stretched another inch. "It's that lady of the hour: Carter's Run."

"Not the *golf course?*" Beth shook her head, her tawny hair following a half beat behind her chin. "Jonas, not on Christmas Eve! Even a workaholic like you needs a night off."

He shrugged, glad they'd come up with an easy excuse for his quick getaway. "The grand opening is April 9, ready or not." *Ready, Lord willing.* Jonas revved the engine and flashed them a wide grin. "Merry Christmas, you two. Good to have you in town for a few days, Drew." Drew's sales territory for Woodstream Corporation—famous for manufacturing Victor mousetraps, among other things—covered three states, meaning the man was on the road more than he wasn't. Beth handled it well, but judging by the way she was hanging onto his arm, she was glad to have him home for the holidays.

By the time they'd moved their car far enough for him to maneuver out of the tight space and onto Church Avenue, Jonas realized Emilie was long out of sight. He pulled up to the intersection and braked, drumming his fingers on the steering wheel. Had she turned left or right on Main? Lititz wasn't that big a place. Maybe eight, nine thousand people, tops. Emilie hadn't gone far. He'd find her, make sure she wasn't freezing her skinny neck off, see she got home in one piece.

Left, then. He turned, steering carefully down the narrow street with cars parked on both sides as he checked one sidewalk, then the other, looking for a tall woman with wavy brown hair. And no scarf.

C'mon, Emilie, I know you're here somewhere.

Seconds later, sitting at the red light at Cedar, he caught a glimpse of her tan coat slipping past an open front door before it closed behind her.

It was her all right. The car out in front had a bumper sticker that pointed to her like a sharp pencil: "You can take Salem women out of class, but you can't take the class out of Salem women."

'Salem,' huh? Bet her other car's a broomstick.

He sighed into the dim interior. *Not nice, Fielding.*

A light came on in the house. She was safe, then. *Good.* Didn't need his help after all. *Fine.*

When the traffic light changed, he slowly drove by the white clapboard house with dark green shutters, a candle in each window, and a stone foundation. *Too bad she's stuck with such an old house.* He almost felt guilty about stepping on the gas and heading for his own brand-spanking-new home with its straight-to-plumb and freshly-painted walls.

Wonder why she picked that place?

As the small house faded from view in his mirror, Jonas sorted through the facts at hand. The property once belonged to Miss Mary Augusta Huebener, the never-married daughter of a Moravian family and the unofficial town historian. *An old maid. Like Emilie, I'll bet.* He grinned at the comparison. These days the house was owned by a missionary couple in Honduras, scheduled to come home on furlough next summer.

Hold it. If his minutes from the last missions committee meeting were accurate, the church was paying rent for some out-of-town professor to live there while he prepared—

No. Not he—she.

Emilie. Dr. Emilie Getz. He slowed down at the square while his mind whirled. Why hadn't he put that together sooner? *Because, Einstein, you assumed the doc was a guy.* So the hoity-toity history professor from Winston-Salem was a *she,* here for the big anniversary.

Well, whaddaya know…

That meant the woman wasn't in town for long—six months, tops.

Just as well, right?

He swung onto Broad Street, surprised to hear his tires squeal.

Right.

No sooner had he straightened the wheel than the cell phone in his pocket chirped. Fumbling with it in the dark, he finally found the right button and punched it.

"Fielding here."

"Wish you were *here,*" a feminine voice purred.

"Here?" he barked into the phone. "Where? Who is this?"

"You saw me at church tonight, remember?"

At church? Had he given Emilie Getz his number? *Nah.* Besides, she'd never sound like this coy little kitten.

The breathy voice came on the line again. "Don't you know who this is?"

Know? No. Oh, no…

They said it in unison—one with a purr, the other a groan: "Dee Dee."

"That's enough moaning and groaning, dear."

"Sorry, Mother." Emilie gripped the phone with one hand while the other gently snipped a dead leaf off her aspidistra. "I hadn't intended to come for the whole day, that's all. I...I need to get back to my research."

Her mother's faint tsk-tsk spoke volumes.

Emilie stared out the small kitchen windows at the fresh flakes slowly covering the sleeping garden that would beckon her come the first warm day. The snowfall was steady, but not enough to prevent her impending drive to her parents' house for Christmas.

"Okay. If it'll make you happy, I'll be there about noon." Emilie sighed, depositing plant debris in the wastebasket next to her desk. "Fine. Eleven, then. But I'll need to be home by six. Yes, I realize your house is home." She bit her lip to stem her irritation. "I meant where I'm staying now...that home, okay? See you shortly."

She eased the phone into its cradle, proud of herself for not banging it down in exasperation. Much as she loved her mother—and she did, she truly did—their conversations of late had been reduced to one topic: her unmarried status.

Never mind the bachelor degree with honors from Moravian College, or her master's. Not even her hard-earned Ph.D. from Wake Forest University merited a brownie point on the home front.

"But I have no grandchildren," Barbara Getz had grumbled on the phone moments earlier. "Surely you don't plan to be an old maid."

"Mother," she'd countered, pruning the ends of an overly vigorous sweet-heart vine. "They don't even use the phrase *old maid* anymore. Not *career girl,* either. I'm a historian, an academic. Is that so shameful?" She'd swallowed hard, fighting to control her emotions. "Besides, I'm *thirty-six,* not eighty-six. Don't throw away those shower gifts you're hiding in the closet quite yet."

Her mother had tried to keep her stash a secret. Said they were items she'd found on sale here and there. Useful household things, that's all. Emilie had counted and knew better: one toaster, one iron, one blender, one mixer, one electric knife.

And one baby blanket. Pink.

Emilie paused in front of the mirror and smiled in spite of her sour mood. *Pink, like the sweater you're wearing this very minute.* She did love pastel colors. Her closet was full of pale yellows, grays, blues, greens, and pinks, all in natural fabrics like cotton, linen, and wool. To her way of thinking, polyester wasn't even good enough for curtains, let alone for apparel.

She smoothed the creases in her winter white slacks and glanced at her watch. Thirty minutes until she had to climb behind the wheel of her venerable BMW, point it north toward Noble Street, and face her mother. Enough time to finish watering the cherished collection of houseplants she'd transported from North Carolina with great care, their leafy green heads covered with a sheet to ward off the cold.

First, though, she'd unpack the last of her research materials and get things in order for this evening, when she'd begin putting together the pieces of the Gemeinhaus puzzle.

Pulling two heavy volumes from a box at her feet, Emilie lugged them up onto the dining room table with a determined thump and an equally forceful vow: Never again would a failure like Bethabara blemish her resume.

"Never!" She slapped another book on the table, punctuating her resolution with a satisfying bang.

Three

Home is where one starts from.
THOMAS STEARNS ELIOT

Bang! Bang! Bang!

Jonas groaned again.

The pounding in his head was relentless. *Bang! Bang! Bang!* His subconscious was shouting at him, too. *Wake up! Haul it outta bed, Fielding. C'mon, get up!*

He pulled an extra pillow over his ears, but the voice in his head only grew louder and more insistent. "Go 'way," he growled. "Lemme sleep." When the pillow was snatched out of his hands, he was awake in an instant—eyes wide, heart beating, fists at the ready.

Two men stood in his bedroom doorway and chimed in unison, "Mornin', big brother."

"What? You…!" Jonas exhaled in frustration and relief as his eyes adjusted to the sight of his twin brothers, Jeff and Chris, strolling toward his bed—dressed, shaved, and wearing a pair of wicked grins. Plastered by Jeff's side, with a stolen pillow trailing from her drooling mouth, was Trix, Jonas' traitor of a dog.

"Figured you could sleep in on Christmas morning, huh?" Chris bent down to rub Trix's ears. "What will the Lord think, this being his birthday and all?"

Jonas collapsed with a grunt, hand over his heart. "Aren't you two supposed to be in Milford?" Trix bounded onto the bed, her shaggy blond tail beating the air with a joyful rhythm, her bobbing head begging to be petted. Disoriented, Jonas scratched his own head instead, trying to make sense of it all.

"You didn't think we'd leave you all by your lonesome self on Christmas, did ya?" Jeff's grin never budged. "No way, brother."

"That's right," Chris chimed in. "Aren't you gonna ask us how we got past your fancy security system?"

"Hey!" Jonas grabbed the pillow behind him and swung it at the nearest target. "Good question, turkeys. How *did* you get in here?"

Jeff rubbed his head in mock agony. "Some blond woman was parked in front of your house when we drove up." He offered a broad wink. "Said you were…good friends." He ducked when Jonas swatted him again. "Anyway, she could tell we were brothers. Said she'd be happy to let us in since she had a key." He lifted one dark eyebrow. "Uh…how come she has the key to your house, Mr. Do-Good Christian?"

Jonas let out a noisy sigh. "Because she sold me this place. I guess she kept an extra key handy." A problem he intended to correct pronto. He'd managed to avoid a visit from her when she'd called last night; now he'd have to face the woman after all, like it or not.

Not.

Jonas nudged Trix off the bed, then reached for a pair of jeans, standing to pull them on, stalling long enough to buy some time and sweep out the cobwebs. "So. I take it you haven't left hearth and home behind to make my own Christmas merry and bright." He yawned, stretching a T-shirt over his head. "Where's the rest of the crew?"

Chris jerked his thumb toward the living room. "They're out there, waiting for you to get decent."

"This is as decent as I get." Tucking the black shirt in his jeans, Jonas followed them toward the front of the house, finally noticing the muffled sounds of activity coming from the living room. It was obvious that his younger brothers—both happily married and settled in their hometown of Milford, Delaware—had gone to a great deal of trouble to transplant their holiday celebration more than three hours north.

Although the twins were identical—dark haired, swarthy skinned—their wives were polar opposites. Diane—cool, blond, and sophisticated—had given Jeff a carbon-copy daughter, plus two dark, rough-and-tumble sons that carried on the all-boy Fielding tradition admirably. Diane was the first one to spot Jonas and nodded her sleek platinum head in his direction. "My, my, look what Trix dragged in."

Despite the rude awakening and his scruffy appearance, Jonas threw out his arms in a general embrace. "Mornin', family."

Connie, a tall, curly-headed Texan with a toddler balanced on each hip, crowed back, "Will y'all look at that mess? Jonas, when was the last time you shaved that sorry face of yours?"

"Huh." He squared his shoulders, assumed his most macho pose, and stuck out his tongue. "Some females like a bit of stubble on a man."

The two women rolled their eyes. "From a distance, maybe," Connie grumbled. "Di and I make sure there are fresh razors at every sink in the house." She lowered her two wiggly bundles to the floor. "Children, give your Uncle Jonas a big hug, but mind you, don't get your tender cheeks anywhere near his chin. It's worse than Daddy's."

In seconds, he was shoved into an overstuffed chair and covered with nephews and nieces, giggling and squealing and ignoring their mothers' warnings as they rubbed their sticky faces along his scratchy one. "Uncle! Uncle!" Jonas hollered, knowing that would only spur them on.

When they finally stopped hugging and tickling long enough for him to catch his breath, Jonas eyed his siblings through the maze of arms that circled his neck, feeling his chest tighten and a catch creep into his voice. "Um...thanks for coming."

Chris shrugged. "Sure. You're our big brother, right?"

Jonas nodded, not trusting himself to say another word, and squeezed the children that were draped across his lap. At that moment, he was as proud of Jeff and Chris as if they were his own sons instead of his younger brothers.

He couldn't fill their father's shoes, not for a second. But he'd tried. The Lord knew he'd tried.

With two of his siblings, those efforts had paid off. But not with Nathan. *Never with Nathan.*

Jonas released his squirmy lapful, grunting as they stabbed him with sharp little elbows and knees. Judging by the look on both his brothers' faces, they were thinking about Nathan, too. "Three out of four of us," he muttered, standing. "Not bad for the Fielding clan. Got just the place for us to have Christmas dinner, too."

While the women marched the children out to their vans to bring in presents and sticky buns, the men moved to the kitchen, trying to look busy making coffee and pouring milk. Leaning on the counter, Jeff asked the unspoken but obvious: "Have you heard from Nate?"

The same question came up every time the three of them got together.

Jonas sighed, his shoulders sagging. "I haven't seen Nate in almost a year. Got a couple of phone calls from Vegas, another one from Palm Springs, but that's it."

"At least he calls you." Chris's mouth hardened into a tight line. "He doesn't give us the time of day. Hasn't for years."

Jonas said nothing, only nodded as he measured out the coffee in generous scoops. The twins—who, at thirty-three, fell between him and Nate in age—had spent their lives marching along the straight and narrow. They'd earned their degrees, joined the Marines, married wisely, and made their late mother proud at every turn—all of which ticked off young Nathan royally. After big, strong Jonas, then perfect Jeff and Chris, kid brother Nathan hadn't stood a chance.

Jonas knew that. Maybe that was why he'd been there for Nate, again and again, even when Nate didn't deserve it, didn't appreciate it, didn't want his help. Period.

Somebody had to do it. Jonas was the oldest; he got the job.

Nate had more talents tossed his way than the rest of them put together, and they all knew it. Awarded a full golf scholarship to Stanford University, he majored in economics and minored in drinking. During Nate's junior year his world came apart at the seams. Kicked off the golf team for a frat party that got out of hand, he dropped out of Stanford and pursued a professional golf career with mixed results. Though he'd passed the PGA's rigorous playing ability test with flying colors and served as an apprentice to some of the best players in the profession, when it came to qualifying for the PGA tour, he'd missed the final cut.

"Next fall," Nate had assured anyone who asked, then stopped by the club lounge to drown his sorrows.

Jonas knew Nate was still drinking, still throwing his career away with both fists. But lately, he sensed it was worse than that. There was a desperation in Nate's voice that no amount of bravado could hide. If Nate didn't darken his door soon, he'd have to find him, bring him home, shake some sense into him.

Rescue him.

The reality hit Jonas like a blow to the solar plexus.

"Jonas, you okay?" Jeff eyed him, concern creasing the dark features so much like his own.

"Yeah, yeah, I'm fine." He jammed the coffeepot in place and pushed the brew button with more force than necessary. "Just thinking about Nate, wondering if he'll call today."

They all knew the answer to that one: not a chance.

"What are my chances of holding even one grandbaby in my arms before I die?"

Barbara Getz sniffed—more dramatically than necessary—then offered her daughter a fresh box of candles for the dining room table. Christmas had been, if not disastrous, at least disappointing. The house appeared older, care-worn. Her mother looked more so. Her dress was neatly pressed but familiar, her apron tied in a severe knot around her too-narrow waist. The hollows under her eyes were darker and her cheekbones more pointed.

Almost as pointed as her words. "After all, Helen has eleven grandkids."

"That's not fair!" Emilie jammed another candle in place. An entire afternoon spent on the same topic had worn her patience down to the nub. "Helen Bomberger gave birth to *four* children, not one."

"One daughter is sufficient—assuming she's married, of course." Barbara lifted her shoulders slightly. "Grandchildren are a natural expectation for a mother to have, you know."

"I know it's natural, Mother." Emilie jammed her fingers into the wavy strands that framed her face, not caring what damage she did to her carefully gathered knot of shoulder-length hair. "Kids just aren't me."

Her mother's eyebrows arched on the ends, creating a perfect V—the same look Emilie saw every morning in the mirror. The older woman's voice dropped precipitously. "Do you mean to say you're not normal, dear?"

"Of course I'm normal!" Emilie circled the room, waving her hands through the air as if trying to grasp at some elemental truth that escaped her. "Husbands are fine and children are fine and all that is…fine. For someone else. Not for me."

Her father's voice floated in from the hallway. "Give her time, Barbara."

Donald Getz, the referee. Her calm, rational, feather-smoothing father.

He stepped into the dining room, as unobtrusive as his faded green sweater and beige corduroy pants. "Our Emilie Gayle hasn't met the right man yet, that's all."

"Pa-paa!" Her groan filled the small paneled room. "Not you too." She was struck with how much shorter he seemed than the tall, imposing man she remembered from her childhood. His hair was solid gray now, his jowls hanging in loose folds around his gaunt face.

He was the same man, yet not the same at all.

His mind, however, ran on the very same track as his wife's.

"We thought you might bring someone with you today." He slipped his arm around her shoulders.

Emilie felt her eyebrows tighten into a V. "Bring who?"

"Oh, I don't know." Her mother's long neck slowly turned cranberry-relish red. "Maybe someone…special."

"Mo-ther!"

The day went downhill after that.

After dinner, their family gift exchange was blessedly short. The two small items she'd chosen with great care in Winston-Salem were opened and acknowledged with appropriate murmurs. Her own present was mined from her mother's closet stash: the Sunbeam blender. Emilie pretended to be surprised, even thrilled with the impersonal gift, already finding a hiding spot for it deep in the recesses of her kitchen cupboards back in North Carolina.

Her patience didn't last until six o'clock after all. By four-thirty she was pacing the kitchen floor, drying her grandmother's china so vehemently that her mother finally snatched the dish towel out of her hands and ordered her to sit down.

"I have a better idea." Emilie grabbed her coat from the back of a kitchen chair and buttoned herself inside its cashmere warmth, her fingers flying. "I'm going home. To Main Street. To work. It's been…Christmas." She sighed heavily and stuffed her hands in her pockets. "I'm here for six months, Mother. We'll try again on a day that doesn't matter so much, all right?"

She was halfway out the front door before she turned back and pressed a firm kiss on her startled father's cheek. "Good-bye, Papa. I'm sorry."

"No need to apologize, Emilie Gayle." He kissed her back, then rested his arthritic hands on her shoulders. "A smart woman like you shouldn't have to wait for a man to wise up and see what he's missing. Why don't you pick out one you like, and ask him?"

"Fine." She bit her tongue to hold back another groan. "I promise. The next single man I run into, I'll ask him to marry me. Okay, Daddy?"

"That's our girl." Her parents stood side-by-side as she marched down the steps, then closed the door behind her with a parting wave.

Home. A mixed blessing if there ever was one.

Fumbling for her keys, she squinted up the street toward Candi Hoffman's house. Emilie smiled, despite the day's frustrations, remembering the summer morning she woke up early and wrapped bathroom tissue around the Hoffman's spruce trees, then took a picture and sent it to the *Lititz Record Express*—anonymously, of course.

It would've been more effective if she'd skipped her return address.

Another familiar front porch caught her eye. *Helen's*. Her second home all through her childhood. In the frozen darkness, the brightly lit house with its cheerful blue door beckoned. A huge fir tree filled the front window, glistening with tiny white lights and decorated with intricate, handmade ornaments carefully snipped from white paper. *Scherenschnitte,* the Germans called it—"scissors cuttings," Helen's favorite craft.

Emilie fingered her keys, considering. She *did* need to pick up that scarf today. Hadn't Helen specifically asked her to stop by? She wouldn't stay a second. Just a quick Christmas hug and home to her research she would go.

Buoyed by the prospect of seeing a woman whose sole mission in life was *not* finding her a husband, Emilie walked toward Helen's place, vaguely noticing a black Ford Explorer and a couple of minivans with Delaware tags parked at the curb. Not likely the older woman had company—not with her four children grown and gone thirty years ago, and her eleven grandchildren married and scattered like grass seed across the plains of the Midwest.

No, Helen would be alone and probably glad for a little company on Christmas.

Besides, Emilie decided with a chuckle, anything was better than running into some horrid-looking man and proposing marriage, just to please her father.

Standing at the gaily-decorated door, she only hesitated for a second before she tapped a never-forgotten rhythm on the wooden panels—*rat-tat-a-tat*—then pushed the door open. A warm, fragrant aroma greeted her like a long-lost friend. "Merry Christmas, Helen!" She almost sang it. "It's Emilie."

"Emilie?"

Jonas' head snapped up, his attention to Helen's homemade sage dressing suddenly diverted. *Emilie Getz? That stuck-up, pale-skinned, cold fish...that Emilie?*

"Who's Emilie?" Jeff popped another forkful of buttered acorn squash in his mouth. After a meager breakfast at Jonas' place, then a morning spent opening gifts and playing board games with the kids, the Fielding family had descended upon Helen's dining room with no more warning than a phone call and a promise to bring some canned vegetables. Even with their pitiful offerings, the woman had whipped up a mighty respectable version of Christmas dinner.

Now it seemed another visitor had arrived with even less notice.

"Emilie is a nice little girl I used to diaper." Helen's wink disappeared among her wrinkles as she stood slowly and called out, "In here, dear," then wobbled toward the front door.

"Diaper, huh?" Chris reached for another roll. "How old is this nice little girl?" When Emilie appeared in the arched doorway, his hand paused in midreach and a wolfish grin stretched across his face. "Ahh. Old enough."

Jonas grimaced. *Easy, brother. Don't jump to conclusions.*

Emilie's wide eyes and slack jaw were his first clue—she was *not* expecting to find him there, let alone toting two look-alike siblings and five kids. Emilie was from Lititz, right? Probably spent the day with family. Whatever the case, she seemed all wrung out—mussy hair, pinched features, drooping shoulders—like she'd suffered through a tough day at the office instead of enjoying Christmas somewhere.

Better tread lightly here, fella. Jonas waved at an empty chair. "Greetings, Dr. Getz."

Helen Bomberger's two chins bobbed up and down with excitement. "Oh, you two already know each other, then?"

Jonas wasn't certain Emilie knew her own name. Her eyes were unfocused and every inch of her face was covered with a faint pink tinge.

"Oh!" Emilie finally murmured, blushing further. "I…I'm…well, I'm…"

"Late for dinner?" Jonas decided Emilie looked good in pink, especially from the neck up. Clearly he'd have to embarrass her more often. "Have a seat. Helen has fed the ten of us all afternoon. Now it's your turn."

"No, no!" Emilie waved her white-dove hands in the air. "I didn't mean to interrupt." She took a step backward. "Besides, I've already had dinner. Couldn't eat another bite."

Yeah, but you should. Several bites, in fact. The woman was so thin, she was almost scrawny. Not his type at all. "Helen doesn't let people sit at her table unless they eat something."

"He's right, Emilie." The gray-haired woman patted the chair next to her. "You're not interrupting a thing. Jonas has spent the last five Christmases here. Hardly company anymore. And isn't it nice his family is in town this year? Join us for sugar cake at least."

Emilie finally slipped off her coat—reluctantly, it seemed—and joined them at the table, carefully spreading a cloth napkin across her lap.

Jonas chuckled slightly at the gesture. *Not taking any chances with runaway sugar this time, is she?*

Stabbing a forkful of broccoli, Chris waved it in Emilie's direction. "Aren't you gonna introduce us, bro?"

Jonas worked his way around the table, putting names to faces, while Emilie's lips moved silently as if she were memorizing them one by one. Finishing the formalities, he cleared his throat and gazed at her downturned countenance. "Just as well you're married, gentlemen. Emilie's already spoken for."

Her head snapped up. "I'm…*what?*"

"Married." Jonas bit back a smile. "Wedded to your history books for the next six months. Right, Doc?" Wasn't that how it worked with these academic types? They lived with their noses in their books and their heads in the clouds?

When Emilie merely nodded with a wary gaze, he explained, "I'm on the missions committee, Dr. Getz. We've been expecting you." *Not you, precisely.*

Not a woman. Must have missed that meeting. He turned toward his brothers. "Emilie has been hired by my church to write a book about our 250th anniversary."

She bristled at that one. "It's my home congregation, too."

A voice drifted in from the kitchen. "And she's the perfect person for the job." Helen reappeared, a generous serving of Moravian sugar cake in one hand, a fork in the other. "Will you be wanting coffee, Em?"

Emilie nodded, her rosy skin beginning to fade back to ivory again. "I'm sorry to be so out of sorts, today of all days." Helen poured coffee into a fancy china cup while Emilie took a tentative bite of her sugar cake.

His gaze followed her fork, tasting the dessert all over again. Of all the good food that flowed out of Helen's kitchen, this stuff took the prize. A shallow pan filled with a rich dough of some sort, covered with thick brown sugar and cinnamon in buttery little puddles. He'd already had three pieces. Would a fourth be too much to ask?

Helen read his mind. "One more square for you, Jonas?"

His grin told her all she needed to know.

While Helen went off to the kitchen, he trained his eyes on Emilie, who'd already put aside her fork, the cake barely touched. Despite the general clamor around the table, he managed to get her attention.

"So, do your folks still live here in Lititz?"

She nodded. "Two doors down." Silence.

A real chatterbox, this one. "You spent Christmas at their place, huh?"

Her narrow shoulders lifted and fell.

Next topic. "Tell me about your research."

Her eyes widened. "My...uh...*which* research?"

Why the frightened doe look? Smiling, meaning to reassure her, he added, "The historical material you're gathering on the church. For the anniversary book, remember?"

She leaned back in her chair, obviously relieved. "Oh, *that* research." For the first time since she'd arrived, Emilie appeared to relax, brushing a few stray wisps of brown hair off her forehead. "I've studied most of the original Moravian settlements in America—Bethlehem, Nazareth, Christiansbrunn, Hope, Salem, and Bethania. And Lititz, of course."

Jeff whistled. "The woman does her homework."

His praise flustered her. "Well...yes. I plan to weave some of their history through the fabric of ours here in Lititz, so local readers can see how it all fits together."

As she outlined the events she'd be covering—Count Zinzendorf's arrival in Pennsylvania and the rest—Jonas listened and observed. *She's smart. Serious. Pretty, in a pinch-lipped sort of way.*

And hurting, unless his radar was way off base.

It was that quality alone that made it hard for him to ignore her—much as he wanted to, much as she wasn't remotely his type. He liked women who were on fire—for the Lord, for life, for people. Emilie Getz was as cold as they came.

Which is where you come in, son.

Jonas didn't move a muscle while his entire being made a radical attention shift. *Lemme guess, Lord. You want me to warm things up. Make her feel welcome. Show her—*

Fullness of joy, son.

Joy?

Show Emilie who I am.

Jonas swallowed a groan, training his eyes on the anything-but-joyful woman sitting across from him. For an instant, they exchanged glances. *Hmmm.* Maybe her chilly exterior from last night had warmed a bit after all.

Whatever the case, his commission was clear. *Got it, Lord.*

The One who made him knew him well: Jonas couldn't turn his back on someone who was hurting. That's why he'd always been there for Nathan. Why he spent three hot weeks on a Central American mission field last June. It was also why he'd found Trix at the Humane Society, a golden retriever with the pain of abuse in her eyes and the limp to prove it.

Emilie wasn't limping, but there was a bruised look about her that made him willing to forget, just for a moment, what a bookish, standoffish snob she was.

Joy, huh?

What the woman needed was a diversion. *Yeah.* Some outdoor activity, full of fresh air and God's creation and...*wait.*

It was perfect.

"Dr. Getz." Jonas tossed his napkin on the table, his fourth dessert a fond memory. "What do you know about birding?"

Her eyebrows formed a distinct *V*. "As in robins and wrens?"

Jonas nodded. "And black-capped chickadees—"

"And yellow-bellied sapsuckers." Jeff added with a chuckle. "Fielding men are a bird-crazy bunch."

Emilie's *V* tightened. "How many are there?"

"Birds?" Jonas shrugged. "Millions, I guess."

"Not birds." The corners of her mouth threatened to curl up. "Fielding men. How many are there of those?"

Chris held up his fingers. "Four: Jonas, Chris, Jeff, and Nate. No need to include Nathan, though." He shot Jonas a sideways smirk. "He's even uglier than the three of us."

Emilie started to say something, then pinched her lips tighter still.

Jonas propped his elbows on the table, his hands dwarfing the fragile coffee cup. "The reason I asked is this is the weekend for the Lititz Christmas Bird Count."

"*Christmas* birds?" Chris groaned. "*Red*-bellied woodpeckers and *green*-winged teals, is that it?"

Jonas rolled his eyes. "He knows better, Emilie. Our dad—" out of nowhere, something lodged in his throat—"that is, our dad was a high school biology teacher."

"Delaware's Teacher of the Year."

"Right, Jeff." He'd almost forgotten that. Forgotten a lot of things. The lump in his throat eased down. "Anyway, Dad taught us everything he knew, which was plenty. He was a bird man from his days as an Eagle Scout."

Emilie made a sound that bordered on a delicate snort. "A bird man who's an eagle? Are you teasing me again, Mr. Fielding?"

"Call me Jonas." He grinned, warming up to the notion of birding with this particular guinea hen. "I never kid around when it comes to identifying our feathered friends. That's the whole idea of the bird count. A hundred years ago, a bunch of sharp Audubon enthusiasts decided Christmas should be for counting birds instead of shooting 'em."

"You still *eat* them, I see." She nodded toward his empty plate and the plucked-clean turkey centerpiece. Her eyebrows had calmed down, but her eyes themselves twinkled ever so slightly. "Are you suggesting I join you for a *Fielding* day?"

Clever girl. He shifted in Helen's direction. "What do you think, Mrs. Bomberger? Can we keep her in line, show her the ropes?"

The elderly woman flapped her hand like a baker chasing insects off a shoofly pie. "Not this year, I'm afraid. The way my arthritis is acting up, I'd be stiffer than a board before daybreak. Planning on counting them at my feeders, though." She pointed toward the kitchen door. "Got fifty pounds of birdseed and two new feeders out back, all set for action." Her rheumy eyes crinkled around the corners. "Emilie is welcome to use those fancy binoculars you got me for my birthday."

"Very generous, Mrs. B." *Heart of gold, this woman.* "So, Doc, I'll pick you up at...say, four-thirty?"

Emilie winced. "In the morning?"

He pretended to look surprised. "Of course. When else would you find a barred owl hooty-hooting at the moon?" He slapped his hands together, anticipating a brisk wintry day at the Middle Creek Wildlife Management Area with a thermos of hot coffee in one hand and a field guide in the other. "Be sure you dress for cold weather. You Carolina girls do own warm clothes, don't you?"

"I'm a Pennsylvania woman." There was a drop of vinegar in her voice. "And yes, I have plenty of warm clothes. Winston-Salem is hardly Myrtle Beach." Her haughty expression was back, which meant his rejuvenation efforts were already starting to work.

"Four-thirty it is then," he reminded her with a wink.

"See that you're not late, Mr. Fielding."

"Jonas."

"Whatever."

His grin widened. *Welcome back, Dr. Getz.*

Four

◆

There was an old owl lived in an oak,
The more he heard, the less he spoke;
The less he spoke, the more he heard,
O, if men were all like that wise bird!
PUNCH

"Rise and shine, sweetheart!"

Jonas emptied the remains of a dog food bag into the plastic dish until it overflowed, then tossed the bag in the vicinity of the kitchen trash can.

"Eat up, Trix, and then we're gone. I intend to surprise a certain bird by arriving early." Jonas pulled on his black parka and a wool stocking cap, then draped a set of binoculars around his neck. Jamming a couple of shabby bird books and a handheld video camera in one roomy pocket, then a handful of dog biscuits in the other, he stuck a glazed doughnut between his teeth and shoved the rest of the box in his backpack.

With so much work piled on his desk, he had no business taking a day to play in the woods with Dr. Stuck-Up. Still, he'd promised the Lord. And Emilie had agreed to come. *Who knows?* Their outing might prove to be more entertaining than he expected.

Grabbing a thermos of hot, black coffee, he headed for the garage with Trix circling his thighs. Like all retrievers, she knew the drill, knew they were heading for a day in the field, and could scarcely contain her excitement.

"In you go, girl." He opened the back door on the driver's side and Trix leaped into the Explorer's roomy backseat, panting and drooling with abandon. Despite the early hour, Jonas let out a noisy whoop. "Won't prissy Miss Emilie love you? Be sure you rub up against her all day long and shed like a...well, like a golden retriever. Got that?" He scratched her behind the ears, a fresh wave of affection washing over him. "Good dog."

That's when the front seat caught his eye. Paraphernalia from Carter's Run covered the seat, the floor, and most of the dashboard of his two-week-old Explorer. *Not good.* Not when he had a passenger who probably didn't know a fairway from a freeway.

The municipal golf course had been his baby from the moment of conception. When he moved to town five years ago to oversee the building of the new Lititz Public Library, he'd taken one look at the rolling acreage that stretched behind the proposed library site and visions of perfectly groomed #419 Bermuda grass danced in his head.

He wasn't the golfer Nate was—few mortals were—but he'd spent enough time on the links to know what an ideal golf course might look like. The thought of developing one, then watching tourists and locals enjoy themselves at a reasonable price, all the while boosting the borough's bank account, made his developer's heart pound with anticipation.

It had taken a year to convince the property owner to sell her verdant farmland, especially when she wasn't willing to give up the 1813 farmhouse that went with it. Perched on a high bluff, its long back windows looked down on an undulating one-hundred-fifty acres and the prosperous town that had grown around it.

Since he didn't need the woman's house, his main bargaining point was obvious: the prettiest backyard she could ever hope for. When he pointed out that another developer would be more likely to scatter three hundred ticky-tacky homes across her valley, she'd caught his vision for par-four holes and sparkling man-made lakes and agreed to sign the dotted line.

But that was only the beginning. Then he had to stand before the Borough Council and convince them a municipal golf course was in their best interest. No sweat. His personally financed feasibility study and profit projections for the borough had them dancing in their seats. The loan managers at Penn Bank were less dramatic, but equally convinced he could make it work and put up millions to prove it.

Once the USGA consultant gave the committee's plans his nod of approval, a steady stream of surveyors, clearing contractors, and ground-chomping dozers came and went through the construction entrance on Kissel Hill Road. Determined to keep his promise to the good folks of Lititz, who worried about a potential eyesore in their historic community, Jonas made sure the architectural team from New Jersey altered the lay of the land as little as possible. The clubhouse was designed in much the same style as the elegant new library he was building, its classic lines echoing the stucco-and-stone Moravian Church.

The golf course would open in April, the library in June. By the Fourth of July, his life would be back to normal, whatever that was. In the meantime, he needed to be on site today—walking the grounds, checking things out—not standing around in a twenty-degree windchill with an ice princess.

Remember why you're doing this, man.

Why *was* he doing this? Because she needed cheering up, right? *Great, Fielding. Another project.*

Except that wasn't fair. Emilie Getz was a woman, not a project. Truth was, he could use a day away from Carter's Run. It wouldn't kill him. Might even be fun watching *Fraulein Doktor* pretend to know doo-doo about birds.

First, though, she'd need somewhere in the Explorer to sit.

With a grunt, he gathered up an armload of notebooks, rumpled architectural drawings, four empty bank bags, and a year's worth of *Golf Digest,* then made his way toward the back door. Nudging it open with his knee, he tossed the contents onto the kitchen floor in a jumbled heap, with good intentions of sorting out the whole mess later.

Much later.

Jonas locked the door behind him and grinned. "Rise and shine, Dr. Getz."

Her copper-bottomed teakettle whistled a cheery tune into the morning darkness as Emilie prepared to break her fast in the usual manner: crisp toast covered with a scant layer of imported orange marmalade, piping hot English Breakfast tea with lemon, and fresh sliced fruit. This morning, a luscious pear waited on her plate, carefully arranged in a creamy white circle.

Almost too pretty to eat. She sighed, slipping a juicy slice of pear into her mouth, and regarded the kitchen clock. *Five after four.* He would be late, of course. Men always were. Since he seemed to be the outdoor type, at least he'd be dressed properly. Black clothes again, no doubt, and a hat of some sort or his pointy ears would freeze with that ridiculous haircut.

Pouring the steaming water into a chubby porcelain pot, she dipped two slim tea bags inside, then dropped the lid in place, followed by a quilted cozy. She'd finish dressing while it steeped, since her clothes were already waiting for her, neatly draped across the foot of her single bed. After darting up the narrow, enclosed curved staircase to the second floor, Emilie donned her lined wool slacks and sturdy boots in no time, then topped them with a high-necked blouse and a heavy brown sweater.

There. She might not know a catbird from a crow, but she intended to look the part of a seasoned birder. The brand-new field guide waiting in her coat pocket would give her away, though she'd bent the cover back and forth several times to make it appear well used. *Face it, Em. Birds aren't impressed with a Ph.D.* Neither was Jonas Fielding, if she'd read him correctly. His two brothers, on the other hand, seemed duly interested in her credentials. They had their older brother's looks, she concluded, without all the arrogance.

What had possessed her to agree to this outing—to spend another day away from her research, sitting in a nature preserve counting birds with a virtual stranger—was beyond Emilie's comprehension. She didn't even know what the man did for a living! Serving on church committees and tallying up sparrows hardly constituted gainful employment.

Obviously Jonas had caught her in a weak moment.

It would not happen again.

Minutes later, sipping her tea in comfy silence, she heard a sudden screech of tires out front, then the bleat of a car horn—not once but three times—shattering the predawn stillness with its rude, insistent blare.

Well, of all the…!

She tossed her cloth napkin on the table in disgust and reached for her blue hooded jacket. "If that's his idea of a bird call, we're in for a very long day." She swallowed her last sip of tea with a jolt when the horn sounded again, catching her off guard. The hot liquid burned a path down her throat, even as she sensed a head of steam building between her ears.

Throwing open the front door with uncharacteristic energy, Emilie lunged over the threshold just as Jonas reached the top step, inches away from a head-on collision. Regaining her balance, she stretched up to her full height, using the threshold to her advantage.

"Mister Fielding!" Steaming hot or not, her breath filled the frosty air between them with an angry cloud of vapor. "Was it your plan to invite all of Main Street to join us?"

He glanced at the vehicle parked at a crooked angle by the curb. "Nah. No room." He offered her a cagey grin. "Just you, me, and Trix."

Trix? So. Another woman was joining them. *Trix. Sounds like a nightclub dancer.* Emilie sniffed. "Very well. I'm ready, of course."

"Of course." He angled one thumb toward the car and pulled the door shut behind her.

She swept past, then paused to give him an appraising glance, eyebrows arched. "Is black the only color in your wardrobe?"

"Yup." His infuriating grin grew more so. "I order two dozen Ts and jeans at a whack from L.L. Bean. No mix, no match, no hassle."

No taste, either.

He followed her down the steps. "I've got you in the back. With Trix. Okay by you?"

"Naturally, I....oh..." Emilie was close enough to see movement behind the tinted glass. Even in the darkness, it was clear Trix was a very large, very active woman. "So...how...old is Trix?"

"Four or five, give or take."

Jonas reached for the door handle while Emilie watched in horror as the backseat passenger smashed her wet black nose and long pink tongue against the rear window.

"Aahh!" she shrieked. Emilie *never* shrieked. "Is that a...a...*dog?*"

"Yup." He yanked open the door, and Trix came bounding out onto the sidewalk, greeting Emilie with slobbery kisses smeared all over her pale white hands.

"Oh...! Oh...!" Emilie was doing her best not to toss her breakfast pears all over the sidewalk as she hastily wiped her hands on the hem of her jacket. "I'm not...well, I'm simply *not* a dog person."

"No problem," Jonas assured her. "Trix likes everybody, even people who don't like her back. Shoulda called her Gracie." He patted the large, yellow beast. "Trix, looks like you're riding in the back all by yourself. Miss...uh, Dr. Getz here says she doesn't like dogs."

"It's not that I don't like them," Emilie corrected him, picking her way across the ice toward the passenger side. As far as it went, that was the honest truth. She *didn't* dislike dogs. She loathed them.

Sliding inside the front seat, she'd no sooner tucked her purse beside her feet, avoiding Trix's lethal tongue, when a deafening blast of music from the car speakers instantly pinned her back against the headrest. Her second shriek of the morning filled the air. "Good heavens!"

Jonas climbed in beside her seconds after the onslaught began. "Like it, huh?" He gunned the engine and shifted into drive, grinning at her as he inched the volume up a notch. "One of my favorite bluegrass CDs. Group of guys from Maryland."

She pressed back harder, trying to escape the noise. "Those aren't...*violins* they're torturing, are they?"

"Nope." The car careened down Main Street. "They're fiddles."

Fiddlesticks. She knew an abused violin when she heard one.

His elbow jammed into hers. "I thought you liked instrumental pieces."

She fought the urge to elbow him back, knowing it was neither ladylike nor appropriate, and shot him a pointed look instead. "Classical music—real music—is more to my taste. Might you have anything softer?"

He touched a round button on the stereo and the disturbing racket disappeared as abruptly as it'd begun. The silence fell on her like a heavy quilt on a cold day—warm and welcome. Emilie tried not to sigh with relief as she mumbled her thanks. To think that she was spending the day with a man who considered that...that *noise* worth listening to!

Minutes later, heading north on Broad Street, he reached under the seat, pulled out an ancient cassette recorder, and dropped it in her lap. "It's not classical music, but I think you'll find it fairly interesting." When she reached for the start button, his hand rested on hers for the slightest of seconds. "Later, Emilie."

It was the first time he'd said her name that morning. She didn't know which startled her more—those familiar three syllables rolling out on a smoky bass note or the brush of his callused palm on her ungloved knuckles.

His hands were large and rough, the hands of a carpenter, yet his touch was featherlight. What *did* he do to earn his keep? She was an experienced researcher; it was time to ask a few well-chosen questions.

"Mr. Fielding, what precisely is your line of work?"

He shrugged. "I play with dirt."

The look on her face made missing a day at Carter's Run worth every second. Shock, confusion, disgust—who could tell? Not him, not in a lifetime. Eyebrows tipped up, lips curled down, chin jutted forward, tiny ears pinned back against her head, she looked like...like...

Of course.

An owl. Emilie Getz looked like an owl. A boreal owl, to be exact. No, she didn't have a light-colored bill or a dark border around her face. But she *did* have the same puzzled expression and erect posture, with no ears worth mentioning.

Except boreals resided in Canada, not Winston-Salem.

"Dirt?"

She even screeched like an owl.

"I'm a land developer." He watched her spine stiffen. "I buy land and turn it into something profitable."

"Then you, sir, represent everything I despise about the world today." Her voice, no longer cool and brittle, burned instead with the heat of conviction. "In the pursuit of commerce, men like you have torn down landmarks, desecrated communities, and run roughshod over history and society and culture and—"

"Emilie, wait. I—"

There was no stopping the woman.

Her shoulders pivoted in his direction, led by that jutting, ferocious chin of hers. "More antiquities have fallen under the blade of your coldhearted bulldozers than historians can count. Believe me, we've tried to stop you." She huffed dramatically, then leaned back against her seat. "I cannot adequately express how disappointed I am to learn that you are counted among their ilk."

Concentrating on two important activities—staying on the road and not laughing out loud—Jonas simply nodded. "I realize that some of my colleagues have gotten carried away—"

"They *should* be carried away!" she fumed, glaring out the window to punctuate her disgust. "Carted off in a paddy wagon! Thrown in jail for their blatant disregard for the history they've carelessly tossed aside under the guise of...*progress.*" She spat out the word like a bit of rotten fruit.

He let the energy of her unexpected diatribe hang in the silent air, its static electricity palpable. Every short hair on his head stood at attention. Before he could stop himself, he said exactly what he was thinking: "Emilie, I didn't know you had it in you."

Her head swiveled toward him. "Had what in me? That kind of anger?"

"No. That kind of passion."

In seconds, she was pink again, forehead to chin, just like yesterday, only brighter. "I'm...I'm not..."

He eased on the brake as they reached the red light at Newport Road. "You're not what? Passionate?"

"No!" She yanked on her gloves, refusing to meet his sideways glance. "I'm not at all sorry for what I said about developers." Her voice was steel cold. "Your...well, your profession happens to be a sensitive subject with me, that's all."

Sensitive? Best he could figure, she was touchy about every subject in the book.

As they passed the intersection and climbed the hill that led north out of Lititz, he studied her angular profile. Even with every corner of her face softened by that porcelain skin of hers, it was clear she'd shut down again. *Blast.* If he expected to cheer up the gloomy professor, so far he wasn't doing too well.

Trix took her cue and laid her head on Emilie's shoulder, offering her own brand of encouragement as she nuzzled Emilie's tightly knotted hair. Emilie didn't move a muscle, Jonas noticed, until Trix made a wild foray with her wet pink tongue and practically swallowed the woman's delicate ear.

"Eeek!" Emilie shuddered and ducked her head to escape the canine's zeal, swatting the air behind her. "Go...go lick *him,* will you?"

Trix would have none of it, Jonas could see that. The retriever had plenty of opportunities to lick him any old day or night, but a hysterical woman—

well, that was too good to pass up. Lunging over the seat to get at her target, Trix ignored his every command. "Sit! Now, sit, girl!" Her obedience school days seemed a distant doggy memory.

Without a traffic light in sight, and Emilie whimpering in a huddle under the dashboard, he had no choice but to pull over on the gravel shoulder and settle things. Throwing the gearshift into park, he turned around in his seat and grabbed Trix's collar.

"This isn't playtime, Trix." Goldens loved nothing more than pleasing their masters, so Jonas made sure she understood he was not at all pleased. Trix slumped down in the backseat with a canine sigh, repentant and humbled, while Emilie slowly rose to a sitting position in the front, easing back against the seat with noticeable caution, still balancing the tape recorder on her lap.

"She'll be fine now, Dr. Getz. Trix loves people, that's all." He steered the car back onto Route 501, checking the rearview mirror to be certain the retriever was still minding her manners. "Once we get out in the field at Middle Creek, you'll see what a well-behaved girl she can be."

Beneath Emilie's calm exterior, he sensed a slight bristle.

"Is that how you like all your females? Well behaved?"

"No, not all of 'em. Just my dogs." *Good grief, is she always this cranky in the morning?* "We'll be on Kleinfeltersville Road before you know it. Meantime, help yourself to a cup of coffee. There's a thermos around here somewhere."

She found it jammed between their seats. Opening it with great care, she poured herself little more than a swallow of the steaming liquid. Even then, she wrinkled her nose.

"Lemme guess." He grimaced. "Tea drinker."

She nodded between sips.

"Figures. You didn't seem too enamored of the stuff they handed out on Christmas Eve."

"No, but I drank it," she reminded him. "The lovefeast is liturgy, not sustenance. When Count Zinzendorf unintentionally served the first lovefeast in 1727, it was meant to be a time of fellowship and worship."

"Funny—" he wrinkled his forehead, struggling to recall a vague reference he'd read in *The Moravian*—"I thought it was lunch."

"Well, yes." She waved her hand dismissively. "It might have started out that way, but even then he could see the spiritual significance of it all."

Jonas couldn't help himself. "You were there, of course."

"Very amusing." She sipped her coffee, then grimaced. "All our research indicates that the lovefeast began August 13, the day the Renewed *Unitas Fratrum* was born."

"If you say so, Doc." Maybe he didn't have all the details down, but he remembered the important stuff. About how the day was compared to Pentecost. About the impassioned, twenty-something Zinzendorf offering a fervent prayer that so moved the assembly that the Holy Spirit filled the place and no one wanted to go home for the noonday meal.

Instead the Count ordered simple foods to be brought and shared.

The first lovefeast.

"Yeah, that was quite a day, Doc." They drove along in a neutral silence for another fifteen minutes, until he turned left along a winding country road, the nature preserve almost in sight. "So. Ready to go owling?"

She peered through the glass into the morning darkness. "Owling? That's a word?"

He turned left at the Middle Creek entrance, heading uphill toward the Visitor Center. "It is to a birder. You have all the bait we need in your lap." He pointed to the tape recorder, then pulled into the parking lot, already filling up with assorted vehicles. "Bring that along, will you? C'mon, Trix, the fun has already begun."

Released from her backseat prison, Trix let out a bark of enthusiasm and leaped through the open door, wagging and wiggling as Jonas snapped a leash on her collar. With other dogs around, it was a necessity. He led the way as Emilie—tape recorder in one hand, Helen's binoculars in the other— picked her way across the stiff grass toward the group of people congregated around a large map. Most of the crew had elaborate spotting scopes on tripods, and for a heartbeat, Jonas regretted leaving his at home. Truth was, though, between a frisky golden and a feisty female, his hands were already plenty full.

An amicable guy wearing jeans and a bulky army jacket was pointing in various directions, dispatching the faithful to their assigned positions with maps that showed the boundaries of their count areas. Jonas listened and nodded, then turned to find an owl-like Emilie standing behind him—eyes wide open, lips pursed shut in a fair imitation of a beak.

He swallowed his second guffaw of the morning. "Ready to find a great horned? That's what you've got on your tape there." He steered her toward the stretch along Willow Point Trail that would be their stakeout.

"I beg your pardon?" She followed along behind him, trying to keep up with his long strides yet maintain a safe distance from the jubilant Trix. "Did you say there's a great horn on this tape?" She closed the gap, firing questions at him as she did. "What kind of horn? A trombone? A trumpet? Why would an owl respond to a brass instrument?"

He stopped long enough to get her complete attention. "A great horned owl, Emilie. A bird, not a trumpet. You'll hear your share of birdsong today, but none of them will be working from the Moravian hymnal. Got that?"

"Well!" She shoved the tape recorder under her left arm and marched ahead of him. "First of all, I didn't hear you properly. And second of all, my specialty is history not ornithology. A person has to learn these things."

"Yes, a person does." He caught up with her in three strides and nabbed her coat at the elbow, careful to grip only fabric and not flesh. "You *do* have a lot to learn, and I'm just the man for the job. You'll see. By day's end, you'll be more proficient than a mockingbird when it comes to mimicking bird calls."

Emilie looked doubtful. "I will?"

"Would I steer you wrong, Doc?"

Her only response was that *V* thing she did with her eyebrows.

With Trix straining at the leash, Jonas waved toward a copse of trees, barely visible in the inky darkness. Separated from the others, he felt rather than heard the subtle sounds of nature awakening around them. Though a great horned was more likely to hoot at dusk, an early morning serenade wasn't out of the question.

"Here, on this log." He sat down and patted a smooth spot next to him, then watched Emilie perch on a rougher patch of bark, putting more distance between them. "Wherever you're comfortable, then."

Out of habit, he uncapped his binoculars, then remembered they were useless in the low light. "For later," he explained, hoping she didn't catch his mistake. "For now, press Play on that recorder, then listen closely. If we're lucky, a great horned out there will hear our mechanical bird and call back."

Slipping off one glove to dutifully press the button, she shook her head. "I've heard of books on tape, but *birds* on tape? I'll believe it when I see it."

"When you *hear* it, you mean."

"Humph."

The tape whirred in silence, then four low-pitched hoots droned out of the small speaker, each one less than a second long. Silence. Then another series of low hoots.

He nudged her foot with his and whispered, "Turn it up."

A slight breeze carried the lone recording of a forlorn owl, hooting at who knew what.

Hoot. Hoot. Hoot. Hoot.

Minutes passed with no other sound but Trix's subdued panting. Finally, in the endless stillness between the taped calls, an answer echoed from the invisible branch of a nearby tree.

Hoot. Hoot. Hoot. Hoot.

Emilie whirled around on the log, almost tipping over in her excitement. "Did you hear that?" She rose and moved in the direction of the sound, her light step barely snapping the twigs underneath her.

He couldn't resist the urge to swing his binoculars up and rest them on the bridge of his nose, adjusting the focus until he had a certain brown-haired woman captured in his sights. Even in the faint light of predawn, he saw the expectancy on her face, the touch of awe in her expression, the wonder at God's creation reflected in her upward, oval-eyed gaze.

His chest tightened—with pride, with gratitude, he wasn't sure what. He knew this much: His father must have felt the same sensation the first time he'd taken Jonas birding thirty years ago in the wooded marshes of the Milford Neck Wildlife Area. Father and son, alone on a quiet summer morning, dead certain the calendar held many more such days for them.

Jonas' throat ached along with his chest. Even after two dozen years, the painful memory had a way of sneaking up on him.

Now, instead of birding with his father, he was spending the morning with a woman who treated his dog, his music, and his profession with equal regard: She hated all three.

Most men would give up on a woman like Emilie Getz. Toss her in the backseat with Trix and head for home. Forget where she lived. Lose her phone number. Change churches. Whatever.

But Jonas Fielding was not most men.

He considered humor-impaired women like Emilie to be a challenge, plain and simple. A stubborn oak that required pruning. A solid wall of resistance that needed dismantling.

A tough assignment that called for tougher measures.

Tough joy. What a concept.

Unbidden, a mischievous thought crossed his mind. A simple way to unstuff the very stuffy professor.

"Psst! Emilie!"

When she turned and shot him a nasty glance, he lowered his binoculars and felt a roguish grin crease his face. Stretching out his hand, he offered an earnest invitation. "C'mon, let me show you something even more…intriguing."

She tiptoed closer. "Is it a bird?"

"Definitely. Ever hear of a black-crowned night heron?"

Emilie shook her head. "No. Is it a common species?"

"Yes and no. Don't see too many around here, usually. Almost never in the winter. It'd be a real coup if we spotted one."

"So, do you have that birdcall on tape, too?"

"Nope." He dug out his bird book with one hand and hid his smile with the other. "Unfortunately we don't have that one on tape."

"Oh." She looked genuinely disappointed.

"Not to worry, though. It says right here—" he opened his book to the herons, jabbed at page ninety-eight, then snapped it shut—"they go *kwawk.*"

Her nose wrinkled. "Quack?"

"No, no. *Kwawk.* Try it again."

He coached her in proper kwawk technique until she got the hang of it. Not that he'd ever seen or heard that particular heron in action. Until now. Sort of.

"You're really good at this, Dr. Getz. A natural birder if I ever saw one." He waved her toward the waterside, where a thready morning light glistened along the surface. "They're fishers, these birds. Go ahead, do the call again."

She obediently tried her best, but not a kwawk was heard echoing back across the water. Shrugging, she started toward him. "I must be doing something wrong."

Talk about a perfectionist! The woman even had to get her birdcalls right to be happy. And she still wasn't laughing at the thing. Time for more drastic measures.

Shaking his head emphatically, he stood and motioned for her to stay near the water. "No, no, you're doing great. All we're missing are the movements."

"We need movements? Oh, surely not—"

He didn't give her a chance to argue. "Most definitely. Head, tail, wings, legs, the whole bit." He bobbed his head up and down to give her confidence. "Your kwawk is flawless. We just need to add the appropriate actions that go with it, and herons will be dropping out of the sky to greet you."

Her face registered the first inkling of doubt, so he plunged forward. "Herons, as I'm sure you know, are related to the *phoenicopteridae* family."

"The *what?*"

Jonas grinned. *Four years of Latin finally paid off.* "Flamingos, Doctor. Surely you've heard of them." And surely she'd see where this was going any minute now and start chuckling.

Her expression, however, was anything but amused.

"I suspect I know as much about herons as you do, Mr. Fielding." She made a sound that resembled a snort and spread her feet apart in a defiant stance, even as dawn was spreading a wintry haze across the skies behind her.

She was a harder nut to crack than he'd imagined, which only made his heavenly assignment more interesting. When his elbow brushed against the video camera stored in his pocket, his cheer-up-the-prof scheme soared to new heights. He and his brothers used to videotape each other doing outrageous bird imitations, laughing their heads off before, during, and after. A bright woman like Emilie would probably get a kick out it, too.

Wouldn't she?

"As you're aware," he began, stalling while he surreptitiously fished out the camera. "Herons, like flamingos, have a particular way of moving." He adjusted the camera in his hand, feeling for the record button. "Ever been to Florida, Dr. Getz?"

Five

He who laughs has not yet heard the bad news.
BERTOLT BRECHT

"I still don't understand how you talked her into this."

Pastor Yeager adjusted his bifocals and squinted at the small video screen in his office. Around the room Jonas counted a half dozen male church staff members, standing with their mouths agape and their eyes glued to the action on the screen.

He was *there* when it happened and even Jonas couldn't believe the shenanigans he'd caught on videotape.

Not that he'd intended to show it to another soul—ever—but after spending yesterday afternoon alone in his den with this footage, howling with laughter, it seemed too good to keep to himself. His brothers would've loved it, but with the twins in Delaware and Nathan in Nevada—maybe—Jonas was left with a drop-dead funny tape and no audience.

That's when he decided to show it to Pastor Yeager after the Monday morning missionary committee meeting, never figuring the rest of the guys would wander in to see what the noise was about. It wasn't any big deal, right? Harmless fun, nothing more.

Oh yeah? Then how come his conscience was ticking like a noisy alarm clock?

All six men watched in amazement as Emilie Getz, Ph.D.—eminent scholar and noted professor, the She-Coon of Moravian Church history—strutted around Middle Creek with her tail feathers pointed north, her beak pointed south, and her arms akimbo in the singularly best imitation of a black-crowned night heron ever seen at the 93rd Annual Lititz Christmas Bird Count.

Or any other bird count, come to think of it.

Jonas couldn't resist announcing, "Our historian-in-residence, gentlemen. In living color. With sound effects."

He eased the volume up so the assembled could hear her well-modulated kwawk, which put Pastor Yeager and his youth director, Kyle Heagey, right over the edge.

"Hawwwww!"

That set off the rest of the group, meaning Emilie's subsequent efforts were lost amid the chorus of hoots—tenors to basses—that swelled through the small room.

Jonas laughed harder than any of them, remembering the impromptu directions he'd shouted across the frozen marsh. "Higher, Dr. Getz. Step higher, that's it. Now, can you bend forward while you—? Oh my, that's perfect. Spot on, as the Brits say. Truly impressive, Doctor. The herons should show any second now."

When she'd paused long enough to realize he was videotaping, he'd quickly explained that it was for archival purposes only, that the Lancaster Bird Club kept such tapes in their files for training future members. "No one but fellow birders will see this tape," he'd assured her, chagrined at how glibly it'd rolled off his tongue. "Only those who will truly appreciate what you've accomplished here today will have the privilege of seeing your heron-ic self in action."

No question, this group truly appreciated it. Three of the ministers were practically on the floor. "So—" one of them asked between gasps—"are you showing this at your next bird club meeting?"

Jonas shrugged, another stab of guilt slicing through his windpipe. The birders met once a month at Franklin and Marshall College in Lancaster. Showing them the tape at January's gathering had never crossed his mind.

Now the idea was tempting as all get-out.

Just kidding, Lord. The minute we're through here, I'll erase the thing. And he would. Absolutely.

On screen, Emilie had just executed her first brave leap through the dried grass along the water's edge. He'd convinced her that herons had a distinctive leap-and-swoop move, which she'd valiantly tried to demonstrate. In her ultra-serious bid to succeed where he'd assured her others had failed, the woman had managed to successfully put five men of the cloth in serious stitches.

After watching an especially awkward kwawk and dip, the roomful of guys embarked on yet another round of raucous laughter, during which the music director managed to blurt out above the din, "Fess up, Jonas. Are you ever gonna let *her* in on the joke?"

From the doorway a woman's voice brought their laughter to an abrupt halt.

"I believe he just did."

Emilie simply watched them, not moving an inch.

Six pairs of eyes turned her direction, then swiftly downward.

Six pairs of feet rooted themselves to the carpet.

Six pairs of hands dove into pants pockets, no doubt lined now with cold sweat.

Like a classroom of slackers on final exam day, the group before her cowered with the awful realization that the jig was up.

The awkward silence was deafening. She wouldn't let herself even look at Jonas. To think she'd trusted the man. *Trusted him!* When he'd asked her to learn a birdcall, she did it. When he'd instructed her in the finer points of heron behavior, she'd thought it foolish, but she *did* it, hoping to please, trying to go along with his agenda. When he'd pulled out a video camera, she'd feared the worst, but convinced herself his intentions were honorable.

How could she have known the entire episode was designed to embarrass her beyond measure? What kind of a man did such a thing?

Her exasperated sigh broke the stillness. She'd have to sort out her feelings later. What to do now with *this* sorry group? That was her dilemma. The women from the office had already lined up behind her, eyes glaring, teeth grinding. These men would be lucky to get one decent letter typed and out the door before next year.

True, that was only four days hence, but the point would be well made by then: *Don't tread on me.*

Pastor Yeager was the first to speak, in a voice so low it was hard to imagine him ever stepping into a pulpit. "Uh...Miss...uh...Dr. Getz. I do hope you see the hu—" He abruptly caught himself. "I mean, the huge...uh, mistake we've made here this morning."

She pulled herself up taller than she'd ever stood before. "What I see, Pastor, is six naughty little boys who've been caught laughing behind the teacher's back."

Around the room, the men's heads nodded and faint smiles broke out on their faces, as though they expected her to laugh the whole thing off.

She dashed their hopes of a swift and painless acquittal with one arched eyebrow.

"The fact is, gentlemen, I do not see the humor in either this video recording or in this situation." Stepping into the room, she strolled among them like a general on an inspection tour, her gaze traveling the length of them, letting disdain emanate from her every pore.

"This congregation, *my* congregation, my own home church—" for a brief second, her throat tightened but she swallowed and pressed on, determined not to lose her nerve. "This fellowship has hired me—has it not?—for the express purpose of researching and publishing a book honoring two and a half centuries of unity among the brethren."

"And the sistren!" a volunteer from the hallway added.

"Suppose we begin by honoring our forefathers—" Emilie nodded at the gathering of women behind her—"and our fore*mothers* by respecting one another's gifts, talents, and personalities. You, Pastor Yeager, have a calling to preach and lead the flock by example. Methinks you can do better than this, don't you?"

He took the opportunity to step behind his desk and drop into his leather chair in obvious relief. "Yes, Dr. Getz, most certainly. I hope you can...forgive me for....participating in..." His words disintegrated into a slight shrug and a properly contrite expression.

A curt nod was her only acknowledgment. "There now. That wasn't too terrible, was it?"

One by one, she went on to point out the relative attributes of the males who stood before her with their egos tucked under their arms like criminals awaiting execution. Rather than the tongue-lashing they clearly expected—and deserved—Emilie granted them each individual pardons. A clamor of genuine repentance rang through the church offices like bells heralding the New Year.

When the men had returned to their desks and the women to theirs, only Jonas and Emilie remained standing. Pastor Yeager jumped up, mumbling something about needing to use the copy machine, and disappeared.

A weighty silence hung in the room.

Neither spoke. Or moved.

Behind the desk, the VCR softly clicked into rewind, filling the air with the whir of regret.

Emilie eyed Jonas as she had the other men. His gifts and talents weren't nearly as apparent as his guilt.

The sudden rumble of his voice, low and warm, caught her off guard. "No offer of forgiveness for me then, Emilie?"

Her heart ground to a halt.

Not "Doc," not "Getz"… Emilie.

Why, oh why, did he have to say her name like that? If he'd behave in his usual, smart-aleck manner, she could handle that. If he mocked her, she could shoot back a few zingers of her own.

But this. She swallowed hard. That steady gaze of his. Those enormous, puppy-dog eyes that put silly old Trix to shame. That rough chin that dipped down like a shy boy's, begging for mercy.

No, this was a stockpile of ammunition for which she had no defenses whatsoever.

Her harrumph, meant to sound superior, came out more like a girlish sigh. "Before I can even consider forgiving you for this…this inexcusable thing you've done, I have one question."

He inclined his head, pretending to look confused when what she sensed about him was an air of surprise. And relief.

Maybe you have a volley or two left after all, Em.

Folding her arms for effect—and to keep her hands from visibly trembling—she angled her chin up toward his. "My question is simple enough: Why?" She pinched off the word before it dissolved to a throaty croak. "Why did you make a fool of me, Jonas?"

My name. She said my name.

Of all the worst times, and for all the worst reasons, the woman had finally said his name. Out loud. Voluntarily.

She was wrong—dead wrong—because there was nothing simple about her question.

Why? He met her gaze and waited for the right words to come.

How could he tell her the truth? That he'd made a fool of her—and she'd hit the nail on the head there—that he'd done it for no other reason than because he *could*. She was so full of herself, so convinced that she could do anything, so determined to take the thing seriously instead of seeing the humor in it, it'd been easy to knock her down a peg or two. Or four.

You're the one who needs knocking down, son.

He didn't need to look up to recognize where that word of truth came from. *You're right, Lord.* He'd brought it on himself.

Clearly the fool standing in that room wasn't Emilie Getz.

Look at her, man. Chin up, arms folded, head held high. The woman was gutsier than any guy he'd ever known. She'd managed to hand those other men their heads in a basket and still leave their egos intact.

Such mercy was not to be his, he feared.

But he would ask, nonetheless.

He cleared his throat, dislodging the foot he'd thoroughly jammed there thirty minutes earlier, and plunged in. "Emilie, I'm sorry. I…well, I didn't—"

"And *I* didn't ask for an apology." Her voice was cool, controlled. "I asked for a reason."

"Fair enough." He folded his arms and assumed a pose identical to hers, though he doubted she'd notice. "The reason I taught you to…well, the reason I videotaped you doing…" More throat clearing. "The *reason,* Emilie, that I showed the guys your…uh, funny little heron imitation was… because…" *Get it over with.* "Because I'm a jerk."

Her tawny brown eyes glowed. "It's all about you, then. Not about me."

"Um…you could say that." *She did say that, turkey.*

"Meaning your let's-amuse-the-fellas act was meant to prove what a macho, in-charge, take-no-prisoners kind of man you are."

He lifted his shoulders. "You could say that, too." He waited to see if she was really listening, or busy loading her next bullet. "But I wish you wouldn't—"

"What you *wish* is immaterial to me, Mr. Fielding." She unfolded her arms and gathered up her bulging briefcase and discarded coat. "I have work to do, and none of it involves you." No longer looking in his direction, she swept toward the door, then turned, no doubt to be certain she had the last word.

"Whatever homecoming efforts you've expended to date have been duly noted and dubiously appreciated." Her eyes narrowed. "Helen may think you're something special, but this woman considers you nothing more than Middle Creek pond scum."

Emilie yanked the door shut behind her with a satisfying bang, leaving old what's-his-stubbly-face to fend for himself.

Only then did she realize she had nowhere to go. Her office was at the Woerner house, not at the church. The last place she wanted to be was standing there in the hall, homeless, when he came crawling out. Or roaring. Whichever.

"This way, Dr. Getz." Beth Landis, waiting a few feet down the hallway, motioned for her to follow, which Emilie did with brisk steps, looking neither left or right, lest she catch the eye of one of the other men she'd summarily dismantled.

"I figured you'd want somewhere to put your things whenever you stop by the church to do research." Beth's sweet, freckled face was the epitome of kindness and innocence. Did Beth even understand what had just transpired in there? For that matter did *she?*

"This will do nicely," Emilie mumbled, trailing behind the younger woman as she directed her to a small empty desk and a sturdy secondhand bookshelf. Studying the room and the girl with equal interest, Emilie decided she was grateful for them both. Though she'd only met Beth Landis briefly when she'd charged into the offices that morning, they'd talked on the phone numerous times while arrangements were made for her sabbatical in Lititz.

Today, though, had been above and beyond duty's call.

"I can't thank you enough, Beth, for phoning and letting me know what that...that..." Emilie tossed her head with a dismissive flip. "What that Fielding fellow was up to. No good, of course. It was kind of you to give me a heads-up."

Beth shrugged off the compliment. "You would've done the same for me." Her angelic smile was tinged with a devilish twinkle. "The minute all the guys started disappearing into the pastor's office, I knew something was up. All I needed was who and where, then I jumped on the phone, hoping you could get here in time to put a stop to it."

"And so I did." Emilie softened her voice, seeing Beth's chagrin. "I take it these good men never would dream of doing such a thing unprovoked."

"Never!" Beth shook her head emphatically. "It was all Jonas' doing. And it's really not like him, either. He's had a...thing about women lately." Her head wagged back and forth again, more slowly. "Unless I miss my guess, it's that Dee Dee woman who's really got his goat." She adjusted the pulldown window shade, letting in more of the slanting, wintry light. "Too bad he took it out on you, Dr. Getz."

"Call me Emilie." She gave Beth's shoulder a light squeeze, already feeling a kinship with her. Beth reminded her of her older students at Salem— bright, settled, at peace with themselves, their teenage traumas long put aside in favor of maturity and a good deal more patience. "How old are you, Beth? If you don't mind the question."

"Twenty-nine." Her laugh was practically a birdcall in itself, though cer- tainly not a heron. A nuthatch, maybe. "Same age as my husband, Drew. We've been married close to ten years."

"Really." Emilie felt an odd catch in her throat. "Children, then?"

Beth began straightening notices posted on a bulletin board, a becoming blush stealing across her freckled cheeks. "Yes, we have a little girl. Sara's four."

"Wonderful age," Emilie murmured, having absolutely no idea what she was talking about. It always worked, though; no matter what the child's age, parents always agreed with her.

Beth did not disappoint. "Yes, you're so right. Four is really fun." The blush disappeared, followed by a clear-eyed gaze. "She's our miracle baby."

"Oh." Emilie wasn't certain what that meant, but murmured in response, "You're lucky to have her, then."

Beth nodded, dropping down onto a straight-backed chair. Her smile returned as quickly as it'd left. "Since Drew travels constantly for his job with Woodstream, God was kind to give me little Sara to keep me company...and busy!" Glancing at her watch, she bolted to her feet. "Good grief, it's almost noon. My baby-sitter will have my head." All at once, her striped sweater was set in motion as she hunted for her purse, then darted for the door. "Mornings are for the church, but the rest of the day is all Sara's. Blessings on you, Dr. Getz." She winked, already halfway into the hall. "And welcome home."

"This is my home, too," Jonas grumbled, ignoring two rock-pushing bull-dozers who veered out of his path as he stomped around Carter's Run, waving his arms at the gray December sky. "That woman shoved me into a dog-house even Trix wouldn't go near."

It wasn't far from the truth. He'd gotten the cold shoulder not only from the women in the church office, but the men on staff had been avoiding him all week, too. As if he had *made* them watch that video. As if it was *his* fault Emilie came stomping in there, all high and mighty. *Yeah, right.*

He kicked a clod of dirt, sending it sailing across his future fourteenth hole. A par-five and destined to be a bear, if the designer's plans were any indication. Jonas punched the chilly air, frustration flowing through his veins like hot water through a radiator.

That woman!

Sure, he'd messed up. Never should have shot the video, never should have found an audience for it. He'd hurt her—the last thing he'd wanted to do—and he was sorry, blast it all. But wasn't *she* to blame for some of this? She could have refused to play along. Could have laughed at the whole idea. Could have made *him* do the funky chicken—well, heron—while *she* held the camera. *Yeah. What's her problem?*

You, fella. You are her problem.

Emilie Getz brought out a side of him he didn't know was there.

It wasn't his good side either.

Right this minute, though, his biggest problem was getting back in the good graces of the 8,280 citizens of Lititz who'd decided his name matched the current status of their golf course: solid dirt.

Thrusting his hands in his pockets, he tromped across the uneven ground, surveying the land with his eye, imagining the finished product. *Three months and change.* That's how long the construction team had. And the landscapers. And the turf crew. He groaned at the thought of all the details that covered his calendar like ants, daily reminders scratched in bold, black ink that no one could decipher except him.

His goal was clear: to give Lititz the best municipal golf course their money—and his skill—could buy. Okay, so he'd never developed a course before. Everybody had a first time, didn't they? He'd consulted the experts, done his homework, put more of his own money in the thing than common sense allowed.

He knew, deep in his gut, that it would pay off. It had to. He'd worked too hard, too long, to let things end any other way.

With one day left in the year and a serious pile of paperwork to crank out, Jonas headed for home, only three blocks west. It'd made sense to live in the same neighborhood. No matter what the weather, he could get from his place to Carter's Run in minutes.

His brick and stucco house loomed ahead, sitting up on a slight rise. Digging in his pocket for the key, he grinned, remembering the calculated look on Dee Dee's face when he'd asked her for his house key back. They'd bumped into each other Tuesday night at the Warwick High basketball tourney, where the Warriors had a great night, beating Garden Spot 56-55.

Dee Dee had taken her personal defeat well. Dangling the key from one long, red fingernail, she'd purred something about hoping he'd have a reason to give it back to her one day, then sauntered off in her too-tight jeans, leaving a cloud of heavy perfume trailing behind her.

What was it with him and women? One minute he was pond scum, the next minute, a nice, fat rainbow trout ready to be hooked.

Go figure.

He bounded up the steps, reminding himself that Dee Dee Snyder had gotten one thing right: This house was perfect for him. The large urns out front and the brass lanterns were her idea, along with the Palladian windows. It was big and classy and brand-new—everything he liked, right down to the easy-care polyester curtains. Admittedly, he owned exactly six pieces of furniture, but that'd come later, when he had time. Once he saw men in chinos toting clubs along the Carter's Run fairways, and grade schoolers filling out their first library cards, then he'd get on with his life.

Pushing open the front door, Jonas heard the answering machine click off. *Blast. Missed it.* He tossed his keys on the desk and punched Play, fully prepared to hear about yet another permit that was required, or an additional demand from the zoning board.

It wasn't about the golf course, but it was a golfer.

His brother.

Nathan.

The tinny-sounding speaker came to life. "Hey, brother Jonas. Sorry I missed you."

Jonas glanced at his watch. *Ten. Seven in the morning, Las Vegas time.* If Nate was still in Nevada.

Nathan's message played on. "I'm headed to Florida. Just thought I'd…touch base. See how you were doin'. I'm…okay."

Jonas felt his throat clamp shut. The kid was lying through his teeth. Something was wrong. Very wrong. He hadn't been Nate's surrogate father for most of his life not to know when he was telling the truth and when he wasn't.

Besides, Nathan never called to shoot the breeze. He only picked up the phone when he needed something.

"Maybe I'll catch you in person next time, Jonas. I could use some… advice. Hit a hole-in-one for me, okay?"

The machine stopped. So did Jonas' heart.

Without a doubt, Nathan was in serious trouble—again—and Jonas had no idea where or how to help him.

Six

Suspense in news is torture.
JOHN MILTON

Nathan Fielding waited, cradling the phone in his hand, one finger hovering over the redial button. Should he call Jonas back? Leave a longer message? Give the man some details?

Nah. What would he say? "Hi, Jonas. Your brother Nate here. I'm broke, okay? Need some money to tide me over…"

Right. Like Jonas had fifty thousand dollars sitting around. Like Cy Porter, his bookie, would take a dime less.

Gambling was the only way Nate knew to raise money fast. He had the scam down pat. Play a round of high-stakes golf with some out-of-town greenhorns. Bet heavily on a few side games he was guaranteed to win. Sundays he'd wager on his PGA buddies to come through for him, watching the crucial game on a wide-screen TV as he clutched a bottle of Miller and felt the adrenaline rush that gambling always delivered.

"They don't call 'em *greens* for nothing," he'd joke when Cy handed over his winnings.

But that was last year, when Nate thought his luck would last forever.

Forever had finally shown up to collect.

Cy had given him extra time, covered for him, lied for him. The more Nate bet, the more he lost. *Fifty thousand flippin' dollars.* No getting around it now. He had to call Cy, to check in. No news was worse than bad news, Cy always reminded him. Today's news was definitely not good.

Leaning against the icy interior of the phone booth, his Chevy running on fumes while it idled outside, Nathan willed his hands not to shake as he punched in the numbers. Asking Jonas for money would be a cinch compared to making this phone call.

The first ring knotted his stomach; the second pulled it tighter still. *C'mon, c'mon!*

A male bark cut the third ring short. "Porter."

"Yeah?" Nate gulped, his bravado fading fast. "It's Fielding."

"You got a lotta nerve callin' here at this hour of the morning, kid. Better be good news."

Nate glanced at his watch. *Eight. Seven in Vegas.* Almost crash time for Cy and Ginger. They'd sleep until one, then crank the party up all over again.

He forced himself to sound confident. "Just wanted you to be the first to know, Cy. I'll…I'll have the money soon."

The man grunted an obscenity. "Heard that one before, Nate. You shoulda never left town, you know. Not smart."

"I had to." Nate heard the desperation in his voice and tried to swallow it whole. "I couldn't raise that kind of cash there."

The man's laugh was ugly, humorless. "No, I guess not. Not the way you've been swingin' that driver lately. Better send somethin' in the next couple days, just to keep the man happy. Hear me?"

Nate's forehead dropped onto the heel of the phone. Between driving all night and facing Cy's demands, his nerves were toast. "I hear you."

"Good. 'Cause if I don't see an envelope in my mailbox by the end of the week, I'll come lookin' for you, Nate. And what Cy Porter looks for, he finds. Got that, kid?"

Five envelopes—all with the same heavenly spire in the corner, all with the same single-digit address on Church Square—appeared in Emilie's black mailbox Thursday morning.

The letters were short, to the point, and neatly typed—if not in fact dictated—by all of the secretaries who'd witnessed the catastrophe now referred to as "Red Monday," the facial shade most often witnessed in the vicinity of Pastor Yeager's office that fateful morning.

Slipping on her glasses—strictly for ease in reading, she explained whenever asked—Emilie opened the envelopes one by one. Little variety in content, she noticed. "Dear Dr. Getz: Please accept my heartfelt apology for the flagrant disrespect..." and so on. The only letter that wasn't typed was from Pastor Yeager. His was handwritten in his wildly cursive script. Rumor had it that his secretary, Suzanne, was so peeved about the whole incident that she'd refused to type a single piece of correspondence for him until he'd posted this one himself.

Emilie refolded each letter and stacked the lot in a tidy pile on her desk, then rested her chin in one hand, staring out the small kitchen windows at the drab-colored sky that matched her mood.

Appeasing as those five letters were, it was the missing one that left her with a nagging sense of doubt. Had she been too hard on Jonas Fielding? On all of them? Was she so unwilling to laugh at herself that she'd allowed a foolish prank to derail her, to provoke her into tossing professionalism aside for the sake of her womanly pride?

Those were the questions that'd kept her up late every night that week, pretending she was searching her books for new information about the Gemeinhaus when in truth she was searching her heart for answers.

The morning had dawned with little more to comfort her than a steaming pot of orange pekoe and the assurance that tomorrow would bring a new year.

No sooner had she reached for her tea than the doorbell rang. Her cup clattered back into the saucer. *Who in the world?* Not many people knew yet where she was staying. The staff at the church was aware of her accommodations. For that matter, her mother had the address, and so did Helen. *And so does Jonas.*

Hastily putting aside her eyeglasses, Emilie smoothed a few stray hairs off her forehead and hurried toward the front of the house, curiosity and apprehension tying her nerves in a knot. She flung open the door, then laughed at her unnecessary angst.

"Beth! What a nice surprise." She stepped back, perplexed at the odd mix of relief and disappointment that welled upside her. "Please, come in. I've just brewed a fresh pot of tea."

Beth's eyes crinkled as she displayed a mouthful of even, white teeth. "You'll have to drink fast, Dr. Getz. I'm here to invite you to join Sara and me for lunch today. At our place." She nodded toward the street. "I come by here every day on my way home, you know. If you don't mind walking four blocks, I can promise you a plate load of killer chicken salad waiting at the other end."

Emilie glanced down at her baggy pants and vintage sweater. "Well…I'm not really dressed for visiting…."

"Are you serious?" Beth's musical laugh bubbled up and over. "You look great. As always. In fact, *too* spiffy for Sara's taste. She'll have you covered with Play-Doh in no time."

"She will? My, isn't that clever." Emilie tried her best to appear enthusiastic, knowing her hesitant tone gave her away. "Are you sure lunch won't be too much trouble?"

Beth grabbed Emilie's nearby coat and deposited it in her arms. "Salad's in the fridge, and my baby-sitter is waiting. C'mon, Emilie, it'll be fun. Any woman who can put six men in their place has some lessons to teach this girl."

"Five men," Emilie corrected, following her out the door, her tea forgotten.

Beth turned back with a quizzical look. "Didn't you get a note from Jonas?" When Emilie shook her head, Beth's eyes narrowed. "That turkey. I told him the other letters were in the mail, and if he knew what was good for him, his better be, too. No letter, huh?" She blew out a frustrated sigh as they walked in tandem up Cedar and circled around Lititz Elementary onto Orange Street.

With school out for the holidays, the playground swings hung in silence, empty and still. Broad Street, though, was bustling with traffic as people left work early to get a jumpstart on the New Year. When they'd safely crossed the intersection, Beth shouted over the din, "Planning on coming to the Watchnight Service tonight?"

Emilie merely nodded, her eyes straight ahead, her thoughts a thousand miles away. What would the New Year hold for her? The archaeological discovery of a lifetime…or one more embarrassing footnote in her unremarkable career?

"Speaking of Jonas…"

Emilie snapped her head toward Beth. "Who said anything about Jonas?"

Beth giggled. "Guess I did, earlier. Anyway, there are a couple of things about Jonas Fielding that you oughtta know."

Looking forward again to mask even the slightest hint of interest, Emilie shrugged. "Not that I truly *need* to know, but go ahead."

"For one thing, he's very much loved in this town. Could run for mayor, if he wanted to."

She felt her neck stiffen. "What does that have to do with me?"

They turned left onto Spruce Street and its tree-lined collection of older homes, many built in the second half of the nineteenth century. "I just didn't want you to think *too* badly of our Jonas." Beth pointed ahead to her clapboard house painted in Williamsburg gold. "He's certainly made himself useful around the church."

"Oh, I can *see* that. When it comes to supplying video entertainment, the man is without peer."

Shaking her head, Beth slid her key in the front door and unlocked it. "Honest, Dr. Getz, that was…well, I don't know *what* that was, but it wasn't typical." She pushed open the door, talking over her shoulder, "You have forgiven him, haven't you?"

"Hmmm." Emilie followed her into the living room. *Forgiving him means forgiving yourself, too, Em.* "The jury is still out."

"Sara!" Beth's voice rang through the house. "Anna, I'm home!"

While the younger woman tossed her coat on a chair and headed up to the second floor, Emilie unwound her scarf, eyes widening at the sight before her. Every single surface was covered with *something*—doll clothes, crayon stubs, hunks of yarn, cereal bowls with spoons stuck to the bottom, and pile after pile of artwork. Pencil drawings, watercolors, collages made from magazine pictures, coloring book pages, construction paper projects, all flowed across the couch and over the dining room table like a blanket of green Georgia kudzu.

From the top of the steps came an explanation for the clutter. "Hi!" A tiny, towheaded girl with a toothy grin peered at her through the banister posts. "I'm Sara. I'm an artist."

"I see that you are." Emilie didn't know whether to applaud the child's efforts or send her to her room without lunch. What a catastrophe of a house! The party responsible for the mess was an exact replica of her mother, with fine, blond hair swirling around her freckled face and dark blue eyes that sparkled with elfin mischief.

Sara bounced down the last few carpeted steps in spritelike fashion, waving paint-covered fingers that begged for soap and water. "Mama says your name is Em-ee-lee, but I gotta call you Dr. Getz."

"Oh, that's not really necess—"

"Good!" Sara interrupted with obvious glee. "I like Em-ee-lee better." Dancing around her as if she were a human maypole, the child stretched out a pair of orange and green hands and plunged them inside hers. "Em-ee-lee! Em-ee-lee!"

Emilie grimaced at the sticky texture, comforting herself with a momentary fantasy involving a warm, soapy washcloth. "I…I'm here to have lunch with you and your mother." With any luck, lunch would first require a visit to the sink.

"Lunch will be yummy," Sara assured her. "Anna made it."

On cue, Beth ushered a woman down the steps—fiftyish with salt-and-pepper hair, wearing a broad but weary smile. "Can you tell Dr. Getz who this is, Sara?"

"She's my morning mama!" the child crowed.

Her appreciative adult audience laughed, then Beth introduced the older woman as Anna Ressler, Sara's baby-sitter from eight until noon each weekday. Pleasantries were exchanged even as Emilie managed to detach her hands from little Sara's firm grasp and hide them in her sweater pockets for safekeeping, hoping the little girl wouldn't notice.

Kids. What a foreign and unfamiliar concept.

She'd never seriously considered motherhood, for several good reasons. Not having a husband was the obvious one. Her academic career was another. This topsy-turvy home decor was definitely a third reason. *Definitely.*

Besides, she had a very satisfying life. Full of research and music and gardening and—

A tug on her sweater brought her back to the task at hand. Sara looked up at her with a wrinkled pink nose that would've done Peter Cottontail proud. "Let's eat lunch now, 'kay?"

"Yes, let's." Not thinking, she offered the girl her hand. *Big mistake.* A still-tacky orange paw dragged her toward the back of the house. How odd it felt to have those small, warm fingers tucked inside hers.

Moving through the house, stepping over the artistic debris, Emilie was amazed to find herself being led by this child, who didn't know her, yet trusted her completely. For a moment—for only the briefest of moments—that little hand felt strangely good. And right. And—dare she admit it?—satisfying, all the way to her soul.

"...Love one another deeply from the heart."

Jonas finished the reading from the *Daily Texts,* then closed his Bible and the small blue devotional. Some days he played catch-up, but it always paid off.

Moravians had been meditating on a daily watchword since Zinzendorf got the thing going in 1728.

Emilie no doubt read hers faithfully every morning.

At 7:05 A.M.

In German.

Emilie. A strange and unfamiliar tightness invaded his chest. Would she be there tonight? Would she ignore him? Embarrass him? Do her best to make him grovel in public?

Snatching off his new reading glasses, he tossed them on his desk and rose to stretch, feeling a stiffness in his joints. Time to hoist some weights, shoot some hoops. Anything to get his mind off Emilie Getz and what he would say if he saw her.

Not "if," buddy. When.

Beth had warned him about the other guys sending her letters. *Letters!* What a waste of time. Pick up the phone. Tell the woman you messed up. Hang up. End of story.

You didn't even do that much, son.

Jonas dropped his head, discovering a new set of tense neck muscles. *I'm listening, Lord. I'm listening.* That was the problem with grumbling right after praying. God was always there, waiting to offer a postscript.

It wasn't like he'd ignored Beth's suggestion. He'd started a letter to Emilie on his computer two or three times, but they'd sounded stiff and nonsensical: "I'm sorry I made you act like a heron." *Ridiculous.* As each day went by, it seemed harder. And less necessary.

"Do it," Beth had insisted. "You of all people owe her this, Jonas."

His gaze landed on Emilie's field guide, left behind on the car seat when he'd dropped her off soon after her leap-and-swoop debut. The tidy new book sitting on his kitchen counter chided him.

Just like Beth did. Just like his own conscience did.

"Love one another deeply from the heart."

Jonas groaned. Clearly, he'd have to give up this watchword business for the year ahead. Too much static from above.

"Love one another…"

"Okay, Lord, okay." His laughter rang through the empty house. "As long as it's *agape* love, that I can handle. And a letter. A short one. Real short." He headed toward the basketball goal behind his house, composing a note of apology in his head as he tracked down the ball and started hitting the boards, determined to get the kinks out of his muscles and a certain wispy-haired woman off his mind.

"Dear Emilie." *Scratch that.* "Emilie. The last thing I wanted to do at the bird count was hurt your feelings when I…" *Nah.*

With every toss of the ball, he came up with a different opening line, none of which were working.

It would have been easier if he didn't care what she thought of him. But he *did* care, blast it. That creamy-skinned, hardheaded woman plain *got* to him, for no good reason. She was intelligent—no, brilliant—not to mention brave and tough when she needed to be. *Like when she stood up to six laughing idiots.*

That's it! He had his opening line after all. When he caught sight of a bright red cardinal silhouetted against the gray sky, the rest of his letter presented itself, right along with the best way to deliver it.

Perfect!

Thirty feet from the net, his one-handed set shot dropped through with a graceful *swish.* Catching the ball on the second bounce, Jonas dribbled and shot again, feeling a self-satisfied grin spread across his face.

Half an hour later, pen to paper, he wrote out the letter he'd already composed in his head:

Dear Emilie:

Yeah, why not? It'd make her feel better, right off the bat.

I know what you're thinking: "Jonas Fielding is an inconsiderate idiot." I'm thinking the same thing. And hoping you'll forgive me for taking advantage of your…agreeable nature.

He chuckled, pleased with himself, then bore down on the notepaper.

It should never have happened, and won't happen again. I hope you can find it in your heart to forgive me.
        Your tarred-and-definitely-feathered friend,
        Jonas

        P.S. If you'd like to do a cup of coffee sometime—make that tea—I'm game.

Could you "do tea"? *Sure, why not?* Anyway, she'd get the message. *So what is the message, man?* Jonas wasn't sure himself, but it felt right. Very right.

Grabbing her bird book off the counter, he slid the note inside next to page ninety-eight, where the heron that'd started it all stared back at him in black-crowned glory. Folded in half, the note fit inside the book like hand in glove, without any stray edges hanging out. Emilie's perfectionist self would surely notice that, earning him a few more brownie points.

He'd sneak it in her mailbox tonight before church.

She'd find it, read it, get teary eyed no doubt, maybe even call him, offering heartfelt apologies and an invitation to tea. At her place.

Word would get around that he'd done the right thing. Beth would talk to him again. Helen would feed him sugar cake again. All would be right with the world.

The problem of how to smooth Emilie's ruffled feathers was finally solved.

"No problem," Beth whispered, nodding at the usher. "We're happy to sit on the side." She slipped one hand around Emilie's elbow and propelled Sara forward with the other, her husband Drew following close behind them.

Emilie bristled as they walked past her favorite pew, now full of visitors, and settled into an empty one that faced the pulpit at a right angle. *Honestly!*

Nothing looked right from this viewpoint. Instead of meditating on the stained glass and flowers, her eyes took in nearly the entire congregation, upstairs and down—children wiggling, parents scolding, choir members filing in. *Very distracting.*

Beth leaned over Sara's head. "Don't you love the Watchnight Service?"

"Usually," Emilie grumbled. *But not tonight.* It was too early in the evening, no lovefeast would be served, and nary a trombone was in sight. "This is *not* how we do things in Winston-Salem."

Beth's eyebrows lifted in surprise. "Really? What's it like at Home Church?"

It was important, Emilie decided, for Beth to understand that not all Moravian congregations shared identical traditions. "The service begins at eleven o'clock and ends when the pastor's sermon is interrupted at midnight with the band playing, 'Now Thank We All Our God.'"

Beth giggled. "I don't think Pastor Yeager would appreciate being cut short by a tuba." At the first chord of the organ prelude, Beth's voice dropped to a murmur and she nodded toward the back of the church. "Well, well. Look who's here."

Tall, dark, and disgustingly handsome Jonas Fielding filled the rear doorway, both his hands resting on Helen Bomberger's rounded shoulders. Emilie couldn't stop herself from watching them make their way forward and find a seat within viewing—but not listening—distance.

Not that she had any intention of talking to the man. He was positively the last thing on her mind at the cusp of a new year. The very last thing.

Beth helped Sara out of her heavy coat, keeping her voice low. "How much has he told you about himself?"

"Who?" Emilie pretended to be confused. "Pastor Yeager?"

Her new friend's smirk was less than subtle. "Nice try, Dr. Getz, but I'm not buying it."

Emilie snapped her chin toward Beth—and away from Jonas. "He's told me virtually nothing. The man moves dirt. Develops things." She shuddered without meaning to. "Hails from Delaware. Has three younger brothers." *Two of whom at least are cut out of the same overtly masculine cloth. Ick.*

"Has he told you about his father, then?"

Out of the corner of her eye, Emilie caught Drew's slight scowl at his wife's question.

Beth obviously caught it, too. "I'm sure Jonas will share everything. When he's ready." The younger woman glared back at her husband, even as a telltale grin gave her away. "You know how men are about…personal stuff."

"I have no idea how men are, about anything." Emilie reached for a tissue and blew her nose with a dainty sniffle. Whatever private story Jonas had stuffed up his T-shirted sleeve, it had nothing to do with her. Less than nothing.

Other than his obvious physical merits, a quick mind, his purported business acumen, a notable commitment to church and family, and the respect of everyone in Lititz—other than that, she couldn't think of one quality the man had to recommend him.

An hour later when she left the church with her watchword for the new year in hand, Emilie was still sifting through reasons why Jonas Fielding held no attraction for her whatsoever. He liked dogs and children. And spending endless hours with older ladies, like Mrs. B. *Well, there you are.* Clearly no woman would find such a man appealing.

Emilie strode down the street, grateful to have sent the Landises on their way so she could enjoy the brisk walk home by herself. Using one gloved hand to hold her scarf in place against the gusty night wind, she dug deep in her coat pocket for the front door key as her borrowed cottage came into view, illuminated by the glowing corner streetlamp still decorated for yuletide.

If she was honest—and she was trying very hard to be so—it was that infernal black-crowned night heron incident that put the nail in the coffin of any potential…well, any *friendship* she and Jonas might have shared. Such a prank was simply unforgivable.

Checking for traffic before crossing the intersection, Emilie was unprepared for the sudden, capricious wind that snatched the long scarf out of her hands. Her world went black as the wool wrapped itself around her face.

"Aahh!" Her muffled scream barely penetrated the cloth as her small ring of keys fell to the pavement. Inches away, tires screeched to an ear-splitting halt.

She froze, not knowing where to turn, not daring to move.

A car door slammed and a male voice cut through the wind and the wool. "Emilie, are you okay?"

Jonas. He *would* find her like that, looking foolish again. She struggled to unwrap her scarf, then suddenly felt it unfurl with a practiced snap.

"Happened to my little brothers all the time," he explained with an indifferent shrug, then scooped up her keys from the roadway. "Sure you don't need a ride home?"

Despite the cold, she felt her cheeks warming. "In case you've forgotten, my house is thirty feet away."

He turned toward her door and mimicked shooting a basketball. "Yup. So it is." Grinning down at her, he swung around and climbed back in his vehicle, then leaned out as if he'd forgotten something. His expression was pure Cheshire cat. "By the way, you've got mail." With that, he slammed the door, steered around her, and sped south on Cedar Street, his taillights winking at her in the darkness.

Honestly! She stomped toward the mailbox, trying hard not to quicken her steps, not to notice the way her heart was pounding with anticipation. So he'd written her a letter of apology after all. *The big brute.* Thrusting her key in the lock, she made herself open the door first, take her purse inside, then slip off her wayward scarf, all before she stepped back out, trying to behave as if she always checked her mailbox at nine o'clock on New Year's Eve.

Reaching inside, she wrapped her hands around a bulky envelope and pulled it out, her curiosity piqued. Carefully opening the flap, she peered inside, then slipped out the contents.

Good heavens. What kind of an apology was this?

It was her forgotten field guide, period. No note attached, no letter sticking out, nothing else in the envelope except her own book.

Well, I never!

Slamming the door behind her so hard it rattled the windows, Emilie marched over to the nearest bookcase and jammed the slim guide onto the shelf, for once not caring if she tore the cover as the paperback squeezed between hundreds of others on the shelf.

It'd be a mighty cold morning before *that* particular book ever saw the light of day again. And to think she'd considered befriending that buffoon! The notion sent her storming up the narrow staircase in a huff, disappointed that a book—one of her most dependable friends through thick and thin—a traitorous book had ended her year on such a discouraging note.

Seven

Friendship is a very taxing and arduous form of leisure activity.
MORTIMER ADLER

"Jonas, be a friend and run this by Emilie's place, okay?" Beth held out a bulging file of papers. "It's taken me days to find this stuff and I know she really needs it." She waved it an inch closer. "Please?"

He dipped his chin in the younger woman's direction and did his best to look put out. "Wouldn't she rather have *you* deliver it?"

"Don't be silly." Beth's freckled nose wrinkled, reminding him of little Sara. Now *there* was a child he'd be happy to claim—unlike his not-so-little brother Nathan, who was playing hard to find. He hadn't heard from Nate since the cryptic phone call about heading to Florida. *Big state, bro. Call back, and soon.*

Since the first of the year, Jonas had made a few phone calls of his own—to Chris and Jeff in Delaware, to a couple of golf courses in Vegas. *Zip.*

That left one option: wait until Nate needed something badly enough to get in touch with him again.

Which reminded him of another person he was waiting to hear from: Emilie. She hadn't called either.

Maybe his phone wasn't working.

"Please?" Beth shook the overstuffed folder at him again.

He groaned in mock agony and took it off her hands. "She may thank you for the info, but the choice of courier won't earn you any gold stars."

Beth's eyebrows arched. "Why? Did you and Emilie have it out when I wasn't looking?"

"Nah, nothing that dramatic." *So*. Emilie didn't tell her about his letter. An uncomfortable knot in his chest showed up out of nowhere. "Fact is, I haven't talked to her in a few days." *Six*. He strolled toward the door, calling over his shoulder, "Make sure Sara wears her mittens. Weatherman says we're gettin' the big one this weekend."

Swinging out the door and down the church office steps, Jonas glanced at the heavy cloud cover overhead and snorted. *Ha!* Who needed a snowstorm when, minutes from now, Emilie Getz would dump her own version of the big chill right on his freshly sheared head?

But she wasn't home.

He rang, he knocked, he peered through the front window into her living room until a Main Street passerby shot him a nasty look. "She's a friend of mine," Jonas mumbled.

When the stranger disappeared into Benner's Pharmacy, Jonas couldn't resist lifting the lid on Emilie's black mailbox. Maybe she'd never found the bird book to begin with. That would explain why no phone call, no pat on the back from Beth, no reprieve from Helen, who'd put him on sugar cake probation until she got word of a suitable apology being offered and received.

Was the book still in there?

He peered down inside. Suddenly, a woman's stern voice behind him barked, "That mail receptacle is government property."

Startled, he flipped the lid down on the empty box. "Really? No kidding."

"I never kid about postal regulations." The uniformed carrier, an older woman with Helen's build but not her sweet disposition, eyed him, patently suspicious. "It's against the law to remove any items from a customer's mail receptacle," she informed him in a clipped, no-nonsense style. "Whether it's mounted on a post or attached to someone's house or stationed on a—"

"Right!" he interjected, anxious to wind things up before they drew a crowd. Already a handful of pedestrians were slowing their steps, obviously willing to be an audience. "I haven't removed a thing. In fact, it's empty. See?" He reached for the lid, then thought better of it when her eyes narrowed.

"Truth is—" he assured her confidently, stuffing his hands in his pockets—"not only did I not take anything *out,* I recently put something *in*—you know, just like you do." He flashed her his most devastating smile. "So, I figured I'd…uh, check on my package. See if Emil…uh, Dr. Getz found it."

His ploy wasn't working.

"Guess she already took it out," he added lamely.

Definitely a crowd gathering now. Ten, maybe.

The woman folded her arms across her uniform. "It's also illegal to put items *in* a residential mailbox without first attaching the proper postage." Her tone was decidedly more sharp. "Did you know that?"

Blast, if she didn't have him blushing! "Uh, no, ma'am. No, I didn't. Sorry."

She brushed past him, shoved one lone envelope in the box, and dropped the lid with a perfunctory slap. "I'll check with Dr. Getz first thing tomorrow and see what she has to say about all this. Your name is…?"

Mud.

"Fielding." He coughed, trying to keep those within earshot from hearing it. "Jonas Fielding. She'll…she'll know me."

"Were you planning on stuffing that in her mailbox, too?" The woman's gaze fell to the folder under his arm.

"Of course not!" he snapped, then caught himself. "Because…it's…too big. Of course."

"Humph." She turned on her heel and marched next door to the Alden House Bed and Breakfast.

"Be sure and try their apple pancakes," he called after her, knowing even those babies, drenched in syrup, wouldn't put a smile on that woman's sour face.

"Show's over," he informed the few stragglers who'd hung back, hoping for another round. "Postage goes up a penny on Sunday," he reminded them, reaching for his car keys. "Forget one extra cent, and you'll have to deal with *her.*"

Driving off toward the work site, his wiseacre grin faded. Emilie had found her book. But had she read the letter? *Shoulda left it sticking out.* However untidy, at least she'd have seen it. When he ran into her again, he'd ask her. Make sure the woman knew he was sorry. See if they'd be doing tea anytime soon. *Yeah.*

Then there was Beth, who wouldn't be happy with him either. Not only did she not know about his truly repentant letter, she'd also fuss at him for doing such a rotten delivery job today.

He grabbed his cell phone and punched in the number for the church. No matter what happened, he needed Beth on his side. Friends were hard enough to come by without losing two in one week.

Nathan never thought about losing. Only winning, and winning big.

He'd crossed the state line into Florida less than three days earlier, and already he'd made a killing on a trifecta at the Orange Park Kennel Club. *Five thousand and change.* Every dime was forwarded to Vegas. Certified check. No traceable address. Only 10 percent of the total, but it was a start.

"Jonas would consider it a tithe." He chuckled as he strolled out of the bank into the bright January sunshine. He hadn't called Pennsylvania again. His older brother wouldn't have that kind of money, and Nathan didn't need another lecture about God right now. If God really loved him, he could sure as spit produce the other forty-five grand. *Yeah. Pull it out of a burning bush or something.*

He steered his Chevy up the entrance ramp to Interstate 95, watching his rearview mirror out of sheer habit. Living out of his suitcase in one of the discount suite motels southeast of downtown Jacksonville, Nathan focused on keeping to himself, biding his time while he scraped together the necessary funds to get Cy off his back forever.

Unless his luck held and the greyhounds raced him into a Tri-Super, that was gonna take a while.

In the meantime, he would play the circuit around a few of the public golf courses in the area—Windsor Parke, Baymeadows—work on his swing, and polish his act for San Pablo, the snazziest greens in town. Danny, one of the pros at Shadow Hills in North Las Vegas, would back him up with a good reference. Say the right words, grease the right palms, do what it took to get him on board at San Pablo Golf Club.

After all, Danny owed him one.

Not nearly as much as you owe Cy Porter.

Nathan banged the dashboard in frustration, then reached for a smoke, lighting it with a practiced flick of his wrist and taking a deep drag on the filter. The nicotine pushed his worries aside while his fingertips tingled and his heart raced, just like those greyhounds, running for their lives. *Just like you, Nate. Doin' the same thing.*

It wouldn't always be this way. He'd get back on his feet, get his game back in the 70s where it belonged. Get back in touch with his family—with Jeff and Chris in Delaware, with Jonas.

Jonas.

Nathan's chest tightened. *Must be the cigarette.* He knew he'd disappointed the twins and his sainted mother. Letting Jonas down had been the worst, though. The guy was a do-gooder of the first magnitude, yet he'd been there for him time and again. Didn't judge him, didn't hassle him. Didn't read him the riot act like Dad would have.

Now his chest really *was* tight. He ground his cigarette into the ashtray, vowing for the tenth time that week he would quit, then turned the Chevy west on Baymeadows Road, his eyes scanning the available options for lunch.

"How 'bout burgers and a movie, Nate?" He said it aloud, just to amuse himself. Just to hear a human voice cut through the silence.

He pulled into the nearest drive-thru lane. Lunch meant something in a paper bag. The flick? Whatever was showing on HBO. And company? Not likely. Life was too complicated to bring a woman into the picture.

"What'll you have, sir?" The sweet voice on the restaurant intercom sounded all of sixteen.

"*You,* darlin'." Nate grinned at the metal box. "I'll have you."

"Excuse me?" Decidedly less sweet now. Older too.

"Just kiddin' around." Even his come-ons didn't work anymore. He sighed and pulled out his wallet. "A burger, plain. Small ice water." *And a side order of luck.* After thirty years, a streak of good fortune was long overdue.

"Run into any other old friends from high school, Emilie?"

Teresa Kauffman, the volunteer behind the desk at the Lititz Public Library, waited expectantly, her soft gray eyes and round features hidden behind an oversized pair of bifocals.

Emilie shrugged and returned to tallying up her armload of research books. "Really, Teresa, I've seen only a few folks from Warwick." She rattled off their names, watching her former classmate's head nod at each one. They were the sort—like Teresa—who'd settled down after graduation, found nice husbands and good jobs around town, attended nearby Millersville University.

Women who had no past to escape, nor an aching ambition that demanded satisfaction no matter what the cost.

The lucky ones.

Scanning the nearby computer screen, the cheerful librarian did her best to keep their conversation going. "How does Lititz look to you, after all these years?"

"More than a few years..."

Emilie groaned at the pesky refrain, then tried to turn the sound into a pitiful excuse for a laugh. "Lititz? It looks…wonderful." And it did. Better, in fact, than when she'd lived there as a child. Gift shop windows overflowed with enticing local treasures, homes and yards were painted and pruned to charming effect, and the landmarks she'd loved had been preserved with great care.

Except for Bingy's Restaurant, torn down to make a parking lot. Bingy's conjured a fond memory of her first genuine chocolate malt milkshake—icy silver container on the side, whipped cream on top. She'd shared it on her first and only date with Brian Zeller. Brian wasn't popular either. Was in truth an awkward, tongue-tied, adolescent mess. But she hadn't known that. He was a *boy*. Plus, he was intelligent and kind and didn't make fun of her. Ever.

Unfortunately, as with the few bright, studious types that came along after Brian, no sparks flew across the milkshake glass. Emilie hadn't spoken with him since…when? Their last National Honor Society meeting, no doubt. In another decade.

"More than a few…"

Enough! It was every bit as annoying as a phrase from some advertising jingle, playing through her head, over and over.

Teresa busied herself straightening up her countertop. "It'll be interesting to see what they do with this place, now that we're moving."

Emilie's attention snapped to the present. "Moving? The library?" She looked around, half expecting to find a Mayflower truck at the curb, and boxes of books by the door. The old house on Broad Street—no longer a library?

"Haven't you heard?" The woman proffered a dark green brochure, detailing the new public library under construction. "We're pleased as punch. The whole town has gotten behind the project, to the tune of a million and a half dollars." A close-cropped fingernail pointed to the architectural rendering. "The nicest library in the state. Least, that's what everybody's saying."

Emilie studied the information, nodding absently as Teresa continued to bubble about the unique design, the spaciousness, the convenient new location on Kissel Hill Road.

"You should swing by, see what's been done so far." Her gray eyes shone. "It opens in June. You'll never miss this old place, believe me."

Who was to say what she might miss? Emilie hated change and never apologized for admitting so. "I might do that," she said, tucking the flyer inside her stack of books. "You've been most helpful today, Teresa. Look for your name on the acknowledgments page, won't you?"

Minutes later, Emilie found herself in the turning lane for Second Avenue. The temperature had hovered around freezing for days, leaving the streets icy and the sidewalks treacherous. Only a crazy person would head for a stark building site on such an inhospitable morning. *Which makes you certifiable, Emilie Getz.* She turned east, toward a library that was probably little more than a hole in the frozen ground.

The lifelong student in her couldn't resist. Libraries and bookstores made her positively giddy.

Winding her way through neighborhoods filled with neat-as-a-pin homes built in the forties, she was surprised to find newer houses springing up on streets she didn't remember even existing. Bearing left on Sixth with a bewildered stare at the construction on both sides of the street, she pointed her car toward the supposed site for the library, fearful of what she might find.

What she found, parked in the area carved out for a driveway, was a familiar black Explorer.

With temporary tags.

But no Jonas. *Thank goodness.*

What was his vehicle doing there, anyway? Abandoned in the midst of a building site for a... *Oh my.* Her eyes took in the bulldozers, the stakes in the ground, and the sign proclaiming, A Great Town Deserves a Great New Library, with the small notation beneath it, Jonas Fielding, Developer and Project Manager.

He said he played with dirt.

He never said he built *libraries.*

Well! Her regard for the man took a marked turn upward. A library, no less, in a field full of corn that would never be missed. Not a landmark torn down, not a slice of history lost, and he'd annexed township land to do it.

Jonas Fielding was building a library!

What else didn't she know about him? Was he everything Beth claimed he was—trustworthy, loyal, hardworking, respectable? Had she misjudged him terribly? Jumped to conclusions? For a woman who prided herself on thorough research, she'd apparently done a poor job investigating Mr. Fielding—something she intended to remedy immediately.

Emilie peered through his car window, checking for anything of interest. Building plans, perhaps—the tiny sketch in the brochure *had* been quite promising—or anything else that might catch her researcher's eye.

Squinting through the tinted glass, she soon spotted her first bit of valuable data. In the backseat, where that slobbering yellow dog usually sat, rested an impressive scale model of the building. Very traditional, very classy. The man had taste after all. *One point for Mr. Fielding.*

The piles of periodicals and sketches suggested that, however sloppy, the man was thorough. *Another point in his favor.* Her gaze traveled to the front seat, where she spied a large manila folder on the passenger side, with a name printed in large block letters.

Wait a minute. That—

"That vehicle is private property," a deep voice boomed directly behind her.

"Oh!" Emilie gasped and jumped back a full foot. It was several seconds before she could breathe properly and turn to face her accuser, now only inches away.

Jonas. The library builder.

"It's against the law to look inside a person's car," he growled, circling around her with exaggerated steps. "Did you know that?"

"I did not." She squared her shoulders, narrow though they were, and stuck out her chin. "Inform the authorities of my actions at once."

His dark eyes sparked. "My, aren't we cheeky, for a trespasser?"

"This is public land, destined to be a public library," she reminded him, using her classroom voice for effect. *Is he getting closer on purpose?* "I have every right to be here…Mr. Fielding."

"It's also a construction site, *Dr. Getz*," he snapped back, though it was more crackle than snap. "A dangerous place."

The only thing that looked dangerous was Jonas.

"By law, it's not open to the public. Not yet." He paused in front of her, inches from the end of her nose. Despite his combative tone, his eyes bore a mischievous twinkle.

"And how do you propose to remove me from the premises?" She let her eyebrows create an especially engaging capital *V*.

Goodness. Were they flirting? *Hmmm.* It felt like they might be.

Which meant this charmingly aggravating, bird-watching, scarf-unwinding man was *toying* with her! And she was teasing him back, for pity's sake! The whole thing was ridiculous.

His eyebrows lowered dramatically. "If necessary, miss, I will remove you from the premises myself. Bodily."

Emilie abruptly turned, hoping he hadn't seen the heat that flew into her cheeks, and pressed a defiant nose against the smoky glass. "I'll leave the minute I get what belongs to me."

"You'll get what's coming to you, all right," he muttered behind her back. "Five mornings in a duck blind—"

"That—" she interrupted, pointing inside the passenger side window, keenly aware of him hovering over her—"that folder is what I want. The one that has my name printed on it, bold as you please."

"Bold as you please?" He chuckled, leaning ever so slightly against her shoulders. "Fine. I can be bold, Emilie." His voice dropped another note. "If you please."

She froze.

The first thing she noticed were his hands, one resting on each arm. And his scratchy chin against her hair. Both were so faint, so tentative, she might have imagined them had she not eased back to see if the sensations went away.

They did not!

He was definitely there and not moving.

Now what?

Emilie had never flirted, intentionally, in her entire life. Especially not with a man like this one. He...he *built* things. Played with dirt. Destroyed historic buildings. He was the *enemy*. Wasn't he?

"Emilie," he whispered against her hair. "I am not the enemy."

Heavens. The man not only built libraries, he read minds.

Her knees began shaking, imperceptibly at first, but then with a more pronounced wobble.

"You're trembling." He seemed surprised, backing up enough to turn her around. With his hands. On her shoulders. "Are you cold?"

"Yes!" A perfect excuse. She tried to make her teeth chatter and succeeded only in biting her tongue. "I need to—"

"Right," he agreed, yanking open the car door behind her. "Your folder, as instructed."

"Right," she echoed, lifting it off the seat in slow motion, then letting her wobbly knees carry her the few feet to her ancient BMW. Her fingers were also shaking, Emilie discovered when she attempted to slide the key in the door.

She heard him walking toward her across the frozen gravel. "Did you lock it?" he asked, clearly amazed. "In Lititz?"

Apparently she hadn't, since turning the key made no difference whatsoever. She opened the door with as much grace as she could muster and plopped into the driver's seat.

He held the door open, leaning in. "Any chance you'd like to...do tea sometime soon?"

"One doesn't *do* tea." She kept her eyes on the steering wheel, her mind fighting one skirmish while her senses mounted a strong defense elsewhere—against his irresistible eyes, his masculine chin, his wide shoulders, his strong hands. The same hands that had pressed against her mere seconds ago.

Taking a deep breath, she forged into battle. "One brews tea, pours tea, sips tea. One does not *do* tea."

"Emilie, I don't even drink the stuff. I was just trying to see if..."

Looking up, her eyes widened. "If what?"

"If you…read my letter."

It cost him to say the words, she could see that. Emilie swallowed her quick comeback and cautiously said what was really on her heart. "Your letter? I was…hoping you might send me one."

He exhaled, clearly frustrated. "I did. A week ago, in your bird book. Page ninety-eight?"

Ohh. "I shelved the book without even looking at it," she admitted, genuinely sorry. "The minute I get home, I'll find your letter and read it." *Immediately. Wearing my coat and gloves.*

"Before you go, I've got one question for you." His top lip vanished in a boyish grin. "Make that two. For starters, what are you doing here?"

He thinks I was looking for him.

"I stopped by the public library this morning and they suggested I visit the site." Attempting to sound nonchalant, she added, "I *do* love a good library."

"You do, huh?" He waved at the bare, snowy field around them, the ground shoved into mysterious forms and shapes of things to come. "It'll look better by June, I promise." His gaze fixed on hers. "The second thing is more of a request."

She sniffed and pivoted her chin back toward the front dash. "Are you referring to the ah, night heron…incident?"

Silence. One beat, then two. "No, I wasn't, actually. But since you brought it up, let me say in person, Emilie, how sorry I am."

He sounds sincere. She sneaked a sideways glance. *Looks sincere too. Repentant, even.* It was enough for her.

With a dramatic sigh, she leaned back against the headrest, careful not to turn his way. No need to embarrass the man further. "It so happens, I'm willing to forgive you. This time." And she was. It felt good to admit it, to get past it. "Suppose we consider that situation…ah, resolved."

"Thanks, Emilie."

She liked the way he said her name, like a three-note song in a bass key. Still staring at the dashboard, she reminded him, "You mentioned something about a request?"

He didn't speak, only reached inside and tilted her chin toward him, even as he slowly leaned down—closer, then closer yet—until their gazes locked and his lips hovered dangerously close to hers.

He wouldn't. Not…not…

His voice was a husky whisper. "Call me Jonas."

Stunned, Emilie watched his features grow still. Serious. No playful wink, no teasing grin.

She matched her tone to his, with great care. "Haven't I done so, all along?"

He shook his head slightly. "Only once."

Could that be true?

"Say it again, Emilie. Please?"

There was no resisting a request like that. "Jonas." Not so hard, especially not when it made him smile so broadly. "Jonas Fielding," she declared, enjoying the sound of it herself. "A perfectly fine name. I'll certainly try to use it more often."

"You do that." Under the shadow of a beard that framed his jawline, she detected the faintest hint of color. He straightened up, letting go of her chin, though the warmth lingered a breath longer. "Thanks for stopping by, Emilie." He nodded at her file, brimming with papers, and a backseat full of books. "Have fun with your research."

"I will," she promised, though she knew not a bit of this stuff would be carted into the house until she tracked down that bird book and turned to page ninety-eight. "See you in church. Jonas."

"I'll keep an eye on your favorite pew. Downstairs. Front and center. Second row. Right?"

Who noticed such a thing? Jonas Fielding, apparently. Suddenly, she felt out of kilter. Her quiet morning at the library had turned into an emotionally charged…something. She twisted the ignition key and felt the heater come alive, blasting her with cold air. "I'll see you…Jonas."

He folded his arms over his chest, the blush gone, the grin back in place. "You already said that."

"Uh…yes. Well, now I'm going." She pulled the door shut with a rattly bang and shifted the car into first gear, preparing to drive off.

But her heart wouldn't let her go without asking one important question. She had to know. *Had to.* Reluctant but resolved, she cranked down the window. "Jonas…what was that all about…earlier?"

"Earlier?" Of course he wouldn't make this easy for her. His arms were still folded, his expression neutral.

She swallowed her pride and plunged forward. "When you...put your hands on...my arms..."

"And rested my chin on your head? I'll tell you what that was, Emilie." He was looking serious again. "A beginning."

Eight

◆

I wonder what fool it was that first invented kissing.
JONATHAN SWIFT

"It's beginning to look a lot like Christmas..."

Beth sang at the top of her lungs, with Sara chiming in every fourth word. Emilie simply stared in amazement, absentmindedly brushing the wet snow off her frozen, red-as-Rudolph nose while she watched Beth bundle up Sara for another slippery ride down Kissel Hill.

Is *this* what motherhood was like? *Fun?* Not bothersome drudgery and getting stuck in the kitchen—but playing in the snow? Making up words to silly songs? Hugging and carrying on like kittens?

It was a revelation, plain and simple.

So was the unlikely friendship she and Beth were beginning to form together. One married, one single; one younger, one older; one happier at home, one happier at work; one fair-haired and freckled, one brown-haired and pale.

And one little girl, the link that drew them closer—one willingly, one not so willingly—while Sara simply loved them both for who they were.

That morning six inches of heavy snow had put a stop to school, not to mention squelching Anna Ressler's Friday baby-sitting plans. Without a sitter, Beth was forced to take the morning off, and in her typical lemons-to-lemonade fashion, convinced Emilie to join Sara and her for a snowy outing.

"You're in charge of the hot chocolate," Beth had announced, then hung up the phone, leaving Emilie in a quandary. Tea, fine. She had half a dozen tins in her cabinets to choose from. But hot chocolate? She hadn't made the stuff in years. Decades.

A quick assessment of her shelves made it clear that whatever ingredients it took to create hot chocolate, she didn't own them. Determined to do her part, she'd dressed as if tackling the Yukon on dogsled, then pointed her BMW toward the nearest grocery store.

Heading west on Main, she'd noticed a shop to her right and slammed on the brakes, skidding toward the curb. *Of course!* "Spill the Beans," the sign said. Surely a gourmet coffee place would have hot chocolate on the menu.

"Three hot chocolates to go," Emilie mumbled through her scarf, fishing out her wallet with gloved fingers. *Would a child want seconds?* "Make it four." Moments later, she'd gingerly carried the cardboard tray out to her car, lodged it in a safe corner on the floor, and eased out into traffic. Driving in snow was a skill she'd left behind when she moved south. With her heart firmly lodged in her throat, she clung to the steering wheel and maneuvered along the snow-covered streets at a cautious ten miles per hour.

Beth and Sara had waited for her outside their house, catching snowflakes with their tongues and jumping up and down to keep warm. The minute she'd pulled up, they piled into her backseat and began singing Christmas carols—with no intention of stopping, Emilie realized an hour later.

She watched Sara whoosh away from her, down the steep hill on her little silver saucer, a bundle of endless energy and boundless courage wrapped in purple outdoor gear. Sara climbed up, then whooshed down. Climbed, whooshed. The hot chocolate, delicious as it was, lasted exactly three minutes.

"More?" Sara asked, her blue eyes round with hope as she stared at the empty cups.

Chagrined, Emilie shook her head. "Sorry, honey. Next time I'll buy twice as many, okay?"

Beth laughed, tightening Sara's scarf before launching her down the hill again. "No way. Next time *I'm* in charge of the cocoa. Really, Emilie. Six dollars! What were you thinking?"

In the snowy morning air, Emilie felt her cheeks glow with unexpected warmth. "I was thinking I didn't want to disappoint a little girl."

From behind her, a deep masculine voice chimed in. "I make a point never to disappoint little girls either." The words were punctuated by the exuberant bark of a golden retriever set free in the snow.

Emilie whirled around, almost knocked over by the slobbering Trix, then caught her breath. "Hello...Jonas."

"You remembered." His usual black attire served as a somber backdrop for the riotous red scarf wrapped around his neck and the broad grin that covered his face. Lowering a sled to the ground, he thrust a silver thermos in her direction with the other hand.

Emilie stared at it, blinking in bewilderment. "Hot chocolate?"

"No." His chin dipped toward her in a pose plainly meant to charm. "Hot tea. I remembered something, too."

"So you did." *Rascal.* Tea, as in "do tea." As in his note that she'd read a dozen times. Emilie took the container, not meeting his enveloping gaze, trying instead to sort out her feelings.

Pleasure, embarrassment, delight, confusion—all vied for her attention while her mind struggled to put together one coherent thought. "What are you...I mean, who invited you?"

"I work here." His arm swept through the air, encompassing the white fields around and below them. "I drove by a few minutes ago—not that anyone noticed, mind you—saw the three of you cavorting out here in the snow, and figured you could use a visitor bearing hot drinks." He gestured toward the foot of the hill. "Your favorite sledding spot will soon become Carter's Run Golf Course and the Lititz Public Library....or have you forgotten that?"

Emilie never forgot anything, especially not a construction site that had provided such a memorable meeting spot two days earlier. While her emotions searched for a foothold, she unscrewed the thermos cap and inhaled the unmistakable fragrance of earl grey.

"Sweetened?"

"Of course." He stuck out his gloved hand, bearing two sturdy mugs. "I'll try anything once."

"No mugs for us?" Beth teased, bending down yet again to knot Sara's scarf, which had been pulled loose by a playful Trix.

Jonas aimed his thumb toward the Explorer. "Would I neglect my favorite mother–daughter team? Sara, see if you can't find a thermos of hot chocolate and two more mugs in the backseat."

The little girl raced Trix over to the vehicle, then scampered back with her treasure, squealing. "Thanks, Whale Man!"

Emilie's eyebrows rose. "Whale Man?"

He ducked his head, a ruddy tint staining his cheeks. "When Sara was three, she decided the Bible story about Jonah and the whale referred to me. You know... *Jonah* instead of *Jonas?*" His eyes shone like sunlight on snow. "It's a common mistake lots of girls make. Even bright ones."

Emilie's brows arched further. "Would you like this tea poured in your mug or down your parka?"

Laughing, he snatched the thermos back and served them both a steaming mugful, while Beth watched with a smug expression.

"It's not what you think," Emilie insisted, silently scolding Beth with a ladylike scowl.

"Really?" Beth winked. "I thought it was tea."

Sara offered a timely distraction with another verse of "Frosty the Snowman," while Emilie and Jonas sipped in awkward tandem and Beth gulped hot chocolate between giggles.

When all four mugs were put aside, Sara grabbed Jonas' gloved hand. "Your turn, Whale Man. Will you fit on my saucer?"

"Nope, we'll have to take my big sled." Even then, there was a lot of Jonas hanging over the edges as Emilie gave them a push and the twosome made a slow start down the slope, picking up speed as they went on their long downhill journey, winding up mere feet from the future library's front door.

While she and Beth watched them climb toward the top again, Emilie shot her new friend a pointed look. "Tell me the truth. Did you invite him?"

Beth's hurt expression told her all she needed to know. "Emilie, I would never do such a thing."

"I'm sorry. Of course you wouldn't." *Shame on you, Em!* "It's just...well, you see, on Wednesday..."

"What about Wednesday?"

"We had a….conversation. Down there."

The twinkle was back in Beth's eye. "A conversation? About bird calls and videotapes, maybe?"

"Maybe." Emilie shielded her eyes from the bright snow and Beth's curious gaze. Should she tell her? *Tell her what?* That she was attracted to—no, no! merely *interested* in—Jonas?

Don't fool yourself, Em.

History qualified as interesting.

This was a *man* she was talking about. A man's man, at that. A muscular, macho, cotton-T-shirt-and-jeans kind of man. A man who built libraries in Lititz, churches in Honduras, and a small but significant outpost in her own reticent heart.

"Emilie, your lips are moving, but you're not saying a word."

She blinked then shook her head, as if coming out of a long nap. "Um…sorry. What were you saying?"

Beth rolled her eyes, then waved at the Mutt-and-Jeff duo heading their way. "C'mon, you two! I'm losing Dr. Getz here."

Jonas lengthened his stride, a look of concern crossing his features. "What is it, Emilie? Are you okay?"

Under her knit cap, she felt distinctly warmer. "I'm fine," she protested as he reached her side. "Just hot."

"Could be the tea." He lifted her cap off with a playful yank, then casually fluffed her hair. "There you go. You'll cool off in a second. It is, after all, thirty degrees."

Not where I'm standing. She loosened her scarf and tried to think of something besides a man touching her hair. *Touching her hair!* It was unthinkably intimate…and altogether wonderful.

"What you need, woman, is a trip down Kissel Hill on your belly. A faceful of snow will drop your body temperature like that." Jonas tried to snap his fingers, then realized he was wearing gloves and chuckled. "Well, you get the idea. You and Sara, on the Flexible Flyer. Okay?"

"Oh, I couldn't possibly!" Emilie stepped backward, her skin chilling quickly at the frightening thought. "I haven't been on a sled in…in…years." *Thirty-six, to be exact.*

"Couldn't be easier," he insisted, guiding her toward the rusty wooden sled that had seen a lot of winters. "You can sit up, if you prefer, and we'll tuck Sara between your knees. Piece of cake."

He settled her onto the slats and handed her a worn rope. "Pull here to turn right…well, you know how a sled works."

No, she did *not* know! Didn't have a clue. *Oh, please.*

A giggling Sara squirmed into place, tipping her head back to check on Emilie, who was feeling a bit numb.

"Such a long way down," Emilie murmured to anyone who would listen.

"Yeah, isn't that great?" Jonas clapped his gloves together. "Best place in Lititz to go sledding. Help me get 'em started, Beth."

Emilie felt their hands on her back, pushing the sled across the snow while Jonas grunted dramatically. "No more Moravian sugar cake for you, woman!"

Humph! He was the one who consumed it by the pan, not she.

"I pushed *you* a minute ago," she reminded him. "It wasn't that harrrr—*aaahh!*" Without warning, the sled took off, tearing down the hillside at breakneck speed.

Snow sprayed around them while little Sara shrieked with joy.

"Wheee-ooohhh!"

Hold it. That was *her* shrieking with joy.

"*Whooo-aaahhh!*" Emilie howled again at the top of her lungs as they plunged downward, while Sara hung on for dear life, her squeal pitched two octaves higher.

Despite her excitement, Emilie remembered to pull the rope left, then right. The little sled jumped to obey her.

It worked. It *worked!*

Toboggans and passengers parted like the Red Sea as Emilie and her charge headed for the bottom, their hairlines packed with snow, their eyes squinting against the wind as the world went by in a white blur.

Sara shouted with glee, "Are you scared, Em-ee-lee?"

"Not meee!"

Jonas watched their descent for all of ten seconds before he grabbed Sara's little silver saucer and threw himself down the hill in cold pursuit.

He could hear Emilie whooping and hollering all across the snowy landscape. *My Emilie? Wailing like a banshee?* This was one miracle he had to see for himself: Emilie behaving like a kid. Emilie having *fun*.

The saucer turned out to be a lousy chase vehicle. He couldn't steer the thing or speed up, he could only hang on, with his bottom pointing down toward the snow, his legs dangling up in the air, and his hands grasping the flimsy vinyl handles with a death grip.

It was fast, though. Mighty fast, spinning like a carnival ride out of control. "Em-i-lieee!" he shouted when she came into view, mere feet ahead of him.

"Jooo-naaas!" She beamed at him as he shot past, her face bright pink, her features covered with ice crystals, her smile wide as the wintry sky.

That smile was the last thing he remembered before his saucer hit a bump and launched him into orbit, headed for deep space.

Mars…Jupiter…

He landed on his back with a jarring thump, his silver saucer lost in another galaxy far, far away.

Neptune…Pluto…

There had to be an explanation for the stars he was counting, laying there in the snow, with two worried faces hovering over him.

"Jonas, talk to me!" A woman's voice. Emmy-somebody-or-other.

"Get up, Whale Man! Get up!" A child. Jumping in circles.

Whales? Maybe he went overboard. Near an iceberg.

"Did you break anything?" The woman again, sounding genuinely concerned. He opened one eye and tried to focus on her face. Such a nice face. Kinda red and frozen, but didn't she have pretty brown eyes? And a nice soft nose, the kind that would squash perfectly if he kissed her.

Had he kissed her? Did he know her? Was she an ice angel, come to rescue him?

The woman was talking again, whispering now. "Jonas, can you hear me? It's Emilie. Oh, say *something*. Please!"

"Emilie," he groaned.

That seemed to make her happy.

Things were coming into focus now, though every drop of color was bleached from his surroundings. White, white, only white. *Oh. Snow. Yeah.* He was in the snow. Sledding.

Here came Trix, licking his face, yanking him into a sitting position. *Good dog.*

And there was the flying saucer that brought him to this planet. *Good saucer.*

He scratched Trix's head first, then he scratched Emilie's head. Emilie sure had nice fur. Curly and brown, not blond like Dee Dee. *No!* Not Dee Dee. Trix. Blond like Trix. *Yeah, that's what I meant.*

The crowd around him had grown, just like when that mail carrier gave him grief about looking inside Emilie's mailbox. When was that? Last year? Last week?

He shook his head, which made things worse. Now there were three Emilies, all wide-eyed with worry. Didn't she have pretty brown eyes, though? And the softest nose. And the sweetest breath, like hot chocolate.

"Kiss me," he mumbled, which she promptly did. Right on the mouth.

The warmth of her lips, the perfect fit of them, the sugary delicious taste, all revived him substantially. So much so that Jonas found himself kissing her back, squashing her nose for all it was worth.

Such a nice nose. Such a sweet kiss. *What's her name again?*

"Dr. Getz, you need to keep him warm and awake for the rest of the day. Think you can handle it?"

The physician tore off a page from his prescription pad and pressed it in her hand. "For the pain, if he needs it. No napping, though, not after a possible concussion. Any questions, call my office." He disappeared, white coat flapping, while Emilie stared at her patient.

The two of them were in a state of shock.

But not for the same reason.

Jonas had done a triple-axel through the air and landed on his head. No broken bones, just strained muscles, the X-ray tech assured them. And one gigantic ache from forehead to toes.

Emilie's heart had done its own flip through the air when Jonas had asked her to kiss him—*kiss him!*—which she'd done. Thoroughly. Publicly. Much longer than necessary for resuscitation purposes, an onlooker had informed her with a conspirator's wink.

Now they were staring at one another, wary and pensive. What had happened out there in the snow? Emilie remembered every single, joy-filled second. The feeling of flying through the air with Sara, of being in control of their destiny with a mere tug on a rope, of seeing the world through a child's eyes, washed white as snow.

Of being soundly kissed and liking it.

Jonas appeared to remember…nothing. Not his crazy, careening trip in the silver saucer, not his travels through time and space, not his crash landing.

And not—it pained Emilie to think of it—not even the high point of the morning: their breath-stealing, heartwarming kiss. It was obvious he didn't remember it, or he wouldn't be glaring at her now like she was a boulder in the middle of his building site, an obstacle that needed removing at once.

"You heard the doctor," she began, perching on a leather chair in his den. They'd propped him upright on the couch with a cooler of sodas and the VCR remote control well within reach. Emilie tried to ignore the dreary setting—a too-new house with no character and even less furniture. *Poor Jonas.* The place had all the personality of a college dorm, right down to the dreadful polyester curtains.

"Yeah, I heard the doc. No napping." Jonas yawned, no doubt just to bedevil her. "I'll be fine, Emilie. No need to watch over me."

What if I want to, Jonas? What if it gives me a strange and inexplicable sense of peace to sit here and keep you company?

Her thoughts were busy, but her words were few. "I see." She swallowed a persistent lump that had threatened her all afternoon, ever since the accident. Ever since the kiss. "Would you rather I left?"

"I'd rather you stayed."

Oh. "Would you like something to…eat?"

He shook his head then by the look on his face, regretted it. "Nah, I'm not hungry. And anyway, you don't strike me as the domestic type."

She shot to her feet. "I'll have you know I brew a mean pot of tea. Might I interest you in a cup?"

He made a face. "I tried that once today already. These sodas are fine for me. You go ahead, though." He chuckled, punching on the remote. "If you can find any."

Jonas watched her turn sharply and head for the kitchen, presenting him with a stiff spine and squared shoulders. *Nice shoulders, though.*

What was she unhappy about? Had he said something unkind when he was regaining consciousness? The doc said he'd been out for a full minute or more. Had he done something foolish, like suggest she try using lipstick for a change or stop pulling her hair back in a knot?

Whatever happened, it had not improved things between them. *Sorry, Lord.* After Wednesday's chat, then reading his letter—and she had read it, hadn't she?—he'd hoped the ice princess might have melted a tad.

One thing was certain: She loved sledding down that hill. Maybe he'd remind her of it, see if talking about it cheered her up.

When Emilie came back in, tea mug in hand, he did his best to look alert. "So, Emilie, tell me how it felt."

Her pale skin grew paler. "How\...what felt?"

"You know. Today. On that snow-covered hill." He smiled, in spite of the pain. "Wasn't it...exhilarating?"

No longer pale, her skin was turning pink. "Yes, Jonas, it was absolutely...thrilling."

"No kidding. Describe the sensation for me." He'd gone sledding so many times, he knew what she'd say: "It was like flying without wings."

"It was..." Her blush had moved from pink to magenta. "It was the most...incredibly...romantic moment of my life."

Romantic! On a sled? With a kid? The woman clearly didn't get out much. "Tell me more."

Her voice was a tortured whisper. "I've never done such a thing before." Her gaze sank toward the floor.

For some odd reason, she looked embarrassed. *Nothing to be ashamed of. Lots of people didn't go sledding as kids.* He cleared his throat. "Look, Emilie, there's always a first time. It gets easier after that."

Her head shot up. "It does?"

"No question. We can practice anytime you like."

Her eyes widened. "We can?"

"Not tonight, of course."

"Oh, of course not!"

"It's downright dangerous in the dark."

"So I've heard." Her swallow was audible. "Did you have a...specific day in mind? For this...practice?"

"Your choice, Emilie."

Her eyebrows formed a startled V. "M-my...choice?"

"Yup." He clasped his hands behind his head and stretched. "Any day you like, just call me."

She looked dumbfounded. "So you want me to call *you?*"

"Yeah. Assuming the weather's right."

"The *weather?*" Her eyes were saucers. "You mean you can only k—"

"Colder the better, don't you think?" He focused in on the NBA game flickering across the screen.

"You're the expert." She stood and put aside her tea, untouched. "I'll... call you, then. Sometime. I guess."

"You do that, Emilie." He punched the mute button and gave her his full attention. "I'd like your second time to be just as memorable as the first."

"Me...uh, too." She offered him a tentative wave, then gathered her coat and bolted for the back door.

"Rebound!" he shouted at the screen before he realized it made his head throb. *Easy does it, buddy.* He settled back to watch the game, even as visions of a blushing, flustered historian spun through his mind.

Fact was, he'd never met a woman like Emilie. Scary-smart, yet clueless. Attractive without knowing it or working at it. Strong, in a quiet sort of way. And stubborn. *Man, is she stubborn, Lord!*

This sledding thing was something else again. Obviously, it struck a chord with her. *Good.* She looked positively dewy-eyed the whole time they'd talked about it just now. If she didn't call him for a sledding lesson soon, he'd call her himself. Anything to hear that wild, joyous laugh of hers again.

Better idea. He'd *buy* her a sled of her own. *Yeah!*

Who'd have imagined the way to Emilie Getz's heart included a Flexible Flyer?

Emilie was a flexible woman, yes. A modern woman, a twenty-first-century woman. But she was not about to call a man so he could...so he could...practice *kissing* her! The idea was long past ludicrous.

Jonas Fielding was *not* the reason she came to Lititz, she reminded herself hourly, and it was high time she got on with business.

The weather was in complete agreement with her decision. Friday's snow dragged on through the weekend, giving her the perfect excuse to stay home and organize her notes for the commemorative book. No one in the church office had asked for progress reports, but Emilie felt obliged to provide solid proof that she was indeed working.

Outside, the icy snow blew, rattling her many-paned windows.

Inside, her fingers flew over the keyboard, creating a highly detailed account of the early years of the Lititz Moravian Congregation. Mary Huebener's writings were scattered across the table for ready reference, along with various publications by the Moravian Historical Society, dog-eared photocopies from the Salem Library, and her own carefully handwritten notes.

The work was exacting and exhausting.

Emilie reveled in it.

Every page, every footnote, turned over another pebble in the hallowed ground of church history. Piecing together the facts at hand, she discovered new truths about the fellowship that had produced the liturgy, the music, the traditions she cherished.

From her viewpoint, history was the essence of religion, its foundation, its reason for continuing to exist at all.

One phrase kept appearing in the myriad texts that gave her pause: *awakened souls*. Awakened to what? In Herrnhut, in Lancaster, in Warwick Township of old, the people gathered because they were somehow "awakened," historians noted.

"Must have been a trombone choir there." She laughed to herself, imagining the early church members being roused out of their beds at dawn by the brassy blare.

But the first trombones from Christiansbrunn didn't arrive until November 1771. Obviously something else awakened their souls. Surely if she kept reading, an explanation would follow.

Wrapped in her warmest wool slacks and sweaters, Emilie pounded at the keyboard for nearly a week, barely taking a break for a few light meals and visits from Beth, who came bearing news from church along with armfuls of additional files.

Thursday's visit included an unexpected question: "Heard from anybody besides me lately?" Beth leaned against the kitchen sink, eyebrows lifted in anticipation.

Stalling, Emilie gathered her frazzled hair in a fresh knot, then slipped in a wide barrette to hold it at bay for another afternoon of research. "No, you're the only company I've had for days."

Beth looked surprised. "No phone calls? From…anybody?"

"My mother, of course. Helen. A couple of friends in Winston-Salem." Emilie wasn't about to tell Beth—or anyone else—what happened on Kissel Hill, let alone the outrageous offer Jonas had made. *Call him, indeed!* Not if he were the last kissable man on earth.

"No need to worry about me, Beth." She guided her toward a cozy, over-stuffed chair in the front sitting room. "I've lived alone for years. I'm used to a quiet house."

Beth shook her head. "C'mon, Em, you know what I'm getting at. Have you heard from Jonas?"

Emilie was appalled when an odd sort of laugh came out—almost like a giggle. *Ridiculous.* She never giggled. "Why in the world would Jonas Fielding be calling me?"

"Because according to Sara, you kissed him in front of God and every-body."

There was no stopping the heat that rose to her cheeks. "Sara said that, did she?"

"Children are notoriously honest. 'Course, I was at the top of the hill and missed the whole thing, but Sara's account was very…um, descriptive." Beth glanced at her watch and unzipped her jacket. "Look, I've got a good half hour before I have to be home. How about *you* tell me what happened. No skipping the juicy details, either."

Emilie groaned, coloring further. "It was beyond humiliating. The man kissed me only because he was confused and in pain. Hours later, he didn't even *remember* it, he was so disoriented."

Beth's bemused expression didn't help things. "The way I heard it, you kissed *him.*"

Well! "Only because he *asked* me to."

Beth's amusement erupted into a laugh. "I thought you said he was deliri-ous."

Emilie uncrossed her legs with a spirited stomp. "Well, he was alert enough to manage two words: 'Kiss me.'"

"The real question is, Em, did he kiss you back?"

Oh, most definitely. It was the very tactile memory of his narrow top lip and generous bottom one pressing firmly and quite intentionally against hers that made the whole scene remarkably unforgettable.

With no effort whatsoever, she could still feel that scratchy chin rubbing along her own, taste the flavors of tea and chocolate mingled together, sense the warmth of him despite his wind-chilled cheeks....

Enough, Em!

Arranging her features such that they gave away nothing, she said simply, "Yes, I believe Jonas did kiss me back. So you see, it was his idea from beginning to end. I was merely a participant."

"Ah, but a willing one, right?"

Honestly! This friendship with Beth was getting more taxing by the minute. "Somewhat." She slipped enough ice in her voice to stem any further discussion. "How is Sara doing, by the way?"

Laughing, Beth zipped her jacket closed and rose to leave. "You can run, Em, but you can't hide. Not in this small town. Sara's fine, of course. Looking forward to more snow tonight, if the forecast is correct." Beth moved the curtain to peer out at the wintry gray sky. "Who knows? We may have to go sledding again tomorrow. Certainly did prove to be an interesting experience *last* Friday." She winked broadly. "Maybe that's why they call it Kissel Hill."

"Now who's being silly?" Emilie pulled the front door open with an exaggerated yank. "It was named after the Kiesel family, among the first local Moravians to take communion the day the Gemeinhaus was dedicated in 1749." *The second Gemeinhaus, that is.*

"Always the historian, that's our Dr. Getz." Beth shook her head as she headed down the steps, then turned back, a pensive look on her face. "Don't get so wrapped up in the past you miss the present, Em. I'll call you tomorrow."

But when the phone rang the next morning, it wasn't Beth, nor Helen, nor her mother, nor the church.

It was Jonas.

Nine

What we anticipate seldom occurs; what we least expect generally happens.

BENJAMIN DISRAELI

"It's snowing," Jonas announced, sounding much too cheerful about it. "You know what that means, don't you?"

No. Yes! Emilie gripped the telephone and kept her voice steady. "You tell me."

"Time for the practice session we talked about. The weather is perfect."

"It is?" *That weather thing again.* She glanced at the window, as if the skies might offer a clue. What did snow and kissing have in common, anyway?

"Are you game, Emilie?"

Yes. No! She gulped. "I...I guess so."

"Meet me at the house. You know how to get here, don't you?"

"I'm sure I'll remember." As if she could forget. "Do I need to...bring anything?" *Courage for starters, Em.* "Hot chocolate, perhaps?" she added lamely.

"Nah, I've got that covered. And Emilie?" She could hear the banked excitement in his voice. "I've got a surprise for you."

"You do?" She hated surprises.

"You're gonna love it, I promise." Jonas paused, his enthusiasm clearly getting the better of him. "I'll give you one hint: you'll be *flying* before the morning is over."

"I see." *See what? See myself flying into his arms?* Certainly not! She scrambled for some legitimate reason to bow out. "Are you sure you've...recovered sufficiently?"

"Healthy as old Trix here." Emilie heard a bark of agreement in the background. "Now listen, Emilie." His cautionary tone pushed her nerves further on edge. "It's nasty out. Dress warmly."

"Dress *warmly?*" Her mind reeled at the thought. "Are we...uh, practicing...outdoors?"

A deep chuckle reverberated across the phone line. "You aren't planning on going sledding in my living room, are you? Granted, not much furniture there, but I'd like to spare the hardwood—"

"Did you say—I mean—*sledding?*"

"Sledding, yeah." His voice was a question mark. "What did you think we were doing?"

Don't ask. "I wasn't sure...exactly."

"You seemed to enjoy yourself last Friday. First time, right?"

"Right." *For a lot of things.* She sighed, her nervous system gearing down, one notch at a time. She'd already said yes. No point backing out now. "What time should I come over?"

"Eleven oughtta do it. The roads are a slippery mess. Take it easy on Cedar Street, promise?"

She heard a soft click, then a dial tone droned in her ear.

"Promise," she said into the stillness of her kitchen, and hung up the receiver, still dazed. How could she have misconstrued his meaning so completely?

Jonas didn't remember a thing about last Friday. Except sledding.

So much the better, Em.

She kept reminding herself of that truth, even as she dressed in a blouse that buttoned up to her chin, a sweater that buttoned down to her knees, and scarves that concealed every kissable inch. "There." She stood in front of the hall mirror, her voice muffled by layers of clothing, her body so thoroughly padded she appeared to have gained twenty pounds. "This should get the message across."

The actual delivery of Emilie's keep-your-distance message was delayed longer than expected. It took fifteen minutes to scrape the ice off her car and four grinding tries before the engine finally sprang to life. Her dependable BMW, kept rust-free from one semester to the next with careful paint touch-ups and plenty of TLC, came through yet again.

Sitting behind the wheel, hot as burned toast from her efforts and over-done attire, Emilie pulled away from the curb, lightly tapping the brakes to test for traction.

There was none. *Oh, wonderful.*

She inched forward, hovering over the gas pedal, as she turned—rather, slid—onto Cedar. A *"slippery mess," Jonas?* Bit of an understatement there. Week-old piles of gray slush, shoveled toward the curbs, lay hidden under last night's fresh snowfall and this morning's treacherous addition: ice.

Clutching the steering wheel, Emilie crawled past the school, then past Trinity Evangelical, noticing how few other drivers had ventured out that morning. A secret shiver of pride ran up her spine. *Brave Emilie and her BMW!* They'd been through so much together, surely they could handle this.

After a steady climb upward, her car crested the hill and started down the other side. *Odd.* The road hadn't seemed this steep before. On many a sunny day, she'd soared over the rise and down toward Marion Street with nary a moment's hesitation.

She was hesitating plenty now—inching forward and inevitably down-ward. Parked cars along the curb, draped with crusty white heaps, loomed closer than seemed prudent. Her destination felt miles away instead of blocks.

From the corner of her eye, Emilie watched a car pull out onto Cedar, fif teen yards ahead. Surely she was going slowly enough to stop. *Surely.* She eased on the brakes, pumping them in slow motion, just like her father had taught her twenty years earlier.

It may have worked then. It wasn't working now.

Her BMW began drifting sideways. The useless brakes only made things worse. Sliding broadside, her speed increasing, Emilie panicked. Steer *away* from the slide? *Into* the slide?

Immobilized, she hung on, eyes widening with fear.

Without warning, the car in front of her veered right, propelling itself over the curb and out of the BMW's path. *Thank goodness!*

In a split second, relief gave way to terror. The rear wheels locked, then hit a patch of ice. Emilie was suddenly facing backward—*backward!*—staring up at the snowy hilltop. With a sickening spin, she turned sideways again. Then headfirst, then sideways. Her world became a revolving blur. The only thing in clear focus was the immovable stone gate of the Moravian Cemetery, waiting in ice-shrouded silence at the bottom of the hill.

"Where *is* that woman?"

Jonas checked his watch again. *Eleven-thirty.* No answer when he called her house. Beth, snowbound at home with Sara, said she hadn't talked to Emilie since Thursday. Helen hadn't seen her either.

The always-punctual Dr. Getz either changed her mind, ran some errands first, or...*nah.* He wouldn't let his imagination go there.

She wasn't in trouble.

Just late.

For the first time in her life.

When his cell phone rang, he punched it on in mid-chirp. "Emilie?"

Silence. "Nooo." The female caller sounded perturbed. "This is the other woman in your life."

The other woman? Jonas held the phone away from his ear with two fingers, as if handling a poisonous snake. *An old girlfriend, maybe? One of his sisters-in-law?* He eased the phone back against his ear. "That you, Diane? Connie?"

"No, silly man. It's Dee Dee."

Caught off guard, he blurted out, "Dee *who?*"

"Look—" she sighed, an undercurrent of irritation rippling below her smooth tone—"I know you collect women like baseball cards, but surely you remember your real estate agent, who—"

"Oh! Dee Dee." *Of all people.* The woman was like a bad penny. "What can I do for you?"

Her throaty laugh sang across the phone line. "I can think of several possibilities, but that's not why I'm calling."

Good. He glanced at his watch again. "Do you mind cutting to the chase here? I'm...expecting someone."

"That brainy historian with the mousy brown hair, I suppose."

Jonas frowned, trying to remember if he'd ever seen a mouse with brown hair.

"Never mind," Dee Dee added with a groan. "Any more details will just depress me."

He heard her shuffle through papers, let out a disgruntled humph, then rattle more pages before she declared, "Aha! Here we go. Remember that property adjacent to Carter's Run, the one you desperately wanted for your clubhouse?"

He remembered, all right. "The one the owner wouldn't sell, at any price we offered?" His one disappointment about the whole project, and Dee Dee the dealmaker had to bring it up. *Talk about depressing.*

"I found another angle, Jonas. Is it too late, design-wise?"

Now she had his attention. "Not if you can give me something definite in the next thirty days." After months of haggling, he'd been forced to settle for a much smaller clubhouse than he wanted—too close to the street, and too small for anything but the basic services. With the additional corner lot, he'd have the first-class setup he longed for, overlooking the entire eighteen holes.

If—and it was a big if—the budget stretched that far.

"How much, Dee Dee?"

When she said the amount, Jonas let out a whoop. "Miss Snyder, you are a miracle worker. I don't even wanna know how you did it."

"Using perfectly legal methods, I assure you. We have a few more details to work out, but before I proceed, I wanted to be certain this would still…please you."

He almost didn't notice the purr in her voice. "Trust me, I'm pleased, Dee Dee. As soon as the weather breaks, I'll have the crew back in here, bulldozers roaring. Keep in close contact with me, will you?"

"That was the idea."

"Good. And…thanks." He punched off the phone, adrenaline pumping through his system. The borough would be thrilled. After he got the full story from Dee Dee, he'd stop by the council meeting Tuesday night, give them the good news.

When the cell phone in his hand rang again, he nearly dropped it in surprise before finding the right button. "H-hello? Emilie?"

"Emilie, huh? So you finally snagged a woman."

He stared at the receiver for a half second, the male voice on the line not registering.

"You there, Jonas? It's Nate."

He gripped the phone harder. "Nathan? Is it really you?"

"Sure it's me. Who's Emilie?"

"A…a woman, here in Lititz." *Who'd better get her mousy-haired self over here pronto before I send Trix out to find her.* "More later on that score. Where are you, man? What's going on? You doin' okay?"

Nate's laugh sounded forced. "I'm in Florida. Jacksonville area. Hitting a few golf balls. Making a few friends."

He knew the sort of friends Nate usually attracted. Guys out for a fast buck, trying to find the right hustle that would put them over the top financially. And women willing to go along for the ride who had nothing better to do than hang on.

Jonas didn't stoop to calling them losers, but they were definitely lost. *Like Nathan.*

"You didn't answer my last question, Nate. Are you okay?"

"Sure." His brother's response was a long time coming. "I'm a little low on cash right now, that's all. Nothing new. I'll manage."

Jonas felt a knot forming in his gut. He knew what Nate would say next, knew what was expected of him, the older brother with all the answers—and all the resources. It no longer made him feel useful—just used.

"Manage how?" Jonas prompted him, dreading his response.

"You know. Find a good club looking for a pro. Florida's lousy with golf courses. Something will open up."

Good. At least he was trying to find honest work. "What about cash in the meantime?" Jonas couldn't hang up without knowing his brother had a roof over his head and three square meals a day.

Nate's chuckle sounded like a spring uncoiling. "Well, if you have any loose bills sitting around…"

Jonas plucked his checkbook out of the clutter that served as his desk, and checked the balance. "How much are we talkin' about, bro?"

The phone line seemed to go dead. One beat, then two. "As much…" Nathan's voice faltered. "As much as you can spare, Jonas. Just for a few…months. I'm talking about a loan, not a handout."

"Right." He'd heard this before. "Is five thousand enough?"

Silence again. "Yeah. Great. Should last me quite a while, let me get on my feet down here, find a nice place…"

Nathan was babbling now, his words a gushing stream of relief. Jonas grabbed a pen and scribbled down the necessary information while he listened to his brother's endless thanks, shaking his head at his own gullibility. No matter what Nathan promised, Jonas knew he'd never see this money again.

The practical, bottom-line, business side of him said it was the worst thing, the stupidest thing he could do.

The generous, protective, big brother side of him said it was the best thing, the most sacrificial thing he could do.

Which was the *godly* thing to do? That's all Jonas cared about. Right now, he wasn't getting a clear word from that sector.

"Where do I send it, Nate?" Jonas printed the address on an envelope and stuffed the check inside. "Done. This'll have to hold you for a while, buddy. I've got a lot of my funds tied up in Carter's Run. Yeah, we're right on schedule." Jonas filled him in, describing the course in detail, elated at his brother's sudden interest in his work.

It was nearly noon when Jonas finally punched off the phone after a final admonition to keep in touch. A pointless exercise. Nate wouldn't call back until he needed something.

The cell phone rang again almost immediately. "Good grief," Jonas muttered, punching it back on. "This better be you, Emilie."

"Jonas, finally!" a woman gasped. "It's Beth Landis."

"Beth?" The muffled sound of traffic hummed in the background. "Where are you?"

"Cedar Street. Some guy loaned me his car phone and—" Her voice was drowned out by a grinding motor in the background. "—been trying to reach you for half an hour. After you called me about Emilie, I started worrying and decided to walk over to her house. On the way—" Beth's words dissolved into a high, thin wail. "Jonas, she's...she's been in a terrible accident."

"An *accident?*" Jonas was on his feet. "Is she hurt?" He jammed the phone against his shoulder and scrambled to find the keys to his Explorer, warm gloves, a flashlight, a blanket, anything that looked like emergency gear. "I'll be there in five minutes. Less." He felt his own vocal cords tightening. "And tell me she's okay."

"We...we don't know yet, Jonas." Beth was fighting for breath. "She's... trapped in the car. The police are here. And EMS. And the fire department."

"The *fire*—?" He yanked on a wool cap, sprinting toward the back door. "Okay. Okay, don't move, don't panic, Beth. I'm out the door. Hear that engine starting? I'll be there in two minutes." He backed down the slick driveway, barely noticing the poor traction as he turned the knob to engage the four-wheel drive. "Make that one minute. Don't cry, honey. Emilie is in good hands. She'll be okay. Just sit tight and pray, Beth. Pray hard."

He tossed the phone aside and pointed the Explorer toward Cedar, his heart pounding, his mind racing. Beth had tried to call him for thirty minutes. *Thirty minutes!* But no, he was too busy buying and spending, too worried about his business and his brother...

The guilt trapped in his throat nearly choked him. *Keep her safe, Lord. Please keep her safe!* He shouldn't have let her drive in the first place. Should have picked her up, for crying out loud. So what if that made their sledding thing look like a date. It *was* a date, wasn't it? Sort of?

In the rearview mirror, he caught a glimpse of Emilie's new Flexible Flyer in the cargo section, propped up with a big, blue bow tied on top. *Too late, Fielding. You're too late.* The knot in his throat sank to his stomach.

The minute he turned north on Cedar, he could see the red lights of emergency vehicles two blocks ahead. Releasing his foot off the accelerator only slightly, he closed in on the entrance to the cemetery, taking in the scattered semicircle of police vehicles and pedestrians congregating around a badly crumpled BMW with North Carolina tags.

He didn't remember parking the car or stuffing his pockets with everything in sight that might serve some purpose. All he remembered were Beth's eyes, wide and weeping, and Sara's small arms reaching toward him as he hurried across the snowpacked pavement.

"Sara!" Without thinking, he grabbed the sobbing little girl and crushed her against his chest, tears stinging his eyes. "I'm here, Sara. I'm here. Everything will be okay, I promise."

Sara shook her head and swung one soggy pink mitten in the direction of the mangled car. "But Em-ee-lee's in there." Her tiny voice barely penetrated through her scarf. "They can't get her out, Whale Man. Can you get her out?"

"I'll sure try, honey." He lowered Sara to the ground in time for Beth to give him a brief hug and a wary look.

"I'm sorry I wasn't..." He shook his head, overcome, knowing how lame his excuse sounded. "I'm…I'm sorry." Jonas abruptly turned toward the accident scene, avoiding the disappointment written all over Beth's face.

I didn't know. Didn't know, Lord!

"Can I help?" He eased his way through the crowd, concerned faces parting to make way for him. Maybe it was his own grim expression that cleared a path for him to reach the inner circle within seconds. Spotting the chief of police, Jonas raised his voice to get the man's attention. "Ted, what can I do here?"

"Unless you got the Jaws of Life in your back pocket, nothing." The older man eased over, his eyes trained on the battered car. "Do you know this woman?"

"Yeah, I do. She…she goes to my church." *Attaboy, stick your neck out.* Jonas pulled off his cap and wiped the cold sweat off his brow. "Has she moved yet? Is she breathing?" Side by side, the two stared at the BMW, crushed like an accordion against a square stone and mortar pillar. Emilie was slumped against the driver's side, her shoulder pinned forward in an awkward and painful-looking position. She was utterly still, her face paler than he'd ever seen it.

Oh, Emilie… Jonas swallowed several times, jamming his hands in his pockets, fighting for control.

Emilie isn't moving. Why isn't she moving, Lord?

Around the accident site were half a dozen rescue workers doing their best to dismantle what was left of the car. A volunteer fireman attempted to pry the door loose with a crowbar while a young woman in an EMS uniform managed to get one arm through the twisted metal, then shouted, "We've got a pulse!"

A murmur of hope circled around him as Jonas inched closer, every cell in his body straining to see her, touch her, hear her voice. Know she was alive. Tell her he was sorry, that he'd messed up, that he—

"It's all about you, then. Not about me."

Her words, spoken in a heated moment in Pastor Yeager's office, echoed in his memory. *No! It's about you, Emilie. All about you, this time.*

Would he ever stop feeling guilty around this woman?

Farther up Cedar Street a horn blared. As the crowd turned to watch another volunteer in a rescue vehicle inch his way down the slippery hill, Ted clamped a meaty hand on his shoulder. "Good news, Jonas. There's the guy with the tools we've been waiting for. We've had wrecks all over the township this morning, you know. Worse than last weekend." Ted raised his voice above the din. "Give the man some room!"

Sliding his vehicle to a dramatic stop, the bearded young man scrambled out of the front seat, then unlocked the trunk and pulled out a hefty power unit and a contraption that resembled a huge set of pliers. "Jaws of Life, coming through!" he bellowed, carting fifty pounds of equipment in each hand across the treacherous ice. Cheers broke out as the team hustled to get the device ready to go, their movements a blur of speed and precision.

Jonas held his breath as the hydraulics kicked in and the metal door on the driver's side began giving way with a piercing shriek. Two inches. Four. "How much space do we need to get her out?" Jonas hollered above the deafening noise of the engine.

"The most it'll give us is twenty-seven inches," Ted shouted back. "I can't tell by looking. How big a woman is she?"

"Not very." Jonas slowly shook his head, his gaze glued to the action mere feet away. "Tall, but kinda skinny. Should be enough room." *Gotta be enough, Lord. Gotta be.*

He'd never felt so powerless. Standing there, unable to help, unable to reach past the jagged wreckage and pull her clear, waiting instead for an experienced crew to do the one thing he couldn't do: save Emilie Getz.

"Emilie! Emilie, do you hear me? We're going to lift you out of the car now. The paramedics are here and your vitals are good, so just relax and let us do the work, okay? That's it. That's the way."

Two firm hands grasped her shoulders while another pair carefully snapped a thick white cuff around her neck. "Ohhh." The moan took an enormous amount of energy. The pain claimed whatever was left. She couldn't focus her eyes, couldn't feel her extremities. Her mouth was dry as parchment, her lips cracked, and the dense, metallic taste in her mouth begged for something wet and cold to rinse it away.

"Water," she croaked, not sure if she spoke the word or only thought it. She tried again. "Water."

A plastic bottle appeared near her lips and she drank greedily. The effort nearly consumed her. "Thank you..."

"That's why we're here, Emilie." A young woman's voice. Soothing, comforting. "Rod is going to maneuver your legs through this opening, while Skip supports your shoulders through the other window. We have a gurney waiting, so don't worry, we gotcha. Okay? Ready, Emilie?"

"Ready."

Voices around her counted to three, then all at once she was moving, being turned and steered like a vehicle careening out of control. "Help," she whimpered, confused. She was sliding. Sliding! Backwards. Sideways. Stop! Stop the car. "Stop. Stop," she moaned.

Finally she did stop, landing flat on her back—a cold white sky above, a cold white sheet below. The voices had faces—faces that smiled down at her, red-cheeked and grinning. "What a trouper you are!" the man they called Rod said, the one who'd guided her legs through the narrow opening.

"Right." Her smile was faint but genuine.

The young woman with the calm voice pushed aside a torn coat sleeve to slip a blood pressure cuff around Emilie's arm. "Good thing you wore so many clothes, ma'am. All that padding probably saved your life."

"Good thing," she agreed, her eyes drifting shut from utter exhaustion. Why *did* she have so many layers on? Was she cold? Was she sick? *No.* She was avoiding…avoiding some…

"Somebody's pretty anxious to see you, Emilie."

A shadow fell across her, blocking the pale wintry sun. She moistened her lips and tried to speak. "Who…?"

"It's me, Emilie."

The voice was low, rough, masculine. Halting, as if caught on a branch. She could feel the warmth of his breath hovering over her. Her eyes opened slowly, weighted down with invisible bricks. "Ohh. Jonas." She closed them again, but not before noticing the tears welling up in his enormous brown eyes as he knelt by her side. "Good," she said, feeling some need to ease his obvious discomfort.

"It *is* good, Emilie. It's…" His voice broke. "Good to have you out of that car and…alive." One lone drop escaped, landing on her chin. Huge, warm, wet. "Sorry." She felt him brush it gently away with one gloved thumb. "How 'bout I follow the ambulance to the hospital? Mind if I do that, Emilie?"

"Do," she murmured, feeling her world starting to spin again. "Please… please…do."

Ten

◆

Anything you lose automatically doubles in value.
MIGNON MCLAUGHLIN

"I dunno what happened, Beth. I just lost it."

"Lost what?" Beth's dark blue eyes twinkled.

"My mind, of course." Jonas exhaled and threw his hands in the air. "My sense of reason. Something."

"Start at the beginning. Tell me how it all took place."

Jonas stared out at the rain pounding on the church parking lot, the last of the snow and ice giving way to swollen gutters and overflowing rainspouts.

Whatever had possessed him to share this with Beth Landis was any fool's guess. He'd vowed afterward he wouldn't tell a living soul. All the way home from the hospital Friday evening, all weekend long, he'd kept his inexcusable behavior to himself. Until this morning when his chest threatened to implode if he didn't get it off there and let somebody else work him over, give him what-for, make him suffer.

Beth and Emilie were friends. That made Beth the most likely candidate for letting him have it with both barrels. Not that she was the shooting type.

Sitting there behind her desk at church, hands busy stuffing envelopes, Beth resembled anything but a shotgun-totin' mama.

"Sit down, Jonas. You're making me nervous, pacing like that. I'm fully prepared to hear every sordid detail." She grinned. "Not that I expect there to be any."

"It's like this." He dropped in her visitor's chair with a determined thwump. "I kissed her."

"Kissed who?"

"Don't be cute, Beth." Which was ridiculous. The woman was the definition of cute. "Emilie. I kissed…Emilie."

Beth glanced up from her envelopes and tried to look disinterested. "Oh. On Friday?"

"No, on the mouth!" He groaned and rolled his eyes. "Yeah, on Friday. At the hospital. That's what makes it so awful, Beth. She was…uh…unconscious."

Beth gasped. "She was out cold? You kissed her without her—?"

"Yes. Disgusting, isn't it?" He stood again, circling the small office. "What kind of man would lean over an injured woman on a gurney and…and take advantage of her like that?"

Beth tossed her work aside and leaned back in her chair, a wide grin inching across her freckled face. "What a minute. Who says you took advantage of her? Maybe she liked it. Maybe she welcomed it. In fact…" She sprang to her feet, cornering him between her bookcase and the office coatrack. "I'll bet she *asked* you to kiss her."

The hairs on the back of his neck rose to attention. "W-what did you say?"

Beth folded her arms. "I said Emilie probably asked you to kiss her."

He gulped. "W-where did you get such a crazy idea?"

"Am I right or am I wrong?"

"You're…right." She *was* right! He blew out a sigh of relief. "That's exactly how it happened. I leaned over to say I'd stick around until the doc came back and she said…uh…"

"Kiss me?"

He narrowed his gaze. "Did she already talk to you about this?"

"Nope. The point is, she knew it was you. Knew what she was doing. So…what's the problem?"

Was the woman dense? "The problem, Beth, is that she didn't know what she was saying. Emilie was…delirious."

She laughed. "Before or after the kiss?"

"That's it. I'm outta here." He grabbed his coat, sorry he'd ever trusted Beth with such sensitive information. Poking his arms in the sleeves with minimal success, he grunted, "I suppose you'll tell her everything we talked about here."

"Relax, Jonas. You and I are friends, too, remember?" Beth edged toward the doorway, effectively blocking his exit. "Look. The only real question here is, did she kiss you back?"

Oh, yeah. He could still feel Emilie's buttery lips molding themselves to his, her soft nose squashing beneath his own, her porcelain skin rubbing his rough beard, her soft sigh against his mouth when he finally pulled away…

"You're smiling, Jonas, but you're not telling me what I need to know. Did Emilie kiss you back?"

He wiped the grin off his face and shrugged. "Yeah, I'd say she kissed me back. But remember, it was her idea to begin with. I was just…handy."

"Right." Beth stepped to the side, giving him a clear shot at the hallway. "My guess is, now you're wondering if she remembers this torrid kiss."

"It wasn't torrid. It was…sweet." That's what she'd said. *"So sweet."* He caught himself before he grinned again. "And that's precisely what concerns me—does she even remember it? I don't wanna have to bring up the subject myself."

Beth checked her watch. "Tell you what. I'm here for another hour, then I'll swing by Emilie's place on the way home and see if she makes a confession of her own."

Jonas buttoned his coat, feeling immensely better. "And you'll let me know?"

"If she brings it up, I'll listen. That's as much as I can promise you." Shivering as the blustery winds outside rattled the old windows, Beth reached behind the desk and bumped the thermostat up to seventy. "The last thing I want is to get between you two."

Jonas paused in the doorway, confused. "Why is that?"

She groaned. "Because you're both stubborn, hardheaded, and strong willed, for starters."

"Both of us?" His fist hit the doorjamb. "You gotta be kidding! Emilie

Getz and I have absolutely nothing in common. *She* may be stubborn, but no way do I fit that description. Absolutely not. Hardheaded? Not this guy. Not in a million years…"

The woman was pushing him out the door. A twenty-something pip-squeak and she was shoving *him* out into the hall. In all his years of dealing with women, he couldn't remember such a thing happening.

"Who told you I was strong willed? Huh? Who said that?" The louder Beth laughed, the more he bellowed. "C'mon, you know it's not true. I am *not* stubborn. Am not!"

The door closed behind him with a firm bang.

Emilie couldn't remember a more miserable Monday morning.

Her BMW was scrap metal.

Her right collarbone was equally shattered and bruised while every muscle ached from the tension that'd seized her body on her endless, downhill slide to disaster.

Worst of all, the insurance agent perched on her living room sofa was scratching down numbers and shaking his head.

"The Blue Book value doesn't look good, Miss Getz."

She rubbed her temple, willing away the headache that had lodged itself there since Friday. "The *what* book?"

"Blue Book. It tells us what your seventeen-year-old car is worth. Naturally, we can only pay you the salvage value. As a courtesy."

"And that amount is…?"

"Pitiful." He told her the figure in dollars and cents.

"Oh, great." Emilie groaned, slumping further down in the overstuffed chair that served as her makeshift hospital bed. "Almost enough for a bicycle."

"A used one, maybe." His chuckle was meant to amuse, but instead grated on the one nerve she had left. "Because you dropped your collision insurance six years ago we don't cover damage to your car. Just the things you hit. Like stone fences."

"I see." So much for frugality.

"Look for your check in a couple of days. Anything else I can do for you?"

"No, you've done enough, thank you." She slid Hamilton's three-pound *History of the Moravian Church* onto her lap, wincing at the stab of pain that shot across her right shoulder. "I'm woefully behind in my research, so if you don't mind seeing yourself out…"

"No problem. He stood and quickly pulled on his coat, heading toward the front door. "Sorry about the bad news, Miss Getz. That's how it goes when things get old and lose their value."

Did he mean her or the BMW?

"Appreciate you stopping by." She lifted a hand as he disappeared from sight, then dropped it on her open book, exhausted from the effort.

How in the world was she going to manage? A broken right collarbone made writing impossible and turned typing into a tedious, hunt-and-peck proposition. Without a car, she couldn't get around to do on-site research, or grocery shopping, or go bookstore browsing in Lancaster.

Or sledding with Jonas. Not that she planned to slide downhill in a moving vehicle ever again.

Her head fell back on the upholstered fabric as vague memories from Friday washed over her. Being pulled out of the wreckage. Seeing Jonas. Watching Beth and Sara smile and cry at the same time. Riding in the ambulance to Lancaster General.

Jonas, looking concerned, asking questions of anyone in scrubs who stood still long enough for him to snag their sleeve.

Jonas, holding her hand, making her laugh in spite of her pain.

Jonas, begging her forgiveness so many times it was ridiculous.

He'd driven her home Saturday morning with Trix in the backseat keeping watch over four bags of groceries for her and a thermos of hot, perfectly sweetened earl grey waiting up front in the passenger seat. Sunday he'd stopped by after the early service with a church bulletin, get well greetings from the staff, and two cheese Danish—which he ended up eating.

Now it was Monday, a workday for both of them. No telling when—or if—she'd see him again.

With the horrid weather, he wouldn't be likely to come knocking on her door today. After the morning's dense fog lifted, heavy rain clouds settled over Lancaster County, resulting in the worst flooding in five years.

At least that's how the noon news anchor described conditions. Emilie stayed high and dry, cocooned inside her little borrowed home with a tuna salad sandwich and a few green grapes for lunch.

Not that the house itself wasn't grand company. She loved the old hall-way clock built inside the wall such that it opened on both sides, put there by Clarence the clockmaker from across the street, who owed the family some money generations ago.

Then there was the bank vault encased in the dining room wall, and the natural wainscoting from the 1840s, and the charming plate rail that circled the cozy kitchen with its scant seven-foot ceiling and eight tiny windows over the sink.

Emilie would happily call it home for a lifetime.

Instead, she'd be Salem-bound come June.

A sharp knock at the back door snapped her out of her reverie. Beth Landis—at least, it *looked* like Beth, bundled up in a hooded red parka—peered in, motioning frantically. Emilie jumped to her feet, then regretted it when her head started pounding and the room tilted sideways. "Hang on," she mumbled, making her way toward the door.

Beth blew in on a stiff, soaking gust of wind. "Whew! Thanks. It's wicked out there." She unzipped her parka and dried her dripping hair with a nearby dishtowel, eyeing Emilie with an affectionate appraisal. "So. How are you feeling today? You look worn out."

"Some encourager *you* are." Emilie shuffled over to the table, doing her best to remain perpendicular. "Have a seat and I'll make some tea."

"Forget that, Doc. *You* sit and I'll make the tea." Beth gently pushed her into a kitchen chair, then busied herself with the necessary ingredients, pulling a generous rectangle of Moravian sugar cake out of her zippered pocket to add to their plates. "Helen sent me home with a whole panful yes-terday." Beth grinned as she peeled back the plastic wrap and sliced the cake in two. "I knew you'd want some."

It was lovely to have company—not just company, a friend—bustling about her kitchen. Emilie observed Beth's cheerfully efficient manner and imagined little Sara sitting just so, legs dangling high above the floor, watch-ing her mother make lunch.

She didn't mean to say it; it simply came out. "Sara is lucky to have you for a mother."

"Think so?" Beth joined her at the table, her task complete, her eyebrows furrowed. "I dunno. I'm never sure if I'm doing any of it right."

Emilie poked at one corner of her sugar cake, not really hungry, wanting to be polite. "I can't imagine having a child under my roof for twenty-four hours, let alone twenty-four years."

Beth nodded, popping a forkful in her mouth. "Pretty scary stuff. No way to prepare yourself, either. When it comes to motherhood, you just dive in. And pray. Speaking of which, okay if we bless this?" She lowered her fork and reached for Emilie's hand. "Would you do the honors?"

"Would I what?" Emilie's hand suddenly felt like ice in Beth's warm grasp.

"Pray. You know, bless our food and our fellowship." Beth dipped her chin and closed her eyes in anticipation.

Pray? Emilie gulped, then closed her own eyes. *Now what?* Should she say the blessing from the *Daily Texts?* Is that what Beth wanted? The words came slowly, mined from childhood memories long forgotten, spoken with the sober formality of her German ancestors: "Come, Lord Jesus, our guest to be, and bless these gifts bestowed by thee. Amen."

"Amen," Beth echoed, then squeezed her hand tighter, adding, "And Lord, while you're here with us, touch Emilie's shoulder. Mend her broken bones and tender bruises. Comfort her with your assurance that all things work together for your good, Lord. Reveal yourself to her as husband and provider and lover of her soul."

"Lover?" Good heavens!

But Beth wasn't done yet.

"Be with Drew as he travels to Atlanta on business in this awful weather. Keep him safe, Lord. I love him so much." Beth's voice wavered, but only for a moment. "Help me be a good mother to Sara. Our daughter is a precious gift. A miracle." She swallowed hard again. "Bless this dessert now, Lord, and our time together. Thank you for my friend, Emilie, and for loving us so completely through your Son, our savior, Jesus. Amen."

They both looked up—Beth with a sheen of tears in her eyes; Emilie with a flush of embarrassment easing up her neck. Whatever that was, it wasn't the kind of thing *she* called a prayer. So personal. So...emotional.

Beth blinked away the moisture in her eyes and dove into her serving of sugar cake and a description of her morning with equal fervor. She'd almost finished with both when she added, "By the way, Jonas stopped by church."

Ohh. "Oh?"

"Monday morning missions committee meeting. He also wanted to find out how you were doing."

Emilie stabbed at one corner of her cake. "He should know. He visited here yesterday."

Beth's gaze softened. "He's being very…attentive then, isn't he?"

"Guess so." *Why is she looking at me like that? Am I supposed to say something? Know something?* "I think he feels a bit responsible for the whole thing. Which is silly. I'm the one who drove my car sideways down Cedar."

"Now, Emilie, you weren't responsible either. It was an accident, plain and simple. Jonas probably wishes he'd come over and picked you up, that's all."

Deep in thought, Emilie cautiously adjusted the sling around her right arm. *Not my fault? Really?* The concept stunned her. It was exactly the sort of reprieve she didn't allow herself.

She stared at the bite of cake on her fork then swallowed it, barely noticing the flavor. "Tell Jonas I'm fine and—"

Laughing, Beth pointed at the back door. "Tell him yourself."

Sure enough, the broad shoulders of Jonas Fielding filled the doorway, jolting Emilie's heart into a double-time rhythm.

"Gotta run." Beth scurried about, gathering her belongings. "Anna Ressler is patiently waiting for this relief pitcher to show up at home base." She yanked open the back door. "C'mon in, big guy. You're right on time. We were just talking about you."

His dark brows lifted dramatically. "Anything…important?"

"Nothing…revealing." Beth flashed the biggest grin Emilie had ever seen on the young woman's face. "See ya." With that, Beth was gone and a sudden quiet filled the kitchen.

A warm silence, full of possibilities.

"Hello," Emilie said finally, finding it difficult to look away from his dark, steady gaze.

"Hello back." He broke the spell at last, staring down at her plate with a wistful expression. "Got any more of that?"

"Here." She pushed it toward him. "Have mine, I've barely touched it. Let me get you a clean fork." Emilie stood, but too quickly. The windows dipped and swayed in a dizzy line before Jonas gripped her good arm, trying to balance her, steering her toward her upholstered living room chair.

"You'll be more comfortable in here." He tried to fluff some pillows around her, succeeding only in jabbing her twice with his elbow. "Good grief, I'm an accident in progress myself."

"Not at all," she murmured, taking a deep breath to slow her wildly beating heart. In the process, she inhaled the unmistakably masculine scent of him. Warm, almost peppery, like wood smoke. "Mmm. Do you have a fireplace?"

He pulled back in surprise. "Yeah. How'd you know that?"

She touched the end of her nose and smiled. "You don't grow something this size and miss the smell of cedar logs on a man's sweater."

"Not a thing wrong with that nose," he countered, staring for a beat longer than necessary. His eyes widened. Hers did too. *What is it? Something. Something about her nose, of all things! Was it too big after all? Too round? Too soft?*

His hand reached forward, barely touching the tip of it then pushing with the gentlest of pressure. She felt her nose spreading, surrendering to his touch. Felt a feverish blush rushing upward toward the same spot. Heard Jonas whisper, almost to himself. "Such a nice nose."

"Such a nice nose?" Just like last time. He remembered!

"Kind of you to say that, Jonas." Emilie was staring at him now, bright pink just the way he liked her. Almost as an afterthought, she murmured, "So sweet."

"So sweet?" Just like last time. She remembered!

He released his hand then, feeling foolish for touching her like that. Still, he'd gotten his answer. She *did* recall their kiss in the hallway of Lancaster General. And—even better—she was still willing to talk to him.

"Hey, I brought something to cheer you up, keep you company. Hang on, I left it outside."

"Outside? In this weather?"

He was already heading back through the kitchen, reaching one hand outdoors long enough to grab the fishbowl he'd left there.

"Get ready for a new friend, Emilie." He strolled into the room and plunked the bowl down next to a precarious stack of research books. "Say hello to Marvin."

She stared at the bowl, not blinking, not speaking.

"Cute, isn't he? And no trouble whatsoever. A little food…" He fished in his pocket for a small canister. "Yup, a sprinkle a day, and Marvin will be a great little friend when it gets too quiet around here." *Which has gotta be most of the time. The woman lives like a nun.*

Emilie's lips finally moved. "How do you know it's a he?"

He shrugged. "I guessed. Does it look like a female goldfish to you?"

Her gaze shifted toward his. "When I was a child, all my stuffed animals were girls."

"You had stuffed animals?" Somehow, he couldn't picture Emilie hugging a teddy bear.

"Dozens of them. All girls." She stared at the fish. "This isn't Marvin, it's Mavis."

"Fine. Mavis. Whatever. You women stick together, have fun, go shopping."

"Go *where?*"

"Uh….shopping." Did he say something wrong? Jonas plopped in the nearest chair, resigned to any diatribe she wanted to dish out, as long as he could gaze at her soft, pretty nose and imagine it giving way under his own.

"Jonas, one does not go shopping with a fish. Besides, I am not like most women. I abhor shopping."

"Is that right? Me too."

They paused, staring at one another in amazement.

"I study catalogs," she explained. "Then I choose the store with the best return policy and buy the most practical, economical model available."

"No kidding. I walk in, get the most expensive one with all the bells and whistles, plunk down the cash, and walk out." He grinned. "Guess we don't have too much in common there, huh?"

"I suppose not." She glanced at a small stack of magazines, then her features brightened. "What about travel? You strike me as a man who'd like to see the world, as I would."

He leaned back, threading his fingers together and tucking them behind his head. "Yeah, now that *is* something we can agree on. I've been to thirty-two states so far—"

"Really!" She seemed positively giddy.

"Yup. Trix and I slept under the stars in Montana, Colorado, Wyoming—"

"Under the...stars?"

"Backpacking." He nodded, smiling broadly at the memory. "A sleeping bag, campfire gear, some grub, and we're golden. Guess where I wanna head next?"

"England?" She smiled, a portrait of anticipation.

"Nah. Bunch of stuffy tea drinkers." *Oops.* "I mean, tea is fine, don't get me wrong. But England is a bit misty-moisty for camping. Good place for hiking, though."

"Quite." She sighed, smoothing her hand across the magazine cover. "I've always thought a walking holiday would be delightful."

"Got the perfect place for you." He paused, building suspense, knowing she'd be knocked out. "One word: Alaska."

"Alaska?" She looked knocked out, all right.

"Glaciers, mountains, caribou, moose. And the northern lights." He drew an imaginary arc above them with his arms, picturing it all. "Someday, when Carter's Run is behind me, I'm heading north."

She twirled a loose curl around one finger and asked in a softer voice, "For good?"

"Nah. A month, at most." He stood and stretched, hearing the crackle and snap in his joints, no doubt brought on by the rain. "Fact is, I'm happy to call Lititz home." He dipped his head to glance out the window. "Except in a soaker like this."

"Isn't it grand?" Her musical sigh filled the room. "I love rainy days. Perfect for curling up with a good book."

Figures. "Give me a hot, sunny day with a couple of sweaty guys and a backboard and I'll shoot hoops till I drop." He grunted, still staring out the window. "This kinda weather only works if you're a duck."

"In that case, quack." She cleared her throat. "Or should I say...kwawk?"

His head snapped around. The woman was smiling. No, *grinning!*

He grinned back. "This is duck weather. Definitely quack. Unless you're a wood duck."

"What sound does a wood duck make, Mr. Fielding? Provided I won't be asked to demonstrate it."

"I can handle that. They have a rising whistle." He let one fly. "'Course, my own brand heads the other direction." He winked and produced a full-bodied wolf whistle.

She immediately looked down at her lap and turned the color of raspberry sherbet.

It wasn't possible.

"Emilie Getz, hasn't a man ever whistled at you before?"

He barely heard her whispered confession. "N-no."

The truth hit him like a freight train: the woman was *shy*. Not stuffy, not prickly, not a stick-in-the-mud. *Shy*.

Shy, he could manage. Beneath that cool exterior beat the heart of a woman who hadn't been...well, appreciated. For being a woman.

He regarded her bowed head with a newfound sense of responsibility. "Emilie, would it be accurate to say you're not accustomed to receiving praise?"

She glanced up, still berry-colored but clear-eyed. "In my office at Salem College, I have a wall filled with degrees, honors, certificates, academic awards, letters from students—"

He waved his hand, cutting her off. "All well and good. Congratulations. But I meant personal compliments. Someone noticing, for example, how much your hands resemble birds."

She glanced down at them in dismay. "Birds?"

"Doves. Small, white doves, flitting around your face when you talk. Nice birds. Honest."

"Oh. Birds."

"And your eyes. The color of that tea you drink all the time. Oval-shaped and full of...life." He'd almost said *fire*. Well-banked, but embers were aglow beneath the surface. *Definitely*.

"And your skin." He was warming up to his assignment. *Somebody's gotta do it, Lord.* "Your skin is like a statue."

She balked. "A *statue?*"

"Yeah, a pure white marble statue or a porcelain doll. Pale and smooth. Very pretty."

Except now her porcelain skin wasn't white, it was pinker than ever.

He tipped his head and squinted, appraising her. "As for your bones..."

"Bones?" Her porcupine look was back. "You are *not* referring to my bony knees, I hope."

"Haven't seen your knees, though I'm sure they're more bonnie than bony." *Attaboy.* He chuckled at his own pun. "You have these interesting cheekbones..."

He dropped to his knees in front of her and placed one finger at the top of her cheek, tracing a line as he talked, feeling the heat of her blush under his fingertip. "They sit up to attention here, then angle along this unusually strong jawline of yours—" She made a tiny huff. "And come to a point at your charming chinny-chin-chin."

She backed away from his touch, clearly flustered. "That should do it, then. We've already talked about my soft nose."

"Which leaves only one feature to discuss." He was gazing at it now. Shaped like a rosebud, full and sweet. Was it only three days since they'd kissed? "I...uh, covered that part...at some length." His gaze inched up to meet hers. "On Friday. After the accident."

"Yes, indeed." Her eyes were unfocused, dreamy. "I remember that Friday afternoon well. I thought *you'd* forgotten, though."

"Forget? Not me. Not likely." He watched her moisten her lips, then, mesmerized, he leaned closer. "Suppose you refresh my memory."

Eleven

Oh love, thy kiss would wake the dead!
ALFRED, LORD TENNYSON

Emilie paused mere inches away from his lips—to breathe, rethink, prepare, *something.* If he needed his memory jogged, she recalled every second in sharp detail. "You were lying in the snow—"

"In the snow?" He straightened, clearly startled. "No way. This was *after* the accident."

"Exactly." She nodded. "Right after you slid down the hill—"

"No, *you* slid down the hill." He rolled his eyes. "Guess you hit your head harder than we thought."

"No, *you* hit your head." *Was the man daft?* "After spinning in circles across the ice and snow—"

"You're right about that part." He nodded. "Round and round, down the hill, crashing at the bottom—"

"Exactly. No broken bones, thank goodness."

"Wait." His eyebrows knotted. "I thought you broke your collarbone."

She stared at him. "I did, on Friday afternoon. But we're talking about—"

"What came afterward," he finished for her. "So then at the hospital—"

"No, it happened before that." The man clearly had lost all sense of time. Then again, it *was* ten days ago.

"While we were waiting for the doc to come back," he clarified. "That's when it happened. Right before the X rays."

"The *X rays?*" Emilie groaned. "You've got me so confused. I'm talking about when, in a delirious state of mind—"

"Right! Without really thinking we—"

"K-kissed."

"Kissed." He sat back on his haunches. "Bingo."

"On Friday."

"Yes, it was a Friday."

"On the hill."

"No, at the hospital. Emilie, are you *sure* you remember this?"

Her headache was back in spades. "I remember everything about the accident—"

"Never mind that. I'm talking about when you asked me to kiss you."

"*What?*" She jumped to her feet, nearly losing her balance. "I did no such thing!"

"You most certainly did." He was standing now, too, no doubt enjoying the height advantage it gave him. His eyes bore down on her. *"Kiss me.* That's what you said. I was there."

"I was there, too, leaning over you when *you* said, Kiss me."

"I didn't say it, *you* said it."

"Listen, you…you!" She was fuming now. Emilie never fumed. "I have a dozen witnesses!"

"Emilie, there wasn't a soul in that hallway."

Would the man stop harping about that hallway? "Honestly, where it occurred isn't the point. The point is, we—"

"Kissed," he stated emphatically.

"On the mouth," she agreed.

"On purpose."

"Just so."

"So?" His dark eyes took on a subtle gleam as he closed the gap between them again. "If we could manage it once—"

"When one of us was unconscious," she reminded him, realizing that with the chair directly behind her there was no avenue of escape.

"Well, we're both quite lucid now." He slid one finger under her chin and gently but firmly tipped it up. "Say it again, Emilie."

Her jaw felt immobilized, though his touch was exceedingly light. "But *you* said it in the first place."

"Whatever makes you happy, woman." He slowly lowered his head. Then his eyes. Then his voice. "Kiss me."

He didn't give her a chance to answer. Or protest. Or think. In the time it took to close her eyes, their lips met.

Now *this*….this she remembered.

It was nothing like he remembered.

That other Emilie was groggy, barely able to put two intelligent words together. *This* Emilie was warm, vibrant, responsive, and tasted like Moravian sugar cake.

Ooh baby.

She leaned forward, yielding herself to him, resting her left hand lightly on his arm for balance.

Feeling less than stable himself, he slipped an arm around her waist, tugging her gently toward him, grateful when she didn't resist his embrace.

Too soon—much too soon—it was over. She pulled back, looking more shy than ever. A telling silence hovered around them which her voice barely dinted. "Now what, Jonas?"

He tried not to appear hopeful. "Maybe *you* say it this time?"

Her back-to-berry blush and downcast eyes squelched that idea in a hurry.

"Okay, then…how about lunch?"

"I've already eaten."

"Come to think of it, me too." He laughed, relieved when she looked up and smiled, evaporating the awkwardness between them. "It's a soggy mess out there. Construction's at a standstill at the work site. Anything useful I could do for you, my wheelless wonder?"

"Humph. You *would* remind me."

"How can I forget?" He gently ran his finger along her sling. "Every time I look at this, I feel responsible all over again."

"Oh, no you don't." She shook her head vehemently and swatted his hand. Strong-willed Emilie was making a comeback. "We've wasted enough time on that subject. With my collarbone out of commission, I can't drive until March anyway, car or no car. Walking around town will do me good. Besides, think of all the money I'll save on gas."

"The ever-practical Dr. Getz." *And ever feisty.* But then, he liked feisty. "Sure there isn't somewhere I could drive you this afternoon?" He'd almost said "kiss you this afternoon," and felt his skin warm at the thought.

Emilie glanced down at her history books, then up at him, a look of expectancy dancing across her features. "Well...if it wouldn't be *too* much trouble, I'd like a ride down to Elm and East Main."

"In this weather?" He made a face. "What's there?"

"Once upon a time, a Gemeinhaus."

"A *what* house?"

"Common house. The cellar was dug in November 1746, but the building wasn't ready for occupancy until May 1748."

"Been there," he muttered. "Those subcontractors will kill ya, every time."

"So, Jonas...might you be willing to take me?" She smiled so sweetly he thought for a second she might be flirting. *Not my Emilie, no way.*

"Yeah." He zipped his coat back on. "I'd like to see the old place." He watched her try to pull on her coat herself, one-handed, before casually offering his assistance. No point making the woman feel less than capable.

"Actually, the log structure is long gone." Her schoolmarm side appeared—minus the wooden ruler—as she warmed up to her topic. "When enrollment dwindled—in part because of bear sightings in the nearby woods—they dismantled the school in August 1765 and reassembled it across from Church Square."

He followed her through the small house and out the back door, holding back a chuckle. "You're like one of those museum displays—push the speaker button and out comes a slew of information."

She did an about-face, nearly smacking his chin with her forehead. "That's what I get paid for, Jonas."

He threw up both hands in surrender. "And you do it well. I'm impressed, okay?" *More than you know, woman. More than you know.* "Lead the way, Doc. *Go-mine-house,* here we come."

Emilie squinted up at the lofty sign, wishing she'd brought her glasses. "Can you make it out?"

Though drenched with rain and surrounded by barren maple branches, the gray-and-gold historical marker staked its claim on the corner of Elm and Main, proudly proclaiming the exact location of the original Moravian Gemeinhaus.

Or so the history books say. She knew better, knew this wasn't the very first spot. That elusive bit of property wasn't much farther east than this one. Tucked in a dusty drawer somewhere in Lititz was a survey map, diary, or letter with the critical bit of information on it, and she intended to find it.

Jonas shot her a sideways glance, then slipped on his own reading specs for all of five seconds. "'It stood 125 yards to the north on the elevation on this side of Carter's Run.'" The glasses disappeared. "That's where we got the name for our golf course—Carter's Run."

"On some maps it's called Lititz Run, but yes, that's the same creek." She peered out from under her tiny folding umbrella. "You're the professional at this sort of thing. Walk us north 125 yards."

As they negotiated the slippery combination of snow, slush, mud, and rain, Emilie took in the surrounding scenery with a sigh of discouragement. The basketball goal on the right, though serviceable, hardly shouted out, Historic Site Ahead. Same with the official auto inspection station on the left, where she might have taken her car twice a year.

If she owned a car. Which she didn't.

When Jonas halted at the intersection of Elm and North Lane, Emilie discovered to her horror that the much-touted grassy knoll of her resource books—the hallowed ground of the original log common house of 1748—was now a humble rest home for deceased and dying vehicles.

"What are those?" Emilie stared, mouth agape.

"A Camaro Z-28—color, black—and an International Harvester Scout—color, rust—with the remains of a snowblade on the front." Jonas looked around. "The pine trees are nice, though. So's the new stone parking lot. And look, a place that sharpens tools. Handy, huh?"

Emilie groaned and her chin sank to her chest. "I'll be certain to drop off every tool I own."

He inclined his head. "Not what you expected to find here?"

She shrugged. "One never knows what surprises might turn up."

Like you, Jonas.

Side by side, they started down a gravel incline, going nowhere in particular, while the rain continued to pound the frozen ground, even as Emilie's heart pounded with strange and unfamiliar emotions.

Dare she tell him what she was really hoping to find—evidence of the very first Gemeinhaus? Could she trust him? She knew the answer to that. Despite his casual approach to life, his integrity was unmistakable.

Would he share her enthusiasm? To find the actual spot—to prove herself right this time—was her all-consuming passion. Would Jonas salute her efforts or find them foolish?

Telling him was risky.

Not telling him was cowardly.

Her decision made, she took a deep breath. "Jonas, what do you know about archaeology?"

He chuckled, kicking at a loose chunk of sod. "I know it involves playing with dirt. Why? Wanna go digging?"

"I might. Look, I'm not only here to write a book for the church." She stopped, locking gazes with him, wanting him to see how serious she was. "I'm here to change Moravian history."

His expression mirrored more than a little curiosity. "This I gotta hear."

Ambling along, oblivious to the inhospitable weather, she told him everything. About Bethabara, about her meticulous research, about her wild theories and conjectures. He listened—really listened—then nodded in all the right places and asked a few hard-hitting questions.

His final request took her aback: "Do I get to help you with this?"

"I'll...let you know." She sighed and offered the most honest answer she could give him. "I'm pleased to know you're interested."

"'Course I'm interested, Emilie. A single-minded woman like you, you're bound to track down the thing and make a name for yourself doing it. I wanna be there to cheer you on."

She stared at the ground, overwhelmed by his support. Even a bit uneasy with it. Had any man—other than her father—ever rooted for her to succeed? As they walked along, she gazed at him out of the corner of her eye, trying to figure out how a man like Jonas Fielding could possibly care about her career.

Let alone care about her happiness.

Without hat or umbrella, he had rain dripping off his stubbly chin. He slicked back his short bangs, revealing a widow's peak—could a man have such a thing?—and a broad forehead, virtually the only part of his face without a constant five o'clock shadow.

"What is it?" He watched her, watching him, and smiled again. "You hate my short hair, don't you?"

"Not at all. You must have a constant battle on your hands, though, holding your hairy nature at bay."

"Yup. One of the hazards of being a Fielding man." His bushy brows wiggled playfully. "Most women like it."

"So I've heard." She feigned interest in an overflowing trash can, lest he catch her smiling. "Is your youngest brother—"

"Nathan."

She looked up in time to watch his animated face grow still. "Yes, Nathan. Is he hirsute as well?"

"Hirsute?" Jonas winked, clearly recovering his form. "Nah, he wouldn't be caught dead in a suit. Strictly golf shirts."

"Don't be clever," she scolded. "I'm talking about—"

"Nate. Yeah, he's hairy. A good-looking son of a gun. The real ladies' man of the four of us."

"That so?" *As if you're not, you dark-eyed charmer!* She still couldn't believe she'd kissed him—intentionally this time—standing there in her rented living room on a rainy Monday afternoon with her arm in a sling *and* without brushing her teeth. *Heavens!*

The whole thing left her torn in two—hoping it wouldn't happen again, wondering how many hours she'd have to endure before it did.

If it did.

Men! A conundrum if there ever was one. In the past, she hadn't found the male of the species particularly...necessary. Not in the emotional sense. Helpful, useful, knowledgeable, even enjoyable in small doses, but *necessary?* Not for her. She had her books, her research, her students, her garden—

"Emilie? Emilie!"

She snapped to attention. "W-what? Did you say something?"

"Yes. Your name." Even soaking wet, his grin was dangerously appealing.

"About four times. Whatcha thinkin' about, Dr. Getz?"

"If you must know, men."

"Oh, *men* is it? Plural, then. Not one man in particular?"

She swiped her scarf at him. "Fishing for compliments is most unbecoming."

He ducked under her umbrella, putting them nose to nose. "But it's perfect fishing weather."

If Jonas wanted to play Go Fish, she'd provide the bait. "What is it you hoped to hear me say?"

"That I'm the first man who—"

"Well!" *The nerve!* She gasped and backed up, taking her umbrella with her. "Jonas Fielding, you are *not* the first man to kiss me!"

He raised a hand in protest. "I'm not suggesting such a thing. You're thirty-six—my age—and hardly an ingenue, Emilie. Of course you've been kissed. Probably better, too."

Probably not. She sniffed and tried to look nonchalant. "You're the first man who did *what*, then?"

"Made you laugh."

She wasn't laughing now.

She was mad. *Or hurt.* With some women, it was hard to tell the difference.

Her sorry excuse for an umbrella was tipped back, rain was dripping off that nice, soft nose of hers, and—unless his eyes were deceiving him—steam was coming out her little porcelain ears.

"How d-dare you s-suggest...!" She was sputtering. He liked sputtering women, liked seeing a gal come unglued once in a while.

Emilie tried again to make her point. "Why, I've...I've laughed many times in my life. The very idea!"

Yup. Mad. "How many times?"

She didn't have a wooden ruler, but she shook the umbrella at him with exactly the same vehemence. "Plenty! Dozens. Hundreds."

"Hundreds of laughs? With a man you cared about?"

"Yes! Well, maybe not...well." She let out an exasperated groan. "The point is, you did not introduce me to my sense of humor."

He dipped his forehead toward hers. "When we met on Christmas Eve, I got the idea you and your sense of humor were, shall we say, estranged." He pretended not to see her eyes become slits, her nostrils flare. "That's why I'm on a mission to make sure the two of you are on speaking—er, laughing—terms again."

Her narrowed eyes popped back open. "A *mission?*"

Uh-oh. Shouldn't have been so up-front about that one.

"That's right." Jonas nodded, rushing to explain himself. "It's a heavenly calling." He lifted one metal tip of her umbrella and invited himself underneath it. "Emilie, I have the challen—uh, the *privilege* of showing you what *fullness of joy* means."

Her anger dissolved into shock. "Are you saying I'm a *project* of some sort to you?"

"Nope. I'm saying the Lord has brought you into my life for a reason I don't fully comprehend."

"Ohh." Her expression softened.

"Part of that reason is helping you lighten up."

When she started to disagree, he barely touched her lips with one finger, amazed at how quickly it silenced her. "Don't argue with me. You and I both know your shrieking-banshee sled ride down Kissel Hill was the most fun you've had in ages."

She shrugged and averted her eyes, fighting a smile. After two beats of silence, she said in an even voice, "You win. Was I supposed to laugh at the Christmas Bird Count, too?"

"In theory." He lifted her chin, eager to see her hidden smile, longing to find forgiveness in her eyes. "Except I blew it. I'm truly sorry, Emilie."

Her smile was in place. So was a glimmer of understanding.

"I know." She eyed him, her breath coming out in frosty puffs. "Joy is more than laughter, though. I find joy in lots of things. My work, for starters."

"Work is good." He nodded, wanting to affirm yet press forward. "But *fullness* of joy is only found in Christ."

A shadow fell across her features. "Do you really believe that?"

"I do." Sensing her pulling away from him, he quickly added, "Hey, don't get me wrong, I love my work. But when it all shakes down, only my relationship with the Lord matters."

"I see." She paled visibly. "Then religion is very important to you."

"Nope. Not religion. Relationship."

She frowned. "You're talking about semantics."

"I'm talking about my best friend."

"Ah." She turned on her heel and aimed her steps toward the Explorer parked on Main. "Jonas, it's too nasty outside to debate such subjects in the freezing rain."

"Agreed." He caught up with her and slipped his arm around her shoulder before she could protest. If words couldn't convince her, a piece of his history might. "I'd like to show you one thing on the way home, though. Okay with you?"

Emilie nodded, not saying another word until they were back in the Explorer, greeted by a dry, wagging golden retriever in the front seat.

"All the way back, Trix," he said firmly, starting the engine. He flicked on the heater and headed east on Main, then north on Oak, where their destination—a concrete bridge—waited straight ahead.

He cleared his throat, surprised at the tightness there, and pointed through the windshield. "That's your Lititz Run, Emilie. Definitely running." Steering his vehicle to a spot a safe distance from the creek's edge, he parked and left the headlights trained on the raging stream overflowing its high banks.

As he stared at the water spilling over the roadway, long-buried memories washed over him with the same chilling effect. *Give me strength here, Lord. You know where I hope to go with this.*

"This is what you wanted to show me?" She peered out the window, clearly confused.

Gripping the wheel, he willed himself to say what needed to be said, for her sake and his own. "It was a day like this..." He swallowed hard and tossed his head back to stem the threat of tears that rarely came but did so now without warning. "A day like this when I lost my father."

Emilie's head pivoted toward him. "Lost him?"

He nodded slowly. "I was twelve. Carl Kreider and I were walking home from school in a wintry rainstorm—icy cold, like this stuff—and came to a swollen creek. As usual, we were behaving like fools, stomping in the puddles, dangling over the rail, when Carl lost his balance and fell in the water."

"Oh, Jonas, how awful!" Her face was ashen. "What did you do?"

"The current carried him downstream faster than I could find a way to get to him. That's when my dad—a teacher, did I tell you that?"

She nodded. The sympathy in her eyes was almost more than he could bear.

"Anyway, Dad was driving home from school, looking for us, knowing we should have waited and caught a ride with him. He pulled over, saw the whole scene, and, before I could stop him, jumped into the creek to save Carl."

"And...he *drowned?*" Emilie gasped, pressing back against the seat in horror. "Oh, good Lord!"

"The Lord is more than good." Jonas closed his eyes, fighting the old doubts that still surfaced on occasion. Like today, of all days. He pressed on, determined to convince not only Emilie, but himself. "The Lord used my dad to save Carl's life."

For a moment, she seemed to hold her breath. "But what about your father? Couldn't God have spared his life, too?"

Jonas' head dropped toward the steering wheel, his forehead landing on one clenched fist. How could she know that was the question that had haunted him for two dozen years?

Nathan held his head in his hands and wept.

It was gone. *Gone.* All five thousand dollars of his brother's money, gone in one disastrous afternoon.

At the hotel front desk Monday morning, he'd sliced open the envelope with trembling hands, almost kissing the check. *Thank you, brother!* He'd waited impatiently at the bank window until it opened at 9:30, all set to buy another cashier's check to send to Cy.

Then it hit him. *He'd double it!* He'd hit another trifecta and turn that five grand into ten. Maybe even have some spare dollars to tide him over for another week's room and board.

But double or nothing turned into nothing. The greyhounds he'd picked might as well have been running the opposite direction on the track. Modest bets turned to bigger ones, until in desperation he put everything in his wallet on the last race.

And lost it all.

It had cost him a whole night's sleep.

It would cost him a whole lot more.

He couldn't call Cy and tell him there wouldn't be a check this week. He couldn't call Jonas and tell him he needed more money. He couldn't call the twins, nor could he call his mom anymore.

And he sure couldn't call his dad.

Nathan exhaled, frustration and anxiety turning his stomach inside out. *Coffee.* He needed caffeine, something to jolt him into action, get his brain working. Wiping away the last of his tears, disgusted with his pity party, he fired up the small coffeemaker, splashing water everywhere as he aimed for the slotted opening on top with a shaky hand.

Not coffee. He needed something stronger.

His mother's voice echoed in his addled brain: *"Your father never touched liquor, Nathan Fielding. You'd be honoring his memory if you did likewise."*

Sorry, Dad.

Nate almost never thought about his father. Not the last few years, baking in the Nevada desert. Not now, basking in the Florida sunshine.

Ten minutes later, *Good Morning America* changed all that.

He was channel surfing—a Styrofoam cup of lukewarm coffee in one hand, the hotel's remote in the other—when a news story flashed on screen about Monday's flooding in the Northeast.

Pennsylvania. Maryland. *Delaware.*

In an instant, he was five years old again. A rainy day in February. An overflowing creek near home. His mother's agonized, tearstained face. The terrible news: "Nathan, your father drowned today."

Jim Fielding, the big man with the dark hair and the stern look and the soft voice, gone forever.

It was Jonas' fault.

At least, that's what Jonas kept saying, until Mother grabbed him by both shoulders and gave him a good shake. "It is *not* your fault, son," she'd sobbed, pulling Jonas tightly against her. "Your father died like he lived, giving his life for others. He's a hero, Jonas. God's man to the end. You couldn't have stopped him from jumping in that creek if you tried."

The way Carl told it, Jonas *had* tried, nearly drowning himself in the process. He'd helped pull Carl to safety, then turned around just as his exhausted father was swept into the swift current, dragged under the icy waters and downstream until he disappeared from sight, leaving his twelve-year-old son stunned and shaking on the frozen banks.

Nate fell back against the scratchy upholstery, battling a wicked hangover, wiped out by the vivid memories. Of Jonas stumbling through the kitchen door, dripping wet, blue from the cold and red from running. Jonas, gasping for air, begging his mother to call the police. Crying that Dad…that Dad…

Nate shouted an expletive and threw the remote across the room. "If he was your man, God, where were you? *Where were you?*"

Twelve

◆

Who said you should be happy? Do your work.
COLETTE

"Where do you turn when you hurt, Emilie?"

That's what Jonas had asked her Monday, parked beside the overflowing banks of Lititz Run.

And there she'd sat, dumbfounded. Had she ever felt that kind of pain, that deep a loss? "I immerse myself in my work until the disappointment goes away," she finally said, realizing how shallow and flippant it sounded.

Even if it was honest.

Emotional situations drained rather than filled her, while her work—teaching, writing, doing historical research—replenished her soul to the brim.

When she confessed that to Jonas, he'd looked at her with an expression that could only be read as pity.

Pity! She would not stand for it.

He was a nice man—very nice, when it came down to it—and their one on-purpose kiss had been warm and lovely—quite lovely, in fact—but Jonas Fielding was simply too inquisitive, too religious, too...*something*, to suit her taste.

Contemplating God was all well and good, naturally. He created the earth and all that was in it, and deserved her attention every Sabbath. But Jonas' description of a personal relationship of some kind with their Creator was another kettle of fish altogether.

And Emilie didn't care for seafood.

She'd come to Lititz for two reasons only: to write a book and to rewrite history. Plunging into both efforts with renewed zeal, the rest of the week had flipped past her like pages in a textbook, filled with the minutiae of dates, names, and places—her stock-in-trade as an historian.

Not feelings—facts.

Not fuzzy emotions—solid evidence.

The reliable, unchangeable nature of such information gave her a sense of security and well-being that no relationship—human or divine—had ever come close to matching.

Each time Jonas called, she made sure their brief discussions steered clear of sentimental subjects. There would be no more kisses, stolen or otherwise. No further questions about her religious beliefs. No more soul-baring conversations. As gently as she could, Emilie made her wishes known: *Keep your distance.*

When he didn't call Friday or Saturday, when his greeting to her at church didn't include one of his boyish winks or an invitation to join him for Sunday dinner, Emilie relaxed and knew her life was safely back on track.

The church bells chimed behind her now as she made a beeline for home, intending to squeeze in another good hour of research and a quick lunch before walking back down Main Street for the monthly meeting of the Lititz Historical Foundation. As a new member, she was eager to meet her fellow history buffs and talk shop, as it were.

Minutes before two o'clock, she climbed the icy, salt-strewn steps of the Schropp House, circa 1793—now the Foundation's permanent home—admiring the stone walls and wide, white shutters along the wooden side porch leading to the entrance.

She was welcomed by a gust of heated air and a friendly greeter who waved her past the downstairs museum and gift shop—clearly she'd be making a return visit soon—and up the stairs to the second-floor lecture room. Finding a seat with some empty chairs around it, merely for breathing space, Emilie slipped off her coat and glove—with her arm in a sling, she needed only the left one—tucked it in her coat pocket, and took out a slim notebook in preparation for the lecture.

Along with the usual green chalkboard and lectern, some forty attendees filled the small room. They were of all ages, she noted, though more had gray hair than not. After a few preliminary formalities, the guest of honor was announced: Admiral William Reynolds, a native of Lancaster. Of course, the speaker wasn't really the Civil War commander. He was a local historian of merit, portraying the historical figure. Emilie delighted in the man's twenty-minute presentation filled with detailed accounts of his naval exploits and friendship with the Keystone State's most famous bachelor, President James Buchanan.

A lively question-and-answer period followed, during which she kept quiet and busied herself making notes, not wanting to intimidate the others with her more scholarly questions.

Joining them in a spirited round of applause at the close of the program, she rose, intending to corner the" admiral" for a personal chat, when a vaguely familiar face turned to greet her.

"Emilie Getz, I can't believe it!"

She couldn't believe it either. *"Brian?"*

Brian Zeller, the other half of her shared chocolate malt at Bingy's Restaurant twenty years ago, stood before her now, hand outstretched. His milkshake mustache had been replaced with a real one, but otherwise the man hadn't changed one iota. Still tall and thin, sporting glasses and a mile-wide grin. "I'd heard you were in town, Em. Welcome home!" His gaze took in her canvas sling. "Hope that's temporary."

"Uh…yes." She shook his hand with her free one, a bit dazed at the alive-and-breathing yearbook picture that towered over her. "How are you, Brian?"

"Terrific. Teaching history at Warwick, of course."

"Of course." A history teacher. *Imagine that.*

She took in his conservative suit, nicely tailored to his still-broad shoulders, and the wire-rimmed glasses that framed an intelligent pair of gray eyes. "Brian Zeller," she murmured. "What a nice surprise to find you still in Lititz."

"Did my B.A. and master at Penn State, but I came back after graduation." He shrugged, still smiling. "What can I say? It's home."

"It is that." She lowered her gaze, trying to see if a wife hovered nearby, then chastised herself for even caring. Though with none in sight, she couldn't stop herself from asking the question. "So, did you marry your high school sweetheart, Brian?"

The reddish freckles that had darkened over the years darkened further. "Emilie, I thought you knew. *You* were my high school sweetheart."

Her heart did an odd flip. "I was?"

"None other." His self-conscious laugh served as a welcome release for them both. "I never got up the nerve to ask you to the senior prom, Em. But I sure wanted to."

"You *did?*" The news astounded her. To think, on that horrid night she'd sobbed herself to sleep she could have been dancing at the Treadway Inn with Brian Zeller. Her brain turned into applesauce. "Really?" She sighed with girlish delight.

"Really." He grinned, and shoved his hands in his pants pockets. "When I moved back to Lititz, I hoped you might do the same."

"Oh?" *Was he suggesting…?*

"But since you were too busy chasing after your doctorate, I had no choice but to marry my Penn State sweetheart instead."

"Ohh." *Don't you dare look disappointed, Emilie Getz!* "And her name is…?"

"Kathleen." He waved across the room at a stunning redhead, who glided toward them with an Audrey Hepburn sort of grace. "Here she is. My wife, Kathleen." He chuckled. "Zeller, of course."

Of course. Emilie planted a smile on her face that quickly withered. "Nice to meet you."

Their introductions made, the two women regarded one another long enough to rule out any threat, perceived or real, then exchanged polite small talk for a few moments.

Emilie hated small talk. Especially with a stunning redhead who barely looked thirty. She was about to make a timely exit, when Brian asked a question that stopped her in her tracks.

"Emilie, have you visited the Heritage Map Museum yet?"

"Maps, did you say?"

"Hundreds of them." He folded his arms over his chest, capturing Kathleen's delicate hand in the process. "Famous ones. Not prints, but originals. Ortelius and Blaeu—"

"Not the 1647?" Emilie gasped. "Of the Americas?"

"That's the one."

Her heart did a merry jig. A map museum in Lititz, of all places! *Could they possibly have what she was looking for?* It was a long shot, at best. Surely the Moravian Archives in Bethlehem had unearthed all the pertinent maps and land draughts decades ago. Still...

She caught herself gnawing on her lower lip, small talk forgotten as she fretted over her carless condition. "I suppose this museum is halfway to Lancaster."

"No, it's halfway down Water Street." He inclined his head. "Remember that old brick monstrosity Clair Brothers bought?"

She lifted her eyebrows. "The what? That who bought?"

He laughed, squeezing Kathleen's hand affectionately. "Never mind, Em, you've been gone too long. It's easy enough to find. Not much more than a block from where we're standing. Open every day but Sunday. I've taken several of my senior classes over there for a tour. Students love the place."

Brian turned to his wife, even as Emilie's thoughts turned the corner and trotted down Water Street. In less than twenty-four hours, she'd be surrounded by history. If the fates were kind, she might find a particular map, one from Lancaster county, created in, say, the mid-1700s. With a particular Gemeinhaus drawn in an unexpected...

Brian's words sounded far away. "...an unexpected pleasure, Emilie."

"Oh! Yes. Indeed it was." She gathered her wits long enough to say her proper good-byes, then hurried down the steps and out the door, turning left instead of right toward home. Even though the museum was closed, she wanted to see the building, know it existed, dream about what secrets it might reveal.

Her steps matched the brisk, rat-a-tat beat of her heart, as the building came into view. No wonder she'd missed it before, sitting back so far from the street like that. She would not overlook it again.

Gazing at the handsome brick exterior and tall gold lettering over the doorway, Emilie smiled and turned on her heel, headed home to her stacks of books and a hot cup of tea. In truth, the sheer anticipation of tomorrow's return visit invigorated her senses more thoroughly than any tea on her shelf or any history text on her desk.

Or any dark-eyed man with a penchant for black.

When the phone on his desk rang twice, then a third time, Jonas tossed aside his pen and grabbed the receiver, prepared for the worst: another disgruntled council member, a new drainage problem, a construction crew running behind schedule, or any other Monday morning headache.

"Fielding here."

A faint chuckle. "Fielding here too. It's your brother, Nate. Still in Florida."

Jonas dragged his hand across his chin, a dozen thoughts running through his mind. At least it wasn't another job site problem with Carter's Run. *Good news there.* But what was Nate's story? No way the guy needed more money. *Nah.* Nobody went through five thousand dollars in a week unless they used it for kindling. *Must be something else.*

He stretched back in his chair, propping one foot on the edge of his desk. "What's on your mind, Nate?"

"Nothing major. Just wanted to…chat, I guess."

"Okay." *Chat? That's a first.* An uneasy silence hummed between them. "You got my check, I hope?"

"Oh yeah! Great. Right on time. Thanks." Nate's rush of words sounded forced. And slurred. The tension between them stretched tighter still. "Look, Jonas, I…I need…"

"Don't tell me. Money." Jonas almost broke the receiver in two, he was gripping it so hard. "I can't possibly—"

"No! Not money. Honest, not money." Nate's voice was strained to the point of breaking. "I need…I need…help."

Jonas unconsciously lowered his foot to the floor and straightened in his chair, aware only of his heart pounding a slow, deliberate rhythm in his chest. "What is it?" He'd almost added "son," his parental instincts kicking into overdrive. "I know you've been struggling lately, Nate. C'mon, let me help you. That's what big brothers are for, right? First you gotta tell me what the problem is."

"I'm…I'm…"

Jonas could hear him gulping for air, struggling to get the words out. *Help him, Lord! Give him the courage to say it.*

"I'm…well…"

"You're what?" Maybe a little levity would help. "Too good-looking?" Jonas made sure the smile in his voice came through. "Too many women chasing you? Too many Florida fathers putting out warrants for your arrest?"

"Nah, nothing like that."

Sensing his brother's embarrassment, Jonas egged him on. "You can't fool me, Nate. You wanna join Hunks Anonymous, is that it?"

No answer.

"Talk to me, Nate, I'm havin' a one-way conversation here."

The voice on the line was barely audible. "Let's just say you're halfway right."

Jonas felt the blood drain out of his face. "Which half?" Surely his thirty-year-old brother hadn't been arrested for corrupting a minor! "Any answer beats no answer, Nate. What kinda trouble are you up against?"

"I'm a…an alcoholic."

It wasn't the answer she wanted.

"Sorry, Dr. Getz, but if such a map exists, it hasn't crossed my desk." The museum curator was a striking man in his late forties with a bushy head of hair and full beard, both platinum-colored. He closed his leather-bound ledger with its carefully printed inventory list and offered her a smile of genuine apology. "I'm sorry we don't have what you need. What resources are you working with now?"

Swallowing her disappointment, Emilie opened her notebook and turned to her bibliography, grateful to have found a kindred spirit, if nothing else. She spread the page in front of him and watched his eyes skim down the list as he nodded in approval.

"Hmmm. You've certainly done a thorough job." He reached behind him and pulled a thick volume from the bookshelf behind his desk. "See if you can't find some reference to the Gemeinhaus that might be helpful in here. Meanwhile, I'll keep my eyes open. Make a few calls." He shrugged, standing to extend his hand. "You never know when something might turn up."

She lifted the heavy book with a nod. "Thanks ever so much for the loan. I'll take good care of it, I promise."

He laughed, guiding her toward the door with a hand barely touching the center of her back. "Of that I have no doubt, Dr. Getz. Hope your luck improves as the week unfolds."

She retraced her steps across the restored hardwood floor, the narrow boards laid diagonally and polished to a gleaming patina. Around her, creamy white walls provided a neutral backdrop for the tasteful display of framed maps, each one individually lit with a recessed spotlight. Enormous, sixteen-paned windows hinted at the brick building's former industrial days, now long forgotten.

The museum was a find, no doubt. She had not, however, found the survey map of her dreams.

Skirting around an antique globe mounted on an oak stand, Emilie nodded to the front desk clerk and stepped out into the chilly midmorning air with a lengthy sigh. Short of digging up everything in a three-quarter-mile radius of Elm and Main, she didn't know how she could hope to find a cornerstone or any other evidence buried two and a half centuries earlier.

Talk about a wild Gemeinhaus chase.

Putting one foot in front of the other, the valuable book tucked under her good arm, Emilie made her way up Water Street toward Main, more discouraged than she'd ever been about a project. Research was all about hitting walls and burrowing under them, but this time her shovel was striking bedrock.

At the top of the hill, the milky gray sky surrounded the steeple of the Moravian Church with a soft matte. Emilie paused to catch her breath—she *did* need this exercise after all—and drank in the tranquil beauty of the sanctuary she'd fallen in love with all over again.

Pale mocha walls and white trim.

Tall, round-topped stained-glass windows.

Huge, stark maples stationed around Church Square, waiting to explode with color come October.

White lampposts, like wooden sentinels, standing guard year-round.

The *Leichen-Kapelle*—corpse chapel—more charming than its name implied, an ivy-covered stone building avoided with fear and loathing by all Moravian children since 1787.

Would the congregation care about her efforts, one way or the other? In its first fifty years, the pioneer community had built and torn down many a Gemeinhaus. Did one more really matter?

Emilie turned toward home, blinking hard. She *could* call it quits. None of her peers knew about her research. Or needed to know, for that matter. If she quietly packed away her notebooks and put aside her dreams, who would notice?

Jonas.

Jonas knew. Would hold her accountable, too. Probably tease her for being a quitter.

Humph. Her stride lengthened and her steps became more resolute. She was willing to do many things, but admit to that…that *man* she was stumped? Beaten? Throwing in the towel? *Not on your life, Jonas Fielding!*

That small bit of property, wherever it was hiding, had her name on it. "*My* name, mind you!" She shook her research book at an unsuspecting cardinal perched on the street lamp at Main and Cedar.

Emilie, who seldom if ever succumbed to her emotions, smiled through a stubborn sheen of tears and stomped across the street, bound on her own holy mission.

Jonas might be heaven-bent to make her laugh. She, however, was equally determined never to be laughed at again.

Nathan still couldn't believe he'd said it, out loud.

Admitted he had a drinking problem. To Jonas, of all people.

His pronouncement had gotten the man's attention. Aroused his sympathy. Unfolded his wallet when Nate mentioned a certain rehabilitation center with a national reputation.

"It's a Christian one," Nate had assured him, knowing that would strike the right note. "They've got trained counselors, group accountability sessions, Bible studies, the whole bit. Thirty days, that's what they say it'll take to sober me up. Get me on the straight and narrow."

A knot of guilt, hard as a peach pit, stuck in Nathan's throat through most of the conversation. Jonas knew he was a drinker, so no resistance there. His older brother didn't know how much he drank or how often, but to a Boy Scout like Jonas, one drink was too many.

It'd taken four shots of Jack Daniels just to screw up the courage to make the call.

And to make him sound convincingly drunk.

His sales pitch was embarrassingly easy: Could Jonas loan him another five thousand? Give him thirty days in rehab before he found a good job, started paying it back?

Jonas hadn't fought him. Nate almost wished he had—made him work for it, let him keep a shred of pride. Not big brother Jonas. He'd gotten choked up. Told Nate he was proud of him for realizing he needed help.

Jonas' only question was how to make out the check.

"They want the patient to provide the money. Nobody else can admit me. I gotta do it myself, willingly." Nate didn't know where he came up with this stuff, but it sure sounded legit. "So if you would, make out the check to me. Yeah, the same hotel address will work. And…thanks, Jonas."

He'd hung up Monday morning with another reprieve on the way. The check had arrived Wednesday. Today was Thursday. Another day at the track for some people, but not for Nathan Fielding. He wasn't planning on messing up this time, no sir.

He'd already spent two grand on a couple of sharp outfits, a haircut and manicure, a one-month lease on a Jaguar. Had to look good before he hit the greens of San Pablo. He'd forgo the booze for a month and concentrate on his game. Make some new friends. Tap some old ones for favors. Mail Cy enough cash to keep him from sending a muscle-flexer to track him down.

Nate's goals had never been more clear.

Thirty days to freedom.

He'd be back in the game with the monkey off his back in a month. If Lady Luck saw things his way, he'd be strolling into his brother's house in Pennsylvania along about March first, toting a suitcase full of designer clothes and ten thousand in loose bills.

Nate buttoned his Callaway shirt up to the neck and smoothed the collar, checking out his look in the mirror. *Yeah.* He still had it. The Fielding charm. Plus the street smarts his brothers never needed.

It would take all that and then some to pull it off.

But pull it off he would. Or die trying.

One more phone call like this—after a long week of phone calls like this—and Jonas intended to ditch the whole project.

Monday, the architect for Carter's Run—an up-and-coming type from New Jersey—decided he was in fact the next Robert Trent Jones and wanted bunkers added to seven holes. *Seven.*

Tuesday, the agronomist from Penn State advised planting another fifty pine trees or risk losing most of his expensive soil—at four bucks a yard—to erosion.

Wednesday, the local jogging club wanted to know why they couldn't plan to use the cart paths for their daily morning run. They could, Jonas assured them, as long as they were willing to wear football helmets and shoulder pads to ward off wayward golf balls.

But it was the latest call that put him teetering near the edge.

With the additional piece of land Dee Dee had acquired on behalf of the borough, Jonas finally had the dream location for his clubhouse plus an expanded driving range.

Except someone had forgotten to notify the superintendent in charge of construction about the change in design, so the crew had carved out space for a *ten*-stall driving range instead of twenty.

Aiming *south*.

Everybody knew practice tees aimed north.

"North! North!" Jonas shouted in the phone until he was hoarse.

They could be fixed. And they *would* be fixed, he was assured. But wasn't Mr. Fielding pleased with his eighteenth hole?

Yes, Jonas had to agree, he was jolly well thrilled. It faced neither east nor west, but pleasantly north, affording a breathtaking view of Lititz and for that matter, of the whole course. And it was a par five, as tradition required.

If they opened on schedule—and they would, absolutely, open for business on April 9—it would be almost two years to the day from the ground-breaking ceremony.

And they said it couldn't be done. Jonas smiled to himself, despite a long, tiring week of hassles and speed bumps. He glanced at his watch. *Nearly three.* Still enough light to head out to the course, see how quickly they were getting things turned around at the driving range. Plenty of time to walk the perimeters of his eighteenth hole and imagine the rest of the course every bit as finished, every inch as perfect.

Emilie almost fainted when she answered the phone and heard the news. The map museum curator waited patiently while she scribbled down the information.

"You're certain this survey map is authentic? Good, good. Dated 1747. Perfect. No, I realize it's already been sold—for how much? Oh, good heavens! And the buyer is stopping by for it later this afternoon? How can I ever thank you for calling me first? I'll be there in minutes."

And she would, too. Her mother, feeling guilty about her only daughter trying to manage without a car, had parked her Toyota out front and deposited the keys on the kitchen table that morning. Emilie hadn't had the heart to tell her that she wouldn't need the car.

But that was hours ago.

Now that the fates had tossed good fortune her way, Emilie needed wheels and then some. *Wings would be more like it!*

She gathered her things in record time, nearly skipping out the front door, then eased her arm out of the sling, trying not to groan as a searing jolt traveled across her not-yet-healed collarbone.

Enough whining, Emilie. You can drive two blocks with this. Grateful the car had an automatic transmission, she steered with a wobbly left hand and arrived minutes later, as promised. She pulled open the heavy glass door with a painful yank and stepped into the semidarkness of the museum.

The curator was standing outside his office, waving her down the hall. "In here, Dr. Getz." She hurried past the collection of maps without a second glance, her eyes focused on the door that would lead to her decidedly brighter academic future. Nodding in greeting, not trusting herself to speak, Emilie approached the sacred map, carefully stretched out under a sheet of Plexiglas.

He offered her a magnifying lens, then stepped back to let her have a look. *Easy, Em!* She forced herself to breathe, to steady her hands, to think like a historical scholar, not a hysterical woman. Bending over the unframed map, she zeroed in on the current Gemeinhaus site at Elm and Main, noting no such building sketched there, then mentally traced due south for three-quarters of a mile, then southeast for one-eighth mile, exactly as one of her primary sources had described it.

There! The black ink square was faint, almost as if it had been blotted out later, but it was unquestionably in the right place. The notation in a sweeping script removed all doubt: Gemeinhaus! She placed her own amateurish map, painstakingly drawn on tracing paper, on top of the antiquarian one. The dimensions were different, but the direction was identical: south, then southeast!

She could drive there. *Drive there!* Right now, this minute, see it for herself, take her measurements, begin to plan the excavation.

And hope it was a grassy backyard or a fallow cornfield—belonging to a fan of historic preservation.

"Thank you! So much. Really." She resisted the urge to hug the smiling curator, then rolled up her makeshift map and practically bowed her way out of the office and back down the hall.

It was all she could do not to shriek with joy. *Joy!*

Ten minutes later, she was elated to find herself crawling up Kissel Hill Road in a borrowed Toyota, following her map inch by inch, marveling at what stretched out alongside her, due east: dirt. Nothing but dirt! Shaped and shoved in odd directions, true, but dirt nonetheless.

Emilie exhaled a sigh of relief when she passed the library under construction. *My!* It would have been criminal to put all that to a stop. Thank goodness her notes indicated a point farther southeast.

She slowed the car, scrambling for her notes. *Top of the ridge.* Yes, there it was. *Steep slope.* Yes, that too. *Facing the road.* Pierson Road, no doubt. *There!* Poking a triumphant finger at her hand-drawn map, she hit the brake and lifted her head, prepared to find her long-awaited Gemeinhaus site, a small piece of land quietly waiting all these centuries for her to look up and see it.

What she saw instead was Jonas Fielding.

The man was wearing a self-satisfied smile and looking off in the distance, paying no attention to her arrival.

Scooping up her tools of the trade, she opened the door with her knee, shoved it closed with her foot, and picked her way across the dirt, realizing for the first time what strange levels and slopes had been carved into the soil.

"Jonas." She raised her voice when he didn't respond. "Jo-nas!"

He glanced over then, regarding her with mild amusement. "Well, well. Dr. Emilie Getz, here to show me her latest research, I suppose."

"You're *standing* on it, Jonas!" She reached his side, breathless with exertion and excitement.

"Correct." He nodded proudly and threw out both arms. "Isn't she a beauty?"

Emilie's jaw dropped. "Then you *knew* all along? That…that this was the spot?"

He nodded again. "Of course. Since the earliest design sketches."

Her voice shot up an octave. "You *knew* and you didn't tell me?"

The gap between his brows narrowed. "Why would I tell you, of all people, Emilie?"

She didn't even try to mask her hurt. "I know I've been rather…chilly of late, but I did think we were still friends."

"Friends, yes. But since when did you care about my eighteenth hole?"

His what? Who had eighteen of anything?

At most, she counted four separate Gemeinhaus locations in Lititz. Nothing close to eighteen.

"You're not making any sense." She exhaled, marshalling every ounce of patience she had left. "Today I saw a map that tied all the loose ends of my research together in one very tidy knot. And this—" she swept her left arm in a circle—"this is the exact piece of property where that first common house was built. Isn't that glorious news? The minute I have the owner's permission, I intend to assemble a crew and begin excavation."

She hadn't noticed his eyes turning into slits. Dark slits at that, except for two fiery spots in the centers.

Why, the man looked like the very devil himself!

"Jonas? Is…ah…something…wrong?"

Thirteen

*A woman is like a tea bag—you can't tell how strong she is
until you put her in hot water.*
NANCY REAGAN

"Beth, you don't understand!" Emilie paced the floor, waving her arms in
abject frustration. "The man was livid. *Livid!* Foaming at the mouth like a
rabid dog."

"Boy, sorry I missed *that.*" Beth's airy giggle didn't help things.

Emilie watched, still huffing, as the younger woman bent over Sara's
purple-and-green masterpiece, murmuring motherly encouragement before
looking up to meet Emilie's flint-sharp stare.

"Look, Em." Beth's voice, unlike her own, was gentle, soothing. "It's been
five days. Maybe he's calmed down enough to discuss—"

"There's nothing to discuss!" Emilie snapped. Emilie never snapped. She
was a cool-thinking, level-headed, facts-not-feelings woman. *He* was a
snarling, ill-trained German shepherd, guarding his precious putting green
as if it mattered, as if seventeen holes of golf weren't enough for any man.
Honestly!

The preservationists were on her side. She'd spent most of Friday evening on the phone with a trusted peer from Moravian College in Bethlehem, describing the scenario, ascertaining what procedures were required to stop construction on the golf course and put together an experienced archaeological crew.

All weekend, she'd sketched and planned, borrowing her mother's car again to drive out to the site and take measurements, make guesstimates. She took the long way around, heading east on Main to Pierson Road, steering clear of a particular house with a black Explorer parked in the driveway.

Things had gone swimmingly until Monday, when she'd spent the better part of the afternoon arguing with a certain short-haired land developer who insisted the steering committee—and soon enough, the whole town—would be on *his* side, eager to see their golf course open on April 9. Fully operational. On schedule. Without—in his words—"any unnecessary dillydallying from a bunch of eggheads."

This morning—Groundhog Day—when Punxsutawney Phil peeped his head out long enough to see his shadow and offer his prognosis of six more weeks of winter, Emilie pictured Jonas at Carter's Run, sticking his head out of the eighteenth hole and making his own dire prediction: six more weeks of stubborn resistance.

Talk about a ground *hog!* The name fit the man to a T.

The Landis living room could barely contain Emilie's mounting fury. Her jaw in a gridlock, she nearly shouted the words. "I just wish Jonas Fielding would…would…"

From the corner of her eye, she watched as Beth's features lost their sparkle and Sara grew quiet for the first time that day.

The silence in the room swelled with the energy of her outburst. *Settle down, Em!* It took a moment to slow her breathing and steady her voice, to gather her scattered emotions and bring them under control.

"Goodness, listen to me carrying on so." She eased down onto an ottoman, carefully skirting Sara's open box of watercolors. "What a frightful way for me to behave, ladies. I hope you can forgive grumpy old Dr. Getz."

Sara's lower lip poked out and her little blond head shook back and forth in protest. "You *are* a grump, Em-ee-lee. But you are *not* old."

"Oh, Sara." Emilie slipped to her knees and hugged the child with her left arm, fistful of crayons and all. "Thank you, little one." Swallowing the unexpected knot in her throat, she whispered in Sara's ear, "How did you know I needed to hear exactly that today?"

From the sidelines Beth chuckled, her sunny disposition back in place. "Kids have an uncanny knack for figuring out adults."

"Even when we behave like children?" Emilie pursed her lips together, slipping back onto the ottoman and smoothing her straight black wool skirt. "I truly am sorry to be so...so..."

"Unreasonable?" Beth's teasing tone softened the truth of it.

"Guilty as charged, I suppose." She lifted her hands then dropped them just as quickly, feeling overwhelmed again. "But isn't Jonas being difficult, too?"

"Absolutely." Beth nodded. "Rock-solid ridiculous, if you ask me." She continued sorting through Sara's box of markers, tossing out all the orphans without matching caps. "He knows you'll haul in the big guns of the academic world and bring his bulldozers to a grinding halt if he doesn't find some way to work things out."

Emilie groaned and shook her head. "There's nothing to work out, Beth." She stood again, fidgeting with her long silver necklace. "As long as there's a tiny hole with a skinny flag on that corner of his property, I can't get to my Gemeinhaus."

"From my viewpoint, Em, you have two choices. One is to fight him tooth and nail, which could take ages and make a lot of folks unhappy with you for interfering with their golf course."

"Well!" Emilie bristled. "They'll just have to swing their clubs somewhere else."

"Now who's being unfair?"

"Okay, okay." Emilie blew out a deep breath, trying her best to stay calm and think logically. "I can fight him—which, believe you me, is my strongest inclination—or I can do what? You said I had another choice."

Beth's grin was anything but angelic. "Win him over."

"*What?* Win him—!" Emilie rolled her eyes. "Are you suggesting I try and convince that...that *destroyer* of antiquities that history matters more than golf? Ha! Some chance I'd—"

"No, Em." Beth rose and planted her hands on her hips, the grin broadening. "I'm suggesting you convince Jonas that *you* matter more than golf."

A host of odd sensations—cold chills then warm, weak knees then a light-headed feeling—assailed Emilie's body. "But I don't matter to Jonas

Fielding one bit! That....well, that whatever it was...ended before..."

Beth ignored her, turning instead to her daughter. "Sara, it seems Dr. Getz is having a hard time figuring out how she feels about Whale Man. What do *you* think?"

Sara's mouth scrunched up into a freckle-framed bow as she studied Emilie for a moment before grabbing a bright pink marker. "Em-ee-lee is this color. I think that means she likes him."

Beth laughed, first squeezing her daughter's hand, then Emilie's. "I think so, too, sweetie. Know what else? Whale Man also likes our Em-ee-lee."

Humph. Emilie, despite her definite blush, would not allow herself to succumb to such sentimental claptrap. "Our nonexistent feelings for one another are beside the point."

"And that's where you're dead wrong, Emilie Getz." Beth's smile faded to a thin, determined line. "Your feelings for one another are the *only* point that matters. Not golf, not history—two people. A man and woman who care deeply about each other, whether they'll admit it or not."

Emilie hated the direction this conversation was taking. Her feelings for Jonas—whatever they were—were *her* business.

Beth, it seemed, was not going to drop the subject. Her eyes resumed their pixieish twinkle. "What if *pretending* to like Jonas would earn you a crack at your Gemeinhaus property?"

Emilie's ears perked up at that one. "What are you saying?"

"I'm saying that hard-driving Jonas, like most men, probably turns into mush when his heart—or his ego—is involved. Couldn't you *act* interested in the man? At least long enough for him to agree to let you do some digging for a month or so, find out if there are any legitimate artifacts there?"

Emilie gazed at her friend's innocent expression, wondering for the first time if Beth knew more than she might admit.

"Are you asking me to flirt? Toss shameless compliments his way?"

Beth grinned. "If you think it'll get his attention, yes."

"He'd see right through that." Those big, puppy-dog peepers of his could peer through steel and melt it in the process. Heaven knows they'd softened her resistance on several occasions—one rainy Monday in particular.

Picturing his soulful brown eyes gazing back at her, even for a second, sent a warm shiver along her spine.

No, Em! No shivers.

She straightened her head, giving her backbone no choice but to join ranks. "We'll have to think of something else, Beth. Another approach."

"Okay, okay." Beth tapped one slim finger on her lips, obviously deep in thought. "Why not give him something he needs but won't buy for himself? Something impersonal, yet friendly. Something like…"

"Like a houseplant?" *Indeed.* Even Emilie saw merit in that. The man's home was devoid of living things, unless one counted that pink-tongued monster of a dog. "He could certainly use a nice fittonia," she murmured.

Beth's brow wrinkled. "You want the man to have a fit?"

"No, a fittonia. A mosaic plant." Emilie nodded to herself, warming up to the idea. "Bright green, white-veined, low growing. I have several along the windowsill in my kitchen. Very easy to care for, as long as I provide a mister."

"Mister who?"

Emilie laughed, realizing only then that she hadn't done so in days. "A mister." She mimicked a hand squeezing something. "You know, for spraying water on plants?"

"Ohh." Beth shrugged. "Sorry. I have ten brown thumbs. You'll probably need to help Jonas on that score as well. Which is perfect."

"Maybe." Doubt attacked Emilie from every corner. Would Jonas think it was foolish? Brazen? Desperate? Conniving?

Was she willing to risk everything to find out?

Emilie smoothed her hand over her hair, as if preparing for a meeting. "So…how would one deliver this plant?"

Beth sighed, reaching for a phone book from the nearby shelf. "One would call a florist. The Hendricks greenhouses are right up the street. I'll bet they've got one of those green fitto-thingies, waiting for you to attach a card and send—"

"A *card?*" Emilie balked. "What would it say?"

"Hmm." Beth gazed at the ceiling for a moment. "How 'bout, 'We had a good thing growing.' Let's—"

"Goodness! I would never write anything that corny." Beth's hurt expression hastened her to add, "Not that it isn't creative. Perhaps if we made some reference to the soil it's planted in."

"Aha!" Beth's smile was triumphant. "I've got it." She grabbed a brown crayon from Sara's collection and carefully printed a long message on a clean piece of sketch paper, then held it up for Emilie's inspection. "Whaddya think? Sounds like you, doesn't it?"

Emilie read through the note then slowly shook her head. "Jonas will think I'm crazy."

"She's crazy about you, son. Isn't that obvious?"

"Helen, have you heard a word I said?" Jonas flailed his arms about him in utter futility, grinding his heels in Helen's well-worn living room carpet as he spun around. "The woman hung up on me yesterday."

Helen looked up from her needlework and blinked in surprise. "Emilie?"

"Yup." He nodded with conviction. "Slammed down the phone right in the middle of our conversation." The fact that seconds earlier he'd called her an "uptight, stiff-necked spinster" probably had something to do with it.

But she'd deserved it, blast it all!

And besides, it'd felt so good when he chewed up and spat out every syllable: *up-tight stiff-necked spin-ster.*

She *was* uptight, wasn't she? Worried about every little thing, but especially her confounded research. *Yeah.*

And stiff-necked? *No question.* The way she jutted her chin out and carried her head like she had books stacked on top. Fact is, her whole body was stiff.

Not always.

Not when he'd kissed her that Monday. She'd bent like a graceful willow when he—

Don't go there, fella.

He exhaled and started pacing again.

Spinster, though, *was* a cruel cut. So what if she was single? So was he. It suddenly struck him that society considered a single guy in his thirties—a bachelor—perfectly acceptable; a never-married, thirty-something woman was an old maid.

Huh. Not much justice there.

Helen swatted him lightly with her cross-stitch pattern book. "Now who's not paying attention?"

He turned in her direction and tried to look contrite. "I'm sorry, Helen. What were you saying?"

She slipped her embroidery needle through the cloth, put aside her handwork, then folded her hands in her lap, looking every bit the proper matron. "If you'd stop waging a war of words with the woman and listen to her heart, you'd know what I'm saying is true. Emilie Getz cares for you, Jonas. I've known her every one of her thirty-six years, and she's never scolded anyone as passionately as she has you. Doesn't that tell you something?"

He leaned against her mahogany mantle, shaking his head. "It tells me that I get under her skin."

Helen's eyes narrowed. "What Emilie feels for you is much more than skin deep."

"Really?" Pretending an inordinate fascination with a Hummel figurine, he avoided her pointed gaze and let the words sink in. *Did* Emilie care? Then why the high drama about a lousy quarter acre of land? Weren't there dozens of other historic sites she could pursue, right here in Lancaster County?

Why this corner of his nearly finished golf course?

Okay, not *his,* exactly.

As good as his own, though. *Like his own child.*

A vision of Sara, her tiny arms wrapped around her daddy's neck, crossed his mind. *No, not like a child.* Not that valuable, not that irreplaceable, not that eternally significant.

It was just a doggone piece of property. But it was his to manage, his to protect.

Helen invaded his thoughts. "Do you know what Emilie wants most in life?"

Jonas put down the figurine, having hardly noticed it, and gave Helen his full attention. "I should know, but I don't." *Love, maybe. Didn't every woman want that?* He shrugged, not wanting to guess incorrectly. "You tell me."

Her tsk-tsk reprimanded him. Her probing question embarrassed him. Her words, though, cut him to the quick.

"Emilie wants to be respected."

He cleared his throat, not sure why he needed to. "I do respect her."

Helen shifted in her seat, recrossing her ankles. "I'm not sure that you do. Not if you think she can put aside this quest of hers so easily. She wants—needs—to be respected for her uncommonly sharp mind. For her carefully orchestrated way of doing things—"

"You mean her picky, perfectionist, drive-a-man crazy way of doing things."

The older woman's head tipped sideways, acknowledging him yet not agreeing. "If that's how you see it, then you truly don't appreciate what she's tried to accomplish with her life. What she wants is respect, but what she *needs* is something else again."

Ah. "The love of a good man, I suppose." He swallowed the grin that threatened to sneak across his face.

Helen snorted. At least it *sounded* like a snort. "Emilie doesn't *need* a man, the way some women convince themselves they do."

Jonas stared at Helen Bomberger as if he'd never seen her before. Maybe he hadn't. Not this forthright, world-wise soul. "Oh?" was all he dared say, hoping she'd continue.

"She needs love, all right, but not from you or any other man." Helen's voice was soft, but her words were filled with conviction. "It's love from the One who made her, that's what she needs most. The one who gave her that fine intellect, who breathed that desire to pursue excellence into her very soul before her lungs filled with a single ounce of air."

Helen leaned forward, as if making sure he was listening. As if he could do otherwise.

"She needs God's love, Jonas. Have you shown her that?"

Had he? Or was it only his own affection—of the flesh, not of the Spirit—that he'd shown her? Selfishly. With little respect, if he was honest about it.

Jonas felt his limbs grow leaden and looked for the nearest available seat. "Helen—" he began, dropping onto the sofa—"God has made it clear that I'm to help Emilie understand the fullness of his joy."

"Good." She nodded, leaning back, looking relieved. "And have you done that?"

"Sort of." *What a lame answer, man!* He exhaled noisily. "I've tried, but I'm not sure I've succeeded."

Helen's smile bore no hint of judgment. "It's a beginning, Jonas."

That's what he'd told Emilie, nearly a month ago. *A beginning.* Trouble was, somewhere along the line he'd lost track of his mission in favor of the miss who'd blustered her way into his life, laying claim not only to a corner of his property, but the better part of his heart as well.

"Now what?"

He didn't realize he'd said it out loud until Helen responded with a gentle but firm list of suggestions.

"Show her respect, Jonas. Reveal God's love in as many ways as your bright mind can devise." She smiled broadly, her straight white dentures sparkling. "Do that, and I believe your little property dispute will take care of itself."

When she reached for her needlework again, he felt dismissed.

"So, what you're saying is—"

"Win her over, Jonas." In the kind, wrinkled face, her eyes twinkled like those of a young girl. "Win Emilie's heart by showing her utmost respect, God's boundless love, and your own gentlemanly attention. No woman could possibly resist all that."

Resistance was futile, even though the invitation was attached to the ugliest little plant Jonas had ever laid eyes on.

No problem. Between his luck with houseplants and Trix's curious chewing, this leafy green whatsit the florist just delivered would be dead in a week.

Jonas tossed his jacket on the kitchen counter, Helen's words still ringing in his ears. *Respect. Love. Attention.* He'd show Emilie that and more—to please Helen, and definitely to please the Lord.

He'd be pleased in the bargain, *if* Emilie agreed to let him press on with construction at Carter's Run unhampered by her fellow history fanatics.

Hadn't his good old Fielding charm unlocked many a stubborn female heart in the past? Jonas grinned and dropped onto a kitchen stool. *Dr. Getz won't know what hit her.*

An uneasiness in his chest told him he was off the mark there. *Okay, Lord. Not charm. Encouragement.* The pressure on his chest lifted as he unfolded the "You Are Invited" note, determined to keep his intentions honorable—and, if possible, his golf course intact.

The message was printed with a brown crayon. *From Sara?*

No. It was signed by Emilie.

Dear Jonas:

"Dear"? Things were already looking up.

Since we seem to share an interest in dirt...

Hence the brown crayon. And the plant. *Clever, Doc.*

please accept this peace offering and an invitation for tea Thursday afternoon at four.

Jonas grinned and scratched Trix behind the ears. "Check this out, girl. She's inviting me to do tea. Gotta be a good sign."
He hated tea.
Thursday couldn't get here soon enough.

Perhaps we can discuss the small parcel of land on Kissel Hill Road and come to a mutual agreement.

"Mutual agreement?" *Bingo!* The whole thing would be over in two days, then. She'd consent to his moving forward without interference and forget all about digging around his practically finished eighteenth hole for her patently fictitious Gemeinhaus.
Sure, the structure might have been there a couple of hundred years ago, but it was long gone. The borough owned the land, free and clear. A little tea, a little sympathy, and she'd see the light. After all, he'd come home to an answering machine full of support from the Carter's Run steering committee, assuring him they would keep it on the q.t. but that they were behind him 100 percent.
If he could convince a dozen men, how hard could it be to persuade one woman?
Jonas continued reading, unable to keep a smile off his face.

Do respond at your earliest convenience if Thursday afternoon will not suit.

It would suit fine. In fact, he'd *wear* a suit, just to demonstrate his regard for her. Earn some extra credits from the professor while he was at it.

First he'd have to buy one. Hess Clothing on Broad Street would have something in his size, right? In black?

I'll watch for your arrival promptly at four at my historic cottage on Main Street.

She *would* have to mention that "historic" part.

Your friend in property management, Emilie Getz, Ph.D.

Ha. "Property Management," eh? *What a kidder.*
The *Ph.D.* wasn't an accidental choice of verbiage either.
Emilie could toss her credentials around all she liked. They'd buy her his respect, joy, and admiration—but not his eighteenth hole.

P.S. The plant is a fittonia argyroneura *and is partial to warm temperatures and high humidity. A kitchen or bath with an east or west exposure is best. Not to worry—I'll present you with a mister on Thursday.*

A what? He shook the letter at the slobbery golden retriever panting at his feet. "I'm the only mister this sister will ever need, Trix. Come Thursday afternoon, she'll find that out."
Speaking of presents, should he take her one as well?
Possibilities ran through his mind and were quickly discarded. Perfume was too personal, tea was too predictable, jewelry was out of the question.
Wait. She liked Mavis the goldfish. Maybe another small pet of some sort. To keep her company. *To remind her of me.* It was Groundhog Day, was it not? Naturally, groundhogs weren't so much bought as they were trapped. No time for that. Still, he was on the right track.
He fingered the leafy plant, amazed when it didn't wither at his touch. Somehow he had to keep the thing alive and out of Trix's reach.
Kitchen or bath, Emilie said.
Easy enough. He'd hang it in the shower.

Emilie missed having a shower.
Her antique claw-foot tub was charming, an antique-lover's delight, but

from a practical standpoint, it was a pain in the neck—literally. When she slid down into the water till the foamy bubbles tickled her chin, the high sides of the tub caught her neck en route and offered no suitable perch once she was immersed in the suds.

Getting in and out of the tub with a broken collarbone was no easy feat either. She was grateful she lived alone, so no one would hear her splashing and grunting about when she struggled out of the tub each morning.

It wasn't morning now, not by a long shot. She'd spent the first eight hours of Thursday cleaning and polishing her little abode until it shone like the electric candles that twinkled in every window, year-round. Having located a recipe for genuine British scones, she'd bravely tossed a batch in the oven and marveled that they'd come out looking quite edible fifteen minutes later.

Lemon curd and fresh raspberries—imagine!—perched in a cool spot near the window, while the ingredients for a mock-Devonshire cream waited on the second shelf in the refrigerator. The dining room table was draped with her favorite lace-edged cloth, one of the handful of household items she brought from North Carolina, set with her best Royal Doulton bone china—the Lady Carlyle pattern, gold-rimmed and delicate. Jonas would never fit his sturdy index finger through the tiny handle in the cup, but he'd no doubt manage.

He'd also be sporting his usual T-shirt and black denim, of that she was certain. Wanting to make him feel comfortable, she'd laid out pressed blue jeans—the only pair she owned—and a plain white, oversized sweater. Her only nod to dressing for tea was a favorite navy silk scarf that would serve as her designer sling.

From her vantage point in the steaming tub, she could barely see the clock across the room. *Nearly three.* Plenty of time to finish her bath, dry and dress, and pour the scalding tea water into the waiting pot. No hurry really, not with a full hour. He'd never be early. Not in a—

Bang! Bang! Bang!

Three sharp knocks on her back door had her scrambling to a full sitting position in the tub, made slipperier than usual by the extra dollop of rose-scented bubble bath she'd poured in the water.

Bang! Bang! Bang!

Not Jonas. It wasn't possible, not an hour ahead of schedule. She squinted at the clock again, wishing her reading glasses were nearby, then steered herself through the bubbles toward the faucet to get a better look at the time.

No! Not three o'clock—*four!*

It *was* Jonas, punctual to the minute.

"Emilieeeee!" She could hear his muffled holler through the small, six-paned window just above her. The back door downstairs was unlocked. Might he let himself in? Come looking for her?

Or would he shout her name until the police came to arrest him for disturbing the peace?

"Em-i-leeeeee!"

She eyed the window, two feet above her shoulder—the shoulder with the broken collarbone. If she could get her legs underneath her, get up on her knees, perhaps she could ease up the window and call down a greeting.

Tucking one leg under her proved to be simple enough. Leaning against her good shoulder, she folded the second leg in place, congratulating herself on her dexterity until the very moment she went face-first into the sudsy drink.

Ker-splash!

Feet pointed up, face pointed down, she surfaced seconds later, sputtering with a mouthful of rose-flavored bathwater. *Ick.* Flipping over on her back, she tried the whole silly exercise again, this time managing to raise herself onto her knees. *So far, so good.* Flexing her good arm, she pushed up the window, wincing at the pain then shivering when the wintry cold breeze hit her bare skin, covering her with goosebumps.

Bang! Bang! Bang! "Em-i-leeee!"

She heard him more clearly now and shouted back. "Jonas!"

The knocking stopped. "Emilie?" She heard his footsteps on the pavement below, coming closer. "That you up there?"

"I'm here." She waved her fingers out the window and heard him snicker one story below.

"You did say four, right?"

"Yes." She felt downright ridiculous in the quickly cooling tub, yet loathed the thought of attempting an awkward, noisy exit with him in such close proximity. "Sorry. I misread the clock, Jonas. If you don't mind letting yourself in—"

"Am I supposed to climb this trellis?" A rustling sound from below launched her heart into her throat.

"No!" Her scream was faint, but sufficient. The rustling ceased. "You'll find the back door open. I'll be down shortly, I promise."

Looking like something Trix dragged in. Nothing she could do about that now. Thank goodness the homemade scones would impress him, since it was a fair wager her appearance would *not.*

Slamming the window closed and flinging herself over the edge of the tub with a graceless lunge, she dressed in record time, choosing nicely flossed teeth over makeup. She heard Jonas moving around downstairs, whistling a tune she didn't recognize—probably one of those bluegrass ditties he considered music.

All too aware of the hour, she fretted with her frizzy, unruly hair only long enough to sweep it on top of her head in an artless topknot, while curly tendrils escaped in every direction.

So be it. It was time to play hostess.

Slipping on a pair of casual leather flats, she hurried down the dark, winding staircase that led directly to her kitchen, where a tea kettle whistled on the stove and a man whistled a tune she finally identified as a Moravian favorite: "Morning Star, O Cheering Sight!"

The music stopped as he turned to face her, wearing a broad smile. "There you are."

Her mouth went dry—drier than scones—and her eyes grew the size of tea saucers. "J-Jonas?"

Fourteen

She who hesitates is won.
OSCAR WILDE

A suit. Not a sport coat and slacks. The man was wearing a *suit!* Black as night, perfectly tailored to his wide shoulders and solid chest, fashioned with lean lines in a subtle, expensive weave that emphasized muscles she didn't even know Jonas *owned.*

Emilie tried to focus her gaze on his, but other distractions kept her eyes busy and her thoughts racing.

No T-shirt, this. His dress shirt was pure white, crisp against his freshly shaved neck, with a sharply patterned tie the color of ripe eggplant. Even his hair was sleek, as if he'd just come from the barber.

Emilie's lips moved before her brain had a chance to intervene. "I had no idea—"

His eyebrows lifted. "No idea that I was coming for tea? But Emilie, you invited me."

"I did?" She gulped. "Yes! I certainly did. Most definitely. Four o'clock, and here you are." *And here I am looking like a church mouse, and you looking like a...a...* Another gulp. "Have a seat, won't you? I'm truly sorry. The time got away from me."

He followed her into the dining room, his new black dress shoes silent against the polished hardwood. "Emilie, you're the most punctual woman I know. Are you sure everything is okay?"

Not okay. Not remotely okay. She concentrated on breathing, knowing fresh oxygen would be the key to staying both vertical and fully conscious.

He paused by the nearest chair where a place setting waited. "Does it matter where we sit?"

She stared at him, mesmerized. "I thought we'd sit here."

"Yes, Emilie." It was his second grin in as many minutes and it matched the suit beautifully, she decided, smiling back.

He pressed his point. "I meant which chair is mine?"

"All the chairs."

She glided back into the kitchen, suppressing an odd, giggly sensation that threatened to overtake her. *Steady, Em!* Pouring boiling hot water into the already-warmed pot, she went through the familiar motions of making tea while fighting a strong impulse to grab the phone, call Beth, and like a lovesick adolescent, describe her "date"—the new, improved Jonas Fielding—in complete and breathtaking detail.

This is not a date, Em. This is tea.

So it was, tea with scones. She unwrapped them, still warm in their cozy basket, and placed them on a serving plate, carrying them into the dining room without meeting his gaze, then hurrying back for the berries and lemon curd.

"Anything I can help with?" he called into the kitchen when she deserted him a third time, her body well hidden behind the white enamel door of the GE fridge.

"Nope," she said simply, snatching two pint containers—one sour cream, the other heavy whipping cream—from the shelf, adding them to the box of powdered sugar on the countertop. Minutes later, her wrist stiff from beating the mixture into frothy peaks, she hurried back into the dining room with a china serving bowl brimming with her own heavenly version of English clotted cream.

"All we need is the earl grey itself, properly steeped by now, I'm quite certain. Then we'll be ready to enjoy our tea."

Tea with a purpose, she reminded herself, feeling her shoulders straighten with a resolute snap. The whole point was to win back her land, if only long enough to thoroughly examine it.

The words ran through her mind like a bit of verse memorized for an exam. *Woo the man and win the land. Woo the man and win the land.* She was on her third mental go-round when she gingerly carried her heavy teapot into the dining room and placed it on the padded trivet with a slight grimace.

Jonas was seated, but seeing her wince, he quickly stood to assist her. "Emilie, you should have let me carry this in for you. Where was my head?"

On top of the broadest pair of shoulders I've ever seen.

She offered a slight smile and slipped into the chair opposite his. "No problem. I'm getting along fine, see?" Tipping the blue sling up for his inspection, she reached for the plate of scones with the other hand. "I made these fresh this afternoon. See what you think of them."

Sliding one on the floral plate before him, his big hand dwarfing the small, triangular biscuit, Jonas eyed her carefully as she sliced it in two, then he did likewise.

Suit or no, the man is still Jonas. The realization calmed her, slowed her too-rapidly beating heart. A man who played with dirt, not with tea sets. A man whose attire today was atypical to say the least.

She, therefore, still held sway in this setting. The linen napkins she'd pressed, the scones she'd baked, the luscious cream she'd prepared…they were quintessentially Emilie.

This was her home, her tea, and her Gemeinhaus they were going to discuss at length. Just as soon as she could get her eyes off his generous Adam's apple disappearing underneath that perfectly knotted silk tie.

"Did you…do all this?" He looked genuinely surprised.

"I did." *Don't blush. Do not blush!* The heat ignored her wishes, sneaking up her neck like a wave of warmth from an opened oven. "Everything except the berries."

Jonas nodded in agreement. "The Lord made those. Did a nice job, too."

She merely smiled and aimed a slice of scone piled with lemon and cream between her parted lips. *Some conversationalist you are, Em.*

Music. *Yes.* They needed music. Right away.

Depositing her napkin next to her fork, she rose with a shaky start, then headed for the living room stereo.

Jonas shot out of his chair. "Uh, Emilie, I meant to tell you, there's—"

"Eek!" Horrified, Emilie pointed at the couch and screamed, sending Lady Carlyle's teacups rattling in their dainty china saucers.

That shrieking-banshee sound again. He'd know it anywhere.

Jonas hustled around the corner into the adjoining room and found Emilie exactly as he'd expected, gasping and pointing at the glass box on her sofa.

"There's a...a...*rat* in there!"

"Not a rat," he corrected, gently taking her elbow. "A guinea pig. It was the closest thing the pet store in Lancaster had to a groundhog." He guided her one step closer and bent toward the cage, hoping she'd join him. "Nice little fella, don't you think? They call it a *cavy.*"

"Good," she said emphatically. "Send it back to the cave from whence it came, please."

"C'mon, Emilie." He straightened and turned her toward him, hoping to get her eyes—and her thoughts—back where they belonged. "Don't you think Clarence—uh, *Clarice*—is rather cute?"

"You thought the fish was cute." She peered around his black-suited arm, eyebrows in a tight *V*, as she assessed the furry, brown creature.

Jonas, meanwhile, assessed her, noticing how every loose hair spilling from the top of her head went its own wispy way. He had a barely controllable urge to curl a lock around his finger and feel its silky texture. "Yeah," he murmured, trying hard to keep his wits about him. "Where is old Mavis?"

"On the piano in the study, making no noise whatsoever." She leaned back and caught his eye. "This cavy squeaks."

"Not much. Mostly he—uh, *she*—eats leafy vegetables and sits there, looking adorable." *Like you, Emilie.* The woman didn't have a dab of makeup on her face, wore dull, frumpy clothes and a ferocious scowl, but blast if she wasn't the prettiest thing he'd ever laid eyes on.

Smelled good, too. *Like raspberries and cream.*

She was frowning at the cavy again, so he took advantage of the moment and closed his eyes, silently inhaling her scent. *Roses. All around her hair.* He tipped his head down for a deeper whiff in time to bump noses with her, looking up.

When his eyes flew open, hers narrowed.

"What precisely did you have in mind, Mister?"

"A mister." His wide grin covered a multitude of unspoken possibilities. "That's what you said I needed. For my *fittonia argyroneura,* remember?"

She made a sharp sound with her mouth—a younger version of Helen's tsk-tsk—and pulled away from him, returning to the room a moment later with a plastic spray bottle in hand. "Your mister, as promised."

"Now, suppose we return to tea? As promised?" He crooked an elbow out for her to take, which she did with some misgivings, it seemed. She hadn't said a word about his suit. Hated it, no doubt. *So much for the old Fielding charm.*

Having escorted her to her seat, he poured their tea, careful not to spill a drop, then joined her at the table, capturing her hand before she had a chance to hide it in her lap.

"How 'bout a prayer, Emilie?" *Sorry I didn't think of this earlier, Lord.*

She looked bewildered. "It's only tea."

"Not a prayer for the food so much." His eyes sought hers, finding in those light brown depths a host of unanswered questions. "I wanted to pray about our time together. For our…discussion."

"Ahh." Her eyes widened at that. "Pray away, then."

Emilie bowed her head, expecting to hear him offer a traditional Moravian blessing: "Be present at our table, Lord" or "Come, Lord Jesus, our guest to be."

As usual, Jonas did the unexpected.

"Heavenly Father, thank you for this…lovefeast, and for the kind, generous hands that prepared it." His voice had never sounded so sincere. It tied a strange and unfamiliar knot in her throat.

A lovefeast, he'd said? Well, there *was* a hot drink. A simple, sweet scone. *Perhaps.*

Jonas squeezed her hand, lightly but surely, and pressed on. "Lord Jesus, we love you so much."

We? The lump tightened. She *did* love the Lord. Didn't she? Wasn't that why she went to church religiously, Sunday after Sunday, without fail? Still…*we.* It sounded odd and felt even more so.

Jonas' words grew softer, and Emilie strained to catch each one, as if somehow her life depended on it. "Lord, more than anything, I want my relationship with you to be right, and my relationship with Emilie to be…right."

Oh. Where was he going with this? She felt her entire nervous system go on alert, as if she'd just heard a train whistle in the distance.

"She's very special to me, Lord. Help us work through our…differences and work on building a right relationship with you."

This time when he squeezed her hand, she squeezed it back. Tentatively at first, then tighter as an unforeseen tear sneaked across her cheek. *What sort of "right relationship" is he talking about?* She swallowed hard, but still the lump persisted.

First Beth, then Jonas—both talking about loving God. It was all so confusing. She sang hymns, she prayed prayers, she'd known the church calendar and its sacred seasons for as long as she could remember.

What relationship? Desperate, with more tears threatening, she gathered up her courage and asked him herself.

What is Jonas saying, Lord?

She was not prepared for an immediate response.

Know me, Emilie.

Know you? She *did* know God, knew all about God.

Know me, Emilie. Know me as you would a husband. I love you, Emilie. Completely. Do you love me?

Tears sprang up from a well hidden in the deepest corner of her heart. With one hand in Jonas' grip and the other in a sling, she couldn't stem the flow trickling along her cheeks, dropping onto the bone china plate with tiny *pings.*

Emilie stared down at the growing pool, mortified, then lifted her gaze to Jonas' bowed head. Had he heard? Did he realize what was happening? For that matter, did *she?*

As if beckoned, Jonas looked up. A moist sheen darkened his own eyes.

He knows! Somehow, Jonas understood what she was going through, what she was feeling. Understood and didn't judge her.

A fresh stream of tears, tasting like warm saltwater, ran across her trembling lips.

She couldn't speak. She couldn't breathe, fearing a single intake of air would turn into sobs that would wrack her body if not her soul. But she had to breathe. Had to, or she would faint.

Help me, Lord!

The dam broke with a great gasp of air and a crushing sense of release. Heat rushed to her face, her neck, as the tears flowed one after another. Unaware of anything but the emotions that were clamoring to the surface—sorrow and gratitude and longing and shame—Emilie simply wept.

Jonas let go of her hand, which she immediately used to shield her face, too humiliated to look him in the eye again. He didn't force her to meet his gaze, nor did he pull back. Instead, he lightly stroked her hair, murmuring words too tender to be heard.

Her heart recognized the cadence of them, though.

The Lord loves you, Emilie. Exactly as you are.

It couldn't be true. *Not like this, Lord!* So plain in looks. So prideful in spirit. So certain she didn't need anyone in her life. *Not even you, Lord. Not even you! How can you overlook that?*

Jonas rested his hands on her head, barely touching her. She felt more than heard the compassion in his whispered words of prayer. Clearly this man knew God. Did she? Could she?

Like a grieving person, Emilie caught herself groaning under her breath. It was the sound of despair, of a heart broken in two. How could God forgive her for not reaching out to him long before this?

She waited, dreading the answer.

I love you, Emilie. Even unto death. All is forgiven.

Everything?

Everything.

Oh! All at once, her heavy spirit had wings. *Wings!*

She found her heart could speak, even when her lips could not.

I love you too, Lord. I do. Truly.

A solemn silence roared in her ears, blocking out anything but the absolute awareness of his holy presence. He was real. And he loved her. It was all she needed to know.

Moments later, after another shuddering sob, Emilie realized her tears were beginning to slow. *Thank goodness, Lord! I've made an utter fool of myself here.*

His voice—and already she was becoming familiar with the sound of it—both warmed and challenged her: *Better a fool for One who loves you than a prophet for one who does not.*

As if fortified by those few words alone, Emilie straightened, unashamedly wiping away the last of her tears. The air around her seemed at once clearer, brighter.

Jonas was smiling—hugely so.

In the living room, a small cavy scurried about his new glass cage. In her centuries-old dining room, the doors of Emilie's own cage had been flung wide open.

Nate slammed the door shut with a violent bang, more pleased than he should have been when a hairline crack appeared in one of the pine panels.

Serves 'em right. The hotel had issued him a sternly-worded notice to vacate his room by morning, threatening to press charges if he didn't produce either cash or a valid credit card to cover the last three nights' lodging.

He only had eight hundred dollars left and two long weeks to go before he supposedly got out of rehab. Jonas couldn't call Nate, nor could Nate call him. That's the way these recovery places worked—Nate had checked all that out before contacting his brother for cash.

It'd been the perfect cover-up, the ideal excuse to borrow money and then disappear. Problem was, the money had disappeared, too. Not at the track—Nate purposely drove out of his way to miss the place—but rather at San Pablo Golf Club. The greens fees were exorbitant. So were meals and tips and a week's worth of new golf shirts at seventy dollars apiece.

Nate did his best to blend in, not wanting to draw undue attention, presenting himself as nothing more than an amiable, dark-haired golfer who'd suddenly started hanging around the clubhouse every afternoon. That's when the CEOs rolled in, ready for a quick round and often looking for a fourth player.

How may I be of service this afternoon, gentlemen? I'm Nathan Fielding, member of the PGA.

Yeah. You and twenty-three thousand other members.

If the men were rank amateurs, he offered tips that made them better. Made them grateful. If they played in the 80s, he complimented their games then made sure he scored a few points lower. Competitive to a man, these business execs liked spending time with someone who gave them a run for their money.

Ever cooperative, Nate took their money and ran with it. In twenties and fifties and hundreds. On side games and long drives and putts. He lost on occasion—it made him seem legitimate—and tucked his winnings away until he could polish off his debts.

It still wasn't enough.

At least the Jaguar was covered for two more weeks. He'd managed without booze, could squeeze by on one meal a day and a handful of mixed nuts at the club bar. Cy grumbled about the measly two thousand bucks Nate had sent, demanding more, but Nate knew how to butter up the man, get him laughing. It was the king-size bed he crashed on at night, the cold shower that shocked him awake in the morning, that's what he'd let slide, figuring he'd pay up by week's end.

The end was near, only hours away.

He looked at the phone by the bed and the number scribbled on the pad next to it. *Rick.* One of the friendlier types in the pro shop. Young guy, maybe twenty, putting himself through the University of North Florida by making himself useful at the club.

Nate knew Rick had an apartment off-campus. Could he talk him into letting him land there for a couple of weeks? Buy some cereal, kick in a little rent, let him borrow the Jag for a night?

He grabbed the phone off the hook, then banged it against his forehead in a pathetic rhythm, punishing himself. *Why?* Why did it always come to this? Asking for favors? For handouts? For loans he'd probably never be able to pay back?

Exhaling the last of his frustration, Nate punched in the numbers and stretched a big, fake smile across his face. "Hey, Rick! How ya doin', buddy?"

He listened, nodding as if Rick were sitting right in front of him. "Same here. Looks like it'll be another two weeks until they finish my condo, though."

It was a smooth lie, one he'd concocted driving past the place yesterday. Snazzy, upscale, the kind of high-rent building San Pablo members would call home. *Opening February 25,* the sign had said. *Primo timing.* His thirty-day blitz would be over by then and he'd already have kissed Jacksonville good-bye.

But Rick didn't know that. Nobody did.

"I hate to ask this, sport, but could you spare a couch and a coffeepot for a couple of weeks? Really? That's great, man. Just great."

Nate tried not to sound too relieved. *Don't give yourself away, Fielding. Don't sound desperate.* "If it's okay, I'll stop by late tomorrow morning and get a spare key. Nah, no stuff to store. One suitcase and a cell phone. You'll hardly notice I'm there."

At least that much was true. He practically lived at the club and owned nothing but the clothes on his back.

"Excellent. You'll let me buy some groceries, right? And help you shave a few strokes off your game? Good. I'll look forward to it. And…thanks, Rick."

He dropped the phone back in place, puzzled he wasn't more elated about the whole thing. Maybe it'd been too easy. One call and he'd nailed a roof over his head and saved a bundle of money.

Nate was a survivor. When he dug himself into a pit, he kept shoveling until he could dig himself out.

Not true, man. You look for somebody else's shoulders to stand on. That's how you get out.

The truth stuck in his craw, like a tough piece of meat.

Maybe he *had* counted on others to boost him up. His dad's shoulders had been stronger than anybody's. Jonas was a poor but dependable second choice.

Not true, Nate. He's been more than a brother to you.

Too much more. That was the problem. Jonas was his conscience. His mother *and* his father. Always wanting the best for him. Always hoping he would change. Nate could hear it in his brother's voice.

Jonas doesn't judge you.

No need. The guy's squeaky-clean life was judgment enough.

Jonas hasn't given up on you.

But he should. After all, Nate had given up on himself a long time ago.

Two-hundred-fifty years to the day.

Jonas double-checked his calendar. *Yup.*

February 9. The day the Gemeinhaus—the *second* one, Emilie would insist—was dedicated and consecrated by the serving of communion. The day the Warwick *Landgemeine* Congregation threw open its doors to Moravians far and wide.

Emilie wasn't the only one who knew her history.

Right this minute, though, Jonas cared only about the woman's future. Her future with the Lord. *Her future with you, Fielding.* No question, that figured into this property fiasco as well.

He shrugged into his parka, planning on a short walk over to Church Square. Emilie hadn't answered her phone at home. Surely she'd be at the church office, today of all days. They'd talked all around the land situation since last Thursday. Now it was time to reach some consensus. Every hour brought them closer to the grand opening on April 9.

"Let's go, Trixie girl." He snapped a long leash on her collar while the retriever fairly rolled her eyes at the prospect of a long walk. Trix didn't just wag her tail, she wagged everything she owned, banging against him as they headed out through the garage.

Jonas took off at a good clip, thanks to his spirited partner, and headed toward Cedar. The weather was decent; temperatures in the low fifties. A silvery gray, overcast sky but no threat of rain. Two blocks away, the bells in the Moravian church spire rang twice and he checked his watch, smiling at the vivid memory of another afternoon. *Three-thirty. Almost tea time, Emilie.*

There'd never be another tea like the one they'd shared last Thursday, not in his lifetime. *Not ever.* He'd arrived on time, hoping to sweep her off her feet. Instead, the Lord showed up and swept her up in his own sacred embrace.

At first Emilie couldn't talk about it, just sipped her tea and sniffled in his handkerchief. Good thing he'd bought a new one to go with the suit. Then she started telling him about how she'd always believed—absolutely and positively—in the existence of God, yet had no clue when it came to *knowing* God in a personal way.

"Like *you* do. Like Beth does, and Helen," she explained, still trying to sort things out in her mind. He nodded, listened, and prayed silently while she talked, wanting so much to say the right thing. To encourage her, as he'd promised Helen he would.

Helen. She'd cried on the phone when he called Friday to give her a full report. "I had nothing to do with it, and you know it," he protested when Helen congratulated him.

"Nonsense," she said, tsk-tsking again. "You were there, you were obedient, and you were used of God. That's as good as it gets, Jonas."

It *was* good. Better than good. Any discussion of mundane issues, like eighteenth holes and Gemeinhaus digs, faded to black in the wake of Emilie's discovery. They'd sat on the couch together—*after* he strategically found a new perch for Clarice the guinea pig—and talked all through the evening, nibbling on cold scones and sliced ham for dinner, then feeding each other spoonfuls of raspberries with cream for dessert.

The evening ended with nothing more than a kiss.

But it lasted twenty minutes.

Standing there in her kitchen, Jonas slipped his arms around her waist, drawing her into a relaxed embrace. His suit coat had come off hours earlier, which meant he felt her fragile warmth through the sleeves of his dress shirt. As if from a great distance, classical music floated in from the living room.

"Johann Friedrich Peter," she murmured, though he hadn't asked. "A Moravian composer." *Of course.* "Eighteenth century."

"One of your favorites?"

"Mm-hmm." The shy look had returned. Her head was dipped down, with her forehead almost but not quite resting on his chest.

Brushing one hand over her soft hair, down to the nape of her neck, he splayed his fingers to cradle her head, then tipped it back ever so slightly. He didn't want her to feel forced in any way, understanding more than ever Emilie's need for control, yet he longed to see her angelic face.

Even remembering it now, walking down Cedar, Jonas swallowed a lump in his throat. Emilie's countenance was radiant that night. Shining like a candle. The only word to describe it was joy. *Pure joy.*

He hadn't put that look there—it was totally the Lord's doing—but he certainly could celebrate it. And Jonas had known precisely how he wanted those festivities to begin.

When he lowered his head, eyes focused on her sweet rosebud of a mouth, she didn't resist. Leaned up toward him, in fact. Met him halfway, sliding one small, white-dove hand up his arm then around his neck.

In a single heartbeat, everything around them disappeared.

The only sensation was her lips pressed against his, a perfect match.

The only sound was her steady breathing. *Maybe not so steady.*

The only scent was her rose-tinged hair and the lingering aromas from their afternoon tea.

The only taste was sweet Emilie.

And the only sight worth seeing was the fullness of joy reflected on her face when she slowly opened her eyes and whispered, "Kiss me again, Jonas."

Whew.

He'd stumbled out the door minutes later, his heart singing, his mind spinning, and his Explorer forgotten as he walked a full block before he remembered that he drove.

Fifteen

♦

When I walk with you I feel as if I had a flower in my buttonhole.
WILLIAM THACKERAY

Jonas' brisk walk with Trix in tow—or was it Trix's walk with *him* in tow?—brought them charging toward the entrance gate to the Moravian Cemetery. As he expected, the Emilie Getz Honorary Rock Pile still waited for the stonemasons to show up and reassemble it back into a solid pillar.

Jonas grinned, in spite of the stark reminder of that icy Friday afternoon. That was one accident, at least, that led to a very happy ending, especially last Thursday.

He'd done everything Helen suggested. *And a few things she hadn't, fella.* Jonas chuckled, trotting past the fragmented gate. *Wait until I walk in with Victor!*

After Mavis and Clarice, Victor would be his biggest surprise of all. He hoped to present it to Emilie sometime this week, in thanks for her anticipated cooperation about his eighteenth hole. Surely, after a kiss like that, the woman wouldn't refuse him anything as paltry as a quarter acre of property.

He followed the paved road up into the cemetery, tugging on Trix's leash to keep her from chomping on the silk and plastic flowers poking from the dirt around the headstones. Familiar Lititz names caught his eye—Klein, Bender, Stauffer, Erb, Graybill—though not a soul was buried here that he'd known personally. Five years in Lititz made him the new guy in town.

As he continued up the steep, curving drive, a cluster of ornate stones on the left caught his eye, including one name that struck a chord: *Landis.* He whistled a command at Trix, then knelt before a small grave marker with a cradle carved into the gray, polished granite.

"Here, Trix." His voice suddenly hoarse, he began reading the inscription aloud, as if trying to convince himself it was genuine. "Clayton Robert Landis. Born March 6. Died March 11."

Only five days. Jonas felt an invisible vise clamp down on his chest. *He would be a little boy of seven now.*

There was more. "Son of Andrew and Elizabeth Landis."

It couldn't be. *Drew. And Beth.* The vise gripped harder.

He'd never asked about other kids. Sara was born soon after he moved to town, and he just assumed…he never dreamed…

Beth. Beth, the woman who adored children, who helped with the nursery and the children's choir, who mothered little Sara like a lioness caring for her cub. Beth had survived the unimaginable heartache of placing her infant son in a casket five days after first holding him in her arms.

Stunned, Jonas rose to his feet, drawing in air with big gulps, his constricted throat and chest muscles fighting every breath. *Clayton Landis.* This little one he had never met, had not even known existed until now, all at once became real to him.

The loss was real, too.

Jonas stepped back slowly, with respect, then turned toward the church, walking forward but seeing nothing, still grappling with the unwelcome news. Trix, aware only of his change in mood, did her best to wrap herself around his legs, nuzzling his hand, nipping his coat with her teeth. "I see you, girl," he murmured, scratching her head.

He had never lost a son, but he'd lost a father.

Either tragedy brought more than enough pain to last a lifetime.

Oddly, Nathan came to mind. A brother who was very much alive, yet lost to him in many ways. The rehab was necessary, no question. The smartest five thousand dollars he'd ever spent. When Nate's month was up, Jonas hoped he'd come spend a few weeks with him in Lititz. See how refreshing life in a small town could be.

His spirits restored at the prospect, Jonas lifted his head and realized he'd almost reached God's Acre, the oldest section of the cemetery. The large, square grounds had no monuments, only flat slabs of marble marking each grave, facing east, with the sexes carefully separated into choirs—men and boys, women and girls. Moravians never died; they merely fell asleep or went home, while their bodies remained buried awaiting resurrection.

No wonder the Easter sunrise service included a triumphant walk to God's Acre with trombones sounding and voices raised in hallelujah. It was not a place of the dead, but of those alive in Christ. Even Trix jogged along at a happy pace, oblivious to her surroundings. She was with her master on hallowed ground. All was well.

On the grassy edge, near the stone and wood archway that led to the church buildings, stood a woman in a light gray suit, her back toward him, surrounded by two others and a man balancing a camera on his shoulder. Jonas grinned, finally recognizing her. *Well, whaddaya know. Emilie Getz.* She'd removed her sling, probably for the camera, and was gesturing in wide sweeps with the other arm.

He lengthened his stride, tempted to call out, yet sensing Emilie was being interviewed. *Something* was happening, at any rate. He closed the gap between them, stopping five yards away to watch and listen as the cameraman from WGAL-TV shouted, "Rolling!"

The reporter, a perky brunette with a vaguely familiar name, prattled on about the 250th anniversary celebration, then turned to introduce her guest. "With us on this important occasion is Dr. Emilie Getz, professor of history at Salem College in North Carolina. Dr. Getz, tell us what this day means to the Moravians of Lititz."

Jonas grinned. *Yeah, tell us all about it, Doc.*

He knew his amused expression might throw off her concentration, so he pinched his lips tightly shut, willing them not to curl up on the ends.

Emilie was the essence of poised professionalism as she leaned toward the microphone. "We Moravians are very proud of our heritage. February 9 is a day for celebrating the leap of faith made by twenty-seven visionary souls, people whose hearts were awakened to the joy of knowing Christ."

The grin escaped. *You oughtta know, Doc.*

Undistracted, Emilie launched into a bright and breezy review of the local congregation, from Gemeinhaus to God's Acre and everything in between. Clearly, Dr. Getz and the Lord were on a roll. The young reporter merely smiled and nodded, wide-eyed at her knowledgeable guest.

When Emilie finished, the reporter abruptly scanned her notes, flustered, it seemed, over losing her place. Finally, she blurted out, "Uh...Dr. Getz, someone at the church mentioned that in addition to the commemorative book you are writing, you are also doing a private research project. One involving a piece of property in town and a possible archaeological dig. Would you care to comment?"

Jonas held his breath. *She wouldn't*. Would she?

No, Emilie.

His grin long gone, Jonas stared at her in silence, willing her to keep this to herself. The committee knew; the community did not. *Not now, Emilie. No comment. Say "No comment."*

He trained his eyes on her, praying she got the message.

She did.

"You've certainly done your homework." Emilie's tone was smooth and assuring. "But since *my* homework isn't finished on this subject yet, I'll save my comments until I have something definite—and definitely exciting—to share with your Channel Eight viewers."

Jonas exhaled, his smile firmly back in place. *What a pro. What a woman!* He listened as Emilie offered a few more interesting tidbits about the church's plans for the year ahead, from picnics to putzing, carol sings to trombone choir concerts. "We'll begin with a special anniversary lovefeast on the fourteenth." Emilie looked straight at the camera. "Do join us, won't you? Ten-thirty Sunday morning."

On cue, the church bells tolled the hour. Four long chimes—on a lower, more solemn note than the quarter hour bells. The musical sound reverberated through the crisp February air as the reporter closed her story with a wide shot of the church behind her and a joy-filled historian by her side.

Watching Emilie bid her good-byes to the television crew, Jonas impatiently started inching her direction. He didn't want to rush her, yet longed to simply touch her hand, reconnect with her. They'd spoken on the phone each day since Thursday and sat together at the second service on Sunday, causing a full hour of rubbernecking around the sanctuary.

She'd hated it.

He'd loved it.

Jonas paused mere steps away and sized up her camera-ready look. The suit was new, a soft gray not unlike the silvery sky above. *Or the granite headstones in the cemetery.* He'd have to tell her about that, about little Clayton Landis. Though maybe she'd already heard. *Women always know these things.*

Her hair was more tamed than usual, gathered into a tidy clump. *Nah. Not a clump. A French something-or-other.* Her lips and cheeks were pinker than he'd ever remembered—not makeup, not his Emilie—and her graceful hand waved through the air as she spoke with yet another woman who'd been waiting for her on the sidelines.

All at once, Emilie turned his direction and flashed him the most dazzling smile he'd seen her display yet.

"Hello, Jonas."

He loved the way she said his name.

"Please forgive me." Emilie inclined her head toward the waiting reporter. "The *Record Express* is here for an interview now. You know…" She shrugged, avoiding his gaze for a moment. "The anniversary and such."

"Sure. No problem." He couldn't resist squeezing her hand, if only for a moment. "Are you busy later?"

"The…well, the *Intelligencer Journal* will be calling at four-thirty for a brief story as well." She was blushing like a schoolgirl. He liked schoolgirls as long as they were his age and single. And named Emilie.

"So, after your media blitz today, might you have time for an old friend?" He tipped his chin down. "One who knew you *before* you became famous?"

"Of course, silly. Besides, I have another houseplant for you. How is your *fittonia* doing?"

"Er….it's good. Yeah, good." *Good and drowned.* How was he supposed to know the shower would wash out all the dirt, or that shampoo and plants shouldn't mix? "I'll take good care of this new one, I promise."

Her eyes narrowed. "Oh?"

Not much got past this woman.

"Emilie, I also need to talk to you about…some things." *Several, in fact.* "Okay if I swing by your house about seven?"

She nodded, already being pulled into another photo shoot, this time with a woman and her Nikon. "See you at seven," she mouthed, then gave the newspaper reporter her full attention.

Trix, patiently waiting her turn, barked with abandon as Jonas scratched her head and pointed them toward home, rehearsing in his mind the words he was going to say, beginning with a prayer request for one very dead *fittonia.*

Emilie watered the leafy pepperface plant with great care. Too much water and the roots would rot. *Then again, it may be weeks before Jonas remembers to give you another drink, little one.* She splashed in a bit extra, pinched off a withered stem, then polished its waxy leaves with a paper towel.

She glanced at the clock. *Ten minutes.* That is, *if* the man was on time. He'd been doing much better in that department, though. *Much better in lots of departments.* He was still wearing his jeans-and-T uniform, but lately he seemed freshly shaved every time she saw him.

"That way I won't scratch your tender skin when I kiss you," he'd informed her when she mentioned it. She'd turned scarlet. Was warming again now at the memory. Smiling too.

Oh, Jonas. The man made her feel sixteen again. *Check that.* Sixteen had been an awful year. In fact, other than one milkshake with the now-very-married Brian Zeller, Emilie couldn't compare any of her earlier experiences with men—boys, really—to the roller-coaster ride she'd lived through in the last few days with Jonas Fielding.

He was bright, attentive, caring, funny. Both devout *and* irreverent, if such a thing were possible. And my, but the man had a way of making her heart beat faster with nothing more than a feathery touch; a dark-eyed glance; a single, chaste kiss. Surely Jonas would see fit to let her press on with her Gemeinhaus research now.

As thrilling as their time together had been—then and since—it was what happened between his black-suited appearance in her doorway and their breath-stealing moments in the kitchen Thursday evening that filled her heart and mind. She was having a hard time putting words to her feelings, but she'd tried on three occasions, with mixed results.

Her mother had wrinkled her brow. "You feel like you know God? Emilie Gayle, what a silly thing to say! You've always known who God is, dear, ever since you were old enough to say the word."

Her father had listened, nodded, and agreed with her mother. *Of course.*

They both perked up, though, when she mentioned she'd been having tea with Jonas Fielding at the time.

"On a date, did you say, Emilie?"

Things had gone much better with Beth last Friday.

"Emilie, you prayed *what?*" Beth's eyes had shone with tears as they'd sat together on her enclosed back porch that afternoon, Sara napping on the nearby loveseat, the house unusually quiet.

Emilie gulped, still uncomfortable with emotionally charged words, no matter how accurately they described things. "I…uh, told the Lord I loved him. And asked his forgiveness for not…well, including him more in my life." *There. Not so bad.*

Beth hugged her neck then asked for minute-by-minute details, which Emilie shared as best she could. Except for that business in the kitchen. She'd start blushing again. *Fie!* She *did* blush again, even without mentioning it, prompting Beth to ask if anything else had transpired.

Emilie jerked her chin toward the back door, feigning interest in the window shade, the doorknob, anything. "Jonas and I kissed, and that's all I'll say about it."

Beth laughed so loudly that Sara stirred in her sleep. "That's more than enough information, Em," Beth assured her in a stage whisper.

It was then, staring out the back door, that Emilie noticed a wire fence enclosing a grove of hemlock and tall, old pine trees in a square area behind the Landis property. "Is that what I think it is?"

"An old graveyard." Beth tucked Sara's blanket up under her chin and smoothed her curly, blond locks. "Saint Somebody-or-other."

Emilie was on her feet, nose pressed against the glass pane. "Of course! St. James. After Zinzendorf preached here, the settlers joined forces— Lutheran, Reformed, and Mennonite—and founded a Union Church. It was named after James because the log church was dedicated in July 1744 on the day of his festival. The log structure is long gone, of course—dismantled in 1771 and used to build a miller's house along Carter's Run—but the graves are still here."

Beth chuckled softly and shook her head. "Do all these facts just live in your head, Em?"

Emilie shrugged. "Afraid so. Four years later this congregation joined with the new Moravian one. A decade later, the first Easter morning service was held right in this graveyard."

Beth's smirk was less than subtle. "With trombones, I suppose."

"No, those came later. French horns were first used in 1763, but the trombones didn't come into use until 1779 when—" Emilie realized Beth was covering her ears and trying not to laugh. "Okay, I'll stop. Really, Beth, you should know better than to throw an historian a bone like that. *With trombones.* Honestly, it's your own fault."

"Mea culpa." Beth joined her by the door. "How many people are buried there, do you know?"

"On record, about one hundred-eighty." Emilie pursed her lips, sorting through her mental file cabinets for accurate details. "The first was a child. Michael, I think."

"Oh." Beth stepped back from the door, as if it were hot. "I...had no idea."

"Yes, it's unfortunate." Emilie turned to add, "Many of the early burials were infants and children..." Her voice trailed off as she gazed at Beth's blanched features and trembling lower lip.

"Beth, are you okay?"

The younger woman sank onto the couch next to Sara, patting her daughter's sleeping form as if for comfort. "I...just never realized there were little ones buried there."

"As there were in every colonial cemetery, sad to report." Emilie perched on a nearby straight-backed chair, at a loss about what to say next. After a few awkward moments of silence, she gave in to the obvious question. "Is something wrong?"

She watched Beth blink a few times in quick succession, then press a hand against her stomach, as if feeling queasy. "I'm...okay. Just caught me off guard, I guess." Her smile was tentative. "Sorry. You were talking about...?"

"About putting you to bed right along with Sara, if you won't argue with me." Emilie surprised herself by sliding her arms under the child and lifting her up, cradling Sara against her, amazed at how light the little girl was.

She moved toward the kitchen, speaking over her shoulder in a soft tone. "Suppose I carry Sara up to her room and you join her for a nap, okay? You look positively wiped out. Hard morning at the church office?"

Beth didn't object, but simply followed her through the house and up the carpeted steps. "I guess. We're getting ready for the big anniversary on

Tuesday. By the way, be prepared for some media interviews, Em. You're our in-house historian, you know."

"Happy to be of service."

The thought warmed her heart, then and now.

Beth's prediction had come true. Emilie had indeed been busy all day today. Bubbling about her Moravian heritage had turned out to be more meaningful than she'd expected. Perhaps because of her work on the commemorative book, which was more than half done. Or because of the last seven weeks in Lititz, living in the heart of the town she loved. Or maybe it was one Moravian in particular—of the male persuasion—who'd put that sparkle in her voice.

No.

She knew better. It was what the Germans had called *Durchbruch*. Her breakthrough. Her awakening. A *change for the better*, her resources translated it. *Indeed*. All that and more.

By any name, it made her more determined than ever to claim the Kissel Hill Road property for the church. Not for her own glory, not anymore. For the glory of the Lord. He'd given her wings and he'd shown her the richness of her roots. Emilie longed now to plant those tender new shoots in the genuine, fertile soil of Moravian history.

Another homely little plant.

Jonas stared at the leafy object in the clay pot and tried to appear elated. "Great! What's this one called?"

Emilie regarded him with a dubious look. "It's a *peperomia obtusifolia*. Pepperface, for the uninitiated."

"That would definitely include me." He poked at the leaf, surprised when it felt like wax. *Lord, don't let me kill this one.* Without a doubt, the woman would take it personally. "I don't suppose you'd consider stopping by once a month and watering this for me?"

She gasped. "Once a *month?*"

"Uh…every week?"

Jonas couldn't tell if she was perturbed or pleased. With Emilie, the difference wasn't always obvious.

"If you think it's necessary, I'm certainly willing."

He watched Emilie press her lips together, as if trying to look put out. Instead she looked like she'd happily swallowed a canary. *Pleased, then.*

Without bothering to hide his own grin, he took her free hand and led her into the living room, settling her on the couch before joining her. Close but not *too* close. The woman was still a tad skittish, like a colt getting used to its legs.

"So are we ready to talk Gemeinhaus vs. golf course? It's time Emilie. Past time, to tell the truth. I haven't got a day to spare if I'm going to have everything finished for the grand opening."

She was picking at some lint on her slacks, clearly buying time. "I thought that after…well, after Thursday, you'd be more open to letting me do some digging." Her gaze lifted. "You know. Just a *little* digging?"

He groaned. "There is no such thing as a little digging when it comes to a golf course, Em. We're talking about fully designed and executed greens here. A serious investment. Besides, you don't know the exact spot you'd need to dig up, do you?"

Though her gaze was steady, her light brown eyes flickered slightly, as if shot through with a ribbon of steel. "Not the exact spot, no. We can make very educated calculations based on terrain, but there would be some…ah, exploratory work, no doubt."

No longer willing to relax against the sofa's upholstery, he straightened. "Then the answer is simple. No."

Emilie's back also stiffened. "It's not a question of *you* saying no, Jonas. You don't own the land."

"No, the borough of Lititz does. And I have the support of every man on the steering committee—"

"Every *man*, is it?" She was on her feet. "I should have known!"

"Wait a minute!" He shot up like a rocket. "This is *not* a male–female issue."

"Oh, is that so?" Her eyes were daggers. "What sort of issue is it, pray tell?"

"It's financial." He threw his hands in the air and started pacing. "It's practical. It's legal. It's—"

"It's historical," she shot back, stalking behind him. "It's spiritual. It's ethical."

He stopped and swung around, startling her. "Emilie, we've been over this before. If you had absolute, concrete proof that these ruins existed underground, I'd be the first one to cheer when the archaeologists showed up. But you're working on theory and conjecture and a flimsy map from two and a half centuries ago, a map you don't even *possess.*"

"I've seen it." She sniffed.

"Well, I haven't, and neither has anyone on my team." A problem he planned to remedy somehow. "Remember how you had to stand before your mentoring committee to defend your doctoral dissertation?"

She glared at him. "How would you know about such a thing?"

Oops. "Never mind that now." He put his hands on his hips, hoping it looked menacing. "The point is, however difficult that day was, it was a walk in the park compared to convincing a dozen businessmen that you need to rip up their five-million-dollar golf course."

Her eyes widened. "Five...*million?*"

"You got it, sweetheart. Major moolah."

Her shoulders drooped noticeably. "I had...no idea."

Emilie's look of chagrin almost made him sorry he'd barked at her. *Almost.*

"Jonas, I need time to think. Talk to my academic peers."

"You do that, Em. But time is a luxury I can no longer afford." *Easy, man. The woman is hurting here.* He consciously softened his voice. "We're getting on with things at the course." Reaching out a hand to touch her elbow, he stopped just short of it when she jerked away from him. "Emilie, after all that we've shared—"

"Exactly." Chagrin moved to pure hurt. "I thought you cared about...the same things I did."

"Many of the same things, I do." He leaned toward her, so slowly he felt certain she couldn't detect it. "I care about the Lord and pleasing him. I care about honoring my commitments to this town. I care about the land and how it's used. And I care about you, Emilie Getz. Quite a lot."

She pointed her chin away from him, so their gazes no longer met. "I'm not at all sure how I feel about that last one."

"I'm very sure." He reached up and gently eased her chin back toward him, tipping it up, lightly rubbing his thumb across her tightly closed lips. "Emilie, you need to know something. I've dated plenty of women in my time—"

"Humph!" She started to pull away, but he held her chin firmly.

"Please let me say this. I've never known anyone like you. So utterly different from me and yet we...get along. Very well." He lowered his head ever so slightly. "I'd say exceedingly well." Lower still. "Don't you think?"

Emilie had apparently stopped thinking altogether. In fact, she was barely breathing. Her eyes were fixed on his and her lids were beginning to droop.

"Don't you think?"

She managed a smile. "Think? Not if I can help it." With that, she kissed him. A butterfly sort of kiss, soft and feminine, landing only for a moment, then flitting away. "Jonas, will you promise me that no matter what happens with the land—"

"Yes. I promise." Then he kissed *her.* Not at all like a butterfly. More like an eagle that unexpectedly swoops down on its prey and won't let go as it soars ever upward.

Moments later, when bird and prey made a safe landing, Emilie leaned back to look him in the eye, her daggers long sheathed. "I have a question for you."

"Me first. Are you busy Saturday night?"

Her eyebrows shot up. "Might this be an actual date you're suggesting, Mr. Fielding?"

"Not 'might be.' Yes, a date. A nice Valentine's Eve dinner at the General Sutter Inn. You game?"

Her smile was a thing of beauty. "Of course, silly man. Will you be...ah, wearing that black suit of yours?"

She did *like it.* "Could be. Now, what's your question?"

Stepping back as if to assess him, she pursed her lips. "You mentioned a minute ago about the oral defense of my dissertation. Frankly, that's not the kind of thing a man who plays with dirt usually knows much about. Where exactly did you get your education?"

"Lehigh. For my bachelor's."

"Ohh?"

He grinned, watching her closely. "University of Pennsylvania. For my master's."

Her face went ashen. "Your *what?*"

"And Rutgers." He couldn't keep the grin from spreading to both ears.

"For my Ph.D. in Community and Regional Planning."

"Your…? You…!" He watched her knees buckle. "You're a….a…"

"Yeah, I'm a doc, too." He steadied her wobbly self with one hand, and nudged her on the chin with the other. "But you can still call me Mr. Fielding. I promise I won't mind one bit."

Sixteen

When you fish for love, bait with your heart, not your brain.
MARK TWAIN

"Emilie, when Jonas walks through your door tomorrow night, I want his stubbly jaw to bounce off the hardwood floors."

Confused, Emilie stared across her stack of research books. "You mean because they're freshly polished?"

"No, silly! Because you're gonna look like a stone-cold fox. Something in basic black, I think, to match that suit of his you told me about. Slinky and elegant and—"

"Beth!" Emilie rolled her eyes. "That's ridiculous. Jonas already knows what I look like. Why pretend I'm someone I'm not?"

"Not pretend—*enhance*. And I have just the place for you to spend the day tomorrow, Em. Enhancing." Beth tossed her coat over Emilie's kitchen chair and dropped down into it with a satisfied grin. "Speaking of things heating up around here, can you believe it's seventy-four degrees in February? I hardly needed a jacket today."

"Don't you dare change the subject on me." Emilie sighed and closed the lid on her laptop computer. Writing—and everything else, it seemed—would have to wait while she straightened out her well-meaning young friend. "If you think I'll let someone smear my face with heavy makeup and tease my hair until it sticks out from here to York County, think again."

Beth propped her chin on her folded hands and grinned. "Too late. I've already made an appointment for you at Shear Sensations for their Grand Spa Escape."

Emilie felt her eyebrows lift straight up into V formation. "Their *what?*"

"You heard me. *Escape.* As in get away from your research for one day and let someone pamper you for a change." Beth produced a colorful brochure and cleared her throat importantly. "Beginning tomorrow morning at eight—"

"Eight?"

"You'll be treated to a one-hour Swedish massage—"

Emilie gasped. "Not the kind where you take off all—"

"Then a luxury facial," Beth interrupted, happily ignoring her. "Followed by a spa manicure—I wanna see some outrageous red paint on those nails, Em—then a spa pedicure. Mmm, my toes are so jealous." Beth wiggled her feet in vicarious anticipation. "After your healthy spa lunch, you'll receive a zippy new haircut and style, plus a full makeup application." She folded up the paper and offered a Cheshire cat grin. "I'm having Drew pick you up at ten of eight, so don't even think about calling and canceling."

Emilie gathered what was left of her wits. "But…but who is going to pay for all this? It must be—"

"Not your concern, my dear." Beth's grin didn't budge. "I took up a collection at the church office this morning. Remember those five male staff members you nabbed, red-handed and red-faced, one noteworthy Monday last December?"

She wouldn't! "You didn't?" Emilie gulped. "You…did."

"Done." Beth nodded. "Their contributions were most generous, though I imagine they're hoping this will absolve them completely from any further guilty feelings." Beth handed her the gift certificate. "You'll be finished about three. I'll pick you up and bring you home in time for a long soak in some exotic bath gel. When the doorbell rings, slip into your sleek little black number and voilà—the man's chin will scrape the floor." Beth glanced at her watch. "Quite an agenda, eh?"

"Your agenda, you mean." Emilie fell back against her chair, still reeling. "Besides, I don't own a sleek little number, in any color."

Beth nodded sympathetically. "Precisely why we need to go shopping. I've already asked Mrs. Ressler to baby-sit Sara for an extra two hours. Suppose we grab a quick lunch, then it's Judie, here we come."

"Judie who?"

"No, Judie *what*." Beth stood, sliding her purse over her shoulder. "It's a store—a very nice women's clothing store—not half a block from your house. Bet you've never darkened the door, have you, Em?"

She shrugged. "I peeped in the window once. Does that count?"

"Oh, brother." Pulling Emilie to her feet, Beth steered her toward the front door. "The next two hours will be the most fun you've had in…in…decades."

"Well!" Emilie tried to flounce out the door and realized she was simply not the flouncing type. "Please limit any references to my advanced age, Mrs. Twenty-something, or Judie will be forced to dress me in crinoline."

By two o'clock, Emilie was dressed in something much softer than stiff crinoline—black silk with silvery satin touches around the wrists and the wide, square neckline. The length was a compromise—mid-calf to make her own paranoid-knobby-kneed self happy, yet with a generous slit up the back to please let's-make-his-jaw-drop Beth.

Emilie slid her credit card across the glass countertop with a shaking hand. "How *did* I let you talk me into this?"

"Talk, nothing, girlfriend. The dress sold itself." Beth scanned the jewelry display, holding up one pair of earrings, then another, before settling on two long, slender strands of black jet beads.

Emilie grimaced. "I wouldn't be caught dead in those."

"Perfect." Beth added them to her order. "I want you to show Jonas Fielding that you are not a woman to be trifled with when it comes to that property *and* that he doesn't know you as well as he thinks he does."

"But he *does* know me. Very well." *Too well.* Emilie hadn't sorted through all her sentiments about Jonas Fielding, Ph.D., but of this she was certain: He knew her well enough to hurt her. The last thing she wanted was to have Jonas take one look at her Saturday night and start laughing.

Nate didn't know whether to laugh or cry, so he did both.

Twenty thousand dollars and change!

He pounded the middle-aged guy next to him on the shoulder and slapped high fives with two other winners, both as delirious as he was.

But not as lucky. They'd only placed small bets. He'd bet the farm—all his winnings for the night, some three thousand dollars—on the last race at Orange Park and *won.* Won enough to keep Cy at bay for another couple of weeks. Enough to buy a few more rounds of golf, a few more outfits, a few more decent meals.

Nate's heart was racing as he headed down to the wagering windows to collect, looking neither left nor right, but making a beeline for the money he knew was waiting for him. *Twenty thousand.* He still couldn't believe his luck was back. *Back, I'm tellin' ya!*

Out of nowhere, a stranger stepped in front of him. Sharply dressed. Musclebound. Intimidating. "You look like a fella who's headed for the winner's circle."

Nate didn't know his name, but he knew his type. He squared his shoulders and widened his stance. "How'd you find me?"

"You're smarter than you look." The guy didn't budge. If anything, he inched closer. "But not smart enough to stay away from the first place ol' Cy suggested I try. So. Got the rest of Cy's money?"

Nate maintained eye contact, wishing he could see if this meathead was alone or traveling with a partner. Only one way to find out and that was start walking. "Why don't you follow me over to the window and see what I can send home with you? For Cy, of course."

"'Course." The man stepped aside only long enough to let Nate pass, then fell in next to him, dwarfing him. *Guy must be six-four, two-fifty.* Alone or with company, he was a solid wall of muscle and bad attitude.

There was no point arguing. Nate knew he would give him the check. All of it. Sign it over to Cy on the spot.

So much for groceries.

So much for clothes.

So much for getting ahead for one lousy minute.

The transaction was over before Nate could add in his head the amount he still owed Cy back in Vegas. But the man slipping the check in his pocket knew, to the penny. "That leaves just under eighteen, Mr. Fielding. When should I tell Cy to expect it?"

Nate wasn't about to admit he'd signed away the last of his cash. Betting required seed money, and his had just fallen on rocky ground.

"Soon," Nate said, trying to sound confident.

"No dice. I need a date."

Nate grabbed one out of the smoky air circling around them. "March 1."

"For all of it, right?"

"Yeah. The balance." Where it would come from was anybody's guess. *Eighteen days.* He'd make it. *Somehow.*

The man turned, thumping a thick shoulder against Nate, not by acci-dent. "Look. I know all about San Pablo and the college kid and the leased Jag, okay?" He bent over Nate, whose own six-foot frame felt insignificant in comparison. "In case you don't know how this works, I get a piece of every dollar I collect for Cy. You're a meal ticket for me, kid. Don't do anything stupid."

Nate exhaled as the jerk walked away, not looking back.

He was running out of options. His fictitious rehab program meant it'd be another ten days before he could pick up the phone, call Pennsylvania.

No. He wouldn't call Jonas. *No way.* Not this time. He'd—

Wait! A better plan hit him like lightning on a starless August night. *Of course!* Should have thought of that sooner.

Well, he'd thought of it now.

Relaxed for the first time in weeks, Nate strolled toward the parking lot, jingling his keys in his pocket, laughing like he'd just thought of the funniest one-liner in town.

"Promise you won't laugh?"

Emilie hesitated in the dressing room of Shear Sensations with a bulky terry cloth towel wrapped around her body, her clothes meekly folded over a chair.

"We never laugh," the friendly woman in the white smock assured her on the other side of the door. "First time for a massage, is it?"

"Y-yes." Emilie gulped and stepped into the room decorated in restful cream and peach with a hint of muted purple. "W-where do you want me?"

She would ask that question half a dozen times through the day as the staff shepherded her from room to room, up and down the carpeted stair-case. The Swedish massage was so relaxing she fell asleep. The facial was an hour of bliss, not to mention an ego boost when the aesthetician praised her "flawlessly clear skin." Emilie knew better, but wasn't it a nice thing to say?

By day's end, her fingers and toes were dripping with a drop-dead red they called Wildfire; her eyes, cheeks, and lips shimmered with their own dramatic hues; and her hair was, if not able to reach York County, at least stretching the boundaries of Warwick Township.

Making the most of Emilie's natural curl, the stylist had worked some sort of magic with hair spray and a circular brush, until Emilie's hair swept around her shoulders in a voluminous, tea-colored cloud.

"Wow!" Beth breathed when she picked her up at three. "Never mind his jaw hitting the floor. The man's whole *body* will sink like a stone." Her gaze narrowed. "Are you prepared to call EMS?"

"Such foolishness." Emilie fought the urge to flip down the visor mirror in Beth's car and take another peek. It *was* rather fun seeing herself done up like a siren instead of a scholar. "Imagine what my students at Salem would say if they saw me like this."

"I'll tell you what they'd say: 'Oooh, baby!' So will Jonas."

Emilie shrugged, a stab of uncertainty popping her small balloon of confidence. "I hope he doesn't think he rang the wrong doorbell."

Beth laughed and turned onto Main Street. "Sure wish I could be a fly on the wall. Or a goldfish in a bowl."

"Or a guinea pig in a glass cage?"

"Right! Like Clarice." Beth giggled. "Honestly, where does the man come up with these names?"

"The Lord alone knows. I hate to think of what member of the animal kingdom Jonas might bring me tonight. Considering how enamored he is of Alaska, I'm prepared for something the size of a car. With antlers."

When they reached the Woerner house minutes later, Beth swerved up to the curb and shifted the gear into Park. "Look, I expect play-by-play coverage tomorrow morning after church. Got that?"

Emilie regarded Beth for a moment, a small lump forming in her throat. "How can I thank you for this...ah, unforgettable experience?"

Beth's eyes twinkled. "Liked it, huh?"

"Yes, but more than that. It made me feel...oh, this will sound ludicrous. For the first time in a long time, I felt like...like..."

"A woman?"

Emilie stared at her, amazed. "Exactly! I've always been so focused on taking care of my mind and its many pursuits. This was utterly different."

Beth nodded. "Good. Details tomorrow, hear?"

"I promise. Give my thanks to Drew for picking me up, okay?" Emilie pushed open the door then turned back. "Your husband said you weren't feeling 100 percent this morning. Everything okay?"

"More than okay." Beth's words were assuring, though her features grew unusually still. "I'll be praying about tonight."

"Thanks." Emilie slid out onto the sidewalk then leaned back inside the car. "Above all, pray the man recognizes me without my sling."

"Emilie?"

Jonas stood, slack-jawed, and stared at the beauty poised in the doorway. "Is it really you?"

She laughed, a throaty, musical, un-Emilie sound, though it suited this enchanting creature to a T. "Of course it's me, dear man. Surely a new dress and a little makeup don't make *that* much of a difference."

Now that's where you're wrong, woman.

Something had happened to Emilie. *His* Emilie went around in simple, tailored clothes. *This* Emilie was wearing a black silk dress that molded itself to her womanly curves—since when did Emilie have curves?—and displayed the longest, most tantalizing neck he'd ever laid eyes on.

Don't think about her neck. Think about her keen mind. Think about her grasp of history. Think about...

He realized the silk-wrapped seductress was tugging at his elbow now, bending toward him, releasing a heady perfume he couldn't place. Gardenias, maybe.

Her voice was silky, too. "Won't you come in?"

Just try and stop me.

A pair of sparkling black earrings danced when he brushed past her. Bright red fingernails flashed through the air as she closed the door behind them. Two narrow black straps were all that held her precariously high heels in place as she glided into the living room, then turned back, her features tinged with concern.

"Jonas, are you feeling okay?"

The words came out before he could stop them: "What have you done with Emilie?"

She laughed again, then stepped toward him, running her scarlet fingertips along his lapels. "One trip to a salon, and you don't even recognize me, Dr. Fielding?"

His mouth was moving; his brain was not. "Did you spend...hours there?"

Her brown eyes, newly accented with a sweep of long, dark lashes, narrowed. "Are you implying that it would take a very long time to make such changes?"

"No, no! I just...wondered." He grinned. A stupid-looking grin, judging by her reaction. Her hairstyle was the most striking change of all. Fluffy and full around her delicate face, daring him to run his hands through its fragrant mass of curls.

Oh, man. Ohhh, man.

He had to say something, now. Anything. "Whatever the time or investment involved, it was worth it."

"Thank you." Her voice dropped. "I think. Suppose I get my purse and we move in the direction of the Sutter." She turned her back to him, bending to retrieve her purse from the floor, and revealed for a too-brief moment an exceptional pair of shapely legs.

Whoa.

Emilie rose gracefully and turned around to face him. "Our reservations were for...?"

His mind was a blank slate. "Dinner."

She rolled her eyes, made even more dramatic by the many colors shadowed around them. "Did the restaurant mention a time?"

"Uh...six." He took his eyes off her only long enough to check his watch. "Soon."

"Then shall we?" Slipping her hand around his elbow, she smiled up at him with lips as crimson as her nails.

Jonas gulped. *Probably the same color as your face, fool.*

He'd get it together any second. *Any minute, maybe.* She was, after all, the same Emilie—the very same woman—transformed by nothing more than a new coat of paint.

Yeah, right. Keep talking, Fielding.

Emilie had never seen Jonas Fielding so flustered.

And to think, *she* was the reason!

They were headed out the front door together—her floating, him stumbling—when Jonas saw his Explorer parked by the curb, gasped, and started digging for his keys, as if he'd neglected something important.

"I…uh…almost forgot. I brought you a present." He unlocked the door, then winked over his shoulder. "For Valentine's Day."

"You did?" *And I didn't get him one, thoughtless me.* "Is it that big thing in the back?"

"Yup. You're gonna love it, I promise. Stand back and let me surprise you, okay?" Jonas blocked her view as he opened the back hatch. Grabbing something in both hands, he swung around and held it aloft with a boyish grin.

"Victor, meet Emilie. Emilie, this is Victor."

She nearly fainted. "Jonas, you wouldn't! You *didn't?*"

He lifted his chin proudly. "I did."

"What is it?" Emilie stared at the heavy cage, aghast.

"A parrot," Jonas informed her as he carried Victor inside the house. She trailed in behind him, still in shock, as an enormous, hanging stand and a bucketful of parrot food followed.

Emilie grimaced at the instant clutter in her living room. "Rather a pricey pet, isn't she…uh, *he?*"

"Usually, yes." Jonas brushed off his hands and stood back to survey his newest living contribution to Emilie's happiness. The yellow-headed bird sported bright green feathers with a few dramatic touches of black and red, a large, hooked beak and four toes—two front, two back.

"The barber that sold him was going out of business." Jonas poured some fresh food in Victor's dish. "Gave me the deal of the century." He closed the door and tapped on the cage with obvious affection. "I've taken care of Victor all week, telling him about you, getting him ready for the big move."

"Oh really?" *An opening.* "Perhaps you'll miss Victor." Her voice oozed with sympathy. "You could certainly keep him at your house. Trix wouldn't mind, would she?"

"That's the point." Jonas shifted his warm gaze away from the brightly plumed bird and toward her. "I have Trix to keep me company. Now you'll have Victor."

Then, for the first of many times to come, Victor spoke. *"Pretty girl!"*

His full-volume squawk ruffled Emilie's feathers. "Good heavens! How often does he talk?"

"Whenever he feels he's not getting enough attention. Isn't that right, Victor?"

"Pretty girl!"

Emilie shivered at the grating sound, noticing how her heavily-sprayed hair barely moved when the rest of her did. "Is there some reason this bird only says *pretty girl?*"

Jonas nodded. "While Don's customers sat around getting a shave and a haircut, if a nice-looking woman walked by, one of them invariably commented, 'Pretty girl.' Victor here picked up on it, and there you have it. Besides…" Jonas' eyebrows wiggled meaningfully. "'Pretty girl' certainly seems like an apropos thing to say in this house tonight, don't you agree?"

She smiled, trying hard to look happy about the whole thing. "But isn't Mavis the goldfish enough? And Clarice the guinea pig? You know how much I'm…enjoying them." She went for an emotional pitch. "Do you think a bird is a wise addition? Mavis or Clarice *might* get jealous, you know."

He shook his head emphatically. "You can watch a goldfish, you can talk to a guinea pig, but a bird like Victor that speaks *back?* Now, *that's* really something." Jonas stepped closer, sliding one hand slowly up and down her silk sleeve. "And *you* are really something, Emilie Getz. Have I mentioned that this evening?"

She found her resistance—to parrots, among other things—melting at his gentle touch. "You *did* mention it a time or two. And while we're on the subject—" she turned toward the door—"you look pretty handsome yourself."

Minutes later, she decided *handsome* was also the right word for the three-story brick building that housed their destination for the evening, facing the town square a short stroll from her front door. The General Sutter Inn was almost as old as Lititz itself, offering food and lodging since 1764.

But it wasn't history Emilie had on her mind tonight. It was the clear and present danger of having Jonas Fielding seated across the table from her, wearing his striking black suit and a devilish smile.

He'd recovered, it seemed, from his initial shock at her altered appearance. Catching a glimpse of herself now in the long windows by their corner table, even she did a double-take.

Emilie wasn't sure she liked all the froufrou. She was quite certain she could never reproduce it. But for one night, it was grand fun watching Jonas Fielding behave like an inept adolescent on a first date.

He was trying his best not to stare at her now. Generously granting him an opportunity to look to his heart's content, Emilie gazed out the arched doorway that led to a brick courtyard dotted with half a dozen old maples. In the warmer months, tables were strewn across the bricks and light meals served. It was almost warm enough for that this evening, another midwinter respite from the cold weather that would undoubtedly return all too soon.

"What's on your mind, pretty lady?"

She looked back at him then, noticing how the masculine planes of his face reflected the glow of the candles gracing their table and nestled in the colonial sconces on the wall. "Pretty? Jonas, you have never called me such a thing since the day we met."

"Shame on me. I'll count on Victor to remind me to do so." His dark gaze roamed over her hair and face, then seemed to settle on her neck.

Too long, too thin. She'd never liked her neck, had always been careful to swath it in sweaters, collars, high necklines, anything to hide its endless pale expanse. *Ick.*

"You realize, of course, I'll never look like this again."

His face was the picture of innocence. "Like what?"

"Honestly, Jonas. I haven't the faintest idea how to make my hair poof out like this, or line my eyes, or paint my nails." She glanced down and realized to her horror that her thumbnail had already suffered a tiny chip. "You'll have to take me as is, I'm afraid."

"Nothing to be afraid of there," he said gently.

She was relieved to see his attention focused on her eyes alone. Nonetheless, she rested one hand on either side of her bare neck, a vague image of embarrassed Eve and her fig leaves springing to mind.

Seconds later, a waiter appeared, pen in hand, and they placed their orders. Black Angus beef for him; roasted chicken, all white meat, for her. Their meals were delicious, their conversation warm but guarded. No discussion about the property, she noticed. If it didn't come up during dinner, she intended to pursue the subject the minute they got back to her place.

One thing needed explaining posthaste. "Are you going to tell me why you kept your…ah, advanced education a secret?"

"A secret?" He managed a blank look. "Everybody knows."

"But *I* didn't know."

"You didn't ask." His eyes twinkled. "Until Tuesday."

She exhaled and tamped down her mounting frustration. "Couldn't you have mentioned it yourself?"

"And missed seeing you toss around your credentials at every turn?" He reached for the coffee cup at his elbow, obviously planning to mask a smile.

"Point taken." She pursed her lips, considering her next question. "Is it customary for a land developer to have a master's, let alone a Ph.D.?"

"Nope." He put down his coffee, his expression decidedly more serious. "Most of my peers at Rutgers had designs on teaching at the university level. I've got enough of my dad in me, I thought I might pursue that angle, too." His lengthy sigh spoke volumes. "After one semester in the classroom, I discovered I liked the hands-on stuff better. Working with local government. Building a community first, making money second." He shrugged. "Guess I'm an overeducated dirt pusher who likes to help people."

And a modest one at that. The humility was genuine, as real and honest as the man himself.

Emilie sensed her chest constricting, right near the spot where her heart rested safely. *Maybe not so safely.* Until now, Jonas had been an articulate, attractive diversion. *Try again, Em.* He hadn't merely diverted her, he'd steered her into deeper waters than she'd ever known existed.

He was regarding her with eyes that held no more secrets. Instead they shone with sincerity and integrity and something else, something at once foreign and familiar and altogether frightening.

Jonas cared for her.

And I care for him.

It was more than that, really. More than *care for* yet not quite *love.* Such a potent word, that. Was there nothing in the middle?

"Emilie, remember the Monday after your accident, the day we sat watching the creek overflow and I told you about my father?"

She nodded solemnly. *As if I could forget.*

He sighed. "It's taken me years to wrestle through the pain of his drowning. Suddenly I was a kid without a dad. Confused at first, then angry with everybody, but mostly with God."

"You were mad at God?" *Could one express such a thing and survive?*

"God is hardly a stranger to anger, Emilie. He knows how to handle it. Especially when it stems from a broken heart, which it usually does."

"But you had a right to be mad." *Didn't he?* "And to be heartbroken."

"Yes." He shifted on his chair to face her more fully. "I just didn't want to live there. I wanted someone to love me as much as my dad did, someone who could understand my anger and forgive it."

Emilie nodded slowly. "So…did your mother fill that role?"

His chuckle caught her off guard. "My mother was a fine person, Emilie, but she could never fill my father's shoes. Only the Lord could do that. See, it was losing my earthly father that sent me in search of a heavenly one."

He seemed to relax at that admission. "'Course, I didn't know that at the time. But since I figured it out a few years back…" He shrugged. "I guess I thought I'd share it with you."

She slipped her hand across the table and touched the strong fingers resting on his coffee cup. "I'm honored that you did, Jonas." *Honored? Is that the best you can do, Em?* "You mean…a lot to me." *Better.* "It's wonderful to know how your relationship with the Lord came about." She felt her skin warm. "After all, you were there when my own took wing."

He nodded, all the tension gone from his face, a wistful smile playing on his lips. "A nice way to put that, Emilie. How are you two flying along these days?"

She chewed on her lower lip, realizing her Wildfire mouth was no longer such a vivid hue. "I've noticed little things. My time in the *Daily Texts,* for example, has been more meaningful. More personal."

"Good. What else?"

"I think about other people more." *Especially you, Jonas.*

He signaled the waiter for their check, then leaned forward, his eyes merry with expectation. "Anyone in particular?"

She pretended to scowl. "Are you fishing for compliments again?"

"I had beef, you had chicken—the only thing left on the menu is seafood."

At that, they both laughed, winding down in tandem to a silent exchange of significant glances.

"So…" he began, then paused, his eyes trained on hers.

"So," she echoed, uneasy with the direction things were going, yet just as eager to press on. The uneasiness won out and Emilie smoothly pivoted their discussion along a different vein. "Your relationship with God is solid. Are all your brothers on the same footing?"

"Two out of three." His voice was low as he leaned sideways to pull out his credit card, the magic between them vanishing like will-o'-the-wisp.

Between Chris, Jeff, and Nathan, she was fairly certain who the prodigal son might be, though now she wished she'd let things move in a more tender direction. Perhaps later. Perhaps not.

Don't be such a scaredy-cat, Em!

They rose to leave, winding through the dining room, drawing attention with every step. Emilie glanced back over her shoulder, then forward again, smiling to herself. Odd as it felt, they made a rather handsome couple in their black dressy attire. Scooping up complimentary mints at the front desk, they stepped out the door onto Main and found the balmy afternoon temperatures had fallen considerably.

Unprepared, Emilie gasped when the decidedly colder night air hit her neck and shoulders. Her silk-and-satin dress was no match for February's changeable weather. "I knew I should have worn a coat," she murmured, hurrying down the steps. Home was only one full block away, but her nonsensical shoes slowed her down, even as her pride kept her going.

They were in front of Benner's Pharmacy when Jonas finally talked her into wearing his jacket, which quickly swallowed her up in its black folds. It held his warmth, though, and his savory scent, both of which made her forget she was wearing such ridiculous shoes.

Seventeen

◆

Everyone's faults are not written in their foreheads.
ENGLISH PROVERB

"Pretty girl! Pretty girl!"

Ten minutes of listening to Victor squawk his one and only phrase and Emilie was ready to wring his ugly little parrot neck. Would have, in fact, if a certain bachelor weren't busy nibbling on her own neck as they sat on the couch, comfortably entwined in each other's arms while a CD of Moravian chamber music played softly on the stereo.

Only one thing worried her: Jonas was even more attentive than usual. Was it just the snazzy dress and big hair? The dramatic makeup and colorful nails? Those things were fun but they weren't *her.* What if he *preferred* her this way? Would he still care for plain old Emilie?

No, Em. Don't go there. Not now, not tonight.

She also didn't have the heart to bring up the Gemeinhaus property and the progress she'd made that week, putting together a knowledgeable dig team. She could discuss that with Jonas on Monday, couldn't she? When he wasn't sitting there in his black suit, looking so utterly appealing? And she wasn't sitting next to him in her silk dress, feeling the most feminine she had ever felt in her purely academic life?

The hour was late when Jonas sat back and studied her, long enough to make her feel uncomfortable with his frank assessment. "What is it?" She huffed and swatted at his tie—bright red this time, for Valentine's Eve—wishing he'd say whatever it was he had in mind. "Out with it, please."

"Will you be offended if I asked to look through your purse?"

"My *purse?* I don't see why…I mean, it's not appropriate." *Really, Em! What would he find in there that matters?* She groaned. "Oh, all right, I suppose." Emilie handed it over, disapproval intentionally drawn on her features.

He seemed not to notice, intent as he was on digging through her black leather bag and pulling out a handful of assorted items that had little in common except that they belonged to her.

"Ah." Apparently satisfied, he put the purse aside, reached up with both hands and began smoothing her hair back with a comb, first one side, then the other, jamming in a few hair pins here and there with no finesse whatsoever.

"Jonas, what are—?"

"Shhh." He tweaked her nose and kept pinning, smiling more broadly with each second that passed.

She could feel her overblown hairstyle growing more tame as he worked, though the way he was poking those pins in there, she feared how it might look when he finished.

"There." He sat back with a nod of satisfaction. "Much better. Next item." He took her old navy scarf—a sling from her weeks of recovery, stuffed in her purse just in case—and tucked it around her neckline.

At least *that* made sense. Cover up all that ghastly bare skin.

Then he took a tissue and patted her lips. Gently, as if he were kissing her with his fingertips, carefully blotting the remains of her Wildfire lipstick. His ministrations did odd things to her heart, sending it off to do cartwheels. Was he planning to kiss her but hated lipstick? Was *that* what all this was about?

Finally, he lifted her reading glasses out of their embroidered case and unfolded them, holding them out to her. "Slip these on, will you?"

Bewildered but willing, she slid them over her ears and eased them down onto the bridge of her nose. Jonas' handsome face came into perfect focus.

"Emilie," he said in a hoarse whisper. "Say something historic."

"Do *what?*"

"Please?" Jonas engaged his most effective weapons—lowered chin, puppy-dog eyes, a slight pout of that generous bottom lip—and added plaintively, "For me?"

"Jonas, this is—"

"Please, Emilie?"

Honestly! How could she refuse such a man?

Clearing her throat, she assumed her classroom voice: "Beginning in 1796, reference is made to the Wachovia Wagons, which managed frequent trips between Moravian settlements in North Carolina and those to the north in Bethlehem by way of—"

Then he kissed her. Thoroughly. Passionately.

She would *almost* say he besieged her mouth, so swift and thorough was his attack, if it hadn't also felt absolutely wonderful.

"Jonas, what—"

A second kiss, more remarkable than the first, left her wide-eyed and speechless. Though not permanently.

"Jonas, *explain* yourself!" She pressed her hands on his lapels, holding him at arm's length.

His lethal grin subsided only slightly. "Emilie, I must confess, when I first saw you this evening, I was dumbfounded."

"I noticed." She tried not to sound smug.

"The women at that salon—"

"And Beth," she reminded him.

"Right, *and* Beth, are to be commended for turning you into a first-rate fox. I was duly impressed, Emilie. Believe me."

"Was?" Hmmm.

"The point is, I would never want you to think that such trappings matter to me."

Emilie blinked. "You mean they don't?"

"Nah." He softly nudged her chin with his knuckle. "That kind of beauty-in-a-bottle stuff wears off. I've dated plenty of supposedly pretty women, so trust me, I know what I'm talking about. *This* is the woman I most admire." He pulled her to her feet and turned her toward the hall mirror. "See? Dr. Emilie Getz, my favorite historian."

Her eyes almost bugged out of her head. "Aaah!"

Her scream woke Victor and started him shrieking, *"Pretty girl! Pretty girl! Pretty girl!"*

Appalled, she shrank away from her reflection. *"Pretty?* Nothing could be farther from the truth, you idiotic bird!" Her hair was tightly pinned in blobs and clumps all over her head, the plain scarf around her neck looked absurd with her fancy dress, and her glasses were meant to assist her reading, not her looks.

Emilie whirled around to face her Pygmalion, feeling close to tears. "Jonas, have you lost your mind?"

"Yup." He gathered her up in his arms, slipping off her glasses and tucking them in his suit pocket. "It seems I've lost it entirely to a woman who doesn't understand how beautiful she is to me. All the time. As is. No improvements needed."

Jonas' voice grew softer with every word until he uttered the last with the slightest of breaths, hovering over her lips, his only punctuation a cartwheel-spinning kiss.

Nathan Fielding had never been without a car, without cash, and without friends.

Until now.

Looking out the grimy window of his taxi, Nate watched the familiar landmarks of Jacksonville flash past him for the last time.

His thirty days in "rehab" were over. So were his chances for scraping together another eighteen thousand in Jacksonville. He'd sold everything he owned but his body. The designer-label clothes he'd hoped to build a wardrobe around were bartered for a bus ticket. His most prized possession—his Cobra golf clubs—were gone as well, sold for a third of what they were worth. At first, he'd hoped to turn the extra cash into a bonanza at the track. By the end, it was barely enough money to keep his head above water.

This morning—Monday, the twenty-second—he'd left a note and a twenty for Rick, ashamed it was so little, embarrassed just to disappear like that.

He'd make it up to the kid, someday, somehow.

Delivering the Jaguar back to Budget Rent-a-Car had been harder still. The young woman behind the counter handed him his paperwork with a toothy smile. "Did you enjoy the ride?"

He shrugged, averting his eyes. "Yeah, it was okay."

It was the nicest car he'd ever driven, but he wasn't telling her that. Not when he had to sneak around the corner and call a cab to get him to the bus station. *Quite a step down, buddy.* The backseat of the taxi was filthy, the driver's language more so. *And you think you deserve better, huh?*

Nate slumped down against the vinyl upholstery and checked his watch. If this guy stepped on it, they'd get to the Greyhound bus station in time for the 5:15. Ironic that he was leaving town via Greyhound. If the greyhounds at Orange Park had been more cooperative, he could have stayed in Jacksonville, bought himself that high-end condo, *owned* a Jag instead of renting one.

Stop daydreaming, Nate.

The cabbie pulled up to the curb, flipped the meter off and barked out the amount, then reached around with an open palm. Nate slapped one of his last twenties in the man's hand and let himself out. No luggage. No briefcase. Just the clothes on his back, eighty-two dollars in cash, a Bible he'd stolen out of the hotel, and a one-way bus ticket north.

Not much to show for thirty days of rehab.

His laugh sounded bleak, even to himself, as he followed the signs for his departure gate, checking his ticket, hanging on to it like a lifeline.

Not much to show for thirty years of living.

That was the truth of it. The sad and awful truth.

He was sober—but only because he couldn't spare enough cash to be otherwise.

He was as lean as he'd been in high school—but only because he was down to one meal a day.

He was safe—but only until Cy caught up with him. He had one week left, and the clock was ticking louder by the minute. Even now he found himself looking over his shoulder, checking for the bozo who'd cleaned him out at the track. He'd said he knew about the Jag. Did he know the lease was up today? Was he watching for him here?

Nate lengthened his stride, keeping his eyes on the Greyhound bus that would take him where he desperately needed to go, a place where maybe— just maybe—he could kill two birds with one stone.

Get the debt to Cy off his shoulders once and for all.

And get his golf game—maybe even his life—back on top.

Handing the gray-haired agent his ticket, Nate fought the urge to scan the crowd around him and simply stared at the open bus door that led to his future.

"You're all set." The woman gave him back his punched ticket. "Arrives at noon Tuesday in Lancaster, Pennsylvania. Pretty place."

"That's what I hear, ma'am." He relaxed—all the way to his soul—for the first time in a week. "Pretty. That's it exactly."

"Pretty girl."

Emilie closed her eyes, remembering. Even now, ten days after their magical Valentine's Eve together, she could still sense Jonas in the room, holding her close, whispering in her ear, insisting his admiration for her was more than skin deep.

Telling her that he valued her fine mind more than her fine features.

Convincing her that he treasured her soft heart more than her soft skin.

Assuring her that he applauded her spiritual discoveries more than her historical ones.

Believing him was easy. This was Jonas Fielding, the most honest, caring, straightforward man she had ever known.

And despite all his arguments about her more intellectual attributes, he had also called her—

"Pretty girl!" Victor hollered, flapping his wings.

Emilie's eyes flew open and she laughed merrily. "The very word, you silly parrot. He called me pretty. And you, mister, should consider yourself lucky you're not sitting out on my porch this morning."

Tossing a covering over his cage, she peered out the window at a frosty Tuesday on Main, then turned the heater up another notch. At daybreak the thermometer in her kitchen window had read a startling twelve degrees. *Twelve!* Too cold for anything but staying indoors, working on her research, and sipping gallons of hot tea.

Without a car—and with Jonas busy slaving over his clubhouse—she was content to be home alone in her quiet, cozy cottage with only a ticking clock to penetrate the stillness.

A ticking clock and one muffled but determined parrot.

"Pddy grrl!" Victor squawked through the quilted covering.

"Well, kwawk to you, Victor," Emilie crowed, laughing as she yanked off his cover. "Kwawk, kwawk, kwawk."

It was only then that the truth hit her: Jonas had presented her with a *bird* and she hadn't even flinched at the possible connection to her disastrous heron routine. The simple fact was, she hadn't thought of it, nor had he implied such a thing. It was just a *bird*. A gift, not a cruel reminder.

The memory of that incident had faded along with the bitterness and every bit of the pain. *Rather incredible, Lord.* Bit by bit, she sensed the less-than-lovely kinks in her personality being carefully smoothed out by a loving hand. Jonas' attentions were a factor as well, but she knew this was something else again.

Something life-changing. Something eternal.

Emilie settled into her favorite overstuffed chair, grateful to have the full use of both arms and hands again. The area around her collarbone was still tender but—according to her doctor—healing nicely. Despite Jonas' odd fascination with her scrawny neck, the man kindly steered away from her injury, prayed over it instead, then headed elsewhere to plant a kiss.

Their friendship—or whatever it was these days—had survived the bird count caper. Their next hurdle was the Gemeinhaus property, which was not, she had to confess, an issue of eternal significance. It just felt like one. A milestone in her career to balance out the millstone around her neck called Bethabara.

Trouble was, Carter's Run was equally important to Jonas. His first municipal golf course. A five-million-dollar budget. A whole town cheering him on to victory.

Did she expect Jonas to put his plans on hold for her?

Was Jonas waiting for her to do the same for him?

Emilie rubbed at her temple, a tension headache popping up out of nowhere. The change in the weather, perhaps. *Or a change of heart.* She looked at her research scattered around her, years of labor with little reward, poised to be published for an academic world that thrived on new discoveries and old digs.

Her peers would applaud. But would the Lord?

All her life she'd considered *compromise* a dirty word, one never used in polite company by a determined, strong-willed woman like her. Now her notebooks full of facts and figures seemed a coldhearted pursuit compared to the very warmhearted Jonas Fielding and the Lord who loved them both.

Her morning reading in the *Daily Texts* came to mind: "Guide us in meeting our deepest needs." *Well, then.* This definitely fell under the deep need category. She could ask, yes?

Emilie looked up and exhaled, as if preparing herself for a daunting task. "Lord, if you're listening—and I know you are—might you offer a bit of guidance here?"

Jonas shoved his calculator aside and ran a hand through his hair. "These figures don't make any sense."

Dee Dee Snyder, dressed in a snug-fitting, jade green sweater dress, perched on the edge of his desk and leaned back at a saucy angle. "Maybe you're looking at the wrong figure."

Oh, brother. He kept his head down, ignoring her blatant pitch. "Dee Dee, you know better."

With an exaggerated groan, she straightened and hopped to her feet. "Okay, okay. A girl can try, can't she? Anyway, rumor has it you prefer plain-faced professors."

"Not all of them," he countered, then grinned. "Just one." *Who is anything but plain to me.* He didn't know which had changed more—Emilie Getz's face or his taste—but she had blossomed into the most breathtaking beauty he'd ever known.

The blond bombshell in front of him might be most men's idea of heaven. For him, she was a business associate in a dress. Period. Emilie, on the other hand, was an incredible intellect wrapped inside an angelic face and form.

Thinking about her this morning made it hard to concentrate on the spreadsheets in front of him. She'd be home writing, naturally, keeping warm on this bitterly cold Tuesday, while he was getting hot under the collar about weather-related construction delays on the site. Finish the library by June? No problem. Finish the clubhouse by April? Big problem.

Dee Dee gathered her papers and stuffed them in her bulging briefcase. "You haven't told me yet. What are you doing with the original clubhouse site that's still sitting there, undeveloped?"

Jonas leaned back in his chair. "To be honest, I haven't given it much thought. It's right next to the new construction. Could give us room for more parking."

She waved her hand dismissively. "Waste of land. You have plenty of parking. What about a free-standing pro shop?"

He'd thought of that one himself, then ruled it out due to cost. "I'll run the numbers again, Dee Dee. Kinda like to finish the clubhouse first."

"Sure." She reached for his desk phone, then paused with her hand over the receiver. "Sorry…uh, mind if I make a call or two?"

"You're welcome to use the phone in the front room." He smiled, but only with his lips. Dee Dee was one to watch. Too chummy, too catty, too unpredictable. In her business dealings, she was above reproach, but in all other areas of her life, the woman was serious trouble.

She sashayed out of the room, swinging everything she owned, while Jonas just shook his head and turned his attention to the Carter's Run master construction schedule. It was filled with scribbled notations, new time lines, and urgent phone numbers—land planners, architects, course builders, his construction superintendent, the borough's attorney—the list went on and on.

The course itself was coming together on time and on budget. Lord willing, they'd be planting pine trees next week—big ones, up to eight inches in diameter—using a tree spade. Jonas couldn't wait to see the giant yellow machines with their hydraulically powered scoops strategically dropping trees all over Carter's Run. Unlike courses that wrapped themselves around prime real estate lots, this was a core course, compact and contiguous, which meant the trees were a key element to keeping it from looking like one big, hilly meadow.

Grass was next on the agenda—#419, one of the fastest-growing, most aggressive of the hybrid Bermudas. For the tees, it'd be #328, a finer-bladed grass. He'd done his homework and was therefore steeling himself for how pitiful the fairways would look at first. Spotty, weedy, nothing like a real golf course. Three weeks after the first sprigging, the mowers would arrive, and with them, the hope of greens to come.

And, of course, there was the clubhouse going up on the recently purchased acreage, thanks to Dee Dee's sharp negotiating abilities. They had the property cleared, the foundation poured, the driveways carved out. It was the wildly changing weather that was doing them in. Seventy-four degrees ten days ago, and now *this*. Twelve degrees did not create ideal conditions for framing a building. There were cracks in the concrete because of expansion and contraction, and the environmental expert kept making ominous noises about potential drainage hassles.

Then there was the biggest challenge of all: his eighteenth hole. His fully designed, nothing-left-but-the-turf eighteenth hole. The one with a hint of history below the surface.

Maybe.

That's what was doing him in. *Maybe*. If he knew, absolutely, that Emilie's Gemeinhaus had once stood there, he would dig the blasted greens up himself. But he didn't know. It wasn't a matter of faith, but of *proof*. Emilie had plenty of the former and hardly any of the latter. Her womanly intuition about the thing wouldn't cut it with the committee. What she needed was that map. He'd considered tracking the thing down himself, if only to get some answers, then realized they might be answers he didn't like.

Which left him in a quandary almost as big as his pounding headache.

If he ignored Emilie's wishes and pressed on with construction, would it hurt her—and their relationship—beyond repair?

Oh, yeah. Dumb question.

If he granted her permission to tear up the course, unquestionably delaying the grand opening, meaning lost revenue and lost momentum for the project, would he have the town—or at least his committee—at his throat?

Count on it.

He needed a serious dose of wisdom on this one. Godly wisdom, not man-made. Today's *Daily Texts* had talked about seeking the Lord's guidance. *Good plan.* A stray memory verse surfaced: "Guide me in your truth and teach me." *That's it, Lord. Exactly what's needed here.*

The dull ache spreading across his forehead ceased at the exact moment a certain pain in the neck sauntered back into his office.

Dee Dee paused inches from his desk, her hands parked provocatively on her hips. "Appreciate you letting me use your phone."

He nodded, feeling the ache building again. "And I appreciate you stopping by with this paperwork."

She seemed hesitant to leave, putting her briefcase back down and regarding him with a bemused look. "I'm always happy to see you, Jonas. In fact…" She glanced at her watch. "It's almost one. Wanna grab a quick lunch somewhere?"

"I'll be honest, I'm not very hungry, Dee—"

A familiar voice from the hallway called out, "Well, *you* may not be hungry, brother, but I'm starving."

Jonas bolted to his feet, his headache forgotten. *"Nate?"*

Before he could blink, his brother was standing in the doorway, ragged around the edges but grinning from ear to ear.

"Nathan!" He covered the half dozen steps between them in less time than it took to offer up a prayer of thanksgiving, then wrapped his younger brother in a bear hug.

Nate. A prodigal and then some. What he was doing in Lititz was anybody's guess. *Doesn't matter. He's here.* And sober, best Jonas could tell. And smiling.

Jonas stepped back, leaving a hand on each shoulder as he gave his brother a once-over. "On the scrawny side, aren't you?"

"Scrawny!" Dee Dee's voice rose into a question mark.

He'd completely forgotten she was there.

"If that's scrawny, I'd hate to see the man after he pumped some iron." Her approving tone sounded more like a purr.

"So," Nate said, checking her out over Jonas' shoulder. "Are you the woman I heard suggesting lunch? 'Cause if my *much* older brother is too busy, I've got all the time in the world for you, darlin'."

Jonas spun around and gave Dee Dee his don't-even-think-about-it look. Smart woman that she was, she picked right up on it.

"You know, handsome boy, I'd love to take you to lunch, but I'll bet you and your brother have lots of catching up to do. Will you take a rain check?"

"I'm more of a Nevada/Florida kinda guy." He flashed her his version of the Fielding grin. "So I'd rather take a *sun* check from you, Blondie."

Dee Dee laughed and gathered her things, shaking her head as she walked out the door. "I'm not sure this town is big enough for *two* gorgeous Fielding men." Turning at the door, she volleyed her parting shot. "Since it seems you're already spoken for, Jonas, I hope you'll give your brother here my phone number. Nathan, is it? I'll be expecting your call."

Seconds later, the front door closed behind her, leaving the two of them in a quiet office, grinning at one another.

"Sure wish you'd warned me you were coming, Nate. The minute my heart stops hammering, you are a dead man."

"Correction." Nathan dropped into an empty seat in front of the desk, obviously pleased with himself about something. "I *was* a dead man. Deader than dead. Lost, blind, the whole bit. But now I'm alive. I'm not lost, I'm found." He leaned across the desk, his tone urgent, pleading. "I see, man. I *see*. Do you get what I'm saying?"

Jonas fought the hope that was building in his chest, not wanting to make assumptions or put words in Nate's mouth. "Nathan, the question is, do *you* know what you're saying?" He slowly sank into the leather chair behind his desk, his senses on full alert. Trix, who'd been watching from the sidelines, wagged her way over, her shaggy blond tail beating the air with a joyful rhythm, her bobbing head begging to be petted.

Dutifully reaching over to scratch her, he looked at Nate—*really* looked at him. His brother's dark eyes, so much like his own, were clear and in focus for the first time in what, ten years? fifteen? Jonas ran his hand over his face, buying time, afraid of being disappointed, yet hoping, praying, he was right.

"Okay, brother, something's happened here. What gives?"

Nathan fell back in his chair, chuckling. "You mean you wanna hear what happened to your bad-boy brother?"

Folding his arms across his chest, Jonas nodded. "Shoot. And start at the beginning."

"How far back do you want me to go?" Nate leaned forward again, his tanned arms resting on his muscular thighs. "You know most of the story. I screwed up, man. Big time. Sixteen ways to Wichita." He shrugged. "I'm... I'm not there anymore, that's all. I...I'm..."

"You're what?" Nathan *had* made a mess of his life, despite every chance for success thrown his way—usually by Jonas. He felt the cords in his neck tighten. "Why are you here, little brother? Hoping for another check?"

Nate looked like he'd been struck.

Sorry, Lord. Shouldn't have been so blunt.

After taking a moment to recover, Nate's wide grin returned. "Don't trust me, huh? Can't blame you for that, bro. I've not exactly been a model sibling the last decade or so. Not like the twins."

Jonas kept his arms folded but gentled his voice. No matter what the guy did, he was his brother. "Like I said, what's up?"

Nate gulped and blurted out, "I...I found God."

"You *what?*" Something like joy washed over Jonas. "Are you...are you serious?"

"Serious as a birdie on the ninth, brother Jonas." Nate stood to face him, his suntanned skin uncommonly pink. "I figured you oughtta be the first to know."

For the second time that afternoon, they were locked in a bear hug, pounding each other on the back, laughing and choking back tears at the same time.

Nate's voice was muffled against his chest. "I hoped you'd be happy about it."

"Happy? You gotta be kidding." Jonas shook his head as he pushed himself away, one hand still gripping his brother's neck. "I've prayed for this for so long I...well, all I can say is, it's about time. Looks like that rehab place poured some sense into you. Worth every penny, bro." He squeezed Nate's shoulder then dropped his hand, smiling so hard it hurt. "I'd almost given up on you, man. I'm glad the Lord didn't."

"Me too, Jonas." He jerked his thumb in the direction of the rest of the house. "Mind if I sleep on the couch for a few days?"

Jonas snorted. "What, are you kidding? My house is yours. Throw your gear in the guest room at the end of the hall." He stretched a kink out of his back muscles, then dropped back into his chair. "Look, I wanna hear all the details on how you and the Lord got your life together, understood? Meanwhile, how 'bout some lunch?"

Nate's eyes brightened. "You buyin'?"

Jonas laughed. "Who else?"

Eighteen

◆

*However small it is on the surface, it is four thousand miles deep; and
that is a very handsome property.*
CHARLES DUDLEY WARNER

The resemblance was striking.

Emilie watched Jonas and Nathan Fielding stroll into church seconds
before the prelude. They had the same height and build, the same shadow
of a beard on their chins, the same broad smiles. Nathan favored brighter
colors than his older brother's basic black, but the men were clearly cut out
of the same bolt of cloth.

While the organist launched into a favorite by Johann Schneider, Emilie
tried not to stare, though heaven knows everyone else was. Nathan wasn't a
surprise to her like he was to most of the others in the congregation. She'd
heard about his sudden appearance four days ago when Jonas stopped by
with Clyde, a male guinea pig.

Lifting the screened top on Clarice's glass cage last Wednesday, Jonas had
lowered a brown-and-white, long-haired partner for the girl cavy to meet,
then dropped the top in place with a wink in Emilie's direction. "I read that
females don't thrive when they're left alone too long."

"You *read* that, did you?" Emilie folded her arms over her sweater. "Where?"

He dipped his chin to meet her gaze. "I didn't know I'd have to cite the reference."

Shaking her head, she feigned disdain. "Such sloppy scholarship will cost you, Dr. Fielding."

"Oh, yeah?" He bent closer. "What's the fine?"

"Two kisses for the first offense." She bit back a smile. "Four if it happens again."

"In that case." He pulled her against him, folded arms and all. "I neglected to tell you where I read about the best kind of pellets for parrots last week. Wanna get all four kisses over with at once?"

And so they had, with Clarice and Clyde paying no attention whatsoever.

Emilie smiled at the memory. With any luck, he'd be quoting more unsubstantiated material this morning.

Across the sanctuary, Jonas caught her in the act of pretending not to see him and wiggled his eyebrows. With eyebrows like his, it was not a subtle move. Everyone in her pew—Beth, Drew, and Sara included—started giggling.

"Shhh!" Biting her lip, Emilie aimed her attention upstairs to the organ, the choir, the stained-glass windows, *anything* to avoid watching the entire church ogle the two brothers walking toward the front. Toward her.

Jonas' stage whisper belonged on Broadway. "Mind if we join you?"

She had no choice but to slide over and make room for them. Not that she minded—not hardly—but her hour of worship would soon turn into a struggle between flesh and spirit. Her spirit longed to have a quiet time of rest in the Lord's house. Her flesh wanted nothing more than to play footsie with Jonas Fielding.

Ah! Nathan filed in first. *Good. Problem solved.*

After Nathan sat down next to her with a friendly nod, his older brother leaned forward and shot her an intense, sidelong glance that made her heart do a quick handspring. *That man!* It was several minutes before she could get her mind fully back on worship. *Lord, this hour is for you. Help me enter into your presence.*

The opening hymn helped, the liturgy even more so. How the familiar words spoke to her now!

"Your love compels us to live not for ourselves but for you."

Emilie let them sink in, even as her lips formed the syllables. The words had not changed; it was her heart that was different. She knew the One for whom she sang. She knew the One whom the liturgy described and celebrated. *Knew him!* Lately, she'd found herself nodding in agreement as she recited the liturgy aloud and reading with more conviction. With—dare she say it?—more passion.

"You fill our hearts with the love of God."

Jesus loved her—loved Emilie! And she loved him back. It was getting harder to be solemn about the whole thing when she wanted to shout it from the steeple: "I am my beloved's, and my beloved is mine!"

That Jonas cared for her was delightful.

That Jesus cared for her was everything.

Aglow with her thoughts, she beamed at Pastor Yeager while he thoroughly expounded page two of his Lenten sermon. He was nearing a key point when Emilie felt a distinct nudge in her ribs. *From Nathan?* She shot him a surreptitious glance, and saw nothing but eyelids at half mast and a slightly slack mouth. Obviously the young man was having a hard time staying awake.

The mysterious prodding couldn't have been from Beth, whose attention was riveted toward the pulpit. And Jonas certainly didn't reach around his brother to poke her.

That left one option...*Lord? Is that you?*

Emilie dropped her gaze to the rack of hymnals, feeling an odd chill run over her. No one else heard their heartfelt conversation, right? This was just between her and the Lord, yes?

The silent inner nudging became more pronounced.

Her stomach tightened. *You want me to do what, Lord? Let go of my land? My Gemeinhaus land? Oh, Father! Surely not.*

His answer was swift and certain: *Not your land, Emilie. My land.*

She swallowed hard when the truth stuck in her throat. Every inch of the earth belonged to the Lord. It was not hers to claim.

To make matters worse, her motives weren't pure and Emilie knew it. She wasn't planning on digging up that ground to please her Creator; she wanted to please herself. To satisfy her pride, to gain recognition among her peers, to get the bitter taste of Bethabara out of her mouth.

Could she let it go? Let it be a sacrifice, an offering to God? Like incense on the altar, like a fragrant aroma?

She could. She *would*. Today, now, right after the service.

One line from the closing hymn—written nearly three centuries earlier, she couldn't help noting—gave her the courage she needed. "Before the hills in order stood, or earth received its frame," she sang, tears springing to her eyes, "from everlasting, you are God, to endless years the same."

After the benediction, with her tears quickly blinked into submission, Emilie took a deep breath and turned to the men on her left, offering her hand and a smile. "You must be Nathan."

Jonas jumped in first. "Brother Nathan, meet Dr. Emilie Getz. The woman I...uh, told you about, remember?"

"So you did." Nate took her hand in his. "I'm Nathan. The *other* single Fielding. So it's *Dr.* Getz, huh? I'm impressed." His dark-eyed gaze, so much like his brother's, lingered on hers for a moment. "Very impressed," he added, squeezing her hand two beats longer than necessary.

Goodness! What had Jonas called him once? "The real ladies' man of the four." *Well!* If Nathan was serious about turning over a new leaf with the Lord, such obvious flirtation was one habit that needed curbing and soon. Otherwise, he'd be breaking women's hearts all over Lititz.

Jonas led them toward the back of the sanctuary, then waited for her outside. The minute she was within reach, he captured both her hands in his, at once wrapping the two of them in their own private world, despite the fact that they were standing at the center of busy Church Square with Nathan and the Landises hovering nearby.

Though Jonas held her at a proper distance, his gaze engulfed her. "You look like a woman with a secret."

"Not for long." She hadn't realized it was possible to grin so broadly that it hurt her cheeks. *Here we go, Lord.* "You and I haven't chatted since Wednesday about that particular piece of property on Kissel Hill Road."

His features lost some of their sparkle. "That's not a secret, Em. That's a conflict. One I keep hoping we'll resolve."

"And so we shall, this very instant."

His bushy eyebrows shot north. *"Now?"*

"Now." Her joy spilled over into laughter. "Jonas Fielding, consider yourself the proud manager of a quarter acre of land with no historical encumbrance on your construction site whatsoever. In other words, it's all yours, handsome."

His astonished expression froze in place. "Are you sure?"

"I am." The peace stealing over her soul confirmed it. "Very sure."

With a loud *"Whoopee!,"* Jonas wrapped his arms around her in broad daylight with a hundred spectators gawking away, and squeezed her so hard she gasped for air.

"Jonas—stop! I—can't—breathe!"

"Oops." He abruptly released her to a chorus of chuckles. "Sorry," he murmured, steering her farther down the sidewalk while Nathan and Drew hung back and got acquainted. "Does this mean your research took you in another direction?"

"You could say that." Try as she might, Emilie knew the silly grin on her face was not going to yield. "I had a little talk with God about that property this morning—"

"In church?"

"Seemed like a logical place to me." Her shrug was nonchalant, but her heart was beating like a kettle drum. "Anyway, this is what the Lord wants me to do: Release my interest in the land and let you press on. There you have it, Jonas. Happy?"

His gaze narrowed. "I'm only happy if you are, Em. I don't cotton to the idea of having you remind me for years to come, 'Look at all I gave up for you, Fielding.' "

Emilie felt her neck grow warm. *"Years to come,"* is it?

She lifted her chin, as though to cool herself, then raised her hand in a pledge. "Will you take my word that I'll never bring up the subject again?"

He offered her a mock bow. "Emilie Getz, you are the utter definition of trustworthy. Of course I'll take your word. After all, you took my parrot."

A guffaw exploded from her lips, a ghastly, unfeminine sound, which seemed to please Jonas no end. "Not only your parrot," she reminded him. "Two guinea pigs *and* a fish."

"And bless you for it." Cupping her elbow, he guided her back toward the church. "Your sacrifice today will not go unnoticed either, pretty girl. On that you can take *my* word."

◆

My word.

Jonas had never seen so many cats. The place was a cornucopia of cats, from tiny six-week-old kittens to old toms with long whiskers and sallow eyes. He hung on to his completed adoption paperwork and moved past the cages, nodding absently as the cheerful volunteer steered him along, chatting about the merits of each feline.

He'd arrived at the Humane League of Lancaster County at ten sharp when the doors opened Monday, ready to bring home the perfect companion for his generous Emilie. A thank-you gift she could actually *pet*. One that would greet her at the door when she came home. Curl up in her lap while she read. Sleep at her feet at night.

It'll be the best pet yet, Em. He grinned at the thought, then realized the volunteer assisting him was ten steps ahead.

"Uh, sorry." Tightening the gap with long strides, he caught up with her, then followed the woman's hand as she pointed to a slender cat with short brown hair and darker stripes.

"This one is part Abyssinian."

"Boy, that's too bad." He shook his head, sympathetically. "Are there shots for that?"

The young woman's eyes flew open, as if she'd just swallowed a bag of cat litter by mistake. "That's a *breed*, sir."

Oops. He recovered by flashing his gets-'em-every-time smile. "You'll have to forgive me, ma'am. I'm not up on pets of the feline persuasion. More of a dog man myself."

Emilie seemed the kittenish type, though. He swung around, surveying the area. "Got any more little fur balls?"

She walked him past the kittens again—all adorable, but frankly, smaller than the guinea pigs. How could something that puny greet you at the door?

He picked one up, marveling at its soft, downy fur, then noticed in a painful instant that hiding underneath the fur was a whole army of sharp little claws. Putting the kitten down in a hurry and nursing his hand, Jonas imagined the furry bundle clawing its way up Emilie's lacey tablecloth. *Not a pretty picture.*

Maybe it was an anomaly. "Do they all have claws like that?"

The volunteer's eyes narrowed into slits. "May I see your paperwork please?" She studied it carefully, making disapproving noises under her breath.

Surely he was qualified to adopt a cat, wasn't he? He loved animals, was a model pet owner. Made regular donations to the ASPCA. He tried his best to look responsible when she handed him back his forms with a huff.

"Very well. A veteran pet owner, just new to cats?"

He nodded emphatically. "That's the ticket. Truth is, I think I need something bigger. Older. Not a kitten at all, but a mature cat."

Her expression softened. "I know just the one." She directed him to a cage in the far corner, then reached in and scratched the occupant between the ears, producing an immediate, pronounced purr. "This is Olive. You'd make my week if you gave this old girl a good home."

Olive was every color *but* green. Black, gray, tan, white, brown, gold— this cat had every genetic thread known to kittydom packed in a massive, fluffy body. One eye was circled with black fur, the other orange, which gave her an oddly maniacal look, like a pirate.

Jonas grinned and took a turn scratching her massive head. "Hello, matey."

"You saw that, too, huh?" The young woman beamed up at him, all suspicions clearly put to rest. "Olive is my favorite. Problem is, she's been here too long. Not everyone appreciates the advantages of an older cat—" she batted her eyes at him—"like *you* do, Mr. Fielding."

He looked over his shoulder, then bent down to whisper. "Are her days...uh, numbered?"

"There's no set schedule for such things, but when the kennel gets crowded like this, and the animal has been here a long time...." She shrugged, her meaning clear. "Olive is friendly, even-tempered, already spayed, only three years old, and ready to make someone a fine pet."

"Sold." He shoved the paperwork in her hands. "Where do I pay my fifteen dollars?" The bargain of a lifetime, this.

Gently easing the monstrous creature out of her cage, Jonas managed to get his hands wrapped firmly around her bulky body, then turned toward the front door, setting his own voice on purr. "You just wait, Miss Olive. Emilie is gonna flip when she meets you."

◆

Nathan flipped the remains of his cigarette at the cement walkway that led to Jonas' front door, then groaned in resignation and retrieved it. *Too classy a street for butts on the sidewalk.*

His brother's place was everything he'd hoped and more. A high-priced two-story in a fancy new neighborhood. *Primo.* He'd had the cab driver swing by the golf course on the trip from the bus station last week, and knew that place was turning into a first-class setup, too.

Nate grinned, despite the dread that tightened his windpipe. *Maybe there really is a God.*

Shivering in the morning cold, watching his breath trail out in steamy huffs, he lit a second Camel, hands shaking as they sheltered his lighter from the brisk March wind.

One thing was certain: There really was a Dee Dee. *She of the tight, green dress.* He grinned at the memory. A little older than him, but age wasn't a concern. Young, old, tall, short—long as they were easy on the eyes, he was game, and this one was fine.

Maybe he'd call her, try and get something set up for the weekend. *And pay for it with what, Nate?* He took a long drag on his cigarette, blowing a curl of smoke out on a frustrated sigh.

Money, money, always money.

According to the calendar in Jonas' stark kitchen, it was the start of a new month. For him, it was the same old money problems, only worse.

March 1. The date had gnawed at his soul for two weeks. Cy expected him to cough up eighteen thousand today. Cy also expected him to still be in Florida.

Nate hadn't told a soul where he was going. Made sure he left no trail of bread crumbs behind him when he disappeared on his Greyhound bus getaway.

He hadn't heard a peep from Vegas. Had almost stopped looking over his shoulder every ten minutes for an unfriendly face. Maybe in a month or two, he could sleep all the way through the night or walk down the street without picking up speed every time he heard footsteps behind him.

The phone in the house jangled. Not Jonas' business line, but the house phone. Nate stubbed out his cigarette half-smoked, tucking the rest away for later, and stepped inside.

Could be his brother, calling to say he'd been bitten by a sourpuss. Nate grinned at his own pun. *Funny, man.* What possessed Jonas to buy his girlfriend a cat was anybody's guess. Moving toward the phone, Nate scratched Trix's head on the way by. "Don't worry, girl, he's not bringing some fool cat into *this* house."

Out of habit, Nate checked his watch before he answered the persistent ring. *Just after eleven.* "Fielding residence."

A male voice blasted out of the receiver. "What are you, somebody's lah-dee-dah butler?"

Cy. Nate almost dropped the phone. "H-how'd you find me here?" *Stupid question.* He didn't need to know the particulars, though Cy seemed quick enough to share them.

"My guy in Jacksonville checked with the rental car gal, who remembered hearing you call a cab for the bus station. Then he found a Greyhound agent who remembered talking to you about how pretty Lancaster was. Only a coupla Fieldings in the phone book. See? Not hard, kid. What's hard is having you do me this way when I've been so easy on you."

Nate gripped the phone. "Look, I'm broke, Cy. Not a dime to my name. Not a penny."

"That's not how I hear it. Hear you're livin' in a real nice house, ridin' around in a brand-new black Explorer, makin' eyes at all the women at church. *Church,* Nate? You goin' religious on me?"

Cy knew everything, it seemed, except why he was in Lititz. Nate started to explain—about his brother, about trying to get in his good graces, maybe work up to asking for a gig at the new golf course.

But Cy didn't care about any of that. He only cared about his money.

Nate tried to sound relaxed. "Cy, old buddy. What's eighteen grand to a high roller like you?"

"I'm not your *old buddy,* got that?" The voice on the other end of the phone had grown cold and sharp, poised to kill like a sheet of ice hanging from a shingled roof. "You're right. The money is nothin'. It's the fact that it's *my* money that matters. The fact that if word gets out that Cy Porter is goin' easy on people, letting 'em get away without settling their debts…well, that's a problem, Nate. How're you gonna solve that problem?"

Nate's mind struggled to function. As best he knew, Cy had never killed anybody. But he'd hurt people. Trashed their houses. Scared their families.

Cy's network spread farther than Nate had ever imagined. He'd figured Florida or Pennsylvania was plenty far away from Nevada.

Apparently he'd been wrong.

"April 1." Nate hated hearing his voice shake. He swallowed and said it again, more firmly. "April 1. That's when I'll have the money, all of it plus interest. Let's make it twenty thousand. Okay, Cy? A little extra for your troubles. Wish I could have it sooner, but it's gonna take some time to…get it together."

The phone was silent. He thought the line had gone dead until he realized Cy's low breathing was still coming over the line. Finally Cy spoke, his voice unnaturally steady. "Is this a joke, Nate?"

Nate's throat tightened again with a jolt. "No, not a joke! No, nothing funny about this. I…just need another month, that's all."

"Sure you're not pulling some April Fool's prank on your *old buddy?*"

Nate's laugh was thin, high and wavery, more like the yelp of an animal in pain. "I know better than to try and fool you, Cy. Thursday, April 1. Got it marked right here." Nate drew an imaginary circle on the wall calendar with a trembling finger. "You won't have to call again. The money will be there, on the first."

"No more second chances, Nate. This is it. Understood?"

Only too well.

Nathan dropped the receiver in place, then sank to his knees on the hardwood floor. Everything ached—his head, his chest, his gut. There wasn't a medicine in the world that could take away this kind of pain.

How did it come to this?

That's what he couldn't figure out. His three brothers were big shots in their communities, their mother had been a saint, their father had been a flippin' hero.

"So what are you, Nate?" He rammed his fist against the floor, then cursed when he bruised it, shouting into the empty house. "What are *you?* A screwup? A write-off? Who needs you, Nate? Who needs you?"

He bent over, hugging his knees. "I'll tell ya who. Not a livin' soul." Long past tears, long past regret. Only the rage and the pain remained.

"Nobody needs you, Nate Fielding." He tore the word out of his throat. "*Nobody.*"

Jonas wasn't there when the phone call came.

The message on his answering machine from Ben Haldeman, the contractor responsible for the initial ground clearing for the course, had been brief but enigmatic. "Something's come up you oughtta know about, Chief. Call me. Soon."

Messages like this one had become commonplace the last few weeks. Most of his work as a developer had come in the early stages—two, three, four years ago. Sell the concept, buy the land, put the players together, get the financing approved, jump through all the legal hoops, fill out all the paperwork. Twenty hours a day of nothing but work.

No time for doing something capricious like driving south to Lancaster to buy a cat for Dr. Getz. Though considering the sacrifice she'd made for Carter's Run, the fifteen dollars was practically a business gift. Grinning as he flipped open his notebook with Ben's phone number, Jonas pictured the look on her face Monday when he'd knocked on her door, Olive in hand.

"Jonas!" Clearly, she'd been overwhelmed with his generosity. "Not another...*pet?*"

He'd smiled and handed over the furry mass. "It's the least I can do to say thank you, Em."

The cat, the litter box, the food, the works. No wonder Emilie was speechless. He'd only talked to her by phone the last few days, always thanking her profusely for letting him proceed without a fight.

What a woman!

It was obvious what was going on. She cared too much to cause him that kind of grief. And he cared about her, didn't he? Sure he did. Enough to drive sixteen miles round-trip for a silly cat.

However fond the memory, though, today was a serious workday. Five weeks exactly until the grand opening. Now more than ever, he was the go-to guy for problems, the point man when it came to taking concerns before the steering committee. His schedule was his own *until* a situation reared its ugly head.

Ben's deal sounded like a situation and a half.

Jonas punched in the numbers and was relieved when Ben answered his cell phone on the first ring.

"Ben? Jonas Fielding. Yeah, fine. What's up?"

"It's like this, Jonas." The man's rough-as-gravel bass rolled across the line. "I'm working on another job in Cherry Hill, New Jersey, with some of the crew who worked for me on your job last year. Sure is a fine place, that Lititz. You 'bout ready for your big opening?"

"Right." Nobody could drag out a story like Ben Haldeman. "And...?"

"And we were talking about weird stuff we'd unearthed on clearing gigs. You know, bathtubs, gravemarkers. Found a '49 Chevy in Lansing, Michigan, once."

"I gotcha. So..."

"So one of the fellas—Gary, I think, guy from Pottstown. No. Not Pottstown. Pottsville. Potts-something-or-other."

Jonas bit his lip. "Uh-huh. Go on."

"Anyway, Gary—I think his name was Gary. Coulda been Greg. Well, he said he'd found the craziest thing on your golf course over there. Too big for a grave, too small for a modern house, he thought. Not exactly a foundation, but close. Walls were eighteen inches thick, Gary said. Lotta pieces of pottery and stuff. Looked real old, he thought."

Jonas felt an uneasy twinge skip up his spine. "Why is this the first time I'm hearing about this, Ben?"

"To be honest, Jonas, you weren't there. This was last June, remember? You were in Hungary. No. Haiti, was that it?"

The mission trip to Honduras. "I left you in charge, Ben, as I recall."

"Yeah, you sure did." His chuckle sounded like an old truck engine on a cold morning. "Jonas, the thing is, we were almost finished the afternoon Gary found this. You were outta the country and I was on another machine on the far end of the course. Down at the ninth hole. Say, did that turn out like you wanted it to? I thought the bunkers were a bit—"

"Yes!" Jonas stood up to keep from exploding. "It's all great, the course is great. But Ben, this news is *not* great. Are you telling me Gary just shoved dirt over this foundation and left it there?"

"Well...yeah. I mean, we didn't have any instructions otherwise. Nothing on the clearing order, nothing on the permits, no red flags in the dirt, no notices posted. You know the routine." He sounded a bit miffed. "Look, we did our job, Jonas. Gary never mentioned it, that day or any other day, until the subject came up here in Cherry Hill. Man, this place is nothing like

Lancaster County. Nothin' but highways and byways and malls out the—"

"*Ben.*" Jonas paused to catch his breath while the man rambled on. "Ben, the question is, where on the course did Gary see this old foundation? Did he remember?"

"Sure. Who forgets a thing like your eighteenth hole? It's the crown of the course, Jonas, you know that. Why, the closing—"

"Thanks, Ben." Jonas sank back in his chair while Ben kept talking. When the older man finally ran out of steam, Jonas assured him, "No, Gary's not in trouble. I shoulda been there, that's all there is to it. Look, I'll take things from here. Thanks for giving me a heads-up. Yeah, you too, Ben."

Jonas hung up the phone with exaggerated care, as if it might electrocute him if he did otherwise. His thoughts were running like shock waves through his system, with the overriding one being this: *Why now, Lord?* Why, after Emilie agreed to let him finish the thing, why did this news have to come today instead of next month, when it would be too late?

For that matter, *now* was too late.

It's not too late, Jonas, and you know it.

He stood, arguing with himself, pacing the room, flailing his arms around him like a windmill gone haywire. If he ignored the news, he would have to live with the guilt every time he looked down into those light brown eyes and that creamy complexion and that rosebud smile.

Anyway, people would find out soon enough. Ben was a talker and the golf industry loved a chewy bit of gossip. If she found out—no, *when*—she would never forgive him.

And that would make two, because he could never forgive himself.

Okay. Suppose he let her have the eighteenth hole? Dig it up, trash the thing, turn it into a historic landmark with tourist buses and third-graders tossing candy wrappers on his clubhouse lawn.

Nah. The whole scenario gave him hives.

But Emilie had made that sacrifice for him. To honor the Lord, she said. Couldn't he make that sacrifice for her, for the same reason?

Lord, I'm willing. Easy to say, hard to do. Impossible to do.

With me all things are possible.

"I know, Lord!" Jonas threw his arms heavenward. "So show me another possibility. Please, Father. I'm trusting you to help me find a way that makes sense."

He ground his fingertips against his temples, willing his brain to work faster, come up with some solution. Whatever the plan, it'd be a lot easier to sell to the committee if he had that blasted antique survey map.

Think, man. Was there another option, another place to put the eighteenth hole?

Ridiculous. Stupid to even consider it.

Still, he started pulling out drawings even as he grumbled, spreading out the architectural renderings to see if maybe, just maybe...

Wait. Of course! The solution jumped off the page. A shot of adrenaline ran through his body at the simplicity of it. One phone call could put it in motion. *No, not one. Two. And a third for good measure.*

He punched in the numbers, so elated it took him four tries to get the numbers right.

A voice came on the line, smooth as silk. "Snyder Realty."

"Good! You're there." His grin stretched wider. Already things were looking up. "Dee Dee, it's Jonas Fielding. Got a minute?"

Nineteen

$$\blacklozenge$$

Life's under no obligation to give us what we expect.
MARGARET MITCHELL

Emilie made up her mind.

She would call the man immediately.

No! She would drive over there, this minute, while the whole thing was fresh in her mind and hot under her lace collar.

Did he think he could get away with this? That it didn't matter to her? That she had no opinion on the subject?

The very idea! Giving her a cat. A *cat!*

Had she asked for a cat? She had not.

Did she even *like* cats? She did—especially when they were owned by other people.

But *this* cat ate more food in a sitting than *she* did. The entire huge bag of smelly cat food was already gone in three short days. Not to mention the multicolored hairs all over her clean upholstery. And then there was this business of changing the litter box…

Well. Jonas Fielding was not getting away with it. Talk about irresponsible! After all, what had *she* so thoughtfully given *him?* Plants. Quiet, unassuming houseplants that ate nothing, drank only a little water on occasion, didn't meow incessantly to be petted, and wouldn't think of shedding or leaving a disgusting mess for him to remedy.

A green plant simply sat there and looked beautiful.

A cat was...was...a *cat!*

In her three days under Emilie's roof, this Olive creature had managed to swallow the goldfish whole, scare the parrot half numb, and choose as her favorite sleeping spot the top of the guinea pig cage, frightening Clarice and Clyde into a stupefied silence.

Victor had stopped squawking "Pretty girl!" and replaced it with an equally annoying phrase he heard Emilie say ten times a day: *"Naughty cat! Naughty cat!"*

And to what did she owe this most generous of gifts? Her heartrending sacrifice of her Gemeinhaus property in favor of a peaceful, God-pleasing resolution with Jonas.

Humph. A cat did not a Gemeinhaus replace.

Jonas needed to understand. And he would, the minute she got to his place and demanded that he take his menagerie—what was left of it, bless Mavis's poor departed heart—and care for the noisy flock himself.

Emilie dressed warmly enough to ward off the breezy March winds and stomped out the back door, Olive meowing in the background as she yanked the door shut. It was eight blocks to Jonas' house. Plenty of time to turn her good head of steam into a full-blown, beginning-of-March roar.

Emilie the lioness. The image alone carried her two blocks in two minutes.

"Jonas," purred the voice over the phone. "I'm always happy to hear from a Fielding man, but I rather hoped it would be Nathan calling. Where is that brother of yours?"

Jonas shook his head. Even in the midst of business dealings, Dee Dee Snyder had other things on her mind.

"He was gone when I got home. Left a note saying he was going out for a walk." To think things through, Nate's note had said.

Dee Dee didn't need to know that.

Jonas hadn't told anyone about Nate's month in rehab, not even Emilie. Wasn't his story to tell. Nate would share it with people in his own good time, if ever. The two of them had hit Hess Clothing for a bunch of pants and shirts yesterday. Poor guy arrived in town with nothing but the clothes on his back, literally.

If Nate wanted to strike something up with Dee Dee, that was his business, but Jonas didn't intend to aid and abet.

He jammed the phone between his shoulder and ear, smoothing out the wrinkled course design drawing with both hands. "I'm calling because we have a situation at Carter's Run and I need your input."

An abrupt knock at the kitchen door interrupted his thoughts. *Nate.* His brother always knocked before he came in. Place must not feel like home to him yet.

After a moment, Jonas heard the back door open and quietly close again. Satisfied Nate was safely in, he spun his chair back around toward the desk and matters at hand.

"Dee Dee, do you remember Ben Haldeman, our clearing contractor from last June? Ben called with some news this morning. Yup. Very bad news, I'd say."

Hearing footsteps in the hall behind him, Jonas hollered out a welcome, then kept talking.

"Seems a fella on Ben's crew—some guy named Gary or Greg. You know Ben, he never can keep names straight. Anyway, this guy found what appeared to be a foundation for a 'very old' building, as Ben put it. How old, we don't know, but eighteen-inch-thick walls suggest it wasn't built ten years ago. Some artifacts too, pottery and such. I'll tell you what I think it is: Emilie's Gemeinhaus."

Jonas paused, detecting an odd noise in the hall. A bump or thud of some sort. It wasn't Trix—she was outside, enjoying the fresh air. Must be Nate scrounging around the kitchen. *Whatever.*

"Guess where this foundation is located? You got it, Dee Dee. Right under my eighteenth hole. Does that beat all? It seems the lady professor was right." Which, despite the hassle, made him prouder than if he'd come up with that deduction himself. *What a woman!*

He nodded at the phone while Dee Dee talked, then interrupted her with a strangled gasp. "*Tell* her? You gotta be kidding. We're five weeks from the opening, Dee Dee. I don't intend to tell Emilie Getz or anybody else, not even my brother. You're the only person who knows this, and that's how it's gotta stay. You, me, and in a couple of minutes, the architect, but not another soul. Got that? I want this thing under wraps."

He listened to her chatter for a moment as he studied the papers in front of him. No way would he tell Emilie Getz. What, and spoil the fun? *Uh-uh.* He'd quietly get things taken care of, then spring the news on her. And boy, would she be *surprised.*

"Listen, there's another property I wanted to check with you about. Yup, that's the one. What's the news there? Huh. Keep me posted and in the meantime, remember—not a word to Emilie."

Emilie had never eavesdropped in her entire life.

She'd seen Jonas on the phone as she walked past the window. Tapped on the backdoor, then when he didn't answer, let herself in. She'd convinced herself it was perfectly all right. Hadn't he invited himself through *her* door a time or two?

Following the sound of his voice, she stepped lightly through the kitchen, reached his open office door, and lifted her hand to knock at the very moment he said those fateful words: *Emilie's Gemeinhaus.*

Her pet disasters quickly forgotten, she froze in place. They'd found it! She was right on this one after all. Right as rain! And it seemed they'd found it in the very spot she'd earmarked.

Surely Jonas would let her dig to her heart's content, now that they knew beyond a shadow—

Wait. What was Jonas saying? That…that *what?*

No. She stood there, stunned, looking at his broad-shouldered back, listening to him admonish that real estate—that *hussy*—to keep the news to herself.

Jonas had said it loud and clear: *"Not a word to Emilie."*

Her spirit snapped in two at that.

Jonas Fielding, how could you?

Her throat clutched into a tight knot. Everything made sense now. Horrible sense. The pets were to keep her busy, keep her away from her research.

And his kisses, what were they? Designed to melt her heart and her gray matter as well? To keep her so off-kilter she didn't care about things like a career. Or a future.

Jonas would never do such a thing!

Jonas *did* do such a thing.

Heartsick, barely able to keep her balance, Emilie tiptoed back through the house. She slipped out the kitchen door, being careful not to let it bang behind her, then sought out Trix for a quick head scratch to keep the retriever's barking to a minimum.

"Good girl," she managed to choke out, realizing she needn't have worried about keeping her voice down. The stiff breeze muffled Trix's joyous barks. Her clandestine visit would remain a secret.

Suddenly, she heard footsteps behind her. Whirling around, she threw her chin up, ready to do battle with Jonas for being such a cad.

The man behind her lifted his hands in surrender. "Dr. Getz?"

"Oh! Nathan." Despite her misery, she found a laugh somewhere deep inside and tossed it out, hoping it might relieve the tension that stretched around them both.

"Emilie, what's the matter?"

He said it so tenderly it triggered the tears that had been threatening for two minutes. "I beg your pardon," she murmured as she dug in her purse for a tissue.

Before she could find one, Nathan graciously extended a handkerchief in her direction. New, by the look of it, and blessedly unused. She pivoted around to mask her unladylike honk, then turned and handed it back to him with a grimace. "Sorry."

His half-smile was melancholy at best. "'Tears, such as angels weep.'"

Her mouth dropped open. "John Milton?"

"*Paradise Lost,* I think."

"You know...*Milton?*"

Tucking the handkerchief in his pocket, he offered a cool shrug. "One of the few things I remember from freshman English."

"Really." Merely talking about academics calmed her spirit a bit. "Where did you study?"

"Stanford."

Well. "A fine school, Nathan." She blotted the last vestige of tears with the back of her hand. "What is your degree?"

The lines around his mouth tightened. "It would've been economics. I made it into my junior year, then...ah, pursued a career in professional golf instead."

Dry-eyed now, she merely nodded, noticing that though Nathan certainly favored his older brother, he had a hardness about him that Jonas did not. "And has golf been a successful venture for you?"

His eyes darkened. "Not particularly. I'm hoping that…that God will have something for me here in Lititz."

How uncomfortable he seemed! A new relationship with the Lord, a new town, no job yet. It had to be difficult for him. Wanting to offer a reassuring word, she patted his arm. "I'm sure Jonas could put you to good use at Carter's Run." Just saying the words made her spine stiffen. "Then again, there are several other courses in Lancaster County. Private ones, I dare say." *Nicer ones.* Ones without a Gemeinhaus on them.

Glancing at the kitchen door behind them, she felt a strong urge to press on toward home and avoid a confrontation she was simply not prepared to handle. "Nathan, I must run, but I have a favor to ask of you."

"Oh?" He looked interested, maybe more so than fitting.

"Would you mind terribly keeping our little visit here to yourself? I was just…walking by and wouldn't want Jonas to think I was making a nuisance of myself. Do we…have an understanding?"

His eyes glowed like embers. "I believe we do, Emilie."

Her sigh was a flutter of relief. "Wonderful. I hope your future here will be…everything you desire."

"Everything I desire," he repeated, his eyes trained on hers, his smile more than a little unnerving. "I hope so too." He patted her arm, just as she had his, though it felt more like a caress. "Your visit will be our secret, Emilie. That means you owe me one."

"Whatever you say, Nathan." She stepped back, oddly uncomfortable, and headed pell-mell down the sidewalk.

"Owed him one," did she? She sniffed at the mere suggestion. His brother owed *her* an apology, an explanation, and a quarter acre of land, in that order.

Nathan watched her hurry down the street, chuckling to himself. Pretty enough woman, but the jittery type. Yeah, he'd keep her dumb little secret—and cash in that chip someday, no doubt.

Strolling into the house, he threw his jacket over a peg in the hallway and wandered into Jonas' office, where his brother was finishing up a phone call.

Jonas groaned. "Phillip, I know this is unorthodox, I know it throws a monkey wrench in your design—I know all of that." He cupped the mouthpiece and waved Nate in the door. "The thing is, if we don't do this voluntarily, some historical society will make a fuss and force us to do it after the fact. This way you'll be a hero, okay? Haven't you always wanted to be a hero, Phil?"

Laughing at the man's response, Jonas sat up and leaned on his desk, apparently winding things up. "Great. You're a pro, my friend. The best. We'll make headlines with this unusual eighteenth hole, I guarantee it. I'll see you at the course Monday at ten. Remember what I told you. Mum's the word."

Jonas hung up and leaned back, throwing his arms out as if to embrace the world and everything in it. "What a day, man. How are you doing?"

Nathan spread out his hands. "I'm breathin'."

Gathering together the messy array of papers on his desk, Jonas stacked them aside, then glanced up, a look of curiosity on his face. "Did I hear you talking to somebody outside?"

Nathan didn't bat an eye. "Just a neighbor. So, Jonas, what's the situation with Carter's Run?"

His brother looked at him with a puzzled expression. "Situation? You mean, are we on schedule? That kind of thing?"

"Nah, I know you gotta be on schedule. You wouldn't have it any other way, bro." Nate tried to keep the resentment out of his voice but wasn't sure he succeeded.

My perfect big brother. Sometimes it got old.

Jonas rocked to his feet and grabbed his car keys. "If you mean what were Phillip Nuss and I just talking about, trust me, you don't wanna know. No offense, but the fewer people in on this one the better. You can keep whatever you heard a secret, right?"

"Oh, sure. I'm good at keeping secrets." *Better than you know, brother Jonas.*

"That's great. Let's go scare up some lunch. Mornings like this can wear a guy out."

Nate followed him out to the garage and they climbed in the Explorer, both seats pushed back all the way to accommodate their long legs. The vehicle roared to life and the CD player along with it.

Nate pitched his voice above the din. "Is that the band from Maryland you were tellin' me about?"

"Yeah. Aren't they great?"

Banging his hands on the dashboard to the lively bluegrass rhythm, Nate merely nodded. *Maryland.* One of the many states he'd traveled through last week. Georgia, the Carolinas, Virginia, then Maryland, and finally here. Nice little town, Lititz. Quaint. Kinda sleepy for his taste, but it'd do for the time being.

One month. Thirty days. Twenty thousand dollars.

He couldn't earn it golfing. Couldn't win it gambling.

There was only one option left.

Emilie fumed all the way home, straight through the weekend, and well into Monday, using her outrage as fuel for her writing project.

The sooner she finished the commemorative book, the sooner she could leave Lititz—and Jonas the fickle-hearted—behind. At the rate she was cranking out pages, she'd complete the project in a total of three months instead of six. Come April 1, with a generous check from the church in hand, she would buy another set of much-used wheels and point them south, toward Winston-Salem, with nary a regret.

The phone rang several times a day. She ignored it.

She went to the early service Sunday morning. Alone.

Her only companions were Olive—who, in truth, was settling down and turning into a perfectly agreeable cat; the ever-quiet Clarice and Clyde; and Victor, who'd also mellowed a bit and only squawked "Naughty cat!" when threatened by a curious paw.

Tuesday morning when the phone jangled in the kitchen, Emilie barely noticed until she heard Beth's voice on the answering machine.

"Emilie? Are you there? Are you okay? I wish you'd call me. I miss you…we all do. All of us."

Humph. Emilie had a good idea whom the *all* might include.

"Will you please call? I've left several messages…"

Emilie sighed and grabbed the phone before Beth could hang up. "Hello, dear. I'm here."

"Thank goodness! I really have been worried, Em."

The exhaustion in Beth's voice made Emilie's ears perk up and a chill run along her arms. "Beth, now *I'm* worried. You sound so...weak. Are *you* okay?"

"Yes, I'm just...tired. So tired. In fact, I couldn't go to work this morning."

Something *was* wrong. Emilie glanced down at her frumpy attire and ran a hand through her unkempt hair, then reminded herself that Beth was a friend and didn't mind about such details. "Look, I'm coming over. Don't pick up a thing around the house, don't scrub the watercolors off Sara's hands, just sit in a comfy chair and leave the door open for me, okay? And I'm bringing lunch. Egg salad work for you?"

It was then she realized Beth was crying in soft little hiccups. "Y-yes, that w-would be great." Beth gave a sniff. "I'm sorry, Em, it's just been so...h-hard lately."

Emilie murmured every comforting thought she could come up with while she worked her way around the kitchen, the phone squashed between shoulder and ear. Praying while she listened, she threw together half a dozen sandwiches, grateful for the tray of hard-boiled eggs she'd fixed that morning, never dreaming how soon they'd be put into service.

The weather felt more like January than March. A bitter wind nipped at her scarf as Emilie made the four-block trek to Spruce Street, praying with each step. *Lord, let her be okay. Help me get my eyes off myself and my own pity party and fill me with compassion for my weary friend.*

By the time Emilie pushed open the front door of Beth's house, her cup was running over with peace and a sense of purpose. She was needed here today, that was certain. The feeling of rightness was remarkable.

"Beth?" she called out, then spotted her and grinned. "Good for you."

As ordered, the young woman was sitting on the couch with her legs propped up. Seated on the floor beside her was Sara, cutting scherenschnitte with her round-tipped scissors.

"I can do this like Mrs. Bomberger," Sara said proudly, holding up her white paper design. "See?"

"A fine job." Emilie overlooked the oddly-shaped edges and nodded her approval. "Mrs. B will be very pleased when she sees it. Did you know that Mrs. B. taught me to do that, too, when I was a little girl about your age?"

Sara's eyes widened and her body grew unnaturally still. "You were a little girl, Em-ee-lee? When?"

She laughed. "Ten thousand years ago. Even before *your* Mama was a little girl." Emilie perched on the end of the sofa and patted Beth's feet affectionately. The woman looked wrung out, her eyes drooping, her skin pale. "In fact, when I was a girl, your Mama was just a baby."

Sara shook her head with exaggerated swings. "No. My Mama could never *be* a baby. She's gonna *have* a baby."

Beth gasped, then frowned. "Sara!"

The little blond's cheeks turned as pink as her sweater. "I forgot, Em-ee-lee. That's a secret."

Tears swam in Emilie's eyes, making it hard to see if Beth was pleased or not that Sara had spilled the beans. "Beth, I had no idea. I'm so happy for you."

And she was, truly. Thrilled to her toes. It was her heart and the cold knife of envy thrust deep in its center that were giving her trouble at the moment. She didn't have a man in her life anymore, let alone the prospect of children.

Why, when it had never mattered before, did it matter so very much now?

Emilie smiled through her sheen of tears. "How wonderful, Beth. When will the baby arrive?"

Beth laughed, in spite of her own spate of tears, and flapped her hand dismissively. "Don't mind me, I cry at baby food commercials these days. Hormones, you know." She blew her nose in a handy tissue, then sighed. "I'm four months along. For most women, the first trimester is the most tiring, but for me, I just stay wiped out. More so with this one than with Sara. 'Cause I'm older, I guess."

Emilie wrinkled her brow. "Four months? I'm surprised you could keep it a secret so long."

Beth nodded, then bent over and whispered loudly in Sara's ear. "I'll bet if you take that brown paper bag of Emilie's in the kitchen, you'll find something good to eat inside."

Sara squealed and grabbed the bag, planting a sticky kiss on a surprised Emilie's cheek before skipping off to the back of the house.

"She really likes you, Em. In fact, she watched the *Wizard of Oz* last night and ran around the house all morning saying, 'Auntie Em! Auntie Em'!"

"'Auntie Em,' is it? I like it. And for the record, I very much like Sara, too." Loved her, in fact, though it felt odd to say so. It astounded her to realize how her opinion of children had shifted completely, from mild distaste to major delight. *Only you could work such a change, Lord. Only you.*

"Emilie, now that Sara's in the kitchen…"

Beth's expression had an intensity that made the hair on Emilie's neck rise. "What is it, sweetie? Why the secrecy?"

"I'm being extra cautious because I…I've lost two babies."

"Oh, Beth! I had—"

"No idea." She nodded. "I know. It's not something I talk about very often. Sara knows about Clayton and Timothy, but we don't dwell on it. We don't want her to worry about me or the baby. God's in charge, and I'll be fine."

Emilie sat speechless. To have conceived and lost a child—twice—was beyond her comprehension. At a loss, she simply took Beth's hand and held it tight, trying to communicate with touch what she couldn't put into words.

"I was in my fourth month with Timothy when we lost him." Beth ran her other hand lightly over her tummy. "That's why I'm not taking any chances with this little one. I pushed too hard with Tim, didn't understand my body's need for rest."

"Don't blame yourself." Emilie squeezed her hand gently. "Remember your own words: God's in charge."

"Mmm, right. With Clayton, it was harder still. He was born full term, but lived only five days." She waved at the calendar, then drew her hand to her mouth, as if holding something inside. "Last Saturday would have been his seventh birthday."

All at once, Emilie was overwhelmed with a sense of sorrow. It seemed every drop of Beth's grief had been poured into her own cup. When she'd prayed to be filled with compassion, she had no idea it would hurt this much.

"Beth, I'm so sorry." It was all she could say and everything she felt. "Thank you for telling me. I…I treasure our friendship."

Nodding, Beth squeezed her hand. "Me too. With Drew gone on business so much, I've been lonely. Knowing you these last two months has really helped."

"You need to let me do more for you, though. Lunch, for example." Emilie stood and offered her hands to help Beth ease up off the couch, then teased, "Can't wait to see you do that all by yourself in the ninth month."

Beth waved her hand. "Uh-uh. You do *not* want to see such an awkward mess. Meanwhile, before I get to the waddling stage, let's eat. I'm ravenous."

Emilie started toward the kitchen, but her heart stopped. *I won't be here for Beth's ninth month.* The baby was due in August, but she hoped to leave town in a month, in April. An unfamiliar sadness washed over her. She'd put down roots again in Lititz so quickly, never realizing how it might feel to yank them out of the ground come spring.

She needed to make the most of this month, then. Do everything she could to help Beth, mend some fences with her mother, pour her heart and soul into her writing for the church. Without a car to tempt her away from her work—or Jonas to tempt her, period—she would surely have time for the things that mattered most.

Joining Beth and Sara in the kitchen, she bit back a giggle. Sara had set the table herself, using three different patterns of plates, Winnie-the-Pooh juice glasses filled with vivid grape Kool-Aid, and paper towel napkins. The sandwiches sat on the plates, carefully torn in half by little hands that obviously had done their best. Emilie applauded with genuine delight. "What a charming table you've set, young lady!"

Sara beamed and pulled out a chair, waiting for Emilie to take her seat. "Daddy does this for Mama, but only in restaurants."

Both women laughed and sat down to lunch, a lively affair made more so by Sara's incessant chatter about what she was drawing these days, her expectations about kindergarten, and her vast collection of stuffed animals.

Emilie had to know. "Are they all girl animals?"

Sara looked at her askance. "No way! You need boy animals too or you won't have any babies."

Goodness! Emilie had no idea little ones managed to figure out such things.

Sara leaned over to add in a confidential tone, "Mama says the boy and girl animals have to be married first though."

Emilie almost swallowed her tongue whole. "Indeed they do. Your mother is a very wise woman." She stuffed an egg salad sandwich in her mouth before she burst out laughing. Moments later, her composure regained, she winked at Beth. "Any Saturday you need me to watch Sara for you, I'm game. The child is nothing if not entertaining."

Beth's eyebrows lifted. "Do you mean that? Really mean it?"

"Sure." *I do, don't I? I'd need an instruction manual of some kind, but...* "Sure, I'd be delighted."

Beth exhaled, a look of joy dancing across her freckled face. "What an answer to prayer, Em! Drew is in Philadelphia at a trade show all week and must stay through late Saturday night for some fancy awards banquet. He begged me to drive down on Saturday and join him, but I thought...well, we don't have family in the area, and—"

Emilie saw where this was leading. "So. You want me to baby-sit Sara for you on Saturday?"

"Yes! That would be such a blessing, especially if Sara could come to your place, like a big girl on her own special trip."

Sara bounced up and down in her seat, waving her sandwich. "Hooray, hooray! I get to go to Auntie Em's!"

"But, Em—" Beth studied her for a moment—"she'd need to spend Saturday night, too. We're driving home Sunday morning in time for church and would meet you two there. Are you sure? I told Drew there was no way, but...if you're certain you can handle it..."

Emilie folded her paper towel and placed it on the table with a decisive pat. "Call the man and tell him he has a date with his expectant wife, who definitely needs a night out." Gulping down a rising tide of anxiety at the thought of this first in her life—twenty-four hours with a small child under her roof—she smiled confidently. "Sara and I will have a smashing time, won't we, sweetie?"

When Sara arrived four days later with her miniature purple suitcase in hand, the first thing that broke was one of Emilie's cherished teacups. Thinking a little girl would enjoy a tea party with her favorite stuffed bear, Emilie had arranged a picture-perfect table of hot tea and sweet treats to greet Sara when she walked in the door Saturday morning.

In her enthusiasm to reach for a cookie, Sara bumped the fragile china cup, toppling it over the edge of the table where it landed on the unforgiving hardwood floor.

"Ohhh!" The child's face started to crinkle.

"Not a problem. Don't you worry," Emilie assured her, hastening to sweep things up, ashamed of the thin veil of tears that appeared out of nowhere. *Honestly, Em! It's a silly teacup.*

One of four she'd ordered from England.

Now there were three.

Convincing herself it didn't matter one iota, Emilie smiled brightly at her charge. "What would you like to do next?"

Sara's eyes twinkled. "I brought my big doll clothes."

"And a big doll, I suppose?"

"Nope." Sara shook her head. "These dresses are for Olive." She jumped up from the table, sending the china clattering, and ran into the living room. "Here, Olive! Here, kitty-kitty!"

Jonas paced around the construction site, ticking off the growing list of major tasks yet to be completed.

Twenty-seven days to the grand opening.

It tied a knot in his stomach to think of it.

You've been down this road a hundred times, Fielding. Relax. Things always looked darkest right before the heavens opened and the sun shone down on a finished project.

This one, though, had taken an unexpected turn. Last-minute design changes always slowed things down. Still, they were good changes. His bigger, better clubhouse was coming together nicely. Seventeen holes were completed with only one left to finish. Sure, Phillip Nuss whined about that one. Golf architects were artists, with a keen sense of how they wanted the course to look and the temperament to insist on it.

Jonas had worn down the man's resistance with the only two carrots he had to offer him: money and publicity. Fact was, they would all benefit from this one: the architect, the course itself, the borough, and, of course, Emilie.

She was the reason behind it all.

He stopped to gaze up at the ominous gray sky and tightened his collar against a biting, wintry wind. *Spring in a week, huh? I'll believe it when I see it.* Carefully treading around the freshly seeded ground toward a hardworking bunch of bricklayers, Jonas frowned when he realized they were packing up their gear.

"What's the story, guys?"

One man shook his head. "Too cold for the mortar, boss."

"Yeah," another added. "And the forecast for tomorrow looks worse."

"Forecast?" Jonas had been practically sleeping on the site; he hadn't flipped on a television or radio in three or four days. "What are they calling for?"

"Snow." One by one, the men looked up at the heavy cloud cover. "Yup. A doozy for March. Six to twelve inches, they're sayin'."

"*What?*" Jonas groaned and smacked his gloves against his legs. "But it's almost spring!"

Twenty

The first day of spring is one thing, and the first spring day is another.
HENRY VAN DYKE

Emilie didn't need to turn the radio on Sunday morning to know what she was looking at outside her kitchen window: *snow.*

A wet March snow, perfect for sledding and snowmen.

Not so perfect for a drive home from Philadelphia.

It was still falling hard as she answered the phone on the first ring, knowing precisely who might be calling and why.

She took a chance. "Hi, Beth."

"Em?" Beth's voice on the other end was incredulous. "How'd you know it was me?"

Emilie glanced out the window again, then winked at Sara, sitting at the table with jelly toast and scrambled eggs. "Oh, just a feeling I had. The several inches of white stuff on the ground helped."

Beth groaned. "We have snow here, too, but I was hoping it would be clear there. Honey, we may have a problem getting home this morning. We have two cars, of course, and Drew doesn't want me driving in this weather. You know…with the baby and everything."

"Absolutely," Emilie agreed and meant it. "When should I look for you? Any idea?" She listened while Beth consulted Drew who, from the sound of his gentle baritone in the background, must have been standing nearby.

Finally, Beth came back on the line. "They're expecting the snow to stop by about three o'clock, and the temperatures to start rising, which is good. No freezing rain or anything like that. In fact, they say we'll be back up in the fifties by Wednesday. Isn't this silly?"

"That's south-central Pennsylvania weather for you. Predictably unpredictable."

Beth paused. "Emilie, I'm so sorry. Guess I should have paid attention to the forecast, but I was so excited about being with Drew…"

"Of course you were. Really, Sara and I are getting along very nicely. Aren't we, sweetie?" She held the phone out for Sara who bounded over and grabbed the receiver, sticky fingers and all.

"Hi, Mama! You okay?" Sara listened and nodded as though her mother could see her blond curls bobbing up and down. "I miss you, too, Mama. But Auntie Em and I are having lots of fun. We popped popcorn and watched *The Lion King* and made paper dolls and played *Candyland*. I won! Last night I got to sleep with Olive in the spare bedroom." She giggled and whispered, "I rolled over on her once, but she didn't scratch me or anything. Mama, can we get a cat?"

Emilie chuckled. "Uh-oh. Better let me talk to your mother now." Easing the phone out of Sara's grasp, she gave the tiny hand a tender squeeze, then lifted the receiver back up. "Listen, I didn't put her up to that cat business, Beth, I promise. Though anytime you want to borrow Olive, just say the word."

"I'll pass. Cat litter and pregnant women are not a good combo."

"Is that so?" Emilie smiled then checked her watch. "We've got just enough time to make the 10:30 service with clean faces. When should I expect you this evening? Six? That's fine. No, really. See you then. Drive carefully, Beth. I'll be praying."

Pray for me, too. She hung up the phone, making sure not a hint of apprehension showed on her face. Somehow she'd managed to entertain an outrageously active four-year-old girl for a whole day. Auntie Em was fresh out of tricks, though, and her house looked like a cyclone had torn through Toys Я Us and dumped the contents in her living room. And to think she'd once foolishly considered Beth a poor housekeeper!

"We need to dress for church, Sara. Did you bring your pretty blue dress, the one with the flowers and bows?"

Sara nodded, jumping up and heading for the stairs.

"Waaait a minute, pixie." Emilie scooped her up off the floor. "Not so fast with those sticky cheeks and fingers. Let's visit the sink first, okay?"

"Okay, Auntie Em." Without preamble, Sara put a jelly-coated hand on each side of Emilie's face and gave her a sweet, smacky kiss. "I love you, Em-ee-lee."

Oh, my. "I love you, too, baby."

Emilie drew the child against her chest, overcome with emotions she couldn't even name. *Is this how a mother feels?* No. That feeling surely surpassed even this.

But this was close. So close.

I want this, Lord.

The realization was terrifying. Foreign. And wonderful. She, who had never given mothering a second thought, at this moment longed to be a mother more than anything on earth.

More tears threatened. *Why now, Lord, when it seems impossible?*

Nothing is impossible with me.

But this, *Lord!* At best, it seemed improbable. Even young Sara knew you didn't get more stuffed animals unless you had a boy *and* girl *and* they were married besides.

Maybe someday. Hugging the child a second time, Emilie carried her over to the sink, trying to concentrate on the simple task at hand when a complex array of feelings and desires swept over her like fresh snow on a late winter's morning.

Sara touched her cheek. "Are you crying, Auntie Em?"

"Yes, I am." She chuckled, wiping away both jelly and tears. "But these are happy tears, Sara, because I love you so much and because I am asking the Lord to give me a Sara someday."

Good heavens, she'd said it out loud!

Emilie gulped. "Uh…but let's not mention that to your Mama, okay? She'll think I'm silly."

Sara sat still while she scrubbed her clean, then shook her head with conviction. "No, she won't. Mama prays for you to be married and have babies."

"She does?" Emilie stopped in midscrub, not sure how she felt about that revelation. Honored and offended and thrilled and scared, all at once.

"Yup." Sara's head was nodding now, as determinedly as it had shook back and forth moments earlier. "Yesterday she prayed, 'Please let Jonas and Emilie realize how much they love each other. And if it be your will...'" Sara paused. "Mama always talks about will. Will who?"

Emilie laughed through her tears. "God's will is something we all seek. It means doing what he wants us to do."

Sara tipped her head. "So he will be happy?"

"Yes, which means we will be, too."

"Oh." Sara scrunched up her face, thinking. "Anyway, then Mama said, 'If it be your will, may they get married someday and have a child as wonderful as our Sara. The end.'"

Emilie's eyes widened. "She said, *the end?*"

"Something like that."

"What about, *amen?*"

"Yeah, that's it! Like they sing in church." With that, Sara hopped down and ran toward the staircase singing the Moravian threefold choral amen at the top of her little lungs. "Aaa-men! Aaaa-men! Aaaaa-men!"

Emilie watched Sara's sturdy legs march up the steps, a prayer echoing in her heart. *Amen, Lord. A husband. A child. If it's your will.*

Could Jonas possibly be the one? Wasn't he keeping secrets from her, purposely covering up the news about the possible Gemeinhaus discovery?

She shook her head, staring out the window at the falling show, trying to sort things out. It just didn't ring true, didn't seem like the Jonas Fielding she knew at all.

Ask him, Emilie.

Well, why not? She knew the truth. If he pretended not to, she would have her answer. If he confessed and had a good reason to keep such an important secret...she might forgive him. *Might.*

He would pay through the nose, of course.

No more pets.

Lots more kisses.

And a shot at that historic quarter acre.

Emilie grinned her way up the steps, humming a doxology all her own.

Jonas was still singing the closing hymn from the early service when he left his adult Sunday school class and wandered onto Church Square.

"Jesus makes my heart rejoice…" Truer words were never written. He'd come to the early service, since rumor had it that was the one Emilie was frequenting these days.

Unfortunately, he'd gotten up early and slid through the snowy, uncleared streets for nothing. No Emilie at eight.

Where is she, Lord?

She'd stopped answering her phone, which made no sense at all. What if there were an emergency?

There is an emergency.

He needed to see her, and soon.

To know she was okay. *Nah, that wasn't the problem.* He needed to know she still cared about him. That was the crux of it. Know she still thought about him twenty-four hours a day like he thought about her, despite Carter's Run's attempts to steal his every waking hour.

Was she jealous of the golf course, of his work? *Uh-uh.* That wasn't like Em. She loved her work, too.

Had she found another man? *No way.* Who else would give her five pets in five weeks?

Was she ill? Homesick for North Carolina? Suffering from cabin fever without a car?

He ran his hands through his hair—or what was left of it after yesterday's buzz through the barbershop—and looked around the snow-covered square, fretting again about how this cold weather bit into his precious construction time.

That's when he saw her.

Emilie. Walking slowly along the sidewalk, hand-in-hand with a child, bending over to talk to…

Sara?

What was Emilie doing with Sara? And where was Beth?

It gave him the perfect excuse to walk up to her. Ask about Beth, say hello to Sara. Look in Emilie's eyes, just to see what he would find there, just to know. *I gotta know, Lord.*

He moved in their direction, marveling at how natural Emilie looked, taking smaller than usual steps, laughing as she walked through the snow with a precious little girl by her side.

Someday, our little girl.

The thought hit him like a two-by-four, knocking him senseless.

He stopped to catch his breath, to pull himself together, even as everything inside him flew apart.

This was what he wanted.

To be a husband. A husband to Emilie.

To be a father. The father of their children.

In thirty-six years, he had never really considered the possibility. Marriage, maybe, but *fatherhood?* To be the man a child looked up to more than any other man on earth? To be a role model? A hero? To be willing to give up your life for your child?

Oh, Father. To be like you.

It wasn't possible.

Nothing is impossible with me.

This could tax the limits, though.

Except there are no limits, son.

Jonas wasn't sure it was possible to put one foot in front of the other, so stunned was he with the realization that he not only wanted to be a parent, but he *needed* to be one.

To honor his own father.

To prove to himself that, with God's help, he could live up to his father's memory—or at least try. And in trying, let go of the guilt of his father's death, which had lurked in the darkest place in his heart for two dozen years.

You knew that, Lord. All along.

I knew. I love you, Jonas.

He was almost shaking with joy. With Emilie—and the Lord—he could let go of that guilt forever.

He could. He *would.*

It was gone. *Yes!* It was gone already.

"Emilie!" His voice rang out across the snow, sending heads turning at every corner.

She looked up. Her smile was tentative, but it was there.

It's there, Lord.

Her smile grew as he hurried toward her, slipping and sliding across the wet snow, almost falling, then catching himself with a wild wave of his arms, wanting only to be near her.

Emilie bent down when he got within earshot. "Sara, I think someone wants to speak to you in the worst way."

Sara stuck out her lower lip. "No way. Men don't wanna talk to kids. They wanna talk to ladies."

Jonas managed to stop without falling, then he and Emilie both laughed, blushed, and trained their eyes on Sara, not daring to look at one another.

"Kids sure are honest," he said, watching Emilie's face out of the corner of his eye.

"They certainly are. Fun too." She caught his gaze and they both looked up, relieved to have made that first connection.

He looked around. "Where's Beth? Or Drew?"

"Stuck in the snow in Philadelphia." Emilie tugged on Sara's wool cap affectionately. "I've been baby-sitting this weekend."

"No kidding." *Is she kidding? Emilie, a baby-sitter?*

He tried hard not to look shocked even though he *was* shocked, right down to his practically bare scalp.

As though reading his thoughts, Emilie's gaze moved in that direction. "My, my. Did the barber charge by the inch?"

Jonas shrugged, embarrassed that she didn't seem to like it. "He got a little carried away, I guess."

"No, not at all." She wasn't smiling, but her eyes were. "I like it. It makes you look very...masculine."

He shivered. It had nothing to do with the cold. "Oh, yeah?"

Now she smiled. "Oh, yeah."

If he didn't kiss her right now he was going to detonate.

Sara saved the day by pulling Emilie away from striking distance and toward the church. "C'mon, Auntie Em. They're closing the doors."

He cocked his head. "Auntie Em?"

"Long story." Emilie offered a gentle wave and turned to follow Sara, still wiggling her fingers over her shoulder. "See you later."

Later? "Tonight, then?" he called out impulsively. "We gotta talk, Emilie."

She didn't turn around, but instead nodded her head, laughing softly. "Yes, we do, Jonas."

He grinned at her retreating back, jamming his hands in his pockets and rocking on his heels. *Wait until you hear what I have to say to you, Doc. Just you wait.*

"Mom." Emilie cradled the phone, keeping one eye on Sara and Olive tumbling on the living room floor like two kittens. "It's Em."

Her mother gasped. "Goodness! Is everything okay? Is your collarbone hurting again?"

"Mom—"

"Honey, if you need the car, I'll have your daddy follow me over there right this minute."

"Mother—"

"Emilie Gayle, I worry about you, alone in that house on that busy street—"

"*Mom!*" She grinned, waiting to be sure it sank in. "I'm fine. Really. I'm also thirty-six, remember? Today, though, I'm baby-sitting and wondered—"

"Baby-sitting?" The wires hummed. "Whose baby?"

"Beth and Drew's little girl, Sara. Who is anything but a baby."

"It *is* easier once they're potty trained." Her mother's tone calmed a bit. "What can I do for you, dear?"

Emilie lowered her voice. "Mom, I've run out of things for a four-year-old child to do for amusement. Short of renting another movie, can you think of something?"

"Well, now!" Her mother sounded pleased as punch. "To think my daughter, Dr. Emilie Getz, would actually think I know something she doesn't."

"When it comes to mothering, you are definitely the pro." Emilie smiled to herself. *Though I hope my turn will come someday.*

"Thank you, sweetheart. Now let's see if I can't come up with the perfect activity. She's artistic, isn't she?"

"Yes, very. I have the crayons, markers, and paint all over this house to prove it." Even after just one day, the messy rooms were beginning to look normal to her. Lived in.

"Do you have this week's *Record Express* handy?"

Emilie reached on top of the fridge, one of the few places Sara hadn't found to put things yet. "The March eleventh issue, is that the one?"

"Correct. Now turn to page twenty—got that? I'm looking right at it, too. See down in the lower left corner?"

"An Easter coloring contest? Mom, that's perfect! Ages four to ten. Great. Thanks, Mom. You're a lifesaver."

"Happy to be of help to you, dear. We're looking forward to dinner on Wednesday night. Planning on...bringing anyone?"

Emilie rolled her eyes, surprised this hadn't come up sooner. "Don't be coy, Mom. I'll see you Wednesday. Three places at the table should do it, okay? Love you, too."

She hung up the phone, studying the rules of the weekly contest. Sara would only be competing against other four-and five-year-olds. *Very fair.* They could use any medium Sara liked. *Sara will use them all.* She could win five dollars, and it was due at the newspaper office tomorrow at noon. *Great!* It was one block from her house. Emilie would see that it was delivered herself.

Reaching into a drawer for scissors, Emilie hummed a line from *Easter Parade,* even as she watched the snowflakes drifting outside her cozy house. *So, Em. Is this little art project for Sara or for you?*

A ridiculous giggle bubbled up and out. *Yes!*

"Oh, Sara sweet." Emilie carefully cut out the contest form with the outline of an Easter egg basket just begging to be turned into a work of art. "Auntie Em has something fun in mind. Come see."

Sara was already at the kitchen door, wide-eyed, a contented cat draped over her shoulder. "Fun? Oh boy!"

Boy, I hope she's hungry.

Jonas sat across the street from Emilie's front door, his whole passenger seat filled with white boxes of fragrant Chinese food that were tickling his taste buds more by the second.

He'd taken a big risk, showing up like this without calling. What if she wasn't home? What if she wasn't hungry? What if she was starving and hated Chinese food?

Next time, call.

And lose the element of surprise? *Nothing doing.*

He was the one surprised when Drew and Beth pulled up in their van. Of course. *Sara.* Emilie and her baby-sitting duties. He was still shaking his head over that one. Probably made the poor child use one crayon on one piece of paper at a time. Eat every bite on her plate. Go to bed at 8:31 sharp.

You're talking about the future mother of your future children.

Jonas smiled. *Right.*

Emilie would be a great mom, especially because she'd have him there to teach her everything he knew about parenting.

Em was standing in the door now, hugging them all good-bye, so intent on what she was doing she didn't even look up and spot his black Explorer, a rather large target on the snowy white street.

Should he get out, say hello?

He hated to interfere with their exchange, slow everyone down.

Let the food get ice-cold. *Yeah, that too.*

In a moment, the Landises drove off, never looking his direction. He felt rather foolish about it now. *Have to apologize to Beth about that tomorrow.* Right now, though, two of his three questions were answered.

Emilie was home and was no doubt famished. If she favored cashew chicken, oriental pork, or sweet 'n' sour shrimp, he'd be one happy man. Grabbing his array of boxes, he headed across the street, his grin growing wider with each step until it threatened to touch both ears.

Emilie answered the door seconds after he knocked.

And promptly knocked him out.

She stood there in the grungiest clothes he had ever seen on any woman, let alone this one. The button-down shirt was missing half its buttons, the jeans had holes in both knees and quit about mid-calf, and her hair was stuck on top of her head with a huge, shell-shaped plastic clamp.

The effect was a cross between Elly May Clampett and Pebbles.

She'd never looked more adorable. If it weren't for the blasted little boxes swinging from his fingers, he'd have hugged her and asked for her hand in marriage on the spot.

The only thing missing was a smile. What she was wearing was more of an *O.* Big eyes, big open mouth, even her nostrils were flared.

"Jonas!"

"Surprise." He really didn't need to say that. It was clear she was more than surprised, she was dumbfounded. "May I come in?"

"In?" She was flustered. "In this house? Now?"

He held up his boxes. "Yeah, if that's okay. While the food's still hot." Glancing around her slim hips, he tried to see what the problem might be. Seeing none, he stepped on the threshold.

"Oh!" She pressed her hands on his chest. "I'm a mess. And the house is…worse. Could you give me about…thirty minutes?" She pressed more firmly against his shirt. He could almost feel his wildly thumping heart beating against the palms of her hands.

Lowering his head, his Chinese food all but forgotten, he slowly kissed her forehead and whispered in her ear, "I'll give you exactly thirty minutes to quit what you're doing to me right now."

Emilie jumped back as if stung by a bee. "Sorry! I didn't mean to…well, anyway—" She tied her hands in a knot wringing them. "Please, Jonas, I'd love to see you. Truly. But I'm…it's…messy."

He finally noticed the living room behind her and whistled. *Whoa.* She wasn't kidding. Cushions were tossed willy-nilly, the lampshades were askew, a chair was turned over, and the dining room table looked like a watercolor war zone. Dirty plates were stacked on an end table, and empty bowls containing what appeared to be the dregs of popcorn were sitting on a bookshelf.

Emilie's bookshelf? A parking spot for popcorn bowls?

"Wow," he breathed. "It looks like home."

Emilie recovered enough to gasp. "Your mother's house looked like this?"

"Only when she was at work." He grinned. "Or took a nap. We always had to clean it up though. Which is what I'll help you do, Em. After we eat. Deal?"

She stepped back, gazing at him in wonder. "You're not…disgusted? With this mess. With…me?"

He put his boxes down and wrapped his arms around her waist, tugging her closer. "Let's get one thing straight: I would never be disgusted with you. Especially dressed like this. You were playing mother today, and by the look of things, doing a bang-up job."

She patted at her hair, as though one pat would put two hundred stray wisps in place. "Honestly? May I at least…change?"

"Nope. Perfect outfit for eating Chinese food. I always end up wearing half of it on my clothes anyway, don't you? In your case…" He bit his lip to keep from smiling too broadly. "You can just burn them."

"Jonas!" She swatted him. "These are my painting clothes. I wear them once every two years."

He leaned over to gaze at her torn jeans. "Are those the same kneecaps you wouldn't let me see in church on Christmas Eve?"

She tried to cross her legs standing up, to no avail. "You…you noticed my knees?"

"When it comes to Dr. Emilie Getz, I miss nothing." He kissed the tip of her nose, then let go of her waist and gathered up their dinner. "C'mon, let's eat. If we can…uh, find a place to sit."

They landed in the middle of the living room floor, the rest of the *Record Express* spread out to catch the drippings. He was right, of course. She did end up having sweet 'n' sour sauce land in several strategic places, while his black shirt and jeans kept his wonton soup drippings in the dark.

Emilie broke open her almond-flavored fortune cookie and offered him half while she read her fortune. "It's meaningless, of course, but just in case it's interesting…" Her eyebrows shot up. "And is it ever." She extended the white slip of paper between two slender fingers, which he playfully kissed before taking the paper.

Smoothing it out with his thumbs, he read aloud, "'Ask and you shall know the truth.' Hmmm. Almost sounds like the Bible verse, 'Ask, and it will be given to you.'"

"I like your verse better." Emilie put aside her chopsticks and napkin, folding her hands in her lap as if to steel herself. "Jonas, if I asked you, would you give me your eighteenth hole?"

He blanched. "What kind of question is that?"

"I want to know the truth." Her pale skin grew paler, her features were utterly still and deadly serious. "I have…reason to believe that my Gemeinhaus foundation may be under there after all. Do you know anything about that?"

"I do." How could he ever lie to her, but especially about this? "I have reason to believe it's there, too, Emilie."

Her eyebrows rose, as did her voice. "And you didn't tell me?"

"I wanted to be sure." *And foolish me, I wanted it to be a surprise.* "I didn't want to get your hopes up after you so kindly offered me—"

"Right!" Her hands clamped on her knees in a defiant pose. "And you also didn't want to dig up your precious golf course if it wasn't necessary."

He waited one beat, then two, while she seethed. She looked so pretty when she seethed, like a feisty lioness. Finally, lest she also develop claws, he admitted the truth.

"I may very well *have* to dig it up, Emilie. And I'm willing to. Honest. Can we leave things like that for the moment until I find out a few more details? Will you trust me?"

This was clearly not what she expected to hear. Her *V*-shaped eyebrows eased back down, her wrists went limp on the floor, and a magical sort of light played around her eyes. "Whatever you say, Jonas. I trust you." She gulped, looking a bit overcome. "Thank you for telling me the truth."

"Emilie, I will always tell you the truth." *Maybe not according to your timetable, but the truth, always.* He slid their dinner out of the way and pulled her toward him, rising to his knees and lifting her up as well. "May I depend on you to do the same, Em? Tell me the truth, always?"

She nodded, her eyes misty. "Always."

"Then tell me this. Are you in love with me?"

Emilie looked as though she might faint. "Am I...?"

"You said you'd tell me the truth." He pressed a tender kiss on each cheek. "And since I promised to do the same, let me tell you this first. I love you, Emilie Getz."

She sighed like an angel might. "Me too."

He couldn't resist teasing her. "You love you, too?"

"No, *you*. I love you, Jonas Fielding." Keeping her eyes wide open, she kissed his lips, one of her butterfly kisses. "Do you even love my knobby knees?"

"Oh, especially those," he whispered, his voice growing hoarse.

"What about my steel-trap mind, Dr. Fielding?"

"Yes, I love that, too." He sat back on his feet, needing air, needing space. The woman was like a fine dish of Szechuan and he knew when he'd had enough. "In fact, if you will, bring that exceptional mind—and everything else, of course—to Carter's Run on Tuesday, March 30. I'm having a press conference you might find of interest. Say you'll come, Em-ee-lee."

Both sitting back, only their knees touching now, hands held loosely together, they smiled at one another.

"Jonas," she said after a heady silence. "Hear me say this: If you want me there, I'll be there."

He nodded, never more certain of anything in his life. "I do."
She grinned and squeezed his hands. "Me too."

Twenty-one

◆

When you play the game for fun, it's fun.
When you play it for a living, it's a game of sorrows.
GARY PLAYER

Nathan stepped up to the uninitiated practice tee at Carter's Run, grateful to be on familiar ground. The place was crawling with construction types putting the finishing touches on the clubhouse. Nobody seemed to notice a lone golfer—a Jonas Fielding look-alike at that—teeing up to hit a few balls.

He squinted up at the bright sky. It was the fourth sunny day in a row with temps in the fifties. On the chilly side for golf, but he was dressed for it. The air was clean and sharp, not too breezy. Even using Jonas' clubs, even woefully behind in his practice hours, Nate was hitting two-eighty to three hundred yards consistently.

Rolling his shoulders to relieve some tension, he shook out his legs and walked through his swing in slow-motion first: *Address. Backswing. Transition. Downswing. Impact. Finish.* Golf was a head game, but it was a muscle game, too, and he was pathetically out of shape.

Whack! The ball soared in a classic arc; his adrenaline soared with it. Man, he loved this game. Loved the feeling of power and freedom on the fairways, the exacting science of the putting greens. Loved the camaraderie of the other players…serious players, pro players.

Players who weren't a has-been like him.

Ten years ago, when it came to choosing practicing or partying, he chose partying. Five years ago, when it came to choosing between the game or the money, he chose the money.

Now the party was over; the money was gone.

And Nathan was in way over his head.

The Christianity bit, for example. That had started out as a lark, a game, a subterfuge to win Jonas over to his side and fast. He knew how religious Jonas was, how wrapped up in his church he'd become. What easier way could there be to make points the minute he pulled into town?

Problem was, it'd worked too well. Jonas believed his story and expected him to pray all the time—not just before meals. How stupid could that be, talking to God? As if he were listening. As if he cared.

Jonas kept dragging him to church, quoting Bible verses, talking about a new life in Christ. Nate wanted a new life, all right. A new life without Cy, *not* a new life with somebody else.

Unless it was Dee Dee Snyder. Too bad he wouldn't be around long enough to pursue that angle more fully.

This week was the big one. "Holy Week," they called it. *Great.* Church seven nights in a row. Not his idea of a good time. Luckily, he had an out: He'd found a job at Hess Clothing. When they'd shopped there earlier, the store manager had commented on his good taste in men's fashion and his knowledge of the better lines. When the guy heard Nate was a former pro golfer with free time on his hands, he'd called to offer him a sales position. "Any brother of Jonas Fielding is okay by me," he'd said.

Just don't do a background check, buddy.

Not that the man would find a criminal record. The two drunk-driving charges from back when he was at Stanford had been dismissed and Nate had judiciously steered clear of the courts since then. He'd also steered clear of a steady job with steady income, choosing instead a life of gambling in the one state that made it legal.

Gripping his club, he went through the motions that had become habit, slowly, then at full speed, turning his frustration and anger into energy for his swing. *Whack!*

He almost chuckled. *Must be plenty keyed up. Hit two-ninety on that one, easy.*

At least he had a job and a place to practice gratis for a week. He almost hated to admit it, but it felt good to be working again. Took a long time to earn a buck, but they couldn't take it away from him.

Cy could. In a New York minute.

And would. Four days from now, on April 1. No fooling.

Desperate times called for desperate measures. And he was nothing if not desperate. *Forgive me, brother.* He'd said it over and over in his mind, consoled only by the fact that it wasn't Jonas' money that'd be missing. It was construction money. Borough money. *What's twenty grand when you're talking about a budget of five million?*

Nate had quietly worked his plan the last two weeks. While Jonas was up to his ears courting his woman and creating his golf course, Nate was busy selling sportswear and suits by day, and talking business with Dee Dee late into the evening.

She would have called it a date.

He called it information gathering.

Dee Dee knew all about the financing, all about the negotiations and the red tape involved with putting Carter's Run together. Smart woman—not an intellectual like stuffy old Emilie, but plenty smart about business. He'd explained to Dee Dee that he'd majored in economics and had an interest in how business worked. In fact, he was enjoying his new venture in sales. Might think about pursuing selling real estate someday.

Would she care to share an insider's view?

She would and did. Dee Dee trusted him. He suspected his earnest kisses helped on that count.

In fact, he'd be seeing her again tonight. They'd agreed to meet at church—since it was Palm Sunday, he'd be expected to show—then they'd slip off to her place for more...sales training. At least, that's how she probably saw it. He saw it as an opportunity to get the last crucial facts straight before Tuesday.

He knew this much: Jonas balanced his books every Monday evening.

Tuesday afternoon, while Jonas and the rest of the world were at Carter's Run for the press conference, Nate would make the necessary changes on the spreadsheet. Wednesday, he'd handle the bank transfer and overnight a check for twenty grand to Vegas. *Thank you, FedEx.*

Thursday, he'd be gone.

Gone where, he didn't know. Or care. Just out.

More than anything, Nate longed to be a free man.

"You are free to go anywhere your two legs can take you, Em," Jonas had informed her. *"Except* in the vicinity of my golf course."

The idea! A full-grown woman being given strict orders not to go anywhere near Carter's Run—for any reason, even with her eyes closed—until March 30.

When he'd first announced his silly stay-away edict two weeks earlier, she jerked her chin up. "Humph. What could I possibly learn with my eyes closed?"

Standing there in his paneled office, Jonas flashed a devilish grin. "Shut your eyes and let's find out."

She folded her arms across her jacket and closed her eyes with a melodramatic snap. "I'm ready, Dr. Fielding."

"Eyes closed tight?"

"You know they are!"

He lowered his voice. "Hear anything?"

She listened to him whisper sweet words in her ear and fought a smile. "I hear a grown man saying some outrageous things about my lips, that's what I hear."

"Even with your eyes closed? Well, well."

They were still shut tight, though that was getting more difficult once he started tracing her features with a single, gentle finger.

She sighed loudly. "I get your point, Jonas. Even without seeing, we still have four other perfectly good senses to work with."

"Yup, and I have two more to engage. What's this scent, do you know?"

"Mmmm. Roses." Her eyelids fluttered at their fragrant perfume.

"Wait!" Jonas put his hand over the top half of her face. "Don't open your eyes. Tell me what color they are."

"Do *what?* I can't tell that with my eyes closed."

"Yes, you can. Try."

She reached up her hand to touch the silky petals, then sniffed again and smiled. "Ah. Pink. Pale pink."

He laughed, that rolling rumble of a laugh that made her toes curl. "Precisely. And how did you know that?"

"Because *you* know I like pink."

"Right. Now, open your mouth, please."

Well! "For a kiss?"

"Nope. For a bud. Not a rosebud, either."

It was her turn to laugh. While her mouth was hanging open as directed, Jonas popped in a swirl of chocolate—a Wilbur Bud—from the Wilbur Chocolate factory on Broad Street. The dark, semisweet candy left her smiling but marble-mouthed. "Mmmm. Yumma! Dat's realla gud."

She opened her eyes then and found Jonas bearing an entire box of her favorite confection in one hand and a dozen pink roses in the other.

"Ohhh." Emilie swallowed the last of her chocolate. "It's like Valentine's Day all over again." She carefully took each generous gift and put it aside on his desk, then wrapped her arms around his neck. "You win. I won't go anywhere near Carter's Run until the thirtieth. But when that day gets here, sir, I expect a limo waiting at my doorstep. Understood?"

It was, in fact, a Lincoln Town Car.

Emilie couldn't believe it when her doorbell rang at quarter to one that sunny Tuesday afternoon. Spring had finally sprung, and everyone in town was oohing and aahing over the daffodils and crocus that were showing their colors.

Her eyes, however, were awestruck by the sleek, solid black automobile at the curb, and the immaculately uniformed young man on her brick porch, holding his hat.

"Are you ready, Dr. Getz? Mr. Fielding insisted you arrive precisely at one o'clock."

"Let me get my coat."

"You really won't need it, ma'am. It hit seventy at noon."

She stuck her nose out and marveled at the warm breeze. "Very well. Lead the way, please."

He did so quite literally, offering his arm to escort her down the steps and see her safely planted in the backseat.

Two things waited for her there, resting on the putty-colored leather upholstery. A stunning corsage—pale pink sweetheart roses—which she carefully pinned on the lapel of her dark navy suit. Jonas had requested that she "dress like a professor." She hoped this was what he meant.

Such a mysterious man! Carter's Run was the talk of Lititz these days, with the opening barely over a week away and the fairways and greens looking verdant and inviting. But the most discussed feature was the eighteenth hole. The entire thing was surrounded with a tall, fence-like arrangement made of canvas. Temporary, of course, but it stirred up no end of speculation.

"Do *you* know what's going on in there, Emilie?"

She told everyone the same thing: "Not only do I not know, I'm not allowed to ask." At which point they stared at her like she was not as intelligent as her degree suggested.

But that was yesterday.

Today was her day—everyone's day—to find out. It was a press conference, meaning photographers would be omnipresent. She'd added a teensy bit of color to her eyes, cheeks, and lips, hoping Jonas wouldn't notice and get out his handkerchief to pat it all off.

She sniffed her corsage and grinned to herself. *If he wants to do so later when we're alone, that's something else altogether.*

Looking out the window at the most beautiful scenery in the world—*home*—Emilie let her gaze drop to the other package in the backseat. A narrow box, the sort one might use for long-stemmed roses, except this one didn't show a florist's name. Only her name on a tag that read in bold print: "To be opened on the ride home. Or else."

Such a rogue, that man. *Or else.* Honestly!

Still, after all he'd done to please her these last weeks, she could leave one little box alone, couldn't she?

Emilie stared at it, tapping one finger on the bright red bow tied around it, thinking.

Nothing said she couldn't *shake* the thing. See if it was heavy or made a telltale noise. She slipped one hand under the box, long enough to realize it weighed next to nothing, then froze when the driver shot her a cautionary look in the rearview mirror.

"That's for later, ma'am. Sorry."

Heavens! Why did she have to get some young upstart for a driver? One with no sense of adventure whatsoever.

"Very well," she said with a sniff. "Eyes on the road, please."

In minutes, they were turning onto Kissel Hill. Emilie pressed her nose against the glass, mouth agape. *It wasn't possible!* How could they have accomplished so much in so little time? Her regard for the project manager's talents shot up another ten notches.

And yet, even with something of this magnitude on his shoulders, Jonas had managed to join her for Holy Week readings at church the last two nights.

Amazing!

That's the word that sang through her heart as they neared the finished clubhouse. The colorful annuals, the fresh sod, the red brick walks, and the creamy tan stucco architecture that matched the library under construction down the street—classic lines that mirrored those of the Moravian church they both loved.

And I love you, Jonas Fielding. She would tell him so, the minute she laid eyes on him. First thing, no matter what.

"There he is!" She tapped the driver on the shoulder and pointed to the pristine white wooden archway that guided golfers toward the welcoming, stone-fronted entrance. Underneath the graceful arch, shaking hands and smiling for the camera, stood Jonas, wearing a sharply-pressed pair of tan slacks and a new Carter's Run golf shirt.

Not, though, in his trademark black.

In pale pink. *My pink!* Her heart leaped in her throat as she lunged for the door handle.

Jonas looked up in time to see her climbing out of the Town Car, handed out by the polite, if a tad rule-obsessive, young driver, who soon faded from view as she moved toward the man of the hour.

Remember what you said, Em. You're going to tell him you love him the minute you lay eyes on him...

It was a silly idea. She would put it out of her mind immediately.

Anyway, there was no time. The minute he leaned over and spoke to the media types on either side of him, their camera lenses swerved in her direction, and Jonas began waving her toward him.

His expression was triumphant, his whole face lit as if from the inside. "Dr. Emilie Getz! Come and meet your many admirers."

There was only one admirer she needed to see.

Emilie walked straight toward him, her navy high heels in dark contrast to the solid white cement beneath them; her tidy knot of hair bouncing a bit as she walked briskly in his direction; her pale pink lips stretched into a smile so wide it made her face ache with joy.

He extended a hand as she approached. "Ladies and gentlemen, Dr. Emilie Getz."

She stopped mere inches from him. "And this," she announced, "is the man I love, Dr. Jonas Fielding." After which the only logical thing to do was plant her lips on his and remain there until people started clapping.

Which the entire gathering did—eventually—with gusto.

The woman was completely out of control.

He loved it.

Loved being kissed by her. Loved being loved by her. Even loved being embarrassed by her very public display of affection.

Why not? She was the new, improved Emilie Getz, and he was one very blessed man.

"Why a light pink shirt?" was her first whispered question when the applause around them faded.

He shrugged. "Because a black golf shirt is too hot."

Quick thinking, Fielding.

Emilie stood proudly by his side while he bragged about her Gemeinhaus research. And about her willingness to forfeit her rights to the land for the good of the community.

"But folks, that sort of sacrifice will not be necessary on the part of Dr. Getz or her peers in historic preservation. If you'll follow me, please."

Pressing a hand lightly against the small of her back, he steered Emilie toward the area enclosed by canvas that was gently flapping in the warm, almost-April breeze.

"Jonas, what have you done?"

"You'll see." *Boy, would she ever.*

He nodded at two smiling clubhouse staff members dressed in matching pink shirts. "Fellas, if you will, kindly tie one of those back for us."

Yanking one huge piece of canvas aside and knotting it in place, they stood aside as Jonas and Emilie walked through the wide opening with the media hot on their heels.

Emilie's eyes grew rounder than a pair of Titleist Pros. "Jonas, you didn't!"

I did.

He grinned down at her, then waved his arm in an arc, taking in the remarkable scene before them. "You are getting a preview of the most unusual eighteenth hole in the world. When Carter's Run opens in ten days, golfers will approach the only bunker in golf history that *protects* history."

Jonas walked the reporters around the putting green, showing them how the designer had cleverly worked around the beginning stages of the archaeological site—a site bordered with a beautiful stone wall to keep golf balls where they belonged. "Which is *not* bouncing off an archaeologist's head. Isn't that right, Dr. Getz?"

Her own head shook back and forth, but the woman was otherwise speechless. Jonas grinned. *Nice change, that.* "While Dr. Getz becomes acquainted with her dig, let me show you our course architect's fine work on the approach to the green."

Clearly Emilie needed time to take it all in. Leaving her standing at her cherished site, never taking his eyes off her for longer than a minute, Jonas shared the story of the acquisition of the larger clubhouse property that had allowed not only a bigger clubhouse but, ultimately, a Gemeinhaus, too. "It's the generosity of our Lititz neighbors, working with us to create Carter's Run, that will make this a golf course of which the entire town can be proud."

Watch it, Fielding, or they'll be asking you to run for mayor.

Shuffling the murmuring group back toward Emilie, he gave them a brief synopsis of the events leading up to the restructuring of the eighteenth hole. "As you can see, ladies and gents, we brought in a crack team to do the initial dig. By unearthing the perimeters of the historic foundation, we were able to adjust our golf course accordingly, allowing both to happily coexist, side by side."

One reporter raised a hand. "If the borough annexed all the land for Carter's Run, do they own this historic section too?"

Jonas was hoping they wouldn't ask this. Not here, not now.

But the Lord—and Emilie—expected him to tell the truth at all times, including this one.

Jonas walked toward a stone marker on the street side of the Gemeinhaus dig and rested his hand on the heavy cloth draped over the stone's engraved front. "The truth is, I bought this property from the borough myself, and—" he could delay the news no longer—"I donated it to the Lititz Moravian Congregation in honor of their 250th anniversary, and in the name of—" he whipped the cloth off with a flourish—"Emilie Getz, Ph.D."

"Jonas!"

The woman attacked him. There was no other word for it. Jumped into his arms from a full trot, knocking them both against the marble and stone marker.

He loved it.

Which was a good thing since that was the photo that ended up on the front page of the *Lancaster New Era,* the *Reading Eagle,* the *Harrisburg Patriot,* and the *Philadelphia Inquirer.*

Above it was the bold headline: "Preservation and Progress Find Common Ground."

"Jonas, after all you've done for me this incredible day, what could I possibly do for you?"

Emilie gazed up at him, knowing there were stars in her eyes simply because she saw them reflected in his darker ones. "The day is young, barely three o'clock. Can you think of something I might do to please you this afternoon?"

Those eyes of his darkened further. "Oh, I certainly can."

"Humph." She aimed a playful swat at his chest. "Think of something else."

"Okay." A sly grin appeared. "Water my plants."

"You must be joking."

He shook his head, leading her toward the patiently waiting limo driver. "It's no joke, as you'll agree when you see them." Digging out his keys, he tucked them in her hand. "Have the driver stop at my place just long enough for you to let yourself in and do your green-thumb duty, then leave the keys on the kitchen counter and head for home. I hate to ask you to do this, Em, but your dozen green friends are wilting under my care. I'll catch up with you at church at seven. Is it a date?"

"Of course." She waited as the driver climbed in and started the engine, not wanting the afternoon to end. "Jonas, I don't know what to say or where to start." Swallowing a lump that had lodged itself in her throat for the last two hours, she pressed her hands against his warm chest, just to feel his heart beating solidly beneath her palms. "You've managed to make not only *me* happy today, but our whole church, our whole *town*."

"Of the three, beloved, you are definitely at the top of the list." Pulling her closer, he bent down and kissed her, tenderly at first, then with a fervency, a passion born of a shared faith and a shared future. When their lips finally parted, he smiled, his mouth still only inches away from hers. "Actually, you *are* the list, Emilie Getz. The Lord told me to show you the fullness of his joy. He forgot to mention that I'd be a beneficiary, too."

With those words ringing in her heart, she kissed his chin, then slipped into the backseat. *Floated* was a better word for it.

The driver shifted into first gear before she saw the unopened box.

"Wait!" She pushed the button that sent her window whirring down, stopping halfway. "Jonas, wait! Your gift. May I open it now?"

He leaned down and looked in, grinning like a big elf. "Please do."

She didn't need a second invitation, tearing off the red ribbon with abandon, then more carefully lifting the lid. It was parchment, rolled up with care, held closed by a wrapper stamped, "Heritage Map Museum."

"Oh, a map! I love maps." She whirled in her seat to face him. "How did you know I love maps?"

He shrugged. "A guess."

With trembling fingers she slid off the paper wrapper and began to unfurl the map in her lap. "Look! In the corner. *Warwick*. Oh, it's a local map. How wonderful!" She looked up at him long enough to blow him a kiss. "Very old, I'm sure. If I can just smooth out—"

Her mouth went completely dry.

It was the Gemeinhaus survey map. Dated 1747.

"Jonas, how…how did you find this? They sold it the day I saw it!"

"Yes, they did." His voice was low. "And two weeks ago when I finally tracked the new owner down, he sold it to me."

"To *you?*" Her mind was reeling. "But why?"

"So I could prove to the committee the Gemeinhaus wasn't a figment of your overactive imagination."

She stared at him. "But look what it cost you! Time. Manpower. Money. Most men would have kept that kind of information to themselves."

The broad shoulders under his pink golf shirt lifted slightly. "Guess I'm not most men."

Now there's an understatement. "So…" She was still trying to put the pieces together. "You'll hang this in the clubhouse, then?"

He snorted. "At that price? Are you kidding? I bought it for the woman who stole my heart."

"The woman who stole your eighteenth hole, you mean."

Jonas shook his head and leaned in closer. "On the contrary, Dr. Getz. You gave it to me, free and clear, remember? Thanks to your map, I found a way to give it back."

"And then some." A tear sneaked out before she could smile and pat it away. "Oh, Jonas, you are amazing. Thank you." She quickly found a tissue and attended to her runny nose, squeezing in another word of thanks between each sniffle.

"And now, before I water this exquisite map instead of your plants, remove yourself, kind sir. Oh, driver." She tapped his uniformed shoulder. "Carry on."

She blew Jonas a kiss as the window closed, then carefully rolled up her map and slid it gingerly back in the box, closing the lid tight. Absolutely nothing could spoil this day. This perfect, sunny, not-a-cloud-in-the-sky day.

The Town Car pulled up to Jonas' house two minutes later. "I'll be back in no time," she promised, sliding out, house keys in hand. Letting herself in through the back door—with permission this time, she realized, feeling a guilty twinge—Emilie found a glass pitcher that would serve as her watering can. She filled it up at the kitchen tap, then ventured into the house, not sure where she might find her leafy gifts.

She couldn't summon plants like she did Olive and Victor, so she'd have to wander from room to room until she found them. None in the kitchen, she quickly deduced. Nor the bedrooms, nor the bath, though rumor had it her first gift met its withered demise there. None in the dining room or living room either, which left only Jonas' large den and office on the other side of the house.

Bluegrass music was blaring behind the half-closed door. *Nathan, obviously.* Odd he wasn't at work today. She knocked so she wouldn't catch him off guard, then pushed the door fully open.

There he is. Hadn't heard her apparently, and no surprise that, with the music so loud. She stepped into the room, then paused, suddenly uneasy. Something didn't feel right. Nathan was sitting at Jonas' desk with his back to her, his hands flying over the keyboard. The oversized screen in front of him was a sea of numbers.

"Nathan?" She spoke without meaning to, then gasped when he swung around with a jerk of his chair and jumped to his feet, the screen going blank as he touched a key in passing.

"What are you doing here?" The almost-black Fielding brows were knit together, storm clouds brooding over eyes that flashed like lightning at sea.

"I…I, uh…Jonas gave me the keys." She held them up in one hand, the pitcher in the other, noticing how the water sloshed from side to side in her shaky grasp. "I stopped by to…um, water the plants."

"Oh, I see." Nathan's expression lightened considerably. "Look, Emilie, I'm sorry I yelled. I just…didn't expect anyone to be in the house." He jerked a thumb toward the stereo. "Shouldn't have had that going at ninety decibels either, huh?" Grabbing a remote control for the CD player off the desk, he stopped the noise with the touch of one button. "Takes care of that problem."

He turned to her and dipped his chin—just like his brother often did—and fixed his gaze on her. "Emilie, will you forgive me for overreacting?"

"Ah…yes. Of course I will." She took a step backward. "Suppose I water the plants in here very quickly…" She craned her neck, relieved to see that there were, indeed, leaf-bearing plants in the room. "Then I'll be gone."

"Fine." He leaned back, and a rush of relief washed over her. "To be honest with you, I'm playing hooky from work today and feeling a little guilty about it." His eyes took on a playful twinkle, and she felt the tension in her muscles begin to relax.

"Emilie, I'd like to cash in a favor, if I could." His grin was most persuasive. "You owe me one, if you recall." Clearly his wink was intended to charm and, indeed, it proved hard to resist.

She giggled slightly and pointed her water pitcher at a thirsty begonia on Jonas' desk. "Owe *you* a favor, you say?"

"From another occasion when you came by our place unannounced. Ring any bells?"

The heat rising to her cheeks answered his question. "Your day off is safe with me. I won't say a word."

He looked immensely relieved. "It'll be our little secret, then. Won't it, Dr. Getz?"

Twenty-two

◆

The best way to know a man is to watch him when he is angry.
HEBREW PROVERB

"Next comes the part where we don't say a word," Emilie whispered, as the hymn concluded and the small congregation found their seats.

Sara, dressed in a somber, dark green dress befitting the occasion, nodded her head then leaned up to ask, "Don't we even sing? Or eat buns?"

"No, sweetie." Emilie smiled down on her dear face. "That's Saturday, the Great Sabbath lovefeast. But this is Maundy Thursday, the last night the Lord was with his followers."

Sara's small nose wrinkled with concern. "If they were his followers, how come they didn't follow him?"

"Because Jesus said, 'Where I am going, you cannot follow me now, but you will follow afterward.' Remember? That's what we all read aloud from our book a minute ago." Emilie gently tweaked the child's freckled nose, enthralled by its miniature softness. "Were you listening, sweet girl?"

"Most of the time," Sara insisted, her voice rising. "But wasn't there a bad guy, who *didn't* follow?"

Emilie pressed a finger to her lips in a silent *shhh*. "Yes. Judas Iscariot, a man who shared Jesus' table that night."

Sara's frown was a work of art, painted across every feature, as she repeated in a loud whisper, "Bad old Judas His Chariot!"

Emilie mashed her lips together until she was certain a laugh wouldn't come bursting out. "Almost, Sara. *Iscariot.* He started out as one of the disciples but lost his way." Straightening up and smoothing her skirt, Emilie watched the men move forward toward the communion table. "Now, sweetie. Will you promise to sit very still?"

Sara did indeed sit quietly while Emilie let the sacred ceremony calm her heart and spirit and prepare her for the weekend ahead. Months ago—a lifetime ago—it would have been nothing more than a Sunday of special music in church, of trombones and Easter eggs in baskets and baked ham with cloves.

Those elements would be in place again this year, but it was the Lord himself, moving among them, that would make the difference. *Correction, Em. He always was the heart of Easter.* She was the one who would finally join the festivities this year, she realized with a wondrous sense of contentment.

There was another first, too. The Fielding family had decided to make Easter morning a reunion of sorts. Chris and Jeff and their wives and kids were coming up from Delaware on Sunday. The first time in ten years that all four brothers would be together.

Perhaps the three older brothers could help poor Nathan, who seemed to grasp the meaning of grace one minute, then throw it away like so much fodder the next.

This afternoon, though, belonged to her and Sara alone. She'd asked Beth if she might borrow her daughter for the early service at four, to be followed by supper at her house. *Cooking for a four-year-old!* The mere thought of it still undid her. Jonas and Nathan were attending the later service at seven, then stopping by for decaf coffee and Moravian sugar cake. Helen's recipe, of course, but baked by her own inexperienced hands.

It'd taken all day—cooking and mashing the potatoes, letting the dough rise twice, and all the rest—but the house smelled divine, like Winkler's Bakery, only better because this house was *home.* A borrowed home, but much loved, nonetheless.

When the service ended, Emilie and her charge stepped out into the cloudy, cooler day, gathering their jackets around them. A whole week of sunshine had spoiled them for certain. Now it looked more like April usually did, with incessant showers.

Emilie squeezed Sara's hand as they strolled down the sidewalk. "Have I told you how proud I am of you, winning the Easter coloring contest with your pretty basket? Your picture in the *Record Express* looked mighty impressive."

The girl beamed up at her, little teeth like a row of fresh white corn. "Daddy framed it."

"Of course he did. He loves his little artist. And I do, too."

It was getting easier to say the word out loud—to Sara, to Jonas, to Beth, to Helen, even to her mother. *Imagine that!* She'd always loved her mother, but *saying* so, putting it into words, was a whole different story. "New, improved Emilie," Jonas called her. The more she understood what he meant, the more she liked it.

They were greeted at the front door by a hungry Olive. Then again, Olive always sounded that way—petulant and scolding. While Sara cheerfully assumed her role as official cat caretaker, Emilie busied herself in the kitchen.

Steering their meat loaf into the oven, she set the timer for a full ninety minutes, then scrubbed two big potatoes to toss on the rack. Green beans went on the back burner to get ready to simmer before she slipped off her apron, satisfied that something approximating dinner would be ready by six-thirty.

You're a regular Donna Reed, Em. She smiled as she moved through the house, looking for one naughty cat and one sleepy girl, knowing they'd be together. Why did these simple domestic tasks feel so natural, so *right?* It wasn't merely hormonal, that nonsense about her loudly ticking biological clock—was it? *Certainly not!* It surely wasn't something as basic as her growing love for Jonas that had her thinking maternal thoughts—was it? *No. Couldn't be!*

She stepped into the living room and paused, smiling all the way to her toes. In the soft lamplight, Sara and Olive were curled up on the couch, both fast asleep. Sara, with damp, blond ringlets around her forehead and her little black shoes still on. Olive, stretched out alongside her, one furry paw resting on Sara's soft cheek.

Emilie etched the scene on her heart, drinking it in like her communion juice, like grace and life itself. Sara was not her own child, but for an hour she could pretend, couldn't she?

The little black oxfords slid off easily into her hands, then she placed them side by side on the floor, two doll shoes. Borrowing the quilt from the back of the sofa, she draped it across cat and child, making sure both had their pink noses showing so they could breathe.

Crossing the room on tiptoe, Emilie pulled a favorite book off the shelf and sneaked back, folding herself onto the end of the long couch, Sara's stockinged feet touching hers.

It was a moment she would always remember as one of perfect peace. Outside, the fading light of an early spring evening; inside, the warm glow of dinner in the oven and candles shimmering year-round in the many-paned windows. A quiet innocence.

At six-thirty, when the stove buzzer went off, Emilie sat upright with a jolt. *Goodness!* She'd fallen asleep, just like Sara. "Wake up, sweetie," she said with a tired yawn, amazed to find her open book beside her on the floor, barely read.

A nap? Me? "It's dinnertime." She flipped off the warm quilt, nudging Olive off the couch, smiling as the furry creature stalked off in a feline huff.

Sara and Emilie moved in slow motion toward the kitchen, where the delicious smells of a home-cooked meal perked them up in a hurry. While Sara set the table—she'd learned to use matching plates now—Emilie sliced the meat, drained the beans, then filled two serving dishes. "So much food for just us two. Suppose we make a plate for Jonas and Nathan to have later, just in case they're hungry?"

There was no "in case." The two men were always hungry.

After Sara's long, heartfelt prayer for every animal in the house—and most of the stuffed ones in her bedroom at home—they dove into their meal. The child ate like she'd never seen food before, packing her cheeks like a chipmunk. Emilie ate with greater poise but no less enthusiasm. Dessert would be sugar cake—later for Emilie, when the men stopped by, but now for Sara before her daddy came for her at eight.

Emilie hated to ask, but had to know. "Does it taste like Mrs. B's?"

Sara nodded, managing to roll her eyes and chew at the same time. "Mm-mm!" she said between bites. That was good enough for Emilie.

The unexpected brrrnngg! of the front doorbell made them both jump in their seats. "Is that my daddy already?" Sara asked, her lower lip in full pout.

Emilie checked her watch. *Two minutes to seven.* If it were Drew, he was an hour early. If it were Jonas, he'd be late for church.

"Maybe it's the Easter bunny," she teased, patting Sara's hand as she stood to answer the door. "You keep nibbling on your sugar cake while I see who's come a'calling."

It was Drew standing on her porch, a tall, lanky man with a smile that commandeered much of his face and eyes brimming with kindness. He stepped inside, instinctively ducking at the doorway, then glanced toward the kitchen. "Is Sara ready?"

"My, you're early." Emilie tried not to sound disappointed. "I was looking for you at eight. Give me a second and I'll gather her things."

He wrinkled his brow, "That's funny. I was sure I was supposed to be here at seven. Sorry, Em."

They both shrugged, chuckling, then headed for the kitchen, where Drew soon had a forkful of sugar cake pointed toward his mouth. Emilie watched them together—father and daughter—and thought of Jonas. Would he embrace fathering with such enthusiasm? Or had fathering Nathan—there really was no other word for it—soured his taste for parenting?

And why are you even thinking such things, Emilie Getz? Had the man proposed marriage? He had not. Had they even discussed it? They had not. Would she say yes if he asked?

In a heartbeat.

That thought kept a private, half-smile on her face through the process of collecting Sara's jacket, shoes, a stray toy, a favorite book. Amazing how one child could require such an armload of equipment.

Emilie hugged her more than once before Sara and Drew drove off, taking a corner of her heart with them. The last thing she saw was Sara's nose pressed against the glass and a small hand waving good-bye.

The tightness in her throat caught her off guard. *You'll see her tomorrow, silly. Then Saturday at the lovefeast, and Easter, too.* Her emotions seemed especially volatile lately. Whatever happened to her calm, quiet, ordered existence?

"I'll tell you what happened," she said to Victor, who was behaving himself in his lofty cage. "The Lord happened. Jonas happened. *Life* happened, you crazy bird!"

Are you talking to Victor or yourself, Em?

"Pretty girl!" Victor squawked back, answering her question.

Laughing softly, she flipped on the stereo to fill the empty house with choral music, then tackled the kitchen, reveling in the simple tasks of washing dinner dishes, wiping counters clean, brushing crumbs into her palms the way she'd watched her mother do a thousand times.

Drying her hands on a towel, she stopped to survey her squeaky-clean domain, enjoying the quiet satisfaction of it, when the sound of a fist banging on wood, mere feet away, snapped her head toward the back door. *Who in the world?* Ignoring the knot in her stomach, she flicked the switch for the outside light and peered through the glass.

Nathan. What in the world was he doing here—alone, at her place—when he was supposed to be with Jonas at church? The clock in the dining room had just chimed seven-thirty. *Odd.*

She opened the back door with the slightest twinge of apprehension. "Hello, Nathan." She took in the sullen features, the slouched shoulders, the downturned corners of his mouth. "I didn't expect—"

Without a word or a warning, he lurched forward and staggered over the threshold, then caught himself on the doorjamb, gripping it for balance, his head hanging down at an angle.

The scent of liquor was faint but distinct. More than anything, the air around him smelled of fear.

"Nathan?" Her heart squeezed into her throat. "Are you okay? Are you hurt?" She glanced behind him, seeing nothing there but the white gazebo in the dusk-filled garden. "Is…Jonas with you?"

"Do I look like my brother's keeper?" His growled words were slightly slurred but clearly sarcastic.

The one that needs a keeper tonight is you, Nate. She'd never seen him in such a state. His eyes were unfocused, his breath was thick, and he desperately needed ten minutes with a sharp razor and a wet comb.

Emilie kept her voice as steady as possible, praying between every word. "Something's happened, Nathan, I can see that. Tell me why you're here, what I can do to help you."

He was unsteady but standing, looming over her, misery and anger vying for control of his features. Any self-control seemed lost to liquor hours ago. "You wanna *help* me?" His eyes narrowed. "You've been too much *help* already. You lied to me, Emilie."

Lied? Struggling to swallow, to keep her tone even, she shook her head. "I'm sorry, but I don't know what you mean."

He swore at her, slamming the door behind him.

"Nathan! Please." She backed up a step. "I need you to wait outside while I call Jonas and ask him—"

"No! Not Jonas." Without preamble, he reached out and snatched her left wrist with one muscular hand, wrapping his other hand around her throat, pulling her against his chest so she couldn't wriggle free.

"You lied to me, Emilie." His words, ground out with barely contained fury, were more menacing than his actions. "You told Jonas about Tuesday." His hand around her throat began to tighten. "You did, didn't you? You told him."

Her heart slammed against her chest. No man had ever been so rough with her. Anxiety and anger washed over her, threatening to drown her.

No! Don't let him bully you, Em.

Straightening her spine as best she could, Emilie said in her calmest, most authoritative voice, "I did not lie to you."

"You were the only one who knew about it, Emilie, the only one who saw me." His voice was a ragged knife; his anger far beyond reason.

But she had to try. "I said nothing to Jonas about last Tuesday. And what would I have told him? That you were playing hooky. That you were sitting at his computer, punching in numbers that were meaningless to me."

His hands, large like Jonas', began exerting more pressure on her wrist, and even more on her throat. "Nice try, Doc. You're too bright not to have figured it out. How else would Jonas know about my money transfer in time to mess it up?"

Her breathing felt pinched. "Nathan...please!" Her voice was high and faint. It was hard to get the words out. She could feel bruises already forming where his fingers manhandled her too-long, too-pale neck.

She had to push through the pain. *Must, Em. Must!* He had to understand. "I had...no idea." He squeezed harder. "Please! I didn't lie. I didn't know....about...the money." She coughed, trying to clear her throat. "Don't do this, Na—"

He cut her off with a curse. "You ruined everything!" He shook her, making her neck crack and ache with each jerking motion.

"I never...I never..." She was dizzy now. Light-headed. The atmosphere in the room was changing to a pale, starry blue. More than anything she wanted to lie down. *Yes, there on the cool floor.* As though from another room, she heard Nathan shouting things she didn't understand. Ugly things, angry things.

That was when she realized, however dimly, that Nathan was in much more pain than she.

"Please…stop. Please…" It was the last thing she remembered saying before the back door flew open and crashed against the cabinets.

Jonas. Roaring like a lion.

"Get your hands off her, Nathan!"

The hands disappeared.

She dropped to her knees, bent over and gasping. Pulling in air like a lifeline, then falling back to a sitting position, her back propped against the refrigerator.

Time elongated. Seconds became minutes.

Jonas looked at her with love and fury in his eyes, concern on his features. Looked long enough to see that she was breathing steadily. Waited until she nodded and waved a dismissive hand that said, "Don't worry, I'm okay," before he turned and slammed Nathan against the counter.

His righteous anger charged the air. "How *dare* you touch her! How dare you hurt her like that!" Jonas was breathing like a locomotive, huffing in angry bursts. "Did you think you could get away with this? With…all of this?"

"She lied to me!" Nathan shouted, pointing an accusing finger at her.

Jonas' voice dropped to a deadly pitch. "And *you* lied to *me,* brother." He dragged in a ragged breath and pushed it back out, the sound echoing his anger and frustration. And disappointment.

"Nate, to think I trusted you." He shook his head, not letting go, still holding Nathan against the counter. Though matched in height, Jonas was more solid. And sober. Emilie didn't doubt his words—and tone of voice— alone would have pinned his brother to the wall. "I trusted you with everything I owned and everything that mattered to me." He turned in Emilie's direction, checking on her again, letting her know he loved her with his brief but potent gaze.

Emilie nodded to let him know she was fine.

She was nothing of the kind, but Jonas had enough trouble on his hands at the moment.

Jonas snapped his head back toward Nate, his voice heavy with regret. "I'm ashamed of you, brother, and ashamed of myself for trusting you."

Nathan met his brother's indictment without flinching. If there was remorse there, it didn't show. The only emotion she sensed, rolling off Nathan like steam, was fear.

Jonas pressed for answers. "Why did you do it, Nate? Why did you mess with the books? And why did I come here tonight and find you...?" Jonas pounded his fists on his brother's shoulders, not hard enough to hurt him, but hard enough.

Nathan dropped his head and shook it. It didn't look like remorse from where she was sitting. It looked like cowardice.

Jonas wasn't buying it. "I asked you a question, son."

Nathan's head shot up, and his voice with it. "I am *not* your son! Can't you get that through your thick head?" Nathan straightened, shoving Jonas back a half step. "I don't owe you, okay? He was *my* dad, too, and he died trying to save *your* friend, and that's all there is to it."

Jonas stepped closer, widening his stance. "Now listen—"

"No, *you* listen! Nobody made you my dad, you got that?" Nathan's eyes were fiercely bright, his anger cutting through his alcohol-induced fog. "You are not my dad and you can't tell me how to live."

"*You* are the one who always calls asking for advice! And for money. Ten thousand in the last two months, Nate."

Emilie gasped at the sum. *Ten thousand dollars! Gone in two months?*

Jonas' tone was as solid as granite. And as hard. "Where did it go, Nate? Looks to me like your rehab time was not well spent."

"I told you I'll pay it back." Nate dipped his head again, bitterness seeping into his voice. "Right now I've got more problems than you can possibly imagine."

"Yeah, and your biggest problem is standing right in front of you." Jonas grabbed his arms, as if trying to shake some sense into him. "Nathan, this afternoon Dee Dee called and told me what she thought you were up to. That's when I checked the accounts, found your digital fingerprints all over them. What you did amounts to attempted embezzlement. That's serious jail time, do you understand that?"

Nathan shrugged, not looking up. "I figured you'd cover for me."

"*Cover* for you? That's taxpayers' money, Nate, not mine. And then there's this business tonight." He turned in Emilie's direction, hands firmly gripping Nathan around the elbows, keeping him immobile. "Did you welcome his company tonight, Em? Was he invited through this door?"

She shook her head and managed a shaky, "No."

Jonas swerved back to Nathan, his jaw tense. "I thought not. So we're talking forcible entry. Plus assault and battery—"

"I haven't got a weapon," Nate shot back.

"Your anger alone is a weapon!" Jonas lowered his pitch but not the intensity. "Your words are weapons and your hands are weapons, Nate. Emilie has the bruises to prove it. Unless you can convince me otherwise, I intend to call the Lititz police and press charges."

"Nooo!" Emilie struggled to stand, then realized her legs were like jelly.

Jonas shook him once, hard, then let go and paced across the room, hands jammed in his pockets, his dark eyes more intense than she'd ever seen them, his brows gathered into a painful knot. His emotions were raw, edgy, and easy enough to read: He needed to move before he hit something, namely Nathan. He needed to understand, to make sense where there was none.

Finally he stood still and simply stared at Nate, waiting.

The air was charged.

Nate said nothing, not even with his expression.

Jonas finally broke the silence with a weighty sigh. "Sit down, brother. We gotta talk. Nobody needs twenty thousand that badly unless they're in trouble. You in trouble, Nate?"

His younger brother lifted his head. His eyes were dead. His mouth was a hard line. "The less you know, the better, Jonas."

"Nah, that's not how this is gonna work." Jonas pulled out a kitchen chair and nodded at it. "C'mon, sit. We managed not to hit each other. Let's talk it through. Figure out a solution."

Jonas dropped into the seat across the table and nodded at the other chair again. "I'm not your dad and never was. But I'm your oldest brother and always will be."

Nate pushed off the counter, moving not toward the chair, but the back door. "Unlucky you!" He yanked the door open and slammed it behind him, rattling the walls of the little house.

The room fell silent except for the sound of Emilie's labored breathing.

She slumped down, as if all the air had gone out of her body at the slam of the door. With her adrenaline already beginning to subside, the pain was back in spades, and with it, more tears.

She managed three words. "Jonas. Get Nate."

"No." His tone was rough, but his touch was gentle. "You're all I care about. I can't help my brother anymore. But I can certainly help the woman I love."

His arms surrounded her, lifting her up from the floor as if she were little more than a feather, carrying her into the living room, carefully stretching her out on the couch.

He knelt on the floor beside her. His voice was like broken steel. "Emilie, I'm so sorry."

"Nathan's fault." It was all she could get out. Oh, but it hurt like the dickens to speak. *Lord, help me!* She smoothed a hand over her throat, trying to swallow.

Jonas disappeared into the kitchen for all of half a second, returning with a glass of ice water. The cold felt good—and awful—in her throat, making the muscles constrict, muscles that already ached from too much pressure.

"Say the word, Emilie, and I'll call the police."

She shook her head so hard it hurt. "No. Doesn't matter now. Help Nate."

The knock at the front door nearly launched her off the couch. Jonas was on his feet in an instant, stalking toward the foyer. Emilie watched him, grateful for his protection, and felt a tiny tug at one corner of her mouth. If he'd had enough hair on his head to do so, it would have been standing on end right now.

"Who is it?" he barked through the solid door.

Let it be Nate, Lord. She swallowed, then winced. *Let him come back, apologize, make amends, something.* The two were brothers, not enemies. Nate had no place else to go, nowhere else to turn.

She lifted herself up on one elbow, straining to hear. *I'm not afraid, Lord. I know Jonas will keep me safe. Let this be Nate knocking on our door. Please?*

But it wasn't.

Not Emilie. Dee Dee.

She was the one who'd turned him in.

Nate staggered along the alley behind Emilie's place, looking over his shoulder for his brother, relieved when Jonas didn't follow him.

Not that he knew where he was going.

He couldn't go back to Jonas' house. Ever. Didn't have enough money in his pocket to buy even one night in a cheap hotel. He could manage without food—his stomach was tied in a permanent knot anyway—but it was a chilly night for sleeping under the stars.

He swung his head back, which made him so dizzy he had to grab a nearby telephone pole to steady himself. *No stars.* Clouds. Rain in the forecast.

The one place he'd thought he could go—Dee Dee Snyder's house was now out of the question.

Dee Dee would never welcome his kisses—or anything else—again.

Nate pulled himself forward on legs that refused to walk a straight line. Maybe he wouldn't worry about what kind of welcome he got. Maybe he'd just go there. Make her sorry she'd put two and two together and come up with four. He'd known she was smart, just not that smart.

Shouldn't have asked her so many questions, Fielding.

Dee Dee's house. He could walk that far. Put one foot in front of the other, cursing her all the way. Yeah, he could make it to Dee Dee's. Knock on her door. Give her the surprise of her life.

He aimed his tottering steps in her direction, his mind reeling with all the things he could and would say to this woman who'd ruined his life, ruined everything.

Cy would come soon, knocking on his door. Or he'd send a buffoon in his stead, with an ugly face and a temperament to match.

Nate turned up another alley, grateful to avoid the main streets where he might attract attention, have somebody see him.

Somebody dangerous.

A children's riddle came to the surface, mined from a memory long left behind for the more serious games of adulthood.

"Knock, knock!"

"Who's there?"

"April."

"April who?"

"April Fool!"

He snickered, stumbling into a pool of light from the streetlamp on the corner. Just as quickly as it lifted, his countenance fell.

You're the fool, man. The biggest one of all.

"Who's there?" Jonas called out again, leaning toward Emilie's front door, straining to hear.

"Drew," came the male voice from the porch.

Jonas sighed, relief crashing on him like a wave, then flung the door open. "C'mon in, man. Glad you're here."

Drew smiled, oblivious to the tension still hovering in the air as he stepped through the door. "I dropped Sara off at home, then realized she'd left her teddy bear here. You know her. Never sleeps without Bear-Bear."

Jonas nodded. "Right. Uh...we have a situation here, buddy." He motioned Drew in, took a quick look out the front door, then shut it behind them. "My brother Nate just left. I have no idea where he went, but a liquor store is the first place I'd look."

Drew nodded, pointing a thumb toward the street. "That explains why I just saw him stumbling across Cedar. You want me to go get him? Drive him home?"

"Please!" Emilie groaned, motioning from the couch.

Drew turned toward her and the color drained from his face. "My word, Emilie! Your neck. What happened here?" He turned toward Jonas, a scowl on his face. "Somebody better start talking, and fast."

Jonas sketched out only the necessary details, watching as Emilie leaned back against the cushions, one hand lightly rubbing her throat.

You did that, Nate. He'd never thought it possible to feel such loathing for his own brother. *I trusted you, Nate. I loved you.*

They had not come to blows, but their words had cut like knives.

When Jonas finished, Drew let out a low whistle. "Thank goodness I came by for Sara early by mistake."

Jonas exchanged glances with Emilie. "No mistake there, Drew. That was God's provision for her safety." The thought of Sara being witness to Nate's cruelty made his stomach clench. *Thank you, Lord, for sparing her.*

Drew finally asked the question on all of their minds. "What are you gonna do, Jonas? Press charges? Issue a warrant? Have him arrested?"

"I can't." Jonas dropped his head, the weight of such hard options bearing down on his shoulders like a heavy wooden cross. "He's my brother."

"Your brother in blood, or in Christ?"

His head snapped up at that. "I wish it were both. He arrived in town, saying the right words. An hour into it, it was pretty obvious Nate was putting on a good show." He exhaled, standing to pace the floor again. "The kid always was a good liar."

"Liars have to face the consequences sometimes, Jonas. You can't rescue your brother like you did Trix."

Jonas turned sharply on his heel, feeling a flush of heat rise from his chest. "He's not a dog, Drew. He's my flesh and blood."

"Yeah, but he's not your responsibility."

"Who'll look after him, then, if I don't?" He heard the anguish in his voice, tasted it in his mouth, felt it in his soul. "C'mon, *who?*"

"God." Drew waited one beat, then two. "Face it, Jonas. Nate is God's responsibility. Always was, but even more so now. He's dug a hole so deep even you can't pull him out."

Jonas sank down on his knees, wrapping his hands around Emilie's. She sneaked one free and stroked his hair, offering comfort and solace with her touch, if not her voice.

He bowed his head almost to the floor. "Father...please..." His words came slowly, drawn from a place where surrender lived, a place deeply buried and seldom visited.

Help me, Lord. Help me let Nate go.

Behind him, Drew lowered himself onto one knee and laid a supportive hand on his shoulder.

Jonas began again. "Lord, forgive me for trying to save Nate when we both know I can't. Only you can." His voice failed him. He gripped Emilie's hand harder. "Nate's in pain and he's in trouble. He won't even tell me what it is. It's...it's so hard to stand by and watch." His heart felt crushed to breaking. "Help me, Father. I would suffer for him if I could."

I have already suffered for him.

Tears clogged his throat. "I love my brother, Lord..."

I love him too, Jonas. More.

His forehead pressed against the hardwood floor. His words were a hoarse and tortured whisper. "What will happen to him, Lord? What am I supposed to do?"

Let him go, son. Let him find his way to me.

Twenty-three

◆

It is one thing to show a man that he is in error, and
another to put him in possession of truth.
JOHN LOCKE

It rained on Good Friday.

The gray, weeping skies and coolish air suited the mood of the day. Melancholy and solemn, a day of sorrows.

Emilie's neck was stiff and striped with bruise marks. The purplish spots were noticeably worse this morning. The painful memories remained equally vivid.

Nathan lunging through her door. Grabbing her. Hurting her.

Jonas bursting through her door. Saving her. Soothing her.

Bless you, Lord, for Jonas. Within the hour he'd be knocking on her door again. *Quietly, this time.* Emilie smiled at the thought.

Stepping from the tub, she patted herself dry, avoiding the mirror, dressing quickly. The weather gave her a perfectly good reason to swathe her neck in an oblong, paisley scarf.

Though her skin was bruised, Emilie was surprised to find her heart was not. She felt no bitterness toward Nathan. If anything, she felt pity. He was a broken man, without a friend in the world, it seemed. Except Jonas, whose love Nate no longer wanted.

As she applied a bit of cosmetic color here and there, Emilie again asked herself the question that had nagged at her incessantly since last night: How could two brothers who shared the same parents and upbringing, much the same looks and intelligence—how could they become such different men?

One a rebel, the other a hero.

One who resorted to physical strength, the other who turned to spiritual strength.

Emilie knew only this: Jonas Fielding wasn't like any man she'd ever known. Her love and respect for him had grown threefold over the last few days. Now she longed for some way to communicate that love. Not merely with words and affection, but in some tangible way.

Show me, Lord.

Jonas rang the doorbell, once and briefly at that. Emilie opened the door with a frisson of anticipation—for the afternoon's meaningful reading service, yes, but even more for the man who would sit by her side, the man who filled her doorway as completely as he filled her heart.

His smile—all boy, all man, all hers—covered every inch of his rugged face. "Hello, pretty girl." His dark, dancing eyes swallowed her whole.

"Jonas."

She was in his arms before he made it inside the house, covering his face with kisses even as the gentle rain covered them both.

"Emilie Getz, what will the neighbors think?" Jonas easily maneuvered them both inside without dislodging her arms around his neck, then kissed her soundly.

For the first time since last evening's painful ordeal, she tossed back her head and laughed. "The neighbors will think I'm the luckiest woman in the world."

His lips pressed against her exposed neck, kissing one sensitive spot, then another, bringing a lump to her throat, one she realized he could feel.

He kissed her there as well. "Don't cry, Em. It's over."

She blinked away the tears that stung her eyes, but the lump was more stubborn, reminding her how sore her throat still was. No singing or reading in the service today for her.

Easing out of his embrace, she touched his cheek, then turned for her coat, adjusting her scarf again. She'd refused to have it looked at by a doctor.

Who went to the doctor for a bruise? She had no intention of pressing charges, so there was no point drawing attention to her injuries.

The bruises would disappear in a few days.

Nathan was already gone.

"You haven't heard from Nate, then?" she asked as they walked along Main, her hand tucked in his, both of them grateful for a short respite from the rain.

His sigh was a heavy one. "Nope. No note, no phone message, no sign of him."

"What about Dee Dee? Heard anything from her?"

"Not since she called and shared her suspicions with me yesterday. For all her faults, the woman came through when we needed her." He turned toward Emilie, his expression more pensive. "Sweetheart, why did Nate seem to think you knew about the money?"

She stared down at her shoes. *Here it is, then.* The question that was never asked last night, the one she'd dreaded the most. The one she'd hoped might get lost in the shuffle.

Steeling herself, she began, choosing her words with great care. "Jonas, remember Tuesday after the press conference, you had me stop by your place and water the plants?" She gulped, seeing his brow furrow. "When I walked in your office, Nathan was there at your computer—"

"Emilie!" He stopped and turned her toward him, his expression incredulous. "Why didn't you tell me?"

"Well...I..." She balled her hands in fists by her side, not knowing how to explain herself. "I was..."

"Tuesday?" Jonas shook his head, clearly dumbfounded. "I could have put a stop to things sooner, maybe have avoided all that mess last night." His eyes widened. "Em, did he threaten you?"

"Not at all. I didn't see him actually do anything. He just asked me to keep it to myself. Said it would be our little secret."

Jonas' face took on a ruddy tinge. "Secret? You're telling me you saw Nathan—"

She jumped to her own defense. "All I saw was him working at your computer. I didn't know what he was doing." Her eyes searched his, crushed by the doubt she saw mirrored there. "He said he felt guilty about skipping a day of work."

"The stuff on the screen, did it look like the spreadsheet for Carter's Run?" She could see he was fighting to keep his voice down as pedestrians walked by, their glances curious, even wary. "Emilie, you know I would never let anyone touch those books except our accountant."

She turned and started walking, knowing he would follow her, that they had to take their conversation somewhere else, somewhere more private. He was next to her in an instant, his long strides forcing her to walk faster as they turned the corner, ending up in the center of grassy Church Square, alone for the moment.

Emilie faced him again, still balling then releasing her hands, close to tears, struggling for control. "Nathan said he majored in economics, Jonas."

"Right. Ten years ago." His voice was tinged with pain. "Did he also tell you he didn't graduate?"

Swallowing didn't budge the knot in her throat a single inch. "Yes...he did."

She felt him pulling away from her. "Another conversation I missed, Em?"

"Y-yes." She exhaled, choking on self-imposed misery. There was nothing to do but confess the whole of it, and so she did. Told him about the clandestine visit, the unintentional eavesdropping, the wrong conclusions, the discussion with Nathan in the backyard, the promises that should never have been made, the scene in Jonas' office that ought to have prepared her for last night but didn't.

Nothing could have prepared her for that. Or for this.

Jonas, the man she loved, was furious with her.

"Let me get this straight, Emilie." He was breathing hard, his face redder still. "You chose keeping a promise made to Nathan over being honest with me?"

"But he said I owed him one, and I—"

"Don't you and I owe one another something?" His voice was still low, but the anger and hurt were unmistakable. "After all we've been through, all we mean to one another." His eyes searched hers for answers. "I love you, Emilie. I believed you when you said you loved me."

It was the last straw. Tears were pouring down her cheeks unabated. "I do love you, Jonas! With all my heart." She reached out her hands, placing them on his chest, needing to touch him, to feel his heart and let him see hers, dangling from her sleeve. "It's just that…when I stood in that hallway and heard you say to Dee Dee on the phone, *Not a word to Emilie,* well I thought…I thought…"

"You thought what?" His words sounded like an accusation, but she sensed something growing behind and beneath them. Awareness, perhaps. Or a touch of guilt.

"You thought what?" he asked again, softer this time.

Her voice trembled, even as she focused her watery eyes on his. "I thought *you* were keeping a secret from *me.*"

Slowly he placed his hands on top of hers, melting away the sharp edges around them, healing them both with a touch. "A secret, huh?" The chagrin on his face reflected his own remorse. "It was supposed to be a surprise."

Despite the tension, her lips began curling upward. "Are we talking semantics again here? Surprise or secret, either way it means being less than truthful, don't you think?"

"I'll tell you what I think." He let go of her hands only long enough to wrap his arms around her, enfolding her in his embrace. His voice was low, tender, and rough all at once, sending a shiver up her spine. "I think you are one brave, feisty, stubborn, wonderful woman."

Ohh. Emilie tucked her head under his chin, loving the way it rubbed against her hair, already like sandpaper at two in the afternoon. She murmured into his chest, not trusting herself to look at him. "And do you think you could forgive me, Jonas? Please?"

He didn't let her get away with hiding. Instead, he leaned back and tipped up her chin, forcing her to meet his brown-eyed gaze. "Forgiven and forgotten. Will you forgive me, Emilie?"

She nodded, then sank back against him, loving the solid warmth, the masculine scent of soap and April rain and something purely Jonas overwhelming her senses.

Thank you, Lord.

There was no doubt where the power to forgive began.

Jonas leaned down and nuzzled her ear. "Uh…probably time to move toward the sanctuary."

Her sigh was pure satisfaction. "Do we have to?"

"Yup." Gently disengaging himself from her, and her from him, Jonas slipped an arm behind her as they headed toward the door, patently ignoring the knowing smiles among the parishioners gathered around the front door.

"Afternoon, everyone," Jonas said as if nothing had transpired on their soggy church lawn, while Emilie pinched her lips tight to keep from giggling. *Giggling, Em! Honestly.*

At that, she stopped short.

Wait. Yes, giggling. She was the new, improved Emilie Getz, was she not? A woman who no longer worried about keeping a stiff upper lip and looking professional at every turn and waving her credentials under everyone's nose.

She was a child of God and loved by Jonas Fielding.

Credentials enough for any woman.

So there! She giggled—loudly—and strolled into the sanctuary, her face beaming until she saw the simple cross, the solemn faces, the dimmed lights, and remembered.

Good Friday.

All joy came with a price.

Tenebrae.

Jonas knew the meaning of the Latin word: *darkness.*

Lititz was shrouded in darkness by this hour. The sun had long set, the rain refused to end. Standing in the vestibule with Emilie, the evening Tenebrae service concluded, Jonas listened to the murmur of voices around him, trying hard to be fully present when his heart and mind were somewhere else.

Searching for Nathan.

The afternoon's reading service—a verse-by-verse account of Good Friday—had been almost more than he could bear, opening with the story of Judas, the betrayer of Jesus, trying to give back his thirty pieces of silver, only to be rejected.

"And he went and hanged himself." The words had clutched at his throat when he read them.

Would Nathan do such a thing? Clearly, his brother was in more trouble than he'd been willing to admit. Where had he gone Thursday night? And where was he now, this minute?

Hungry? Thirsty? *Dead?*

Jonas' grip around Emilie's shoulder tightened. The past hours, full of suffering and sorrow, washed over him afresh.

Where's my brother, Lord?

He and Emilie had called everyone they thought might have seen Nate—including the police—then spent the rainy hours between today's services driving the streets of Lititz, looking for a thirty-year-old man wearing navy pants and jacket, a yellow golf shirt, a two-day beard.

Wherever his destination, Nate hadn't taken any clothes or a suitcase. They were all still in his closet at Jonas' place, waiting for his return.

Come home, Nate. I love you, brother. All is forgiven. Just come home.

Emilie looked up at him, her expression creased with concern. "Jonas? You don't look well. Shall we leave?"

He nodded, suddenly anxious to be away from the hubbub and alone with Emilie. Though he was lousy company, she seemed glad to be with him, supporting him with silent glances and warm hugs. What a gift this woman was! It brought the slightest of smiles to his face when he remembered the gift he'd prepared for her on Resurrection Sunday.

But this was Friday. The day of shadows.

Until they heard from Nathan, the joy of Easter seemed a long way off.

Darting across the square, skirting puddles and mud, Jonas kept Emilie close to his side, memories of Thursday night in her kitchen still taunting him. *If I'd been there earlier...* Truth was, he wouldn't have been there at all, would have been in church, except that Dee Dee called with her bad news and Nathan never showed up for dinner.

Jonas had wanted Emilie to know the sordid story and so drove directly over to her place, never dreaming he'd find his brother with his hands around her neck...

Was it possible to love someone yet loathe their behavior?

Yes, son. It is.

Of course.

Starting the engine, Jonas lifted Emilie's hand and pressed his lips to her palm in gratitude, then without a word, steered the Explorer through the misty, wet streets. Around the square, the glow of the streetlamps was diffused by the moist air, creating large, pale circles of light.

If anyone was in need of light tonight, it was Nathan. *Help us find him, Lord.*

They arrived at his place minutes later, any hope of finding Nate there quickly dashed. The porch light was off, the drive was empty, the mailbox had no note tucked inside. Following him through the back door, Emilie carefully deposited her wet raincoat across the clothes dryer in the laundry room.

Her purse put aside, Emilie stretched up on tiptoe and kissed his forehead. "Mind if I brew some tea?" Her voice still sounded rough around the edges. Weak and strained, threaded with pain. It ravaged his heart to hear it.

He said the words again: "I'm sorry, Em."

With a wave of her hand, she went about her tea-making duties. "Enough of that, handsome. None of it was your fault. I'm praying we find the man before he hurts himself. Have you checked the answering machine?"

"Three messages," he called out from the den a moment later, and pushed rewind. Long ones, from the sound of them. Emilie joined him, dropping into his lap on the desk chair as he pushed the playback button.

"Jonas, it's Dee Dee. I've been out of town since we spoke Thursday, so I just got your message. Sorry I missed you. Look, I haven't seen Nate. I...I hope it was appropriate to tell you about my discussions with him. Was I right? Did he try and pull something? Jonas, I'm...sorry. He's a cute guy, but he's trouble." Dee Dee's throaty laugh rolled out of the tiny speaker. "He may be a Fielding, but he's not you. Tell that professor she's one lucky dame."

Click.

Jonas grinned and leaned over to whisper in Emilie's ear. "Is that what you are, Dr. Getz? A lucky dame?"

"Humph. Luck had nothing to do with it."

He erased Dee Dee's message, relieved to know she'd been gone Thursday night. Nathan might have tried to pull the same stunt at her place that he'd pulled at Emilie's. Em might be willing to let it go, but Dee Dee Snyder would have seen Nate behind bars within the hour.

If she'd lived through it.

Nathan was trouble, all right. More than Jonas had realized.

He pushed the start button for the next message, which had his complete attention from the first sentence.

"Nate? It's over, kid. Do you understand what I'm saying? We're talking months of patience on my part, covering for you. This ain't a bank, Nate, and I ain't a loan officer. Twenty thousand on April 1, that was our agreement. I waited all day. No check. Time's up and I'm tired of waiting, Nate. So long and good riddance."

Click.

Jonas stared at the machine, stunned.

"What was all that about?" Emilie slipped out of his lap, ignoring the teakettle whistling in the kitchen, reaching out to push replay instead.

The message was even more disturbing on the second listen. No name, no identifying noises in the background, nothing except an older man making a threat that sounded anything but idle.

"Save that one, and let's see if the next message sheds a little light on it."

It did more than that.

"Jonas Fielding? This is the Lititz Borough Police calling at 7:08 on Friday evening. Mr. Fielding, we just picked up your brother, Nathan Fielding, on a charge of public drunkenness and disorderly conduct. Unfortunately, he resisted arrest, so we're going to need to keep him locked up here for a while. Thought you might want to come down and talk some sense into him. Bring him a change of clothes and an electric shaver while you're at it. The guy's a mess."

Click.

Jonas couldn't have put it better himself. Nathan *was* a mess.

Nate's curly brown hair was matted to his head as if he'd slept in a mud puddle. *Probably did.*

His bloodshot eyes were glazed over with a veneer of alcohol.

His hands shook, making the steel cuffs around them jangle.

His clothes reeked of perspiration and worse.

"I brought these for you, Nathan." Jonas handed the officer standing behind his brother a small bag of clothes and the shaver, as requested. "You're welcome to check these, Officer. Feel free to toss what he's wearing after he changes."

"Uh-uh," Nate mumbled, barely able to lift his head. "Good clothes."

"Not anymore, brother." Jonas shook his head, pulling up a wooden chair and straddling it backwards as he sat, resting his chin on the back. "Are you gonna tell me where you've been the last twenty-four hours?"

Nate stared out the small, barred window. "You don't wanna know."

"Actually I do. I spent a long, sleepless night wanting to know."

Nate shrugged, unwilling to meet his gaze. "Somewhere dry."

"Not dry enough, looks like." Jonas dropped his voice. "Nate, we got a phone message from your twenty-thousand-dollar headache."

His brother's head shot up at that, terror gripping his face. "Cy called?"

Cy, huh. "Never gave his name."

Nate exhaled, aging in front of his eyes. "What did he say?"

"I wrote down the message so you could explain it to me." Jonas handed him the note, carefully printed. "The part I'm worried about is the 'good riddance.'"

"Yeah, well, don't worry about it. I'm safe as long as I'm in here, aren't I?" Nate tipped his head back, taking in the spartan surroundings. "Like I said Thursday night, brother Jonas, the less you know, the better."

"What I know is, you are in a heap of trouble sitting right here, with more waiting when you get out. Bigger stuff. Dangerous stuff." Jonas rested one fist on Nate's shoulder, not meant to comfort or threaten, simply a way to make contact with a man who'd suddenly become a stranger. "Nate, how can I help you when you won't tell me what's going on?"

Nate's eyes focused on his at last. Defeat and discouragement poured off him like sweat. "It's like this: I owe a bookie in Vegas twenty grand. He has every right to collect it."

"Maybe to collect it, but not to threaten you."

Nate slumped in his chair. "You don't know Cy."

Things were finally starting to add up. "So that's what your little...uh, bookkeeping adjustment was about, then?"

"I was desperate, Jonas." Nate looked like he meant it. "I never wanted to hurt you." Looked like he meant that, too.

Hard to tell with a habitual liar like Nate.

What now, Lord?

He could walk out that door, climb in his Explorer and never look back. Let Nathan pay the penalty for his mistakes. Jonas felt a knot of righteous indignation building in his chest. Since when did loving somebody require paying all his debts?

The silence in the cell was deafening.

I paid all yours, son.

Jonas sat up, gripping the back of the chair. *But he's not even sorry, Lord. Probably lying through his teeth.*

He brought his thought pattern to a grinding stop, a grim smile stretching across his face. As if he were always repentant. As if he never stretched the truth.

You know the truth, Jonas. Tell him. Tell him about me.

"I need you to wind this up." The officer standing behind them looked up from his clipboard, pointing at his watch. "Five more minutes, okay?"

Jonas took a deep breath, exhaled a prayer for guidance, and fixed his eyes on Nathan's dark brown ones, so much like his own.

"Brother Nate, I know you don't know or care about God right now."

A guilty look stole across Nate's flaccid features.

"Sure, you showed up in February singing a sweet gospel tune, but it didn't take long for you to hit a sour note. I wish like anything it'd been the real thing, Nate. Chances are good you wouldn't be sitting in here."

"I don't need a sermon, Jonas."

"Couldn't agree more." Jonas stood, flexing his leg muscles. "What you need is a Savior." He folded his arms over his chest, regarding his brother with fresh eyes. "Know what today is, Nate?"

His brother lifted his shoulders. "Nah. Lost track."

"Good Friday."

Nate snorted, leaning back to look at him. "What's so good about it?"

"Two thousand years ago, a man died on your behalf, Nathan. An innocent man died so sinners could be set free."

"Oh, free is it? Yeah, I'd like that." Nathan staggered to his feet. "You're so perfect, Jonas. You gonna die for me when Cy comes lookin' for me? You gonna pay my debts? You gonna set me free?"

Jonas swallowed the knot in his throat. "I would if I could. Fact is, I'm not good enough. I'm a sinner too. Jesus died for both of us. I was in a jail of my own making. Made out of anger and bitterness about dad's death—"

"Save your breath for somebody who cares." Nathan swung at the air in front of Jonas, then stumbled toward the wall, propping one shoulder against it. "Look, if you wanna do somethin' useful here, pay Cy off. I'd be much obliged. His address is in my wallet. They got it at the desk. I'll pay you back somehow, count on it."

I'll pay his debt, Lord, but only if you say so. Jonas felt his chest tighten. "Nate, I'll look into it."

His brother's eyes took on a hopeful glow. "What about helpin' me get outta here? Can you do that?"

No. Leave him to me, son. Go.

The vise in his chest turned another notch. "I've already given you the key you need to be set free. Without that, you'll still be in prison, no matter where you are."

Jonas took a step toward the door, dreading what had to come next. "I love you, Nathan. Always have. Always will. No matter what you do, you'll always be my brother. When you're ready to talk, come find me."

Now, Jonas. Leave him. Nathan is in my hands. Go.

Jonas did the hardest thing he'd ever done in his adult life.

He turned his back on his brother, put one foot in front of the other, and walked out. He left Nate behind bars, without a nickel to his name. And he stopped at the front desk only long enough to slip a small piece of paper out of Nate's wallet and into his own.

Twenty-four

◆

An egg is dear on Easter Day.
RUSSIAN PROVERB

Emilie tossed and turned in the predawn darkness.

Trombone music filtered through her subconscious.

Behind her closed eyelids, sunlight sparkled across Church Square. Everyone was dressed in white. *No. Only she* was dressed in white. A long, white gown, radiant as the sun at noonday.

Jonas was wearing black, naturally. His black suit? *No!* A tuxedo. *My, my.* He stood in place, smiling, as if waiting for her to join him.

Sara was covered in pink lace, head to toe, bearing a basket of delicate flowers. When had the child worn anything so fancy?

Near the front, a very pregnant Beth sat, glowing, in a pale blue dress, Drew proudly stationed beside her in his Sunday best suit.

One would almost think they were attending a summer wedding.

The trombones grew louder. What is it they were playing? Nothing remotely like "Here Comes the Bride." It sounded more like a hymn. An Easter hymn, perhaps? Yes, written in 1708, she was sure of it. "Jesus Christ Is Ris'n Today."

Hmmm. Odd choice for a wedding.

On the other hand, if it were Jonas she was about to marry, they could play the theme from *Lassie* and she would be happy.

Emilie stretched and rolled over in her sleep, grinning. Trix would like that for certain.

The trombones grew louder, crowding out her pleasant dream until she sat up in bed with a start, one hand fumbling for the alarm clock.

Easter music.

It wasn't her wedding day—it was Resurrection Day!

She squinted at the clock, then tossed her covers aside and leaped out of bed, her feet barely touching the floor for the next twenty minutes as she dashed from bedroom to bath, dressing for the Easter dawn service at God's Acre, while the trombones played on.

"Lucky for you, sleepyhead," she chided herself, one eye on the clock. Without the trombone choir making their way through town from three in the morning on, she might have slept through the whole service. Instead she pulled on warm clothes and ratty old shoes, then hurried down the gloomy street.

Temperatures hovered in the forties and a light rain was falling. Emilie was relieved her new Easter dress would make its debut later in the morning. At six—in the dark—Jonas would have to settle for her at her frumpiest.

He was waiting for her at the side door of the church, scowling dramatically and pointing at his watch until she ran up and planted a kiss on his surprised face. "Sorry I'm late, dear man." She curled her hand around his elbow. "I was having the most marvelous dream."

"What was the occasion?" he murmured, steering her through the door.

"Our wedding," she said airily, swallowing a giggle when his eyes turned to saucers.

"Uh…are we getting married?"

She shook her head and lifted a finger to her grinning lips. "Hush now, the service is about to begin."

Welcomed into the sanctuary by the trombone choir, they joined the crowd of several hundred packed into the sanctuary. The mood was quiet. Reverent. Emilie closed her eyes, letting the sacred morning surround her. Pastor Yeager stepped into the pulpit, arms raised, face triumphant.

"The Lord is risen!"

The congregation trumpeted their response, "The Lord is risen indeed!"

Soon, with the instruments and choir leading the way, the congregation quietly filed out, headed for God's Acre, much like the early Moravians had done in Herrnhut in 1732. The history and the majesty of the simple procession filled Emilie's heart as fully as the antiphonal music filled the air. Those leading the group played their instruments first, echoed by those following, the notes lifting everyone's spirits despite the soggy atmosphere.

Walking side by side with Jonas, Emilie longed to speak a word of comfort to him. All day Saturday he'd been polite but taciturn, almost brooding. Silence was the order of the hour now, so she could do nothing more than squeeze his hand and pray he'd share more with her later, perhaps when his brothers arrived in time for the Easter egg hunt.

Proceeding through the stone archway leading to God's Acre, they were handed a program and joined the other worshipers gathered around the old, flat gravestones. The minister faced due west, the congregation faced expectantly east—though it was unlikely they'd have a true sunrise to gladden their hearts this dreary morning.

For Emilie, thoughts of the resurrection alone sufficed.

You are risen in my heart, Lord. You are risen indeed!

By seven, they walked back toward the square. Some headed to their cars, while she and Jonas wandered into the social hall for a light breakfast served by the youth fellowship. Helping themselves to coffee and buns, they found a warm corner and sat across from one another, knees touching beneath the table, their gazes locked across the tops of their coffee mugs.

After dutifully sipping her hot drink for as long as she could stand it, Emilie finally gave in and asked him. "Jonas, are you ready to talk about Nathan yet?"

A hint of a smile tugged at the corners of his mouth. "Sorry to be so mysterious about it, Em. Yesterday was tough. Not knowing if he needed bail or when his hearing will be." He groaned and bit off a piece of roll, chewing in thoughtful silence.

"If you followed the Lord's leading, you did the right thing, Jonas." She threaded her fingers through his, marveling again at the strength and gentleness of his hands. "Though I must say, it feels backward for *me* to be giving *you* spiritual encouragement."

His sudden, broad smile shone like the sun bursting forth on a bleak horizon. "Emilie Getz, on this day of all days, it's the best gift you could give me."

"Speaking of gifts." She stuffed her hand inside her jacket pocket, relieved when her fingers closed around the bulky package. "I've been pinching my pennies lately, saving up for the perfect Easter present for you."

I hope this is right, Lord! Emilie slipped the box in front of him and held her breath as he yanked off the gold paper and lifted the lid.

"A new bird book!" He grinned and reached over to tweak her nose. "You rascal. Does this mean we're going birding sometime soon?"

"You and Trix are, for sure." She gulped, nodding at the gift. "There's something else. Inside the book."

"Bet I know where to look, too." He laughed and flipped to the section on herons, where a plain envelope waited for him. "Clever girl."

"I learned from a master." She gazed at him, drinking in his warmth, sending it back in waves. "Go on. Open it."

He slid out the gold foil card and flipped it open. "A gift certificate! For…for…" She watched his Adam's apple dip up and down twice. Watched him blink, hard. Watched his eyes move back and forth from her to the certificate to her again.

"Emilie, you didn't!"

I did. "Round trip airfare to…"

"Alaska!" He shook his head in wonderment.

"You deserve it, Jonas." She pointed at the fine print. "It's good through the end of November. Surely sometime between Honduras and Thanksgiving you'll find a few weeks to get away."

"No doubt. Thanks, Em." He slowly shook his head. "Only problem is, it's for one passenger."

She bristled. "Of course it is! It would be unthinkable for me to join you unless we were planning on getting married this summer. Which we're not, of course."

He smiled an elfin smile. "Of course."

Their breakfast finished, they moved back over to the sanctuary for communion at eight, after which Jonas dropped her off at her house then zipped down Cedar toward his place. They both needed to change in time for the rest of the morning's festivities.

Emilie pulled her new outfit over her head, holding her breath. Another investment item from Judie. Pale pink angora in a straight sheath of a dress. The long sleeves made her feel modest. The wide, boat neckline and deep V in the back did not, though the woman in the shop assured her it was perfectly appropriate for church or anywhere else.

She fussed with her hair, recapturing the style of Valentine's Eve with some success, and added more makeup than usual especially on the bruises on her neck. Her good pearls would help as well, a triple strand that filled in her neckline and reminded her fondly of Barbara Bush. Stepping into her tallest black heels, Emilie climbed down the dark, steep staircase with great care.

Waiting on the dining room table was yet another investment. A broad-brimmed hat in the very same pale pink, touched with satin ribbon and a tiny spray of white silk flowers.

Easing it onto her head, Emilie tilted the brim until it was parallel with the floor, as the woman in the hat shop had insisted, then stood before the mirror in the hallway. And grinned.

Even if she only wore it once—today—it was worth it to feel so gloriously feminine.

She hovered by the front door, waiting for a black Explorer to come into view. When Jonas pulled up, she swept open the door in her best imitation of Grace Kelly and glided out, delighted to find him standing at the bottom of the steps with his mouth hanging open.

"Emilie! You…you…!" He gulped. "You…!"

She smiled in a genteel manner, lips closed, eyebrows lifted. "Yes, me." She sighed as musically as possible, moving toward him. The brick steps were not conducive to gliding, but her entrance had produced just the reaction she'd been hoping for—a sort of bumbling paralysis.

He recovered in a moment and opened her door. She lifted off the hat, realizing there was no way to steer both it and her tall body inside gracefully, then climbed in, carefully placing her new beauty in the backseat, praying for a minimum number of blond dog hairs to attach themselves to her chapeau.

She turned her attention to the man behind the wheel, who looked every bit as polished in his black suit—not a tuxedo, but close enough—when a pale pink tie caught her eye.

"And I suppose the tie is to commemorate the grand opening of Carter's Run in a mere five days?"

He grinned. "What else?"

"Not a thing I can think of." She waved at the street ahead, wishing she'd gone all-out and worn gloves. "Carry on, Jonas, or we'll miss your family's arrival."

Which was another reason for the new addition to her wardrobe. She'd met his family at Christmas, long before she and he were an *item,* as Beth called them. Making a good impression was on her mind, though if she only impressed the man at her elbow, that suited her fine.

They parked where they could on the crowded street, then headed up the sidewalk, Emilie with her hat squarely on her head; Jonas bearing a large Easter basket boasting a soft, stuffed bunny and one huge plastic egg in the center. "For Sara," he'd explained, swinging it next to him like he always toted such a thing.

The rain had given way to hazy skies and warmer air, though on Emilie's back it felt a bit breezy. When she stepped in front of Jonas to cross the street, she heard him whistle under his breath.

"Man, do I like the view from back here."

"Jonas, please!" She whirled around, hands on her hips. "I checked the three-way mirror at the store and thought it looked quite demure."

"You're right," he chuckled. "De-more I see, de-more I like."

She would have swatted him if they weren't almost at their destination: the picnic grove behind the Sunday school building. "Behave yourself, sir," she cautioned, hooking his elbow. "There are children afoot."

Youngsters of every age dashed about the damp grass. Little girls ruining their white Mary Janes with bright green stains. Little boys soaking their pant legs in the nearby puddles. Emilie, ignoring the headaches such shenanigans would give their mothers, found the scene utterly enchanting. *Someday, Lord.*

Across the parking lot, she spied two Jonas look-alikes moving toward them. Good heavens, would Lititz ever be the same with three Fielding men in one setting?

Three, not four.

The realization caught her by surprise, taking a bit of the sparkle off her morning, if only for a moment. *Poor Nathan.*

"Emilie Getz, you remember Chris and his wife Connie? And Jeff and Diane? Welcome, everybody."

She extended her hand, giving each one an affectionate squeeze. The women were warm and gracious, complimenting her dress as she did theirs, without any trace of giving her an is-she-good-enough-for-our-Jonas? once-over.

Jonas, on the other hand, embarrassed her nigh to tears asking her to twirl around so his brothers could see her dress from the back. She graced him with a V of her eyebrows to match.

"Honestly!" she huffed, and the women nodded sympathetically. "Suppose we get down to the business at hand. Namely, an Easter egg hunt. Are you children game?"

Five little Fieldings, ranging in age from three to six, nodded enthusiastically and took off with their baskets to join the growing circle of kids preparing for the egg hunt, wet grass or not. Jonas followed them over, making sure they were properly registered.

From a distance, Emilie observed him with the children, feeling a warm tingle move through her system as she watched him swing Sara into his arms, then present her with her gift basket. He seemed intent on telling her about the egg inside, no doubt containing a special present for later, judging by the way he was wagging his finger.

Seconds later, he was back by her side as the woman in charge blew a whistle, silencing the children with remarkable speed. "The youngest go first, please. Threes, that's you. Go on now." They toddled out, a bit confused with it all, till the fours soon followed, quickly showing them the way of it. Sara, in her adorable flowered dress with the full skirt and multiple petticoats, showed them off prettily each time she dipped down to scoop up an egg.

Less than ten minutes later, it was over, as giggling children returned to their parents who duly noted their efforts and counted their eggs. The Fielding clan had done well, gathering two dozen eggs among them.

"And here comes Sara," Jonas called out, seeming more exuberant than one might expect from a man at a child's Easter egg hunt. "Whatcha got in the basket, sweet Sara?"

"A bunny!" She held it up. "His name is Peter!"

"Oh, for Peter Rabbit?" Diane asked, wiping the wet grass off her own daughter's patent leather shoes.

"No, for Peter the apostle," Sara said with conviction. "He was a follower of Jesus who really followed him. Not like that bad guy, Judas."

"Good for you, Sara." Jonas hovered over her basket, peeking inside. "Got anything else in there?"

"Eggs." She grinned a pixie grin.

"Regular old eggs."

"Yup," she sang out. "Except this one." With that, she lifted the oversize plastic egg out with great care. "It's pink," she announced importantly. "And it has a name on it. Look."

Sara held the egg up high.

It did indeed have a name on it, Emilie noticed. *Mine*. "Is that egg for me, then?"

Sara nodded. "Whale Man said it is. Oops." She blushed. "I wasn't supposed to tell."

Jonas tousled her hair and winked at his family, gathered in a loose circle. "No problem, sweetie. Emilie would have figured that out soon enough. Go ahead." His voice softened. "Open it. We have a good twenty minutes before church starts."

Emilie shook it first, wanting to stretch out the suspense. For a woman who hated surprises, she'd learned that when Jonas Fielding was involved, they were always wonderful. Eventually.

She gazed at him now, trying to read his expression. Dark eyes trained on her, crinkled in a smile. Smoothly shaved chin begging to be touched. A grin broad enough to melt any woman's heart.

"Please, Emilie?"

He didn't have to ask again. She gently pulled the two halves apart, holding them as if they contained real egg whites that might come spilling out in a gooey mess.

One half was empty.

The other half had three small, gold keys, all different sizes and shapes.

"What...?" Emilie poured them out in her hand, holding them out for all to see. "Am I to wear these on a necklace, Jonas? Charms, perhaps?"

"Well, you are a charming woman, but no, that's not what I had in mind." In two steps, he was by her side, close enough that she could feel his warmth, catch a whiff of his aftershave, sense one hand sliding around her waist.

"Now this key—" he began, holding up a flat, ordinary one—"this fits that." He pointed to the parking lot, where Chris had positioned himself next to an older but sturdy BMW in powder blue. "Behold your new wheels, Emilie Getz. Used, of course, but only because brand new doesn't become you, Madame Historian."

Her carefully lined lips dropped open. "For me? A...car? Jonas, you didn't!"

"I did." He grinned and lifted out the second key. "This one should look familiar."

She stared at it for a moment, then fumbled in her purse for its twin, holding it up with a gasp. "They *do* match! It's a key to the Woerner house. The place I'm renting," she explained to his family, who exchanged knowing smiles. Were they in on *everything*?

Jonas lifted his broad shoulders in a nonchalant shrug. "You can call it the Woerner house if you want to—for historical reasons—but according to the deed, which is now in your name, there's not a reason in the world it can't be forevermore known as the Getz house."

"*Jonas!*" She was having trouble breathing. "What about the dear people who—"

"The missionary couple? They asked the church to sell it for them." He grinned. "I helped. Dee Dee handled the paperwork." He patted her cheek, no doubt feeling the heat that had pooled there. "You seemed so at home in your little Main Street cottage."

"Well...I am, but...*Jonas!*" She looked for somewhere to sit down before she fainted, then realized fainting was the least of her worries.

"Oh, but Jonas!" *This is not good, not good at all.* "What will happen to my precious house when I have to go back to Salem College and...and...?"

"That's where this third key may come in handy." He stood in front of her now, toe to toe, effectively blocking the others from her view, as if he wanted her all to himself.

Jonas Fielding, I'm yours for the asking.

Had her gift communicated her love for him, as she'd hoped?

Did her eyes tell him so now, as his so eloquently expressed?

Might the warmth of her hand, enveloped by his, let him know that he made her heart beat faster, her skin grow pinker, her toes start tingling?

Does he know, Lord?

Yes, Emilie. He does.

"Jonas," she whispered. "Kiss me."

Without a moment's hesitation, he leaned forward and pressed his lips to hers, obviously not caring for a moment that they had an audience.

Nor did she.

"Emilie," he whispered back. "Kiss me."

Which she promptly did, with pleasure. "Now about that key. What does it open?"

His eyes twinkled. "Don't you know?"

She held it up. "It's a rather large key, I know that much. Not the type that fits in a car or a house, and anyway, you've already amazed me with those." Studying it, she took a few educated guesses. "Something valuable?"

"I hope you'll think so."

"Is it old?"

He laughed at that. "Old enough."

"Is it big, this thing it opens?"

"Some have said so, yes."

Emilie racked her brain. "Is it breakable?"

"Most definitely." His eyebrows knit together for a brief, stern look. "I'll count on you never to do so."

"I wouldn't dream of it," she assured him, then shrugged. "Jonas, I'm afraid I've run out of questions and still don't know what this might open."

"The truth is, Emilie Getz, it's already wide open and waiting for you to move in. Permanently. I'll tell you what this key opens." He whispered two words in her ear.

"Oh, Jonas!" Now she really might faint. "Are you saying...?"

"I'm saying marry me, Emilie Getz. Make my heart your home."

He slipped his arms around her, tickling her bare back because he was a Fielding, then gently kissing her because he was Jonas. "Say yes, Emilie. Say you'll come home to Lititz for good. And come home to me, forever."

"Yes, Jonas." Tears were poised on her lashes, making everything around her shine like stars. "I will."

"That's it! I heard an 'I will!'" announced Chris, creating no small amount of ruckus among the assembly. Emilie stepped back, startled to find herself suddenly surrounded with hugging, cheering Fieldings. Had they truly been there all along? Somehow she'd only had eyes for Jonas, who was now enduring backslaps and high fives with his usual aplomb.

"So." Diane flashed a toothsome smile. "When's the wedding?"

Jonas held his hand up. "Not so fast. The woman just said yes."

Emilie shook her finger playfully. "But the woman is not getting any younger."

His brows arched. "Are you saying you're in a hurry?"

"I'm saying I can't wait."

A grin covered his face. "Name the day, pretty girl."

She laughed and patted his chest. "August 13, then."

"Of course." He rolled his eyes, ignoring the crowd jostling around them. "Another historic Moravian anniversary, right?"

Grinning so broadly her cheeks hurt, she nodded. "So it is."

As they both leaned forward to seal their plans with a kiss, the church bells began to toll the half hour, calling all to worship. Their lips touched briefly, then Jonas took her arm and led the way as the Fielding clan moved with the crowd heading toward the door and a glorious celebration of Easter.

When they came around the corner, Jonas saw him first.

Nathan.

He was standing a dozen feet back from the front door of the church. Waiting, it seemed. His expression was blank. His attire clean but casual, not chosen especially for Easter Sunday.

"Oh, Nate!" Emilie held her breath, not knowing what brought him there, fearing another painful confrontation to spoil the most amazing day of her life. *Selfish, Em! Just pray.*

She watched Nate blanch, stepping back as all three brothers and assorted family members came sweeping around the corner then stopped, obviously as surprised as she was.

Jonas went forward first, arms outstretched. "Nate. Welcome." She heard the elation in his voice, felt the eagerness in his stride as she hurried to keep up with him. "You managed to talk them into letting you out, eh?"

Nate nodded solemnly. "Looks like I'll be doing some community service for a few weeks."

Jonas nodded, clearly pleased. "Good, good." He tipped his head toward the door. "You'll join us this morning, then?"

"No. I just knew I'd find you here." He looked down then, as if at a loss for what to say next. "Look, Jonas—" he glanced up, his skin ruddy—"I have a pretty good idea what you did yesterday."

"Oh?"

"That slip of paper is missing from my wallet. Unless I'm wrong, I think you paid my debt. In full."

"Is that right?" Jonas' smile was warm, without judgment, without pride.

Nathan's eyes filled with unshed tears. "Jonas, you…" His voice was raw with emotion. "You saved my life, brother."

"Someone did that for me once, Nate. I'm simply returning the favor." He held out his hand. "Sure you won't come to church with us?"

"I'm sure." Nate stepped back, but Jonas snagged his elbow and pulled him forward.

"So be it. Another Sunday, maybe. Meanwhile, there are two guys and their families here who will take me apart limb by limb if I don't let them get a shot at you."

Jonas stepped aside as Chris and Jeff moved forward. Emilie eased closer to Jonas, swallowing hard. *Here come the Marines.* She watched their broad shoulders and muscular arms embrace Nathan, one by one, in a manly bear hug. None of them were crying, but none of the four brothers were dry-eyed either, Emilie noticed, sniffling herself.

Jeff spoke first. "Nate, you look…good. We're glad you showed up today, brother."

"Got that right," Chris chimed in, punching his arm.

Nathan nodded, the set of his mouth firm. Too firm, like he was holding something in.

Help him, Lord.

But he said nothing, only listened as the twins brought forward their children for inspection, followed by a brief hug from Diane and a Texas-style squeeze from Connie.

Jeff reached out and tugged Jonas back into the fray. Since her arm was tucked in his, Emilie inadvertently stumbled into their circle as well. Jeff winked at her. "Heard about the newest addition to the family, Nate?"

Nathan's eyes met hers. Steady, not blinking. "Congratulations, Emilie." His volume dropped in half. "I'm…sorry…about Thursday."

The lump in her throat wouldn't budge. "Me too," she managed to get out, hanging on to Jonas for support. "I…I wish you'd join us for church, Nate."

"Not today. Another time, okay?"

She knew there would be no other time, could feel him pulling away from them, disconnecting. *Don't let him leave, Lord!*

"I gotta go." He backed up, stepping right into Helen Bomberger's path as she scurried up the walk toward the sanctuary.

"Oh!" Startled, the older woman abruptly stopped, her Easter bonnet knocked to the ground. Nathan's face turned a brighter shade of red as he steadied her, brushing off her floral crown and handing it back to her with a slight apology.

"Sorry," he mumbled, then turned back only long enough to say, "See ya," before he straightened his shoulders and started down the sidewalk toward Main.

"Call me, Nate!" Jonas hollered above the chime of the church bells.

Nate didn't turn back, only lifted his hand and kept walking. The three remaining brothers exchanged looks that spoke volumes—and decades—then gathered their families around them, even as Jonas pulled Emilie closer and slowly followed the crowd toward the narrow wooden doors.

He stopped on the church steps and tapped his brother on the shoulder. "Save us a seat downstairs, will you, Jeff?"

His younger look-alike shot him a knowing grin. "See you inside, brother," he said with a chuckle, then disappeared through the doors.

Emilie, meanwhile, couldn't stop watching Nate, separating himself from his family with every step. "What will happen to him?"

"I think God isn't finished with Nathan Fielding yet." Jonas gazed at the retreating figure for a moment, sighed heavily, then slowly turned back toward her, his features softening. "But he's doing a mighty fine work in you, Emilie Getz."

She basked in the warm glow she saw shining on his face, and touched his rough chin. "I had a good teacher."

He grinned and kissed her finger. "Takes one to know one."

"Oh, Jonas!" Her heart was so full she feared she might faint. "I can't wait until you are my...husband."

Husband! The very word gave her chills.

His eyes darkened. "I can't wait either." He leaned against the sanctuary door, assessing her. "Come August 13, beloved, have you any thoughts about where you might like to set up housekeeping?"

She felt her eyebrows hit *V* formation in record time. "My house, of course."

"That old place?" He winked. "How 'bout I bring my new curtains, at least?"

"No!" She ducked her head when an usher shot a stern look out their direction and dropped her voice to the faintest whisper. "My antique curtains are fine. You may, however, bring your Explorer."

"Such a generous woman." He tipped his head. "You'll serve coffee for breakfast, yes?"

She nodded. "And tea. I expect you to feed Trix and the rest of our menagerie, though."

"Deal. Long as you water the plants."

"Humph." Her chin jerked ever so slightly. "I thought you liked playing with dirt."

"Mountains of dirt, not little clay pots. That's your department."

"Very well." A more serious thought crossed her mind. "Speaking of departments, I suppose the folks at Salem will be able to get along without me."

"Their loss will no doubt be Franklin and Marshall's gain." His grin was a lethal weapon. "I happen to know they have an opening. In the history department."

"Oh?" She managed to sound nonchalant, even as her heart soared. *Thank you, Lord!* "That might be a good fit."

He tapped her hat playfully. "Speaking of which, this bonnet of yours is a perfect fit."

"You think so?" She lifted her hand to the brim and tried hard not to sound pleased as punch.

"I do. And underneath it is the most intelligent, beautiful, joy-filled woman I could ever want for a wife."

"Know what?" Emilie laughed as the church bells chimed the quarter hour and without a moment's hesitation, tossed her hat into the fresh April air. "I think so too!"

Helen Bomberger's Moravian Sugar Cake

1 package (or cake) yeast
1/4 cup lukewarm water
1/3 cup Crisco shortening
1/4 cup sugar
1 egg
1 1/2 teaspoons salt
1/2 cup mashed potatoes
1/2 cup scalded milk, cooled
3 1/2 cups flour

Crumb Topping:
1/2 pound brown sugar
1 1/2 tablespoons flour
1 teaspoon cinnamon
1/4 cup butter in small bits

Add yeast to lukewarm water, set aside. Cream shortening and sugar. Beat in eggs. Add mashed potatoes and salt. Add yeast water to cooled milk and add that to mixture. Add flour and mix until it forms a solid dough. Knead the dough only until smooth. Place dough in large greased bowl, cover with cloth, and set in a warm place. Let dough rise 3 to 4 hours, until it doubles in size. Pat out dough in two greased 9 by 13 pans and let rise again for another 1 1/2 hours. Poke holes across the top of the dough in 2-inch intervals. Fill holes with bits of butter and cover entire cake with crumb topping. Bake at 375 degrees for 15 minutes. Makes two 9 by 13 pans.

Dear One:

What a thrill it was to write this second novel for you!

I hope you've fallen in love with Lititz, Pennsylvania, my hometown and one of the most charming boroughs in America. It was pure joy to walk those streets again—in person doing my research and in my mind as I wrote the book. Thanks to the *Lititz Record Express* that landed on my doorstep weekly, I was able to make the dates, times, places, even the weather conditions, as accurate as possible. The characters are fictional (though you'll never convince *me* of that!), but the streets and businesses are delightfully real. Come visit Lititz in the heart of beautiful Lancaster County and see for yourself.

Even more than the town itself, *Bookends* is the story of the Lititz Moravian Congregation, where as a child, I first heard of God's love for me. When I tell people I grew up as a Moravian, they often pat my hand and murmur, "I'm so sorry. Is that a cult?" (tee-hee!) The Moravians are in fact the oldest of the Protestant denominations, predating the Reformation by sixty years. Perhaps your only exposure to the Moravians has been spotting one of our many-pointed white stars shining brightly on someone's front porch at Christmastime. Within these pages, I tried to give you a deeper glimpse into the rich spiritual heritage that the Moravians—originally known as the *Unitas Fratrum*—bring to the world.

Moravians are fond of proclaiming as our watchword: "In essentials unity, in nonessentials liberty, and in all things love." What a perfect rallying cry for our two main characters, Emilie Getz and Jonas Fielding! Although these two began like "bookends," facing life in opposite directions on every point, I loved watching the Lord turn them toward one another and toward him—You too? Emilie's journey was a joy to behold, and Jonas positively stole my heart. (My dear husband Bill has insisted on taking it back...)

Thank you for spending Christmas through Easter with me in Lititz. To view our *Bookends* scrapbook full of photos, please visit my Web site at *www.LizCurtisHiggs.com*. I'm also honored when readers take time to drop me a line, and love to keep in touch twice a year through my free newsletter, *The Laughing Heart*. For the latest issue, please write me directly at:

Liz Curtis Higgs * PO Box 43577 * Louisville, Kentucky 40253-0577

Until next time...you are truly a blessing!

OTHER BOOKS BY LIZ CURTIS HIGGS

FICTION FOR WOMEN
Mixed Signals

NONFICTION FOR WOMEN
"One Size Fits All" and Other Fables
Only Angels Can Wing It, The Rest of Us Have to Practice
Forty Reasons Why Life Is More Fun After the Big 4-0
Mirror, Mirror on the Wall, Have I Got News for You!
Help! I'm Laughing and I Can't Get Up
"While Shepherds Washed Their Flocks" and Other Funny Things Kids Say and Do
Bad Girls of the Bible and What We Can Learn from Them

FICTION FOR YOUNG CHILDREN
The Pumpkin Patch Parable
The Parable of the Lily
The Sunflower Parable
The Pine Tree Parable
Go Away, Dark Night

On the Air

WITH LIZ CURTIS HIGGS

Popular radio personality Belle O'Brien is weary of looking for happiness "town to town, up and down the dial." A phone call from smooth-talking Patrick Reese sends her packing once more. Tune in for smile-out-loud humor mixed with an entertaining cast of characters, heart-tingling romance, and a touching story of forgiveness.

Belle O'Brien's radio show is a solid-gold hit, but her love life is an off the charts disaster—until a man with a past offers her a future.

Mixed

Signals

LIZ CURTIS HIGGS